TINSMITH
~1865~

FLATS JUNCTION SERIES
BOOK 1

SARA DAHMEN

TINSMITH 1865

Promontory Press
www.promontorypress.com

ISBN: 9781773740416

Cover designed by Edge of Water Design
Typeset by Spica Book Design
Interior Artwork Copyright © 2019 Sara Dahmen
Printed in Canada

0 9 8 7 6 5 4 3 2 1

To Bob, Marilyn, and all the tin tinkers,
and my husband,
who understands how the stories burn and glow
and gives me the time to write them.

DAKOTA
TERRITORY.
Tinsmith 1865
FLATS
TOWN
YANKTON
BROOKINGS
YANKTON

PECK'S PATENT IMPROVED MACHINES;

TIN, SHEET IRON, BRASS AND COPPER WARES,

For which a Premium was awarded by the American Institute, Oct. 1843.

The Subscribers having purchased of SETH PECK & CO., the sole right to manufacture PATENT TINMAN'S MACHINES, as hitherto made, by them, and also having recently become the assignees of *Letters Patent,* recently obtained by O. & N. PECK, with the sole right to manufacture Machines after that Patent, continue to carry on the business at the old stand of SETH PECK & CO., in SOUTHINGTON, CT.

The Subscribers would here say that Mr O. PECK, has had nearly 20 years experience in the manufacture and invention of these Machines, and he in company with N. PECK, flatter themselves that with the experience they have had, and the study which they have bestowed on said machines, have produced an article WELL and NICELY adapted to all kinds of work which TIN-PLATE workers and STOVE dealers may wish to perform. The men employed in making said machines, have also had a number of years experience in the employ of SETH PECK & Co. Also, that this is the only establishment in the United States where said Machines can be manufactured without infringement on said Patents.

The improvements for which Messrs. O. & N. PECK, have obtained *Letters Patent,* are valuable, inasmuch as one Machine is made to perform the work of two, by simply adding extra faces to the rollers by means of screw and wrench. The *Large* and *Small Turning,* and *Large* and *Small Burring* Machines may be accompanied with extra faces of Steel or Iron, as may be wished by the purchaser, of different thicknesses and circumference adapted to different or all kinds of work. The *Setting down* Machine, is also essentially improved; and also the *Grooving Machine,* the rollers of which are made much larger and mount the work much easier than the old kind. The Shear or break to the *Folding* Machine has been improved so that locks of any width under ½ inch may be laid over. For further particulars Tinners are referred to the Machines themselves, as it would be impossible to describe them within the brief compass of a hand bill.

The Subscribers would only add that in the quality of Stock, of which they are made, and the various and complicated uses to which they may be applied, their Machines are vastly superior to any which ever have been, or are being made in the World.

The Machines will be warranted complete in every respect, and be forwarded on order to any part of the United States, or the Canadas, without advance on the Factory prices, except freight and insurance, and no machine will be sent abroad until found perfect by actual trial.

The Prices of Machines appear below. Applications for entire or parts of sets may be made to the subscribers, or to either of the following Agents and the Machines will be promptly supplied. Any person forwarding a good draft on N.Y., or a certificate of deposit from a Solvent Bank not liable to discount, for sets or parts of sets of Machines, and directing in what manner the machines shall be forwarded, will have the machines sent as directed—it being understood that in no case is the freight, storage, or *any* charge to be made to the Manufacturers by Agents or Purchasers; but in all cases the Purchasers pay such charges.

The Subscribers also manufacture Machines for locking and forming Stove Pipe, and Machines for making Eave-troughs or Gutters.

AGENTS.

MAINE.
THOS. TOLMAN & SON, Portland.
ALBERT NOYSE & CO., Bangor.

MASSACHUSETTS.
MOSES POND & CO., Boston.
REUBEN RICHARDS, do.

CONNECTICUT.
C. SIGOURNEY & SON, Hartford.
J. & E. NORTH, Berlin.
J. & W. BULKLEY, do.
F. ROYS & CO. do.

NEW YORK.
PHELPS, DODGE & CO. N. York.
LOCKE & CARTER, do.
STOKES GILBERT & CO. do.
E. CORNING & CO., Albany.
WILLIAM AUSTIN, do.
E WATTS, Rochester.
OWEN O'NIEL, Utica.
KELLOGG & CO., Troy.
SIDNEY SHEPARD, Buffalo.

PENNSYLVANIA.
JAMES PARK & Sons, Pittsburgh.
WM. ROOT, Harrisburgh.
N. & G. TAYLOR, Philadelphia.
NATHAN TROTTER & CO., do.

RHODE ISLAND.
JOHN A. HOWLAND, Providence.

MARYLAND.
WELLS CHASE, Baltimore.
E. PRATT & BROTHER, do.
N. & E. L. PARKER, do.

GEORGIA.
B. F. CREW, Augusta.

OHIO.
W. & R. P. RESOR, Cincinnati.
SELEW & CO., do.
S. WHITAKER, Cleveland.

KENTUCKY.
WALLACE & LITHGOW, Louisville.

TENNESSEE.
BENJAMIN WELLER, Nashville.

LOUISIANA.
SAMUEL LOCKE, New Orleans.
SLARK, DAY, STAUFFER & Co., do.

ALABAMA.
CALEB PRICE, Mobile.

MICHIGAN.
S. SHEPARD, Detroit.

MISSOURI.
O. D. FILLEY, St. Louis.

☞ The Agents will generally have on hand sets of Machines for examination.

Extra faces can be added or not at the option of the purchaser; they will be sent however unless otherwise ordered.

PRICES FOR O. & N. PECK'S MACHINES.

	Prices for old kind full set, $80.	
Full Set, $90.		
Folding Machine, 15,50	Folding Machine,	$14,18
Grooving, do. 12,25	Grooving, do.	11,42
Setting down do. 9,75	Wiring, do.	9,60
Wiring, do. 11,50	Setting down, do.	9,56
Large Turning do. 8,50	Large Turning do.	8,40
Small do. do. 8,55	Small, do. do.	8,40
Large Burring do. 8,00	Large Burring do.	7,62
Small do. do. 8,00	Small do. do.	7,62
Extra faces for Machines. 8,00	Extra Burr Rollers,	3,20
$90,00		80.00

PECK, SMITH & CO., Southington, Conn.

JANUARY, 1846.

PRESS OF ELIHU GEER, 26 STATE STREET, HARTFORD.

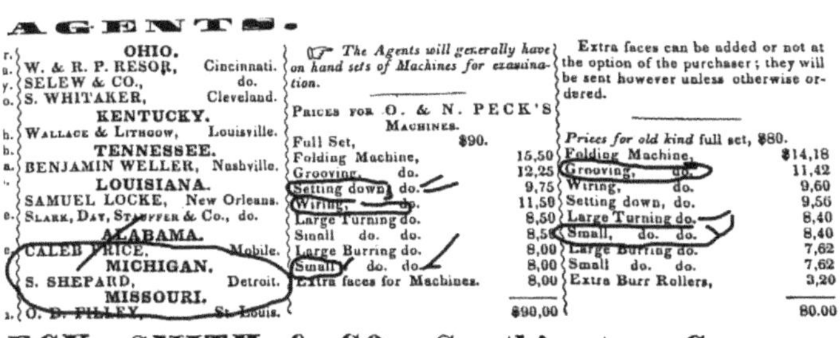

AGENTS.

OHIO.
W. & R. P. RESOR, Cincinnati.
SELEW & CO., do.
S. WHITAKER, Cleveland.

KENTUCKY.
WALLACE & LITHGOW, Louisville.

TENNESSEE.
BENJAMIN WELLER, Nashville.

LOUISIANA.
SAMUEL LOCKE, New Orleans.
SLARK, DAY, STAUFFER & Co., do.

ALABAMA.
CALEB PRICE, Mobile.

MICHIGAN.
S. SHEPARD, Detroit.

MISSOURI.
O. D. FILLEY, St. Louis.

☞ The Agents will generally have on hand sets of Machines for examination.

Extra faces can be added or not at the option of the purchaser; they will be sent however unless otherwise ordered.

PRICES FOR O. & N. PECK'S MACHINES.

	Prices for old kind full set, $80.	
Full Set, $90.		
Folding Machine, 15,50	Folding Machine,	$14,18
Grooving, do. 12,25	Grooving, do.	11,42
Setting down do. 9,75	Wiring, do.	9,60
Wiring, do. 11,50	Setting down, do.	9,56
Large Turning do. 8,50	Large Turning do.	8,40
Small do. do. 8,55	Small, do. do.	8,40
Large Burring do. 8,00	Large Burring do.	7,62
Small do. do. 8,00	Small do. do.	7,62
Extra faces for Machines. 8,00	Extra Burr Rollers,	3,20
$90,00		80.00

ECK, SMITH & CO., Southington, Conn.

PRESS OF ELIHU GEER, 26 STATE STREET, HARTFORD.

14 August 1853

To my Friend Wladislaw Salomon,

Greetings. Jozefa and I received your Letter when you wrote of your impending Journey west from Philadelphia. I hope you have arrived in Safety and you will write when you can of your Life.

We are settled in Chicago as we were when I last wrote. Jozefa has found many Friends with the Polish here and the Children are growing well, as is the Business, though I envy your continuing Adventures. Jozefa does as well. She sends her Regards to Monika.

In Friendship,
Stanley Kotlarczyk
Chicago

06 November 1862

To my Friend and fellow Smith, Stanislaw Kotlarczyk of Chicago, Greetings from the Dakota Territory.

I have asked my Friend, Harry Turner, the Owner of the Mercantile here, to write this for me.

We departed Independence for the Dakota Territory in Spring. I have a Smithy in Flats Town, which is Well-Placed on the new Wagon Trail. With the Homestead Act, we now have some Land, though I do not know how to Farm. The Territory is growing each Year. You might Wish to come West with your Family soon.

Monika sends her Regards to Jozefa.
Yours in Faith, and in Friendship,
Wladislaw Salomon
W

18 December 1863

To my Friend Wladistaw Salomon,

Greetings. We have received your Letters, and considered Plans to join your Family. However, my Sons are off to War, and we Dare not leave Chicago until they are Returned to us. I do not know when or how we will get to Flats Town.

In Truth, we are very Distraught by this War, and with two Boys fighting, I know Jozefa worries that our Wojciech will need to Enlist in time. You are Fortunate you will not need to send your Children to Battle.

In Friendship,

Stanley Kotlarczyk

Chicago

12 November 1864

To my Friend and fellow Smith, Stanisław Kotlarczyk of Chicago, Greetings from the Dakota Territory.

I have asked my Neighbor, Joe Greenman, a Good Man, to write this for me. We are growing quickly here in Flats Town, as Fort Randall to the West continues to be Important and Yankton is booming, especially as it is the Capital of the Territory. There is Much Need for more than the occasional Tinker that comes around every other Summer, and you and your Sons would find enough Work to keep all four of you busy should you come West.

The Wagon trails go through here to stop in a traditional place at the old buffalo jump, and there are new Arrivals often. They are building a Railroad in the East, which we are sure will run through Vermillion next, then Yankton and then Flats Town.

Our Banker says we will then rename the place Flats Junction. You will find the rail will Bring more Work and materials will Arrive quickly. Perhaps buy a New Machine if you can Afford it. The Novelty will draw customers Quickly, and I will Advertise of your Skill before you arrive. Send Word of your decision so I might Prepare for you.

Do not Speak of this to Jozefa, but know there are small Battles still Fought on the Plains between the Army and the Natives. While none have been in Flats Town lately, it is the Wagons they will sometimes Target. There is Danger in coming, but the Rewards for life here are far Greater than you would Imagine.

Yours in Faith, and in Friendship,
Wladistaw Salomon
W

18 January 1865
To my Friend Wladistaw Salomon,
We will come to Flats Town as soon as Tomasz and Ludwik return from the War. Jozefa and I are Agreed. If you might secure a Building for us, we hope to come out in the Spring.

I will make Inquiries about the Travel and a Wagon. Jozefa is glad to know there are Polish where we go, and we hope there is a Church as well. The City is growing fast, and there are more Craftsmen every Month. We will be glad for the Work in the West.

My son Tomasz will bring his Bride out if the Marriage can be made in time. Look for us in the Spring.

In Friendship,
Stanley Kotlarczyk
Chicago

8 March 1865

To my Friend and fellow Smith, Stanisław Kotlarczyk of Chicago, Greetings from the Dakota Territory.

I have asked Father Jonathon, a Good Man, to write this for me. He is the Priest in Flats Town. You may tell Jozefa.

A Building is secured for your Family. It is not much. A Barn on my Property I can Provide. It will take much Work to make it a Home and a Shop, but with your Sons to Help, I am sure it will Suffice. Please tell Jozefa I Apologize I cannot offer More.

Be Well and Safe on your Travels. I will watch for you in the coming Months.

Yours in Faith, and in Friendship,
Wladisław Salomon
W

Wagon Road

DAKOTA TERRITORY

30 June 1865

CHAPTER ONE
30 June 1865

The dust rolls inside my skirt. It feeds the layer sifting to the bottom of my stockings and digs itself into the cracks of my heels. I can smell it, breathe it, taste it. It has no color until it gathers in the creases of my neck. Then it is a chalky black, though the sand and land around me are dun and red and tan.

We're rounding up early today. The head of the wagon train curves back around toward us at the rear, snaky and wobbling as the oxen lumber and low, and the horses scatter.

"You better get back there and get ready for supper," Tom mentions, jerking a fat thumb behind us into the stifling shade of the wagon's box, and stretching a stiff leg over the top of the seat. "See if you can manage dinner decently tonight."

"It's not like there's much I can make," I retort. "Flour, beans, rice, and root vegetables."

"For once you might figure out how to put all those things together and make something taste like real food, so."

"'*Real*' food?"

"It can't be as hard as you make it out to be, Marie," he complains. "Mother always—"

"Shut up."

I don't need another reminder of Mother. And why does Tom need to mention her anyway? It's not like he was there at the end.

"Well, get back, so," he says again. "Or Father and Al will be griping worse than me."

Clambering over the seat and under the rain-stained canvas, I wince as I climb around the trunks, and hit my shin on one of Father's boxes.

"Damn!"

"I heard that!" Tom calls through the flap, his shadow hazy and grey against the soiled fabric. The wagon churns below me. The thin wood has warped along one side, grinding and smashing against the iron band of the wheel on the right as he swerves the bull team to match the others in a rough circle.

"Well, damn anyway. It hurt," I say quietly, rubbing my shin on the small box holding the treasured burring machine. Tom must not hear me the second time, or else he's concentrating and doesn't care. I glance down, and suck in my lips. The new tinsmithing machine is a heavy lump snuggled in a revered pad of cotton wadding and rags. I've wanted to turn the gearbox once, just to do it. To prove I can. There's no chance any of my two brothers, or Father, will let me touch such a beautiful, gleaming, efficient wonder, but if I'm quick enough, I can take a peek before I need to jump out and start unloading the camp kitchen for dinner.

They won't see what I'm doing. Tom's busy with the oxen, and Father will be guiding one as well to help. And heaven knows where Al is at, walking somewhere behind us. It's now or never.

I unwind the fabric, noting the black stains of slippery grease on it, and feel under the edge of the blankets for the base of the machine. My fingers shake. I'm petrified I will drop and break it, rendering it useless and my father's investment lost. It was incredibly expensive—almost eight dollars—and with it is our future.

Opening up the rest of the sack, the round wheels and choppy gears of the metal are revealed, and I reverently lift up the burring machine so I can settle it onto my lap. My apron is already stained with food and grime, so the extra grease does not make much difference. I tuck the short, fat, stake end into my thighs, and hold on tight as the wagon lurches again. Running my fingers along the perfectly cut iron, turning the crank, and watching the round plates slip and slide past one another, I sigh. It's beautiful. I'm no trained artisan by any means, but I can understand the wealth and hope tied up with such a thing.

Pinching up the fabric in the box open, I heft the machinery in one palm, the comforting weight of the iron matching the strength of my wrist, just as the wagon box pops up once more and the slippery oil on my fingers gives way. With a fat, deadening thump, the burring machine smacks the brass edge of the trunk at my hip, pounding onto the iron stake plate nestled between the boxes, and smashing into my foot.

"*Pieprzyć go! Fuck it!*"

"What are you swearing at in there!?" Tom bangs on the edge of the wagon from the outside, and I yank up straight, my heart pounding, my breathing coming fast and hard, and the heat of the wagon receding into a quiver of chills.

Please don't let it be broken ... Prosić ... please ...

"Marie?"

"Dropped a ... box!" I call out, hoping my surly older brother doesn't think to poke his head in just yet. He can't. He ...

I pick up the machine and turn it over in my hands. A pebbling tremble runs down my fingers, my heart drops, and my mouth cottons. The slender wrought handle, which should crank the disks together, is bent inward, the curl of it gouged from the stake plate, and the threads pulled halfway out of the socket.

My God! What have I done?

I cannot take another breath without the panic breaking loose, and the strange chill sprints up my arms, matched by the thin river of sweat burrowing along the blades of my shoulders, and down the crease between my breasts.

The wagon slows, and Tom stands. Al's voice mingles with Father's, and without another thought, I tunnel the burring machine deep into its packing. Worry splits my head, shame and disappointment in my own clumsiness worming into my chest.

"Marie, you making food?" Al yells in, the canvas dampening his shout.

"I am!"

I shuffle toward the camp kitchen box, letting the shake of my hands flicker through me as I start taking out the big skillet and pot, my mind skittering over the lines of the machine. It was supposed to make the journey to Dakota Territory without issue, but I've destroyed it.

Is it an omen? Will we be shattered during the thirty-day journey to Flats Town too? Or is it a sign of what's to come once we reach the end of our trip?

Pressing my lips tighter together, I sort through the box of turnips and try to pretend that I haven't touched the damn machine at all.

CHAPTER TWO
3 July 1865

"Oh, damn! Not again!"

I stare at the stew. The bubbling broth is thick with ever-available flour, but I've forgotten to add rice.

"Ha! Ruined soup and a curse, too, sister?"

I swat my oldest brother as he walks by, surveying the scene and shaking his head.

"Don't torment. I'll have it fixed in a moment, just see if I don't."

"Pah. You always say so." He keeps teasing, grabbing a crust of hard bread off the makeshift sideboard.

"I'm right at least half the time," I press, and he laughs with a mouth full, walking over to the fire to poke it with the iron. "Tom, I'm not such a bad cook."

"You're not, Marie, really," he obliges with heavy sarcasm, and then stuffs the rest of the crust into his jaw, gnawing and smacking his teeth together.

Father comes around the corner of our wagon, carrying a small bag.

"Trading a tin box for some onions," he says proudly, his Polish accent heavy and thick on hard-won and imperfect English.

"Who has onions?" I wonder.

"Cooley's."

Tom frowns. "Pfft. We have stores of vittles enough," he reminds Father. "Why go wasting good made tinware for some vegetables?"

Without pausing, Father bends down and opens the burlap. Round, globular, onions cascade out of the sack, breaking their translucent skins as they tumble onto the packed dirt of the prairie. I catch one up and inhale the pungent flesh. The first thing I think about is how well they will be to make a soup I likely won't ruin.

"I'll add one to the stew," I announce, and am rewarded with Father's brilliant grin.

"Ha! Do you even know how?" Tom asks.

I push away my irritation, and answer as calmly as I might. "Even if I didn't, I'll figure it out." I sound defiant anyway. He shrugs it off.

"Well, that's something, then." Tom sighs and disappears behind the wheel spokes. Undoubtedly he'll re-count our stores of goods in his head as reassurance as he goes to check over the wagon. We'd bought the lighter prairie schooner for our month-long journey at the railhead in Marshalltown, Iowa, but it was quickly made and needs repairs nearly every night.

Turning back to the blackened pot, I make quick work of the biggest onion on a nearby rock, and add the savory spongy bits to the stew. Father watches me the entire time, and when I finish, he smiles again. It has been long since Father has smiled so much.

"You do that deftly as your mother did," he mentions, and the compliment makes my fire-ripened cheeks flush further. "The saving of a soup. She could always save a soup ..." The memories choke him, and he falls silent. After a moment, he walks away toward the deepening shadows of the wagon circle. I press my lips together and turn toward the onions. At least the cutting of them will give my misty eyes their own excuse.

While stirring the different pots and skillets, churning the rice, I glance at the hardening vegetation around us. We flatten the prairie grasses quickly with our encampments. The ocean of grass, and the smudge of trees on the horizon dips and flows, while the feathering road stretches westward where others have already traveled. The clumsy wagons create a shield against the emptiness of the plains, and the flaps of linen against the frames are tempered by the noise of two hundred bodies preparing to eat. There are many of us, and we leave a trail of graves, black campfires, and garbage every night we make a circle.

I wave tentatively to Agatha Cooley, who usually camps next to our wagon. She grins at me, and I try to match her enthusiasm, but the truth of it is I am too choked with worry about the machine I've broken and the terror twisting through me each night on the prairie.

The tension always mounts as we settle in for the evenings. Will the night be peaceful? Will we wake with a camp full of corpses? Illness? Fire? Will a troupe of angry Indians find us? Have they been trailing us? The litany of questions is unstoppable. Even with the peace the government promises, horrifying stories trip and ripple around campsites on their own accord.

The smoke billows around my skirts, black and brown, and yet finally smelling like something resembling edible food. Would Mother be proud I've salvaged it? Would she be giggling with Agatha Cooley and still pull off a delicious meal? Likely. How I wish she were here!

I rock back on my haunches, and finger the grease stains on my apron, wondering what would have happened had we stayed at the railhead in Marshalltown after riding the train from Chicago. Suppose we had never started this meander through the undulating grass and bluebell sky. Would I marry? Would we find work?

Nearby, the older Cooley children start to chant one of the walking songs from earlier in the day:

> *With a merry little jog and a gay little song,*
> *Whoa! Ha! Buck and Jerry boy,*
> *We trudge our way the whole day long,*
> *Whoa! Ha! Buck and Jerry boy.*
> *What though we're covered all over with dust,*
> *It is better than staying back home to rust,*
> *We'll reach Salt Lake some day or bust!*
> *Whoa! Ha! Buck and Jerry boy.*

I do not hear my brother Albert come up, but suddenly he appears on the opposite side of our campfire, his eyes glittering with energy.

"And where have you been? Certainly not helping around here!" I sputter, feeling disconcerted to have my mulling snapped.

11

"Making the rounds, as always," he says calmly, and takes off his hat. The line of the brim glows. Both of my brothers have a deep crease along their foreheads, where dust and reddened skin meet a gash and then a sallow swathe of virgin flesh before touching their scalp. Al's hair is burnished and tarnished gold in the campfire glow. Above us the early stars pulse and rotate with blue-white gleams. Everything feels bright and stark on the prairie. Will it be the same in Flats Town?

"Anything worth noting around camp tonight?" I ask.

"Naw, not tonight. So, let me help you now, *siostra*," Al offers, reaching to grab the spoons and knives. The onions in the skillet are a mix of clear and opaque, their shimmering whiteness sparkling against the patina of the blackened cast iron. They look ready. I add them to the stew, and hope it'll pass the stomachs of my menfolk.

Father determines we will say a prayer over our food, just as we used to do when Mother was alive, so even in this rough and tumble space we bow our heads. He murmurs his offering, but I am too far away across the fire to hear what he says.

As we eat, Al relays what he has learned from the other wagon drivers. A small pack of wolves was spotted. Some bison are on the horizon to the far north.

No Indians so far.

The papers simultaneously call them awful and noble savages. Like so many others, my men believe the Indians to be less than us, and their ways barbaric and strange. Father thinks they should all turn to Christianity, and their problems with us will be solved and there won't be fights at all anymore. Tom is not so straightforward. He knows battle, even saw our middle brother Lou die on the field. Sometimes he says things that make me think he sees how people come of different minds, and ideas can grow and fester even between whites, just as it was in the war.

But the war in the south is over, and Tom is returned even if Lou is buried in the South. And the war in the Plains is over too, so they say.

"What did you pay for the onions?" Al's light question makes Tom frown and breaks up the conversation about the specter of the Indians.

"I trading them." Sometimes, when Father speaks with emotion, his accent sits heavily on his tongue, adding to the fact that he never fully mastered English. When he admits guilt, it is also very much pronounced.

"How?"

"*Ojciec* decided to trade a box." Tom glowers from his corner next to the wagon. He slouches over against the spokes, and his boots splay out so exterior wear marks where he walks on the outside of his feet are visible.

"It is being fine." Father shrugs and his tone brokers no further debate. The wind picks up and stirs his beard, cropped shorter than usual in practicality for the journey west. His jaw pushes out from under the bushy brows and fat mustache, and he settles deeper into his seat. I curl my knees up under my chin, and hold in my own thoughts as best I might. It doesn't matter if the boys ever have issue with Father. They'll lose any argument they make with him, and my voice will only get lost if I add it.

"We do not be needing to arrive full of stock," Father finally continues. "Walter and his son do not require us so— that is never part of our plan. Besides, we have the machine, to take much time from our hands, to allowing us making many more pieces quickly. You knowing this."

My throat closes. Yes. The machine that is hiding *and broken*. Will they believe it was done during the jostling of the journey? Surely none of them will suspect me? The guilt flattens my lungs. I should speak up. But how? My cowardice shames me, but I don't want to admit defeat or wrongdoing, and my tongue sticks.

Father's confidence in an argument is unshakable. My brothers deflate, but not for long. Tom speaks up.

"And what if we use up all our tin right away?"

"We will not. We be having enough."

I think of the crates, heavily bound and full of metal, in the back of the wagon. Father himself oversaw most of the packing in those frantic weeks in early June, after Mother passed and just before Tom returned from his years serving in the Board of Trade Light Artillery regiment. Al had managed daily tin orders and had sold furniture so we could all leave on the railroad three days after Tom stepped back into the tinshop on June twenty-second. I still recall the blasting arguments shaking the walls of the shop and house when my oldest brother had realized not only that Mother was gone, but we were to leave Chicago only a few days after his return.

But leave we have. The train took us from Chicago to Marshalltown, and there we bought the schooner, filling it with the outlandishly heavy boxes Father had packed all by himself throughout the nights after Mother's death, holding all the tin sheets and the machine, too.

I know the machine cost the equivalent of a month's wages because the boys talk about it endlessly. The *broken machine*, now.

I gulp down my fear. I hope this journey is worth it. I hope we find the work Walter the blacksmith promised. I hope my brothers are able to set up their own shops somehow, as they've always planned. I hope Father is truly happy again, if only for distraction..

As the night builds and the stars burn brighter, my brothers shift, their bellies heavy with hot soup. Tom leaves our campsite to take his turn as part of the early watch. Al rolls out blankets and curls around the fire, already used to the bumpy, hard, ground.

"The onions did well. *Dobranoc. Good night.*"

I look up at Father, where he stands over me. He is treating me as he would have treated Mother. My heart feels as though it bleeds.

"Good night," I echo.

He turns on his heel and disappears into the wagon. I hear the wooden box creak and pop as he shuffles around the narrow space at the back. He will likely sleep next to the machine. I think he feels better when it is nearby, even if he must sleep in a cramped and musty place.

Damn. My luck will be that he pulls out the machine and notices it's broken!

I glance up at the moon. It is only half-full. Soon it will wane to nothing but a slip of a fingernail crescent. It is brighter out here, and some nights the moonlight is as brilliant as day. The bed of starlight tracing across the heavens is clearer and truer than the yellowed, stinking lights of Chicago. If I stopped worrying, I might actually enjoy the beauty of the west.

CHAPTER THREE
5 July 1865

The rifles sound like firecrackers. At first, that's what I think they are: firecrackers left over from a July Fourth celebration, likely tied to the tail of someone's cat or dog for the fun of it. I roll over and hit my temple on a pebble.

"Damnit!"

"Hush!" Al hisses, sitting up and barely visible against the smoke of our half-dead campfire. "That's shots."

"Shots? Pft. Someone's drunk." Tom groans, turning in his blanket. "Shut it, both of you. I'm just into bed myself. Damn, I hate the middle of the night watch."

"It's better than the first watch," Al grouses. "I've been on that this week, and I can't wait for next week when—"

"Be quieting!" Father pokes his head out of the wagon back. "It's a gun."

As he mentions it, another round of shooting goes off, and the flash and burn of the powder and flame on the far side of the wagon circle sets off a scream among the women and children. It ripples through the night, and bursts into each camp. I close my lips together to keep my own sounds in check, but a whimper escapes all the same.

Then the whoops begin. They are eerie, and echo around us. It sounds as though a thousand Indian braves are staring at the huge circle of wagons and yodeling. My scream matches the others, and I shrink down, feeling cowardly and completely unable to survive all at the same time.

"*Święty piekło! Holy hell!*" Tom jumps to his feet, his bulk moving faster than I've ever seen. He is white as paste, even in the moonlight, but his face is tight and hard under the beard. "Where's our guns?" He shouts hoarsely to Father to pull out the cartridge boxes and powder horns.

I creep on all fours toward the wheels, wincing hard as each shot rings out. The next round of whoops fills my ears and stops my eyes. I'm blind, dragging my silly feet and my hands through the dirt, my toes hitting every rock, and my fears colliding in one unspeakable swallow.

How many are there? Will they scalp us? Shoot us? Kidnap us?

Will they torture us?

Dearest God, what were those stories on torture again? The running, the gauntlet … was that the Plains Indians or another kind? *Why can't I move faster?*

This is what I've feared the most on this journey and now it's here.

It's happening!

Jezus! Help me! *Maryja, Matka Boża*! Mary, Mother of God, save me!

The wagon wheel is scant cover, and Father's bulk shifts and tumbles out, the gleaming tin cartridge boxes and

the hard horns of powder spraying from his fingers. One
bursts open at the cap, and the dull, black, gunpowder flies
up like tiny black gnats, disappearing into the grass.

"Where's Marie?" Father shouts as he goes, and Tom
points toward the shadow of the wagon.

"Here!" I call, but my voice sounds small and lost
amid the spreading gunfire. Shapes swarm on the far end of
the wagon circle, flickering black and gold and red around
the half-eaten fires, and the racket of more rifles shooting
into the blank wilderness around us covers half my yell. Did
Father hear?

"Stay here!" Father orders, and he vanishes into the
dark with Tom. I grip the hard wood spokes of the wheel,
and jump so high I hit my head on the bottom of the wagon
box when a body dives next to me.

"What—?"

"Shhh! It's me." Al rearranges himself and crouches
nearby. Even in the dark, his face is slick with sweat and paler
than Tom's. When his arm pushes against me, the tremor of
his body shakes into mine, and I instinctively put my arm
about his shoulders.

More whispers and rustling syphon through my ears,
sighing and soughing, and at first I think it's Indians creeping
up at our backs. I jerk and turn as best I can in the cramped
quarters, but the prairie is washed in moonlight where it
slowly opens onto the land. The clouds scuttle away and all
the stars reveal their glory. The grassland is empty. There are
no Indians, at least not behind us.

At least, not that I can see.

There are more whispers, and I finally notice many
families hiding inside and under their wagons. The Cooley's

have six children still living, and all of them are huddled around Agatha. In the strange, shadowed, dark, they look like a teeming mass of strange half-beasts, and my mind wanders to the pictures I've seen of the Indian savage in newspapers back in Chicago. Fear cranks into my mind again, and I strain to hear more whoops and hollers. The gunfire continues here and there, but suddenly settles considerably.

"They've scared them off, it sounds," Al echoes my thoughts, and shrugs off my arm from his shoulders. "I should … maybe go see?"

"Stay here!" I hiss. "What's the point? You don't have a gun ready anyway."

"I can grab the extra from the wagon—"

"Damn it, Wojciech!" I use his given Polish name as Mother would have done, and it draws him up hard and quiet at once. "There's no reason to go right now. Stay here."

"So I … can protect you?"

"Something like that."

Another rustle stalks the shadows behind our wagon, and I lunge on instinct when I feel the box above us creak.

Someone is stealing in! Someone's taking our food! Our goods!

The burring machine!

I scream without realizing I'm screaming, until the sound of it rips through my throat and rakes it raw. Pounding my hands on the underside of the wood, I stand faster than my feet can move, and whack my head straight on the bottom of the wagon.

"Get out!" I screech. "Out! We've got a gun!"

The motion pauses, and out of the corner of my eye, I notice the teeming Cooley clan has frozen.

"*Wynoś się! Get the hell out!*" I smack my hands against the side of the wagon, uncertain if I dare to climb in. I have nothing! Nothing but my voice!

Is it savages? Is it—?

The shards of broken, brittle, grass crackle again, and I spin once more, my heart suspended completely in the back of my chest, my hands going up and out to protect my face.

"Marie! It's us!" The whisper is hoarse.

I let my hands down slightly, and take in the black shadows of Tom and Father. My arms are shaking and my stomach twists. Is it relief or is it fear?

Who the hell is in the wagon?

"What's going on?" Tom's voice is very soft, and his dark eyes are trained on the back of the wagon.

"Someone's inside." My eyes spin toward the wagon, and I remember Al is still huddled under the box.

"Who?"

"How should I know?" I back away slowly, staring at the hulking frame. The campfires on the other side cast a barely visible red edge to it, and it's impossible to see in through the fabric. The wagon moves again, and I round behind Tom, glad of his large height for once.

"Al's under yet," I murmur into his back. "Be careful."

"Shit! Al's under the wagon!" Tom mutters to Father and another man who joins in. "Watch it."

The guns slide in unison, curving onto their shoulders. The dull silvery steel of the Bridesburgs capture the bit of fire-light and glow gold on the lock plates. I suddenly wonder if I'm overreacting. Maybe there's no one in the wagon. Maybe my own foolish, womanly eyes … But no. Al felt it too. I'm sure of it.

20

"Come out careful. There's multiple guns on you now. If you come out peaceful we won't fill you with lead," Tom calls.

I wait, breathless, my blood still pounding erratically. Behind and around us, more men slip forward, guns trained on the wagon.

The machine! Our goods! Our food!

We still have nearly two weeks to go, we need our food …

My place is taken by a few more of our wagon neighbors. I can't see over the manly heads anymore, but Tom is still in the front, calling lowly, and with growing anger.

"Get out!" someone finally yells. "Show your face, you damn coward!"

The cry picks up at once, and a gun goes off into the air, and women scream, and it's all very confusing and dark and the bodies around me press and pitch forward, jostling and shouting until I'm spit out at the back end of the mass.

"Al!" I shout, hoping my brothers hear me, hoping they remember. "Be careful of Al!"

No one hears me, though, not even Father, and in another minute the wagon is crawling with men. The screaming and yelling and shouting only get louder and higher when Tom appears at the back, with his black beard flying and his black eyes burning, and he throws a body deep into the crowd.

"There's one of our Indians, boys!" he bellows, his face a mask of stiffness and strange, contorted rage.

There's a scuffle and more shouting, and then a tall, lanky man is spun upwards, his wrists twisted tightly behind him with someone's raggedy scarf, his thin, gaunt, cheeks purple and red.

"You can sit with the others and wait your trial," Franks, the wagon master, declares from his place among the shadows. "First light."

The thief disappears within the crowd, and the shouting melts away slowly and carefully, though at least two more muskets go off without warning. I jump both times.

"What the hell were you thinking? He could have stabbed you! Shot you!" Tom fumes, shaking my arm suddenly. I glance up at him and pull my lips in, pressing them against my teeth to fight any retort careening through my mind.

"My Marie is being very brave, I am thinking," Father says quietly, just as Al slowly, reluctantly, crawls out from under the wagon.

"You alright, too?" One of the last of our neighborly helpers grasps Al's forearm and yanks him up.

"Fine."

"Pfft. Of course he is. He sat hidden in a little black hole and let our sister do the screaming," Tom says.

"I thought it was Indians," Al says sullenly, and turns toward his wadded bedroll.

"It wasn't Indians!" Tom says to Al's back, but our youngest brother refuses to speak at all, which is saying something. I stare at Tom and Father and their rifles in various stages of readiness, and inhale a shaky bit of night air. Fatigue pummels into me all at once, and I let my mouth go loose.

"If it wasn't Indians, what was it?"

"A couple of the drifting men, pretending to be Indians to scare people on one end, only to have the rest of them try to steal from the wagons on the other," Tom explains.

"A good notion, too, if the man doing the stealing is smart enough to pick a wagon that's empty."

"Ours was empty," I remind.

"Well, but you were under it and not being shy about screaming," Father grins at me briefly.

I shudder slightly at the memory of the fear that had split my mind in half. Suddenly the bent burring machine feels a paltry, small, thing in the face of all the scrabbling and worry and very real violation of our private traveling house.

"Pah! Marie's not shy about letting anyone know she's nervous," Tom scoffs, and moves toward our fire and away from the gloomy night.

"So not Indians," I repeat, needing to say it once more.

"Not being Indians," Father agrees, his heavy hand guiding me toward our beds as well.

"Now what—what happens to the men doing all the mischief?" I ask as we smooth out our blankets once more, and Father smashes around the coals to bring more heat out from under their layer of black, ashy chips.

"We are waiting for Franks to get a court together tomorrow. It will be being like Chicago, with a jury and judge and even having witnesses, and someone is likely having to be standing and be speaking for the guilty."

"But they'll be found guilty, won't they, Father?"

"They'd better," Tom growls from his corner by the wagon wheel. He's a huddled shadow. Al is flat and tight as a board on the other side of the fire. "No question. Guilty." Tom puts his head behind his arms and looks upward. "And then they'll hang between the wagons. I hope they use ours. Ha!"

CHAPTER FOUR
8 July 1865

"Morning, Marie."

I crack an eye. Al grins at me from across the fire. He is always the first one up, as if the sun sets his sleeping and waking. He makes the coffee and starts the fire, and the two of us share a cup before the others generally make an appearance. I appreciate it; I am not very good at making the morning brew.

"Sleep well?" he asks, twisting his mouth.

"That's a bad question," I retort.

We have about seven days left before we reach Flats Town. For all I'm worried about the hard work needed to build a new life, and though I fear the roughness of the west against the ease of the city, I'm barely able to think for the fretting consuming my thoughts as my feet pound the dirt each day.

Sitting up and pulling my knees to my chest, I wait as Al pours the smashed beans into the large tin kettle along with water, and sets it over the fire. The normalcy of the morning settles my nerves. Thankfully, the coffee will not take long to boil; the tin is thin.

Al tosses two mugs next to the fire, and places a small clay bowl just inside the ring of fire. I do not need to look to know he is planning to repair the soldering on the two pieces of crockery. They were leaking yesterday.

"Going to try your hand at it?" He cocks his head at me, the yellow hair sticking up at all angles in the morning haze. Out of all of us, he is the brightest, the beautiful child, with dark eyes and fair hair. Mother used to say we had some Austrian blood somewhere in the family, and Al is proof of it. The rest of us are the usual mix: dark brown hair, dark black-brown eyes, swarthy skin, and built for strength and power and hard living.

"Why should I try any metalwork when there are three tinsmiths around here?" I ask, raising my eyebrows.

"If you learned a bit of it, there'd be four," he intones, rehearsing an old argument. There is little need for me to learn the trade, what with Father, Tom, and Al all able to do the same work, and even Lou before he was killed. I admit I've absorbed more than is ladylike—it was hard not to, when the smithy was in the same space as the kitchen hearth—but I have had no hand at practicing. I have often wondered what it would be to bend the silver and gold of the tin and copper, and make it grow and sing beneath my hands. There is a type of art, a magic to it. A touch. It is a small curiosity, of course, to wonder whether I'd be any good.

Now that I broke the burring machine, it's obvious it is not my place to even touch part of the family trade. What a horrible smith I'd be, if I can't even keep machinery safe in my own hands! I dread when Father opens up the box and sees the mangled handle.

What will I say? How much apologizing will be enough?

Al stares at the small bowl of tin, waiting and watching. The shift and slow buzz of bubbles starts in the coffee pot, filling the air between us. The beans are overly toasted, but the deepness of the brew makes my mouth water.

"Ah … nature calls." My brother suddenly announces his bodily functions, stands abruptly, and heads off into the tall grass on the edge of camp. I am grateful he thinks to find privacy. Some of the men around the wagons have no issue with marking wheel spokes with their own urine, just like a dog. Like Tom does.

The coffee simmers and sighs, but I do not hear the telltale sound of a true boil. Though the drink is not ready, the tin soldering is. The small beads of tin shot run, liquefied and shining like brilliant quicksilver. Al is still not back, and I try to cinch in the curiosity yanking at my senses. Wouldn't it be something if I might surprise him with a repaired mug? He's teased me enough about it.

Why not?

Slipping over to his side of the fire, I take care to not rustle my skirts too much, so that I do not wake Tom. Surely, it is not so difficult. I have heard them talk about smith work my entire life, watched them assemble tricky orders out of the corner of my eye, and fondled the tools with my own hands when no one looks.

Still, I have not handled the metal itself. Is there a good trick to it? An artisan's magic? I pick up the mug closest to me and try to find where it needs repairs.

There. Along the edge of the handle on the base. I see the fine crack in the seam, where the burr has pulled away from the bottom, and the soldering has worn away. No wonder it was leaking beer last night.

I press my lips together and glance at Al's small tinker kit. There's a battered tin container of rosin flux, and I open it carefully, wondering how much should be used. Pinching a small chip, I drop it inside the interior of the mug, where any globes of excess will be easily hidden. Placing the piece on an edge of the iron grate over our fire, I dip a scoop of molten tin out, and quickly dump it into the heating body.

Is that it? Exhilaration and tension choke my thoughts, chasing away the other worries and concerns festering in my mind. I peer into the mug, the morning fire blazing along my cheeks and my neck. Is it going to be warm today or am I just nervous? I push my lips together hard and tight, and jiggle the cup again.

"Take it off the fire."

I jump. Al is at my shoulder, glancing inside the mug. He wordlessly hands over my slab of sheep wool, and I take the heated piece from the flames. Inside, the tin is wetly soft, spinning along the edges and curing into the crack.

"Blow on it, Marie," he instructs, his hands hovering over the cup. I send cool breath into the fresh solder, and watch it harden almost immediately. There are small chunks of leftover rosin inside, a light brown residue clinging to the metal.

Glancing up at him, I give a little smile. "And that's it?"

He has a lopsided grin, an endearing trait that kept all the young women running to him back in Chicago. To me, he looks forever like the little toddler I had to chase to save from falling into the fires and touching the hot coppers.

"That's it. You've done a good tinker job."

"How long were you watching me?"

"How long does it take to piss?"

He crouches down and takes the warm mug, wiping off whatever excess rosin he can, to keep from needing to chip it off bit by bit later.

"You don't mind I tried it?" I feel more than a little exhilarated. Is it that I didn't mess up something for once? Because failure didn't worm its way into my actions? Or is it because for the first time in weeks, as I concentrate on smith work, I wasn't buried under the strain of constant questions about our future?

"Marie, I've been after you for years to try your hand at tin. You did a fine job of it. No one will be able to tell, at least not right away." He inspects my work again, frowning slightly, but then his youthful, beardless face clears, and he sets the tinwork down, satisfied.

"Can I … should I try it again?" I try to mask the eagerness in my voice. The euphoria of creation, even though I did nothing but fix a small piece of crockery, sits in my belly and tingles my bones. Al hears the nuance anyway, and grins saucily.

"Can you do it before Tom or Father wakes?" We both of us know how particular they are to provide good work. They're both sticklers for tradition, among other things. If I were a true apprentice, I would never be soldering. Instead I'd be carting fuel for the brazier furnace, slowly tracing and cutting patterns, or just cleaning pots for re-tinning.

I don't wait for him to reconsider, and immediately set the second mug on the iron.

"Now you're hasty. You don't know where to repair, and you forgot the flux."

I close my eyes at my foolishness and take the handle quickly before it gets too hot. "Alright then, where do I fix this one?"

"How are you supposed to learn the trade if I give you all the answers?"

This mug is harder, and I feel an urgency to finish the repair work before the others poke their heads up. The sun turns the sky a soft grey blue, with a pale peach blush pulsing along the horizon. Soon the whole camp will be awake.

Al must feel the pressure as well, because he does not wait long before reminding me to check the lap seam along the vertical ends of the body.

His intervention is just in time. Father snaps his head out of the back of the wagon as Al is blowing on the fresh solder.

"Is coffee being ready?"

I nod, and stand to pull out more mugs, the clink of the tin bringing Tom awake as well. Before long, the four of us gather around the campfire, chasing away the morning chills that come with the dampness of dew and mist and uncertainty.

CHAPTER FIVE
9 July 1865

Tom grinds his teeth, a sound I can hear clear across the fire. It grinds my nerves. Father ignores him, and pulls his letter from Walter in his lap and gazes at it, his fingers brushing over the words. He traces the lines making out my mother's name, a gesture so small and intimate that I feel as though I am betraying a confidence by seeing it. Looking away, I feel the same old tug at my own heart when I think of her. Josie, he had called her. His Josie.

"Looking at the damn letter again?" Tom says, noticing the paper. "Pah. If it weren't for that, I'd be married by now." He turns away, and gazes across the dark plains, clearly not interested in actual conversation. He left Sonja in Chicago, with barely a chance for a soft word of love between them before Father whisked us off to the west. I wonder if he thinks of her often.

How much of his thoughts linger on the war he fought? Some days Father talks of it, and of how glad he is Tom is home. No one speaks of Mother when he does, or how my brother missed her deathbed. Tom has no vision of her wasting from the strangling yellow fever she suffered, shortly after mingling along the river with some neighbors.

Always social and brightly popular, Mother never turned down a chance to gossip with the other Polish in our area. But the last time, she'd come down sick, and no doctor could fix her. That much was clear by the end.

"Well, then, my little Marya," Father says softly, putting an arm around me suddenly, using my given name in a small gesture of affection. I fall into his steady, thick, middle, enjoying the comfort and familiarity of it. Father seems as though he will never die. He is solid and real and forever. He smells like sweat and horses, fire and cooking oil, with the heavy tang of metal always lacing his fingers. Like my brothers, the cracks of his hands are filled with the black of soot and rosin. It's a stain that never completely cleans up, even after rigorous scrubbing.

"Do you truly think that we will be successful?" I ask him. I wish to ask so many more specific questions. I want to know why he took us west, why the minutes after Mother's death were filled with a frenzy of packing. I want to ask about Flats Town, and old Walter the blacksmith, and what he thinks of Tom after the war.

Father nods. "Successful? We will be succeeding. Walter not tells me false."

"Likely he's lonely for some good, lively, discussion in his own language," I say, and Father chuckles. The tickle of it jumps under my cheek, and I shift so the button of his vest pocket doesn't dig into my skin.

"I am sure he will be liking that, too," he agrees. "And it is nice to be building a town. It is better than leaving something, knowing it is broken."

He speaks of the diaspora of our country. He is one of many who chose to pick up the family and come over after the Uprising in '46, right as the potato crop festered with the first wave of blight. My father, forever a tinker and a fixer, still agonizes over leaving. I think he feels it a personal failing that he did not stay and work to reconstruct Poland.

Sometimes I wonder if and how life would be any different there. I was not yet born when Father sold his tools and snatched us out of Krakow. They had hiked overland to Bremen, choosing a ship to New York before pressing to Chicago. Two of my older siblings died on the journey over. Mother never spoke their names, and in deference to her, Father doesn't either.

"Is Władisław a very dear friend, then, Father?" I refer to the letter, edging the soft paper with a rough forefinger. The sensitive question still feels like an intrusion, but Father actually answers.

"He was," Father amends. "We were training much side by side in Poland. He in iron, and me in tin. We worked together on many swords in our apprenticeships. That was creating a deep bond that is forging with metal. It is a partnership, a trust. I was being lucky to have him as my friend, as I do now. I was young, once," he says, with much wistfulness in his voice.

I bend down to kiss his forehead softly.

"I know it, Father."

As I pick my way to bed, I see Al and Tom are both sleeping, their heads turned against the cold toward the fire. The flames, previously roaring for the evening meal, settle themselves to a rolling ember pile of orange. Soon the moonlight will take over, and the stars, and then the pale shivery color of night will wash over us.

My own rest takes its time to creep over me. The camp is never completely quiet. Sometimes children cry out: a sharp, piercing, shrillness cutting the night. And there is always the shifting, coughing, and crackling of old campfires. There are murmurs of the men who are in charge of keeping watch, and soft sighs of coupling. In the fluttering shadows, I can see the undulating limbs of their passion, and I wish, someday, it might be me who is held by a man. I think I might like it.

Would Mother have found this charming, the way she always found good in everything? She would have likely seen the adventure in it all: to strike out across the land into a more daring world filled with danger and excitement once more. She could make anything seem bright and full of laughter. Would that I were as light-hearted as she was, and as luminous. Her eyes could twinkle at Father and pull him out of a brooding mood when he worried over a customer's intricate request. She could keep Tom from grumpiness, her tenderness toward Al was always just the right touch of mothering.

I know I will never be as lovely as my mother, nor as flirtatious. She was dark-haired, like me, but her beauty was deep and true. Without Mother to put her polish on my manners, I feel dull and clumsy even chatting with the Cooley family or other young women my age. I wish I was like Mother.

I can wish, I suppose. I close my eyes, and head to the edge of sleep. In the far distance, the coyotes howl their warbling yips to the sky. Their presence is soothing, if only because it confirms there are no Indian raiders sneaking up from the heaving hills that crest and roll and stretch around us.

CHAPTER SIX
12 July 1865

"So?"

He lifts up the copper boiler. "No leaks yet."

I allow a full smile to spread across my cheeks, and then pinch them down with my hand. My fingers are dirty and coarsely rough—worse than they've ever been—but Al is not helping my attempt at humility because he is smirking with something akin to pride.

"It's all my doing. I knew I'd be good at—"

"What did you do?" Tom is awake, rubbing a stout, wide forearm across his forehead as he sits up.

Al's face stops mid-chortle, and he turns to address our older brother.

"Made coffee."

"You don't make the coffee," Tom sits up. I wonder how long he's been listening. I think I've been quiet enough, but I can't stop a shiver of delighted fright spinning down my spine. It really is not an issue if I've been learning some craft on the side, but I know my Tom will think it's foolishness and a waste of time, and likely will discourage it. He will say it is ill-bred. Or, he'll tease mercilessly. And remind me how I'd do better to work on my cooking than play with metal. He'd be right.

Al lays his head down on one shoulder. "How would you know who makes the coffee every morning? You're always sleeping anyway."

We stand next to each other, as if ready to brace one another against any accusations, but Tom just sighs heavily. "It's too early to argue."

He gets up and heads toward the tall grasses, unbuttoning his fly as he goes.

I rummage into the food box. It is meager pickings this late into the journey, as we haven't packed the full amount of food for pioneers going all the way to Oregon. Instead of hundreds of pounds of flour and coffee, dried beans, peas, and vinegar, we took the minimum. The tin and tools and stakes take up too much weight for more than the barest cupboard needs. If I had fresh meat, I could try to make *kielbasa* or *kishka* sausages as Mother would.

"Marie, what's for breakfast?" Al asks.

"Probably porridge," I admit, and he groans.

The porridge itself is ready quick enough once the water is hot, though I end up overcooking it slightly. I dish out the grey slop as Father, Tom, and Al settle in, and they fall to the meal hungrily. For all their complaining, the outdoors and the heavy travel make them ready to eat near anything I make, even when it is burned.

Father finishes quickly and hands me his dishes, which slip and rattle as I move them into the water, and the bit of food left glides off, smooth and silky and slimy. I'm looking forward to a proper kitchen, where I might find my hand at making meals, and to have the ease of a solid hearth. There are dreams of roses and cornflowers and lily of the valley rising above the ground around my door, and geraniums in windowsills. A sentimental part of me wishes to put myrtle and rosemary in the ground in the hopes I might make my own wedding bouquet. I want a space to make into a home for everyone, as if by living in such a shell of a place, I might find some mastery in being a true homemaker.

I think of the meager stove sitting in the back of the bed, covered in sooty blacking against the elements and rust. How will I make such a thing useful to heat and cook?

Tom and Al polish off the last of the meal behind me, just as Father leaves to speak to Franks, the wagonmaster. Tom absently taps the edge of his knife against the edge of the tin plate as he starts on his coffee. It is an old tick of his, and much of our kitchenware has dents along the sides due to his repetitive bounce.

"Stop doing that." I turn and rip the plate out of his fingers.

He raises his eyebrows. "*Jezus*. What's got into you?"

"Nothing."

He glances at me skeptically.

"It's not my place," I mutter, "to speak up about how I feel."

"When has that ever stopped you from saying it anyway?"

"Since we left Chicago."

"Have you found a sweetheart on the trail you don't want to leave?" Al teases. "Worried about our arrival in Flats Town tearing you apart?"

Tom snorts into his coffee. "Marie's a bit young to have a sweetheart."

"I am not," I huff.

Tom stretches as he balances his empty plate on a knee. He has a hole in his left armpit. I will have to remember to mend it. Mending and sewing I am rather good at, at least. "I guess not."

"Well, what does that make me otherwise? Already a spinster at eighteen?" The complaint is out before I can stop it, and I bite my tongue afterward. It does no good to moan about my lot in life, and truly I have no men who seemed interested me in Chicago—nor on this wagon trip west—but the knowledge that no man pays me mind is disheartening. Perhaps Mother was overly kind when she would say I had a smooth face.

"I suppose we could let you marry, eventually," Tom considers aloud.

Al nods thoughtfully. "Once we settle down and are able to meet most of the men."

Their seriousness makes me pause. Surely, they are giving me trouble to make me rise to argue. I try not to take the bait, but it's no use.

"Of course, you'd be the ones to manage who I marry."

They turn to me together, one pair of eyes wide and the other narrowed.

"Of course," Al echoes. "What else do brothers do for their sisters?"

"It's Father's job to worry on that," I say. Tom shakes his head.

"Maybe he gives permission, but we can be sure to control who courts you, Marie."

I scoff, and move toward the dishpan. "Well, thankfully your job at protecting me from suitors does not overtax you."

Tom actually chuckles, and Al grins.

I turn from the sudsy water and stare. "What's so damn funny?"

"Oh, Marie! Pfft! If you only knew! There were three fellows in Chicago and at least five here on the wagon train who have wanted to court you." Tom's voice is almost merry.

Surprise yanks at my gut, and I round on them.

"What is this? You're teasing awful." It does not do to explain to my brothers how much it hurts when I am not noticed by any of the available young men. Their gaze always slides over me, as if I'm unworthy. If only they knew how lusty my dreams can be. If only they stopped to speak to me! And in Chicago? I was lucky to get more than a polite greeting even from the other Polish boys in our neighborhood.

"Oh, yeah, there's lots of men asking about, so. At least five here on the trip west. Maybe six?" Al glances at Tom. "But one was quite old. Forty, was he?"

"At least. And then there was the one looking for a wife to manage his five children."

Al raises his fingers, closing two. "And there was the one younger than me wanting a bride to prove his manhood. And the bald one who wanted a wife before he reached his destination as he'd heard women were scarce where he was heading."

"And don't forget the pretty one."

"You two must have been dreaming up this little tease all day yesterday. Very nice. It's not nearly as funny as you thought." The whole discussion makes me grumpy.

"We're telling the truth, Marie," Al says earnestly, and his tone takes me aback.

"These men? They ask you to court me?" The dynamics of the male realm are beyond me, but I would think anyone who is truly interested in marrying me will approach Father.

Tom twists his thick mouth into a smirk, but he is not unkind. "Pah! Of course they do. We're the brothers. Easier to ask. Until they realize neither of us are going to approve of them. Lou did the same, back before the war. Keeps Father from having to tell everyone to stay away."

"But …" This is a morning of revelations, it seems. They cannot be serious, though there can be no other reason for their confession. "But … *why*?"

"Why what?"

"Why should you tell the men here to stay away from me? Or the ones back in Chicago, whoever they were? What if I *want* to get married?"

"You don't want to marry any of them," Tom says dismissively, and gets to his feet.

"Isn't that for *me* to decide?" The men they list certainly don't sound like solid matches I might desire, but to have the choice taken from the start is what sets my blood to boil.

Tom sighs. "We're getting to Flats Town in a matter of days. I'm sure there will be men there who will marry you. Just don't tell them how horrible you are at cooking—ha!"

"Oh, I see it, then!" I snap a dishtowel angrily in his direction, barely missing his back as he moves off toward the oxen. "You just wanted to keep me around until you married, never mind I might want a beau of my own!"

Tom does not bother to answer my accusations. He walks away, as stoic as ever, but Al comes up and slides his plate on top of Father's dirty one.

"It's not that at all, Marie," he says quietly. "It's that none of them were truly good enough for you."

He follows Tom off to the wagon, and I wipe my hands down my apron front, and a long line of water stripes the fabric along the seam. In my pocket a small round of tin rolls. A piece of solder must have dropped in this morning. Soon, I'll have my last lesson from Al. Disappointment and uncertainty shatters into me. Will my brothers tease the same in Flats Town? Will I miss my tin lesson? I don't know if I want to find out.

CHAPTER SEVEN
13 July 1865

The morning fills with mist again. It is unearthly and ethereal and effortless, floating around Al and me as we crouch by the fire. I feel hidden and ensconced in the cool dampness of it.

The tin kettle needs a new spout. The current one is bent and crooked from a tumble out of the kitchen box. Al uncovered the wide wood container of tin scraps last night while Father slept, and pulled out a piece large enough to cut the cone for this morning.

"It's not really fair," he tells me. "You're trying to learn without the benefit of a shop—without all the right tools and patterns. But I'll take off the solder from the old spout if you want to cut out the shape."

He's etched out the pattern on the tin, and I can barely make it out. It is a line of silver in the greyer metal. The spidery, flowery, blooms of hot-dipped tin over the surface of the steel sheet glimmer and roll. I hesitate. The yearning to make it perfect swings in my chest, but causes me to tremble and shake instead of holding a steady hand as I would wish. Pressing my mouth tight, and taking a deep breath, I start to cut.

"Do the excess first," Al murmurs, his eyes on the kettle. The bubble of solder drags out of the seam that he's heating.

The straight snips are unwieldy, but I've grown used to them. I prefer the many different pliers in Al's leather tinker kit, but for this I must use the larger tools. The straight part of the pattern slices off in buttery softness, shearing away cleanly. I pause at the curved bottom, worrying again. I've managed the knack of pushing into the tin so I do not create any unnecessary burrs, but I know I've the wrong snip to do a good job of cutting the rounded base.

"Al. You should do this part."

He shakes his head, still concentrating on removing the old spout. "You can figure it out. Keep the cuts short and small and tight."

His confidence in me feels ill-placed. Doesn't he realize I'm going to make a mistake? That I've a knack for wrecking work? That I'll ruin it? The edge of the tin bites into my finger, cutting into the thick flesh at the base of my palm's side, but pausing while I cut will certainly make for a rough piece of tin if I lose my place.

I finish, feeling triumphant, and then hold up the metal for Al to inspect. He peers at it. The milky white of the morning light makes everything feel close and warped. We are suspended in a land of cloud, and my sense of accomplishment is muted, too.

"That's very nice, Marie. Now comes the hardest part."

"Why?"

"We've got to form it, and I don't have a way to get

the blowhorn or needlecase stake out. Father's sleeping on top of the trunk."

"Well, we have to fix it now. You can't make coffee in that." I point at the deconstructed pot. The solder has started to pop apart down the main seam where Al has roasted the metal to break off the spout. The coffee kettle looks completely wrecked, though I know it isn't.

"Why don't we find a stick? There should be some twigs somewhere around here," he offers.

"You'll be scratching the *cyna tin.*"

We both jump and jerk around. Father materializes, a grey, looming, shadow through the morning fog. In his hand is the necessary tool, the long skinny end of the needlecase stake sticking out sideways from his fist. His face is unreadable, and he wordlessly hands it over to Al, who grabs the heft of it absently. We stare in unison at Father, who turns around immediately and disappears back into the wagon, somehow as soundlessly as he had climbed out. He rummages around, the scrape and scratch of boxes catching and protesting as he does.

Al and I stare at each other. How long has Father listened to us? All morning? Every day we worked the metal?

Al stabs the end of the stake into the tough ground, pushing at the center so he doesn't warp the slender ends. Once it is deep and immobile, he shows me how to curl the sheet slowly so I do not create a bend that hardens the metal. It is careful work. By the time I finish, the mist is starting to clear, and Father appears once more, carrying a worn gunny sack.

My heart stops. *The burring machine.* He'll see it!

Palming the iron deftly, Father peels the fabric back, revealing the black gleam of the machine, and wonderment at the perfection of its gears enthralls me once more, for all I know it's broken. My instinct is to reach and caress it, to see if I dreamed the damage, but I curl my fingers around the band of my sleeve.

"You be needing a burr once you are soldering the edge," he nods toward me, focusing first on the tin in my hand, and then meeting my eyes directly. "Go ahead."

Al, still tongue-tied, hands me the box of rosin pieces while I hold a lap seam together to flux it. We've already put a small clay bowl of tin into the fire, and it is curdled and molten. I spoon in the tin, watching it run downward and drip into the flames. A single bead of it is caught at the edge and I shake it slightly, satisfied when it plops and fizzles off.

"Very nice, Marya." Father's voice is low, affection apparent as he uses my Polish name. Turning, I watch him carefully unwind the rest of the burlap, and the burring machine is completely revealed in all its expensive glory. The round curving slope of its handle, and the tight click of the gearbox is slickly glossy. None of this beauty hides the bent handle and jumpy gear box.

"What is this?" he exclaims, and though he's obviously, immediately, distraught, he still has the presence of mind to keep his voice quiet. His outburst is a rasping choke.

Al jumps up. "What?" He freezes as he stares over Father's shoulder. "It's ruined!"

Misery collides with guilt in my head and I close my eyes, willing the scene to be different. If I'd not been so clumsy, or carelessly curious, the machine would be whole! What a horrible excuse for a woman I am! I can't cook or bake. I can't do my family's trade …

"Marie—look at this!" Al motions, but I'm stuck, my bottom sewn to the earth. I don't want to see it again. I don't want to look at what I've done.

"Marie—"

"You are knowing of this, *corka daughter*?" Father fires at me. My silence is palpable and tactile; I'd usually be the first to speak of such a worrisome issue. The dagger in his words makes me want to cry, but instead I push my palms into my eyes and keep my lips together.

"Damn it, Marie! It's our one machine!" Al says, stating the obvious and sounding panicked. "Did you ... how did you break it?"

"I didn't mean to." The admission scorches my mouth as I give in, unable to lie, unable to think. There's no fix to this, no way to take it back, and no point in giving any false story. Why? Why did Father bother to bring out the machine right now? He could have left it there, safely packed, until we arrive in Flats Town. He'd believe, maybe, that it happened on the journey ...

"You are breaking this machine, and are not thinking to tell us?"

"*Pierdolić! Fuck!* Tom will—"

"That is enough bad words," Father cuts into Al's frenzy, and the pause hanging between us is so heavy I must look up. When I do, I wish I hadn't. Both of them stare at me, rampaging anger, disbelief, and hurt flickering between them and blasting into my body. I sink my head down again, but I cannot ignore the weight of the iron as Father places it on my toes slowly. It presses on them even through my sturdy leather boots and the gears inch into the bones of my feet.

"I'm sorry," I finally say. "I didn't mean to drop it."

"You *dropped* it?"

"You are thinking only now to be telling us?"

I nod, resignation pouring through me in a cascade. "I was ... I was too afraid."

"Too stubborn, you mean," Al mutters.

"I'm not!"

"You are!"

"You are dropping this machine. When?"

I stare up at Father's deep brown eyes, and look past the heavy lines of his mouth, and the creases of his forehead. Honesty cancels desperation, and I sigh.

"The first week of the trip," I admit. "I was ... I wanted a chance to touch it. I didn't think I'd ever get to use it, and ..."

"You dropped it," Al finishes, looking forlornly at the machine, which is still a mystery to all my brothers, the workings of it a puzzle half the time.

"The wagon hit a rut, and I was just putting it back, and—"

"You should be telling us this," Father shakes his head. "You should not be hiding such a story."

That he's right makes me feel all the worse.

Al runs a finger along the iron, and then plops glumly next to me. "So it's a waste."

"Oh Father—I'm so sorry! I'm—"

"It is done, Marie," he says shortly. "I am not knowing what to tell you. I am being very disappointed in you. This is being a horrible thing you did."

"I know. I know!"

"It is being so much lost. I cannot easily be buying a new one. The West—"

"*I know!*"

Father stands, and his heavy bulk, and the wide, fleshy shoulders slump. "I am not able to be speaking to you, Marie. Not now."

He walks back to the wagon, the machine hanging from his hand like a piece of old used iron instead of the wonder it is. The horror of what I've done eats me alive inside, and Al's silence is almost as painful as Father's reprimand.

Finally, Al sighs. "Well, we still need to fix the spout, I guess. I'll do it."

So I'm found out, and watch with disappointment of my own and despair as Al does the work I'd hoped to do.

I knew eventually it would happen, but to have my mistake discovered burns even more than the slices on my fingers. The shame of it near paralyzes me. I don't believe I will ever touch the trade again with confidence.

CHAPTER EIGHT
15 July 1865

The clattering of the wagons, and the hustle and shout of many men combine with sidestepping horses and plodding oxen. Chaos swirls around us as we peel through the line of bodies and animals when we jumble into Flats Town. Most of the wagon train will camp on high ground on the northeast end of the town. Franks told Al that it is an old buffalo jump, where the Sioux would run the bison off to their deaths. For the wagons, it is one of the safest vantage points from all directions to make a long two or three-night camp, and is, to the best of my figuring, the reason Flats Town exists in the first place.

There is an overwhelming scent of wood. The air pulses with sawdust. It lies finely across every surface. Maybe I have traded the dust of the prairie for the dust of the trees. Everywhere there is construction and bashing activity. Father is certainly correct about one thing: this is a town that is determined to grow.

48

Father says he will return once he finds Walter Salomon, and has taken Tom with him. Al is with the oxen. My job is to stay inside the wagon to guard our things against the press and rumbling wheels. But no matter my duty, I still wish to be outside and see more of Flats Town. I wish to see what the women are wearing, to get a peek of the main street.

I'm trying to keep my willfulness in check. It is the least I can do so Father will forgive me for bashing in the burring machine. My anxieties gnaw at me, though, and I remind myself how we survived the entire trip without anyone getting eaten by a wild animal, or even sustaining an injury. There wasn't an Indian raid. If we can manage all that, perhaps we have luck enough to survive and be successful. Will I find satisfying work? Happiness? A home? A place to call mine?

Maybe I will find friends, and Father will continue to be happy even though he misses Mother, and the boys will get their women and build their shops. These hopes whirl within me, a maelstrom of uncertainty and worry.

"Marie." Al's head, downy and bright, sticks around the corner of the fabric flap. "Father's on his way."

Clambering down from the back of the box, I instinctively draw near Al as we wait. Father seems misty and soft-edged within the pillows of dust. He is not alone. Tom strides too, a wide wall of prideful thickness, and beside them is another. Walter Salomon is older than Father, his hair and beard a sooty, snowy, white, and he is even taller than Tom. His shoulders, arms, and torso are thick and round, and his black eyes glitter.

"Welcome to Flats Town," he says, surveying us carefully. He looks like a giant, and his words trip over themselves. Like Father, Walter Salomon did not learn to disguise his accent, though his English seems pure.

We wait, thinking there will be more to this abbreviated speech, but he seems disinclined to be talkative.

Tom steps forward. "*Dziękuję Ci. Thank you* for your welcome. This is my youngest brother, Wojciech, and our sister Marya." I stare at Tom. He notices, and gives a grimace. The formalness feels as awkward as it sounds. Why bother with our official Polish names? Isn't the west supposed to be American and new?

Walter nods at us but does not rejoin.

Father jumps into the stretched silence, and rubs his hands together, the old energy roaring through his wiry strength.

"Well then, we can be going. Walter says he was putting a stove in for the winter. When we are hooking up ours, we will be cozy."

The blacksmith nods amiably at Father, and turns back into the heart of town. Al and Tom grab the oxen's heads and we move as one to follow Walter. Around us, the other wagons have already melted into the path heading up to the old Indian hunting ground. One other wagon is staying, like us, and parked in front of the closest saloon, a freshly painted new building called *The Powdered Keg*. It's the Winters family: Matthew, his children and wife Mary, and Mary's widowed sister Doris Tucker, along with Matthew's dashing brother, Tommy. Today, Tommy's sporting an elaborate mustachio for the arrival into Flats Town. Doris giggles at him and shoves her fluffy breasts into his face as he lifts her easily out of the wagon. Tommy ignores her completely as he eyes up a group of cowboys passing by, copying their swagger as he follows the rest of his family inside the *Keg*, only losing his balance as he walks through the door.

There is a solid main street stretching west and east: wide, flat, and with a curve at the end emptying to more homes. The *Powdered Keg* saloon sits across from several buildings. One is a big mercantile. There's a bank and a small post office, and about fifty children scrambling around the alleys between sod homes and freshly sawn board homes. Is there a school? I peer between the dust and the houses but cannot see one. A church on the far west is in the middle of gaining a steeple, and I see the telltale spire of another chapel ahead of us.

A hugely busty woman cuts Tom off, and he curses in Polish just loud enough for us to hear him, but the woman pays him no mind and hustles into the bank without pausing. The wind shifts from behind us, and suddenly the potency of a tannery's smell swarms the air. Instinctively, I put my sleeve to my nose, and my eyes water. We take a dirt path between the general store and the bank and onto a narrower, newer road that runs parallel to the main street. I see the darkened windows of a makeshift bordello, and inhale the stink of the saloon and a dilapidated mess hall spills greasy smoke of bacon gone black. A middle-aged man sweeps the back porch of the general store. It seems he's doing so as an excuse to watch us straggle into town, because he's staring at everyone instead of at his broom.

A sprawl of houses creeps around the outskirts, where the prairie's silky grass slowly melts into distant trees up on the old buffalo jump. The wagons there are creamy blobs, their canvases swaying in the breeze. Some farms pepper the fields about, lumpy sod buildings sagging and flat. While there is comfort in the town's growth, I almost wish I could go running up to the wagon train, and let it carry me to the end of the line and back again. Being in Flats Town is so final and finishing. There's no returning to Chicago. I'm a pioneer now, a woman of the west with absolutely no way to go back on my own. My life must pick up its place and grow. The knowing of this does nothing to quell my worries.

Will they think I've gone insane if I start to sob? Will my brothers shake their heads against my fears?

"New?"

I start, and pivot on my heel as I walk, finding the sharp eyes of a very slim, middle-aged man who is staring at my chest instead of my face.

"I … I'd think that was obvious," I say shortly, glancing up to see if Tom or Al notices I'm accosted by a stranger. They don't, their attention stuck on pulling the oxen carefully through the path around a ramshackle old church-like building with new stairs built up to the door. Scrawled into the wood is the word "SCHOOL."

"Sass, is it?" he spits to the side and grins at me through yellowed teeth.

"I'm not sassy!" I retort.

"Ohhh, and spicy too!"

"Horeb Harvey, get your ass over to the lumberyard before Mikey decides to finally fire you!" A young man at a cooper's bench yells across the streets, and my companion makes a wrinkly face.

"You my wife now, young Franklin? You watch your own business!"

"I only know that Mikey O'Donnell's temper is worse than Lettie Zalenski's and you don't need me telling you that that's saying something."

"I'm going, I'm going," Horeb leers at me just as a wide hand claps him hard on his shoulder.

"Ain't. Go on." The new arrival, a chubbier, thicker, man who looks to be the same age as Mr. Harvey, with a mop of blonde hair going grey, peers at me from under shaggy brows.

"How do." He tips fingers to his forehead. "Gilroy Greenman."

I press my mouth together hard, and then open it to offer some polite niceties, but Gilroy Greenman steers Horeb away from my side swiftly before I can answer.

Alone again, I let out a breath and glance around the second street. Some of the buildings in this area are made of wood in various stages of aging with long, sloping porches. Two cowboys speak earnestly to a well-dressed man next to a blunt-sided livery in the distance ahead, and a group of young women are making eyes at the two ranchers. Their gowns are surprisingly fresh and pretty, but the fashions are at least a decade old if I remember correctly from Chicago.

Men in leathers stroll past, their heads together and the tops of their hats kissing as they bend toward one another, heading toward the mercantile. I catch snippets of their conversation—"railroad" and "bison"—and then they are gone, into the general store.

We hear the blacksmith shop long before we see it. There is a ringing of metal hitting metal, and the blow and belch of smoke from the forge. It is an unmistakable and homey smell, and a small part of me relaxes. For how strong and quick this town is growing, I am at once grateful and amazed there is no other tinsmith already here peddling wares.

"Tadeusz. And Jimmy, too. They are arrived." Walter announces.

Two younger smiths turn from their work, heavy aprons stained with black, and their faces sweating even with the coolness of the morning. One is tall, massive, and broad like Walter, and the other slim and sinewy, with a bounce to his movements.

"This is my son, Tadeusz," Walter gestures to the taller of the two. The likeness is obvious, though Walter's beard is white and his son's is black.

He approaches us, his hands absently wiping on his leathers and his eyes searching us all: perhaps measuring his height against Tom, and his weight against Father, and judging Al's grin. His gaze flickers over me as well, a cursory, uninterested, swipe, and then he shakes Father's hand, a grim half-smile tracing his face briefly.

"Finally. You've come." He releases Father, and gestures behind him. "Jimmy will be glad to hand off his work to you." We all look about and see the pale white glimmer of tin against the sooty grey of the workshop.

"You be taking care of tinware then?" Father's eyes narrow, and he looks to Walter for confirmation.

The older man nods, and a rueful smile grows. "We've been acting as blacksmiths and tinkers both. Repairs mostly, as anyone wants new they have to order it through a wagon master or relatives back east. It will be a relief to let you handle the softer stuff. We don't have the touch of it."

"So long as your repairs don't be leaking, maybe you are being able to get away with it." I can see Father already wishes to inspect the bit of tin in the shop to fix it himself, to save the weaker metal from improper hammering and puckers from dented stakes and anvils.

"There have only been a few complaints," Walter admits, then waves his hand. "Tadeusz is right, Jimmy. No need for you to keep working on the tin. You may as well start heating some of the rods for shoes while Tadeusz and I take them out back. Consider your apprenticeship to move up a peg."

The younger man smiles, a bright, brilliant flash of white happiness reaching across the space. "That sounds just fine, sir." He is so pale and small compared to the Salomons. I wonder who his people are, or how far he traveled to take this apprenticeship.

Once again, we march behind Father and Walter, though this time we add the steps of his son, who falls in between us.

"So, Tadeusz, is it?" Al is, of course, the first to jump into the quiet.

"Father uses it. Call me Thaddeus."

"Not Ted?" Al's flippancy feels out of place against the serious face of the blacksmith's son, who instead sends a withering glance.

"No."

"Well, we go by Al and Tom. And Marie." He gives our English names. As always, I am just a heartbeat behind in the list. "We know you won't remember our names right away—"

"Marie, Tom and Al," he recites back. "I'll recall."

The building is behind the combined house and blacksmith's shop, with a wide patchy lawn hemmed in by fences for the smithy's small farm. I immediately see the worth of our location for all that it is borrowed from Walter. There is a meandering stream bubbling across the property west to east, serving as both water for the people, animals, and hot iron. Though it seems drafty, and the roof looks as though it will only last another winter or two, the wide front doors of Walter's extra building open into a generous cavern.

No one says it, but I can feel the thread of anxiety still running through each of us. Though we will not have to build a new house, and a new shop this season, the amount of labor needed to make the place fully livable is enormous. When the word 'barn' had been mentioned, I had expected a round-roofed, long, structure familiar in the fields of Wisconsin and Illinois, perhaps stained a deep red-brown. This is nothing like that. The rough, planked, walls have shrunk with time to leave wide gaps, the ground is churned dirt, and hay rots in the corners. Holes of light puncture into the dim space. Suddenly, I shiver against the imagined cold of winter that will blast through the wide spaces between the boards, and imagine the ceiling give way to drifts of snow and ice.

How much work will we need to do before my brothers can set up the kettles and the tools? Concern gnaws at the corners of my stomach, and I inch a finger into my mouth, worrying at the corner of a nail.

"Tadeusz, why don't you show them the place?" Walter offers, and my brothers string out behind Thaddeus as he explains window repairs needed, and the ventilation to be created, and how we can salvage the handful of rough tables stacked along a dusty wall.

I'm not a tinsmith, for all my lessons with Al, and though I wish I could listen and think about the placement of stakes and tin sheet, I must be silent. Strangely, I feel chafed by the restrictions of my sex. How odd. I've never felt so constrained before. I must truly be spoiled by the freeness of the wagon train!

"Stanisław. So. I must tell you." Walter's voice, though not as melodious as his son's, carries to me where I wait by the doorway.

"What is it?"

"This space. I do not own it. Not any longer. I did when I last wrote to you, but I had to sell it."

"Sell it? Then we are not staying here?" Father's voice holds ill-concealed panic.

"No, no. I managed to speak to the new owner and he agreed to leave you here, at least for the winter."

"What is he wanting with a barn if not to be using it?" Father sounds as incredulous as I feel. Without meaning to, I start to inch closer to listen better.

"He wishes to own as much land as possible. He is a rancher. I owed money … I needed hard cash, not just traded goods. Selling the land was the best way to get it. You'll find the banker here—Percival Davies—drives a hard bargain."

"Do we be needing to meet this new landlord? Paying rent?"

As Father asks, Walter has the grace to look uncomfortable. Father, nearly a full head shorter, glowers up.

"I don't know. I don't think so. Yet." Walter rubs his hand around his neck. "He or his son will probably be around at some point to negotiate. Old Oddvar knew you'd be coming in soon enough. But it's a good space, Stanisław. It is." This is a plead, a beg. "I wanted you here for many reasons."

"It is a right time to be coming," Father amends. "We can be going in then, and be seeing your wife. Monika—yes?"

Walter still looks uncomfortable, and now his long mouth tightens further under the greying beard.

"She's gone, Stanley, a few months past. Like your Jozefa. Died of the dysentery."

"*Mój Boże, człowieku. My God, man.*" Father does not press his sympathy further, but his voice goes deeper. I know if I glance over again, he will be standing there, forlorn himself, and buried in memory. They are quiet for a long moment, and I feel the history between them settle and ferment. I think if Mother were here, she might have embraced Walter, for all his surliness, and would have promised to take care of him and his son as well. I seem to always know what she would have done, but can never make my mouth or feet follow her ghostly footsteps.

"It is a strange thing, is it not, to be here in a growing country exactly as we'd hoped, but to have lost so much?" Walter finally speaks again against the murmuring of the boys in the back of the barn.

"We have our sons," Father reasons, as if determined now to stay cheerful in spite of the low news. "And I have Marya."

They fall silent once more, and the deeper roll of Thaddeus's voice bumps toward us. He explains the best way to get lumber: sweet-talk old Mikey O'Donnell for a good price on planed wood by offering any nice knives we have on hand—the man has a penchant for collecting them. Or barring that, offer to help his wife Lara organize a church social to get good credit. Or there is the bank if we need money for lumber.

If! We need a full loan to pay for the repairs on this oversized shack! This so-called barn structure has a lofty, beamed ceiling, and feels like it has been vacant for many seasons. The twirled straw and grass nests of mice in the corners wilt, and the wooden slabs along the walls are going gray with years. The wind pokes through the open knots of the planks by the one easterly window facing the short prairie and wood beyond the farmyard. It's big, surely, but it's dirty and musty and the wood is half-eaten by termites on the north end.

I wonder how we can possibly make this feel like a professional shop, let alone a home.

We can't. At least, not without help.

I sigh inwardly, and press my hands into my skirts, chewing the insides of my mouth. I know the sinking in my gut is the chafing of the unavoidable. I am to be relegated back to the hearth and the kitchen. Al will not have time to teach me much more tinning, and my brothers will marry and drift away, leaving me to care for Father without Mother's bright tinkling joy to lighten the days. My future is not undesirable, but I feel disjointed with it. I wish I could create, to feel some sense of the euphoria I had when tinkering with metal. I wish to have that confidence again, somehow. A silly dream, I know.

Father paces over to the door, then draws back, surprised to see me so near. I smile at him lightly, but he shifts his chin to the side, eyes narrowed.

"You are being here standing the whole time, Marie?"

"I have," I admit, bending my head slightly in guilt of eavesdropping, but I'm not so embarrassed I can't speak up. "And … Father. We can't afford the lumber, can we?"

Father glances away at once, and Walter looms behind him, his face unreadable and flat.

"We can't do this!" I whisper, hoping the boys don't hear me. "We need a better place!"

"There isn't one. Not right now," Walter inserts himself into the conversation, and a brief bout of resentment flashes through me with his interruption.

"What do you mean, there's no other place?" I ask, resting my arms across my chest and meet his eyes frankly. "There's not an empty house we could use? Something better than this piece of *gówno shit* that will need a loan just to make it livable?"

"The words you are using my daughter!"

Walter's white-tipped eyebrows reach his hairline, but he holds his tongue.

"Well, it's true!" I hiss against the rumbling of the four young men on the far end of the room. Hasn't Tom at least done any of the math needed for the repairs? "It's useless! We can't stay in a big old shack!"

"You could take out a larger loan and build something from scratch," Walter says tightly.

"I am not wanting a loan first thing in coming."

"We'll need one if we stay here," I say, worry mingling with stubbornness as I pull myself up, almost able to look at Father in the eye. "We can't have it both ways—and lumber isn't free!"

"Marie, I am knowing what it is taking to make this good to live."

"It'll take weeks! All the rest of summer or fall, won't it?" I glance around. "Does anyone know how to repair the roof? It's too much—"

"It is being better than nothing." Father cuts me off, and glances at Walter. "I am sorry, my Jozefa is always very bright, and speaking her mind and was teaching my daughter to be so, but she is not here to be telling Marie when it is no good to speak of such things."

My lips smack together, and I hold in another unbecoming cuss, fuming at Father's response and the hugeness of the task ahead of us. The two old men stand silently for a long moment, shifting their feet and looking anywhere but at me or one another.

"We'll help you unload the wagon," Walter finally offers, as though it will take the sting from all his disappointing information. "And get your animals unhitched. Jimmy will have started the meal. An apprentice is good for more than the grunt work."

"Well, then," Father sighs. "Marie, why don't you start to be unloading?"

Knowing my words will fall needlessly at this point, I move woodenly into the wagon and pull the lighter items down: the copper and tin lanterns, the rolls of bedding wedged between the larger crates, and the travel-bitter blankets. Then the small box holding the ruined burring machine.

Oh heaven. What will these blacksmiths think of me and my stupidity?

The boys join me soon, jostling and clamoring with Thaddeus among them.

"Hah! Tonight, we'll get a break from your cooking, Marie," Tom thunders jovially, as he takes some of the smaller boxes down. "Thaddeus says Jimmy has a way in the kitchen."

"He does," the blacksmith confirms, his gaze resting on my hands as I shift the next few items toward the edge of the wagon. "Some of the best cornbread and roasted rabbit around."

"Well, it doesn't take much to find someone who might outmatch me in the way of the hearth, be it woman or man."

Thaddeus finally meets my eyes, the greyness of them cutting me shrewdly, but he does not answer. Al and Tom jump up beside me, taking the edges of the bigger boxes, and waste their power and strength trying to shift them alone before deciding to heave together. I am in the way, so I climb out in the usual clumsy half-jump that never fails to catch the edge of my skirts.

I was hoping I'd do laundry finally, and get out of these grimy, dirt-caked clothes soon after we arrived. Not likely to happen as I'd wished. There is too much to do. Too much to figure. Too many pieces to organize before I can think of laundry.

The three young men quickly create a heave and swing of the big boxes, and their shoulders strain and legs bend with the weight of the tools and the cumbersome burden of the stakes. The smoke of the nearby forge hits me as I pry open the top of one of the crates, and mingles with the smell of the wood in the air. Suppose Father is incorrect and I'm right. Suppose we will need to pay rent to a new landlord— rent we will not be able to afford until, perhaps, the spring. Suppose the barn is too drafty for the winter. What if there is not enough work? I dig into the unpacking of our goods and our livelihood, and apprehension wells inside of me, choking my lungs more than the plumes of smoke ever could.

CHAPTER NINE
20 August 1865

Bess, Clara, and Grete. And Sadie.

I try to remember the names of the young women who have come to call. They're all in their early teens, though Clara's calmness and styled hair twists more like a woman's, and her dress stretches with a pregnancy just starting to show. She tells me she is married to a farmer, and Grete giggles whenever she speaks of a Lawrence Fawcett. I'd like to flatter myself that it is me they wish to befriend, but likely it is the news that two new young bachelors have arrived in town.

"We'd heard that you'd be coming for months," says the brassy blonde called Sadie. "And we thought we'd stop by on a Sunday and see how you're getting along. Mother sent some pie. Figured you weren't up to making much as you're not completely set up." She cradles bakery in her arms.

"Tell your mother I'm grateful." I glance around us, where old boards are patched vertically with new against the weather, and the partitions of one long wall along the back of the space boasts half-erected bones of what will soon be actual, real, private quarters. It's taken us far longer than it should to organize ourselves, between building, setting up shop, and handling orders pouring in.

"Will you be a-joining vun of the churches, you know, a one of dem?" Bess asks through a thick Germanic accent, craning her neck to get a look at my brothers. She must catch one of their eyes, for she blushes and glances down quickly but not before readjusting the fit of her chemise bodice.

"Bess Martin! You're supposed to be sweet on Franklin!" Sadie says briskly, though her eyes rove over my brothers as she speaks.

"Vat? So he is still my sveeetie, but I can be a-looking, no?"

"I should tell Franklin he's got competition—"

"It is a-nothing serious to be a-looking—"

"So, church?" Clara interrupts, raising her eyes at me, and slapping Grete, who has been batting her eyes at Tom as he walks by with another board.

"The church?" I hesitate. "I suppose we'd join the Catholic one."

"Of course. St. Aloysius. We go there as it's the only one," Clara tells me. "They're building a Lutheran one, finally, so we can attend our own services."

"Perhaps, then." I have no idea how strict Father will be. It was Mother who had been religious. We've been in Flats Town a few weeks, but it feels like far less.

"Oh, but church is the best place to be social all week," protests Sadie, who still is holding the food to her chest. I wonder if she will forget to hand it to me for all she is making eyes over my shoulder at the boys. Irritation bubbles in me.

So it will be like Chicago after all? Church, niceties, girls chasing my brothers? Does that mean I'll still have no beaus too? Will I still struggle to have friends?

"We …" I pause, and squint against the late afternoon sunset streaming through the open door. Clara watches me straight, but the other three gaze at the pulling muscles of the young men whacking hammers and patching the walls and framing the door for the entry into our private area, where we will put the rough-hewn beds and the kitchen. Pressing my lips together, I speak loudly.

"We'll come to church, I'm sure. And when Tom's *woman* gets here, there will be a wedding as well."

Sadie deflates a bit, and Grete steps back, though Bess still props her bosom over the scratchy new work countertop and smiles amiably at me.

"I vill be a-looking for you and your family at the church, then."

"And welcome, truly," Clara adds, grinning. "You'll have to speak to Lara O'Donnell about joining church groups. She'll be glad to get more hands for making bakery goods for the socials."

"Maybe. That would be—"

"Hey Marie! There's another big box or two that we haven't got to unpacking, but Father says he wants it done now." Al's rescue comes a bit late, and he nods absently at the four girls. Sadie remembers to hand over the pie as an afterthought, her eyes following Al.

"What about *that* brother? Is he taken?" she asks pointedly. Busk stays crackle as Bess and Grete whip their necks to stare at Al again.

"No. But he's very young."

"He doesn't look too young," Sadie says and Grete nods vigorously.

I shift the pie on the board and smile tightly.

"Thank you. And your mother," I say. "It'll help with the meal today for sure."

Their backs trickle through our overlarge doorway with a few last suggestions about Mass and insistent welcomes. If there are so many men around in the west, why are these girls coming to make eyes at my brothers? They should stay away.

Once they're gone, I turn around and poke Al reproachfully. "You might have told me I was needed sooner to help unpack."

"You have to talk to *some* girls," he says, shaking his head. "You're going to have to actually work to make friends here, they won't come with Mother's prodding."

"What makes you so wise?" I say off-handedly, stinging with the truth of his words and his measure of my character.

He grins and shrugs. "I'm not. I just know what you're bad at: cooking, baking, having friends, getting a man to notice you—"

I hit him on the arm hard, and he winces slightly.

"You're being a *pierdoła asshole*."

"Well, Father *does* want the last big crates opened."

"I'll run this into the kitchen in the big house first." I jerk my chin toward the back of the home that serves as both living quarters and forge for the trio of blacksmiths. "Jimmy will be glad for something to help with feeding us all tonight."

"Pah! Especially since you don't really help him much," Tom mentions, as he walks by with another plank over a meaty shoulder.

"I *know*!" I grit my teeth against rising to the barb. It doesn't help that it's true. I've found more to keep me busy since arriving to put off the role of the hearth, and so far, I've been successful. August is hot and dusty, and we've had no time to breathe against orders we've yet to fill in a shop not yet made, on top of trying to set up the workroom to everyone's particularities. My head swirls with the repetition of what must be done.

I'm thankful we still eat with the blacksmiths in their more organized kitchen. Jimmy is quite accomplished at making foodstuffs as well, which puts me to shame when I try to help, and there's no shortage of teasing, ribbing, and heckling.

Soon I'll be stuck doing nothing but food: planting, cooking, preparing, storing. My life will be consumed by the push and pull of mealtime. Walter's stove is already hooked together in our shop with the crimped black tin stovepipe, and our smaller potbelly in the back. Father says if we stay more than one winter in the building, he will build a fireplace so I might cook larger meals easily. Tom says a fireplace won't make my cooking better and doesn't want to haul the rock for it. Al just shakes his head.

I wonder why we'd consider moving out of the building in the spring. We've taken a huge loan from the bank just to buy lumber to repair the damp walls. With all the money we've poured into this wide space, I have no idea why we'd ever leave unless we had to!

Walking through the crunchy grass toward the smithy, the ring of hammers strikes true and loud around the air. Sliding in, I watch Thaddeus and Jimmy pull the metal from the depths of the red fire. The hot, burnt, orange glows on the edge of the thick band of iron. Nearby, Walter moves iron into vats of water. On the wall, a few swords cling to nails, curved and crafted beautifully. I suppose they carry some of Walter's pride.

I wait, knowing the ire that can come from work interrupted when the metal is hot and ready. Walter straightens when he sees me, but does not speak. The clang and bang of the smiths fills my ears. Thaddeus moves with a heavy power combined with fluid strength, while Jimmy's body strains with the weight of the hammer and the control needed to set a solid blow. It does not help that he is a bit shorter than his masters, but he takes it in stride with a determination and drive that I admire.

As they finish with the iron, they turn as one. Thaddeus submerges the metal quickly in the vat of water nearby, and the steam rises and billows around us. When it clears, he and Jimmy both notice me. The bigger blacksmith glances at me slightly, then turns back to the fire. Jimmy's smile blazes through the dirt.

"You baked a pie, Marie?"

I want to hug him for saying so without sarcasm or surprise. I settle for a full smile in return.

"No, no. One of the town girls brought it over. I thought to leave it here to keep the sawdust out of it."

"It won't keep much cleaner here," Jimmy gestures to the soot around us. "But cover it up with a cloth and set it by the hearth and we'll cut it up with dinner."

I move through the forge and balance the pie as I open the door beyond the bellows, where their living quarters tuck behind the forge. Stepping through and closing the fat pine slab door to block the drift of coal dust, I adjust my eyes, and take in the now familiar space. There is one large unmade bed along the far corner and another opposite it that is neat and orderly. The loft is for food storage and Jimmy's cot, which peeks over the edge in a messy array of sheets and quilts. The kitchen is nothing more than a big hearth with a banked fire, a long narrow trestle, and a large wooden worktable where I set the pie.

On the other side of the door, the rumble of Thaddeus' voice mixes with Jimmy's lighter one as instruction on creating the exterior of a wheel continues. Flats Town does not yet have a wheelwright. I pause, listening to the careful and simple explanation. I miss my discussions with Al about tinware, and the passion I felt, briefly, about creating something with raw skill.

I should apply that same passion into making food. Maybe I'd get better at it.

Walking out the back door so I can reach our so-called barn without bothering the blacksmiths again, I pause, and take in the small farm the Salomons run. The fences are tidy and the animals seem fed and content. It's the chickens running wild across the grasses, looking for seed and fall bugs that I hate, and one attempts to peck at my boot while I stand unmoving. *"Odpieprz się! Fuck off!"* I growl at the bird, who doesn't seem to care I'm a moment from kicking it in the head. Shaking off the shiver of dislike shimmying down my spine, I keep going along the yard. Father's boxes are waiting.

Beyond the meandering stream and the matted yard is the prairie, flat and dry, and the trees building up from the horizon where the old buffalo jump reaches for the sky. The trees inch close to the north of our rented property. I wonder what it will all look like in spring, as I am determined to put out flowers around the edge of our new house-and-shop. It doesn't matter that it's not really ours. It will feel like a good Polish home, then.

Heading toward the extra-wide door, I realize the hammering and shuffling and tinny pounds have stopped. Perhaps it is closer to the day's end than I had figured.

As I round the corner and go inside, I stop short. Both of my brothers huddle over the last of the large boxes with Father in the center. There is a contained, quiet, reverence to the vision, as if they are barely breathing.

"What is it?" I ask lowly, and Tom shifts so I might get a view.

My heart stops when I see what the box contains.

Buried in oiled padding and tucked around wadded fabric are several machines!

I think back to the burring machine I obsessed over, secretly touched, and then broke. It sits in its own box yet, unopened. Everyone knows it's broken and they will not speak to me about it at all. Their silence is worse than their tease.

And now ... now to know there are more!

Here I thought the burring machine is the most precious thing we own. It's not. Not at all. It simply must not have fit in *this* box. Amazement pounds through my body, and I can't take a full breath. My stomach gurgles with shock.

It is a *fortune*.

"Where ... how?" I find my voice first amid my brothers' incredulous stares. Father looks up at us all, his eyes sparkling and proud.

"It was a good decision to be buying these, I am thinking."

"How did you pay for this, Father?" Tom asks, urgency peeling into his tone, layered with the shock. "What did you do?"

Father's eyes go dark at once. "Do you be saying I am coming by this dishonestly?"

"No!" Tom backtracks immediately. "Pfft. That's not what I meant, you know that. I mean … do we have a large debt to pay? How did you afford this? We didn't even have money for lumber to fix up this place, and have that heavy loan from Percy Davies at the bank to show for our poverty, and now to know we had … *these*?! Pah!"

"It seems very expensive," I add, counting the money up in my head as best I can.

Father does not answer anyone at first. Instead he unwraps each piece reverently. There is a beautiful new beading machine, with several different beads for multiple designs to change on the knobs. A very long, flat, wide, grooving machine is buried under a wiring machine and a used turning machine.

I had pored over the broadsheets that boasted of these items back in Chicago, thinking on how rich and lovely it would be to own such fantastic inventions. I knew it would help my brothers, and save Father much time with a hammer. They were novelties, and unaffordable. My brothers had dreamed of using them, but we had all believed our scrupulous parents would never buy such luxuries when there are so many boys to help with the trade.

The contraptions glimmer with a deep black shine, and I reach to touch the one nearest to me: a tight, compact, wiring machine.

"Don't touch it, Marie!" Tom barks sharply. "We all know what happened the last time!"

My fingers shrink back and curl into my palms at once. "I have apologized more times than I can say."

"But it's broken, damnit. Father has already said he'd sent for another."

"What?" I swing to stare at Father. "How? With what money?"

"There is being no complete shop without a burring machine, my daughter," Father says quietly, his eyes burning into the pure black of the oiled machines in the box. "I must be having one no matter the debts I am getting for it."

"But—"

"But you won't get to do much with it when it arrives," Tom says sharply. "We can't trust you."

I push my lips together and rest my hand on the wiring machine, cupping the body of the iron in my wide palm, and glare up at Tom. He grinds his teeth and turns away. But touch is all I dare to do. I don't trust myself, either. More debt! So much more debt, all because of me!

"Father. It's so many!" I say slowly, reaching to caress unconnected beads. Father slowly pulls out the turning machine, with its wide circular front wheels curving back toward the gearbox. Tom's eyes finally start to glow, too. He's probably thinking how quickly and easily he will be able to grow his own specialty with such tools.

Al bounces between us all, the excitement of such riches enough to send his youthful passion into a tizzy.

I'm beyond envious. They'll get to use these inventions … while I cook.

"Father must have found an old cache and we've run away with it to the west so we aren't discovered!" Al suddenly crows. Father shoots him an annoyed glance.

"It is certainly not being so, Al. No," he finally admits. "No, it was your mother."

The mention of Mother makes us pause. Father's eyes go misty, but he smiles at all of us with a mixture of defiance and pride.

"Your mother was having some money tucked away."

"Surely Mother hadn't wanted to haul all of this out west?" Tom says, astonished.

"Your mother had some craving for adventure, *tak*. And … I am having my reasons. It is true we did be having a thought to be moving west with all of you, and your bride." Father glances at Tom, who looks away. "I thought to being together—as a family—and being something different, where we are all sharing the tools, and be working in a so big tin-shop. Not like in the city where so many old ways are sticking or dying. Here, we could be being together."

"You mean … never have our own shops? Never be a master?" Tom gapes at Father.

"No, no." Father raises his hands and pushes against the air between him and us. "You would be becoming masters, so. We are dividing the specialty work, but with such tools and machines, we are having many very good smiths under one roof and be being so much productive than ever before. It is a new idea, yes, but it is saving … well … then again, my Jozefa was never being ordinary."

He looks away from us, and then down at the machines. I squat down low, and gently run a finger along the hard edge of the grooving machine. It is a powerful thing, and large. I can imagine Mother and Father planning this elaborate future, thinking the journey and the tempting tools would serve as enough to keep us together as a family. Perhaps they had even hoped I would marry another smith to stay within the circle of artisans. Mother had many large dreams to go with her large laugh.

"You might have told us!" Tom finally explodes. "And hell, Father! You had no reason to rush—"

"Walter's offer was coming before you are arrived from the war. We were to be going west, it is decided before you returned. Your mother … and yes, I am rushing west to be beating the bad weather and I am wishing to escape memories of your mother, among other things," Father admits. "It was very nice timing for everything excepting your marriage."

"All stay here in the shop?" Al says weakly, palming iron beads and clicking them together. "Never be on our own?"

"It *is* a crazy idea." Tom rubs his wide palms against his temples and into his disheveled hair. "Pfft. It's too much."

He walks out into the growing dusk, away from us and the haphazard shop.

"It is a lot to consider, Father," Al says, looking out into the deepening dark after Tom. "I don't know how it will work. But I can tell you that Tom won't like being told what his future holds."

Father spreads his hands. "That is being the point. It is a pioneer way, you are seeing?"

"I see Father's points, too," I offer.

Al sighs, sounding older than his years. "It doesn't affect you, Marie."

We all jump when Jimmy rings the iron bar from the back of the house. Al shakes his head and walks out toward the smithy, leaving a deep, rippled, silence in his wake.

"You are understanding, Marie?" Father finally asks me directly, his strained smile cracking.

I shrug and nod, trying to be supportive. "You've been so happy, Father. Now I think I know why," I say quietly. "You've been living Mother's dream. Without Mother."

Once again, the quiet drops between us, but it is an almost peaceful one at that, perhaps each of us remembering the sparkle and adoration Mother brought to our lives. Likely if she were here, she'd smooth the ruffled egos of my brothers. She loved us all—she loved the *family*—and I think I can understand exactly why Father wants to keep her hopes alive, even though she is gone.

"You'll be wishing to try these, Marie," he finally says, and bends down to touch the cold, greasy, iron. "You are having a hand for the metals. I am not forgetting."

"Oh! But—I thought ... I would, but I'm supposed to set up the house." Shock shimmers through me again, though it is warm and jittery.

Will I be truly allowed? It's more than I expect. I'm still responsible for a broken machine, and additional debt now, and worst of all, the disdain of the boys.

"I thought I wouldn't continue. It was something for the journey, but not here. You don't ... need me," I say. "I enjoyed every minute of learning. But I'm supposed to handle the food, and the baking, and the stupid womanly things. I know my place."

"If we are having truly much successes in the way I hope, we can be getting a cook, Marie," Father breaks into my thoughts, and I think I hear him wrong. My eyes grow big with the suggestion, but Father seems serious. What an idea! It would be exhilarating to be rid of the hearth, and exchange the stove for the brazier.

What foolishness. It is an impossible thought. Father is being kind, and offering some sort of forgiveness in his words I am sure. He doesn't mean it other than he doesn't hold a grudge. I know I cannot actually exchange my place for another. It's not the woman's way.

Dakota Territory

1866

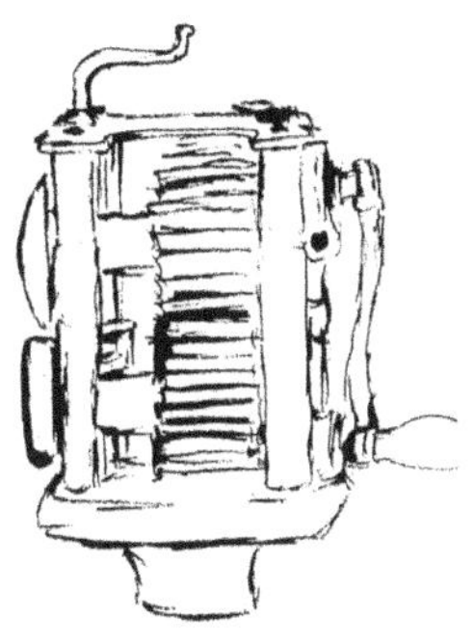

CHAPTER TEN
10 February 1866

Tom posted letters to Sonja last fall after the local harvest festival, and had received a note back. He checks for more letters this frigid Saturday morning, though nothing has come in months thanks to the horrible weather. I do not know what he told the girl. But he's sending another missive now, and it feels a silly expense to keep spending postage on a sweetheart who doesn't write back very often.

The crusty thickness of snow and ice cracks beneath my boots as I do chicken chores. Some days, things melt and stick, and other days I can barely breathe the cold air without tears prickling at my eyes. Weather in the Dakota Territories is certainly unpredictable.

There is a touch on my arm. Jimmy sidles alongside me, his eyes twinkling and merry against the bright sun jumping from the snowbanks.

"Marie, how are you?"

"I'm well, thank you." I feel shyness well in my stomach, but am flattered he gives me attention in the way a boy flirts with a girl. His green eyes look at me with wonder, as though I am the first young woman he's ever noticed.

"So, is your family happy yet with the tools your Father brought?" It is the topic that never quite ends: the adoration of the machines. Walter, his son, and Jimmy come in often to touch the metalworking, and exclaim over the iron gears.

"Oh yes."

"It is … special … to see how much you care for the tools your family uses. A man would be happy to have a woman to have such passion." His cheeks flush.

"Does your family care about your own passion about blacksmithing?"

Jimmy shrugs. "My parents both died on the wagon trip out, and my siblings and I were all broken up among the different families on the trail. There's no one to care."

It's a usual story, but not one I like to hear anyway. "I'm so sorry."

"It was long ago, Marie, and I was just a toddler. I don't even know their names."

"So your last name is your adopted one?"

"Yup. And they live in Vermillion and have so many of their own mouths to feed, I skipped out to find apprenticeship chances almost five years ago. But anyway … you're doing well?"

"Yes, yes, of course. We are trying keeping up with the first round of orders," I say, thinking on my rudimentary bookkeeping. Father is determined to start from scratch, and to start paying our loan back to the brisk, exacting, Percy

Davies, so I have been entrusted with watching the numbers and making note of customers and any trade of goods. It is an easy enough task, and it gives me a sense of belonging within the family business, even if my fingers are dark with ink instead of rosin.

"I've the meal ready," Jimmy says amiably. "Come on in."

As we walk into the blacksmith's house, his hand lightly fingers the small of my back, where my skirt and shirtwaist meet, hidden from other eyes. I hope my cheeks do not flush overmuch at this, and I don't mind his touch. I think, too, of Jimmy's easy smile, and feel a curl of wonder in my chest coupled with some warmth. It feels very nice.

"I've never fixed one!"

We walk into Thaddeus's ire and I stop cold when he pins me with his frustrated gaze.

"*You* broke this, and I know you all want it fixed so it works a tiny bit with a jig until the new one arrives, but I've never touched a damn tinsmithing machine, and now you need me to reheat it and bend it back?"

His anger pierces the room, but Tom takes his seat and sighs loudly.

"You know it's easily done, Thad. Just heat the iron and push it back into place."

"But the threads on the top, by the crank? I have to get them just straight." Thaddeus turns the machine in his hands, and the iron piece looks dwarfish. The burring machine has been unusable. But there's a little give on the handle, so I know Father hoped it might mend. Every time someone curses if they run the handle around, it is like they are cursing me directly. And now Thaddeus does, too.

Pressing my lips together, I meet the blacksmith's face and line up my shoulders. "Do you doubt you can do it? What about your father?" I glance at Walter, who looks strangely nervous by the request.

"No, no, this is best for Thaddeus. He should learn such delicate work."

"*Doubt?* You think I can't do it?" Thaddeus glowers at me, and stands abruptly. "I can't get the dent out of the iron, that's for sure."

"It needs straightening, just for a season before the other arrives. You probably don't need to heat it so much," Tom mentions.

"Oh, so now you all can tell me how to do my job?" Thaddeus strides to the door separating the forge from the house.

"Dinner time!" Jimmy yells at his back.

"Shove dinner," comes the shout as the door slams. Then the wild head pokes back into the room for a moment. "And if Marie's making it, I don't want any."

CHAPTER ELEVEN
7 March 1866

"I'll need the full set of kettles by the end of the month," Toot Warren lists. "And I want bigger sizes than the ones what went bad before you all came to town."

"Bigger?" I panic, but hold my fears in check by folding my mouth tightly over my teeth. "We'll have to use extra tin."

"Yup."

"More expensive." I'm torn between dissuading her and needing the money. The tin sheets are already getting low, and it sounds like there'll be no deliveries until May's first wagon train comes through, and then we must somehow scrape the money to both order the sheet and pay for it. The new burring machine should arrive, too, and more bills with it.

But we *need* the money from all orders. Father says there is rent, which he pays to our landlord through the bank, and also the loan for all the lumber and necessary food credit. Percy Davies is not giving us much leeway. We're too new in town. We are so deep in debt, none of us feel secure.

"Look, I'm all for saving money where I can, but my son's wife Elaine handles the books at the Rusty Nail and she says I can have what I wish. I'm the best cook in town," Toot says matter-of-factly, folding wizening arms over her flat bosom. "Don't you want my business then?"

"Yes, yes!" I say and pull the book near, flipping to the Warrens' page. "It's only they are very big pieces."

She gazes at me through narrow dark eyes and sniffs. "You need to be more grateful for the work, I think."

I press my mouth together again, and then try to smile as sweetly as possible. "We are. More than I can say."

She sniffs and watches me scratch in the book before her spry, bendy body disappears out of the shop and into the street.

Jimmy arrives at the door just as old farmer Henry Brinkley barrels in and pushes past the apprentice.

"Here for my order!"

"It's not ready," I snap, then swallow the retort and plaster another smile on my face. Behind me, I can just feel my brothers' eyes and Father's disapproval. Am I too honest with the customers? Mother had always sent everyone away with a laugh. Here's another area I'm lacking.

The old farmer draws his round stomach up and humphs. "I told Susan it'd be ready. And I'm not making a trip in from the farm again for just a piece of crockery. Where's the damn teapot?"

"I—it's not ready yet. We're still ... setting up."

"Then I want a discount."

"I didn't give you a date it'd be ready. There's no reason to give you money off," I push back, feeling my feet plant harder into the packed dirt.

"But—"

"You don't need any money from what I hear," Jimmy pipes up, coming beside the grumbling older man. "You sold a good chunk of southern farmland to the bank."

Old Henry swings to Jimmy. "I made a damn good deal with Percy."

"Sure, sure. So you don't need to save a few pennies."

"It's the principle of it."

I lift my chin. "So take your wares to another smith."

The man looks frustrated, and I take some small pleasure in pushing back, but Father sidles up and smiles apologetically.

"You are needing your wares?"

Henry squints. "I'm going to be back in town in a month and expect to have the teapot ready. With a discount."

"We'll do our best," I tell him.

"It will be ready," Father adds. Henry ignores me and nods at Father before stalking out, and I let my breath go in one, long, affronted huff.

Father only looks at me mournfully and shakes his head. I turn away, unable to meet his eyes and see the reflection of my failures in them.

"You like to make pretty pictures, don't you?" Jimmy leans over the countertop at the shop, his forearms sliding next to mine, brushing against me lightly.

I blush, and yet leave my arms where they are. I rather like the touch and affectionate moments between us, for all they are still quite innocent. Some nights I imagine that

Jimmy is a bit less careful, and the remembering of it now makes me squirm with embarrassment.

"I don't draw much," I say to his question, glancing down at the bookkeeping notes, and the scribbles I have in the margins.

"Like this. It's not even an animal or a flower, but a scroll pattern." He points. "It's very pretty, Marie."

"Thank you," I say, smiling into his eyes.

He grins back. "Anyway—dinnertime soon. Think you can manage it?"

"I hope I can. What time is it? There have been so many people today."

He chuckles, gently poking me in the shoulder. "I'm teasing. It's done already. You all can come over and eat."

Tom saunters up. Perhaps he has been listening behind me this whole time. He stares at Jimmy, at the tightness of our arms, though our bodies are separated by the counter's wooden frames.

"Jim, what are you?"

"Ah … an apprentice blacksmith?"

"So not truly an artisan yet." Tom nods once. "And— your heritage?"

Jimmy seems to understand the deeper question. "I'm not Polish, no, but I'm Catholic as you know."

Tom's nostrils flare a little, then he passes through. Father and Al follow wordlessly, and as they go, Jimmy cocks his head.

"Shall I walk you over?"

I want him to, but then I don't. It's a little strange to have a young man's rapt attention. Folding my lips over my teeth, I nod and we hike across the yard through the bits of debris, animal feed, snow, and slush to the back door of the blacksmith's house.

Inside, the stifling warmth makes me sweat at once. Father and Walter speak earnestly and with serious brows, and the smell of hot stew, old bread, and fire swirl around the room.

"We're to eat," I mention to the two older men. "But do you need some time?"

"No, no, Marie. You might as well be hearing it. It's the Army," Father says, glancing around at the boys. They all stop moving around the kitchen to listen. Even Jimmy pauses dinner preparations. His hand absently stirs the large iron oven over the fire.

"What of it?" Tom asks, picking at the black dust under his nails, his booted feet on the bench across from the table.

"There is being a notice in the papers Harry Turner is posting in the General," Father explains slowly. "The Army is to be asking for volunteers, recruits, and militia before a General is arriving in Fort Laramie. They are stretching so thin across the territories as it be, and needing help since the War between the States were taking manpower. But mostly they are saying they be looking for able bodied men, for whatever they are planning to be doing this spring."

Tom leans forward. "This in retribution against all the Indian raids out west? Dry Creek and Little Powder River? That's what they're doing—Pah! Building a western army. What about the treaties?"

Father and Walter gaze at the young men clustering around the table. I try to shrink out of the intensity radiating from each of them: Tom and Thaddeus, and even Al and

Jimmy, for all their youth. Do they thirst for the fight, as if they are unstoppable and immune to an Indian's arrows?

Why the fervor?

My brothers have no need to jump into such a fray, to put their lives in danger. Why would they leave the family when we've been here less than a year? There's just barely been time to set up the shop and handle whatever customers I haven't offended. Why should they leave a good, solid, craft that will give them respect? What have the Indians done to us?

Unplanned, I say such a musing aloud, and the hearty, heavy, murmur of masculine chatter stutters.

"Pah! It's not what the Indians have done so much, though some of it is awful," Tom says to me, his condescending tone familiar and grating. "There will likely be payment. You remember the money the Army sent back during the war? Good money." His eyes glint.

"We can make do with what money we're making."

"It's not enough, not fast enough," Tom says bluntly. "Even with the machines. And the most important is still broken, even with Thaddeus tinkering."

Fire races across my forehead at his implication. "We can get money if we get orders like Toot Warren's today. Eventually we'll have enough."

"And you giving your opinion to every customer doesn't help," Tom reminds me.

"But—"

"What do you know, Marie? We need to pay off the loan before we can dream of getting ahead here. And then see what happens to our ... 'family' business."

I twist my mouth shut, and decide to push my way out of the menfolk before I say another word. Taking the spoon from Jimmy over the hearth, I stir with vigor and anger mixed.

"So then, I might have to re-enlist." Tom looks around at the room, including everyone in his bright gaze. "To wherever they need us. Maybe they'll use my trade this time."

Father sounds outraged. "You are having no need, Tom. You already are giving your time to the Army."

"You think just because you've managed to drag us out west without any choice that you can still have control? That by teasing us with fancy machines, we'll do as you say and mind your word for the rest of our lives? And now we have debt! How can I ask Sonja to marry me while we're paying some old man rent and the bank interest for lumber, and can't even afford new tin easily plus an expensive machine?" Tom's argument jolts into the room, hard and mean. I wonder if he's more upset by the loan or Father's rule.

"We need to make money," Al puts in a word, though he sounds uncomfortable. "And ... we like doing what we please, Father, without all the planning. We're not your young boys anymore."

I take the other kettle from Jimmy's inert hand, our fingers brushing. He gives me one of his grins, but it is distracted, and he moves closer to the conversation while I am left with the stew. Damn. I hope I don't ruin it.

"If Carrington is to be going to Fort Laramie, and if the Army is being looking for volunteers, you still are having no need to go," Father insists, his tone harried. "You are all each a good tradesman. You should not be wasting such skill. Craftsmen should to stay in the towns, to be creating. Officers at the Fort Randall won't be wishing to be losing local metal workers to some crazy march out west and beyond. You are not even knowing where you will be sent!"

"So then, this is true." Walter finally speaks. "The talk is they plan to establish more forts in Indian Territory. And while I am sure they will need some sort of rudimentary crafting, it's not like they need artisans to do it."

"Pfft. They'll want us," Tom says confidently, nodding at Thaddeus, who nods back. "Not only are we tradesmen, but I at least have some fighting experience."

"You're being *głupi foolish*," Father complains. "For what? Stay here, where it is being safe and you'll be making a good living."

"Not really. Not until we get ahead. It's not working, Father. I'll come back and pay off the debt. Marry. In the meantime, you can take care of the new materials when the tin order comes in, and Marie can do any tinkering repairs." Tom's reasoning stops the conversation once more. I feel all the eyes in the room settle into my shoulder blades. They twitch under the scrutiny. What does Tom mean by this announcement? It goes against the grain of everything he's said since he discovered the broken machine.

I am afraid to turn around. I have not had a single moment to practice since we've arrived in Flats Town. There are so many preparations for winter from candle making to spinning, and I thought Al kept most of our teaching moments quiet.

There is a thick clearing of throats, and then Walter speaks calmly.

"So, then, Marie knows something of the trade?"

"Both the tin and the copper," Father says, and I turn to look at him directly. He stares at me, a softness to his eyes and to his voice. Is he actually proud of me?

"I taught her most of it," Al says, unwilling to be left out of his place. "She's even used the machines."

"Is she any good?" This is Thaddeus, incredulous and skeptical.

"I haven't had nearly as much time to practice as I'd like," I shoot at him, lifting my chin.

He raises a hand in defense against my zeal. "It is just not common—*anywhere*—for a woman to … *choose* to be a smith."

"I haven't chosen anything. There's no *choice*." I wave my hand at the meal bubbling over the fire and shrug.

"I'd like to see how you do," Jimmy inserts. He beams at me, and a smile traces itself across my face and a warmth flutters in my chest. I nod once and turn back to the stew. So far, it still looks edible. I focus on that, and hope the speculation about my crafting slips away.

There is another fat pause in the room, then Al pipes up.

"If Tom and Thaddeus are going to help the Army build a new fort, I want to go too."

"You're being too young," Father dismisses.

"I'm sixteen!"

"Who will be helping me and Marie around the shop? I cannot be letting all of you go."

I feel Al's displeasure pour out of his energetic bounce, which is only magnified when Jimmy adds his voice.

"I would also like to go."

"What have you to prove?" Walter sighs. "So then, besides, you too are young as well."

"I'm almost eighteen." The admission is embarrassed, and I am surprised. He is younger than me. I am nearly nineteen. It is not so strange a match, though. Then I feel myself blush darker while I bend over the food.

I'm speculating on a future with Jimmy!

Walter sighs loudly, and my heart sinks as fast as it has risen. "I have no hold over you in your adulthood, Jimmy, though I'd say you shouldn't. We've put in enough time to train you. I'd not like to see all the years go to waste."

"They won't. I'll use the trade."

"I do not be thinking you all must be going," Father says again, as if making the decision for Walter and Jimmy and Al altogether. "There is being no need."

No one answers, and I look down at the soup again. It looks done. I hope it's done. Does he add seasoning? I can't remember, and have no notion of what would taste best. Seasoning is something every good Polish woman should understand, but I'm at a loss. As I stare at the chunks of potato and venison, parsnips and onions bobbling like hopeful boats, there is a presence at my back. Jimmy's eyes smile at me once more, a laugh and twinkle in the green.

"We should add something. Thyme or some oregano for the meat." He reaches above me to take a sprig from the dried herbs hanging from the ceiling upside down over the hearth. The action inadvertently brings him closer, and I feel his chest brush my shoulder. I blush again, and am thankful the fire glow hides it.

He brings down the seasonings and adds them, breaking them up in his hands. Burn marks—fresh and pink—scamper along the outside planes of his palm with the whiter lines of old scars from the forge along his forearms. I think of my own slim scars, still healing to white from tin edges. Jimmy and I seem more alike each day. At least he does not think it odd that I've tinkered.

"How does that smell, then?" he asks, and I lean over the hearth to take in a whiff of the dinner.

"It's delightful."

"Yes. Delightful." Is he teasing? Yes, *delightful*. I realize he is gazing at me instead of the meal. How has he been so quickly captivated? It is not as though I have many charms to recommend me. His attraction washes over me, drenching me with earnestness, and I want to both draw away and lean into it. Should I feel flustered? Should I feel more certain of my own response? Believing he might truly like me blooms fresh and buoyant in my stomach. I don't know if I care about him romantically; I just know I'd prefer to be wanted the way Father wanted Mother.

In a strange, unexpected flash, I remember walking around the corner of the wagon once, and seeing Tom pressed against one of the unmarried girls, her skirt high above her hips. I do not know why this memory floods me now, but as Jimmy's eyes run over me, I wonder if such a passionate embrace is in my future.

"Jimmy! Stop ogling Marie and serve us the damn food," Thaddeus thunders from the table, and we jump in unison. The note of anger in the big man's voice cuts hard.

Jimmy takes over the heavy pot of stew for the table, and I pull out the three-day bread and break it out across the men. When I finally sit, Walter raises his glass.

"It is not just Stanisław who will be changing things around in his shop, then, it seems." He juts his chin toward Tom, who nods back gravely. It seems it is already understood that he will join the militia and march toward Fort

Laramie and Indian Territory. "It is my Tadeusz who bears congratulations. He is now the master smith."

Thaddeus sets down his beer suddenly. He looks winded and wary at once.

"*Ojciec*. Father. *You* are the master smith of this house."

"Not anymore, *mój syn my son*," Walter says, and while there is fondness in his voice, I see he slides his glance away from Thaddeus. "So then, I have decided to retire."

"Just like that?" Thaddeus' voice is generally louder than most, but now it booms, mellifluous as one of the brass bells we wish we could forge. "Today, you've decided you're through? You're going to stop working the bellows, and leave the work to me?"

"You do nearly all of it anyway," Walter says, and then lifts his glass higher, as if trying to close the argument. I cannot help but stare first at Walter, then at Thaddeus. He is winded, breathless, and, unsurprisingly, very angry. My brothers, who have come to know Thaddeus well over the many weeks, look between father and son, their glasses stuck at various heights. Father recovers from the uncomfortable moment first.

"That is quite ... *timely* ... Wladisław," he observes, and clinks his mug with his friend. The two older men drink deeply, and each of my brothers takes a sip as well. Only Jimmy and Thaddeus remain motionless until the bigger smith turns, his long, large torso contorting on the bench to do it.

"I suppose that means you are no longer the apprentice. Congratulations, Jimmy."

Thaddeus does not drink in celebration yet, though Jimmy himself slowly raises his beer in a small salute to Thad and takes a moderate sip.

94

The silence is thick and demanding. I wonder truly if my brother means to go further west to enlist and meet up with Carrington, and I wish he wouldn't. We need Tom here to help make wares. What if the Army doesn't send money for a year or more? What good will his absence be then? Father and Al will have a hard time keeping up with the orders even with my measly help.

Then again, I have no choice in it, no matter how I'd like to worry or argue. The knowledge of this doesn't help my mood.

"So then, the Wells Fargo will be here this spring as soon as the snow clears, early enough, should you want to send further instructions to your bride before you go," Walter mentions to Tom. "Since they bought out Butterfields Overland, they're the only ones who come through as the weather allows."

"I'll write Sonja from where we're sent. Wives usually can come out, so we'll marry at the fort. Or we'll send her here, and when I get back we'll have a wedding. We'll have the money for it by then. Pah! For doing *any*thing we want."

"Weddings indeed," Jimmy murmurs, and presses his thigh next to mine. I pretend not to feel it, but I smile into my cup.

"I don't like it," Father says sullenly.

"Can't stop me. It's the Army life for me yet, and I'll be plying our trade as it is, Father, just getting paid by the government to do it," Tom says loudly, and pours himself and everyone else more beer.

Suddenly, my older brother is boisterous, as if happy to have a prosperous plan away from Father's tinkering, though Al carries a pensive light. Jimmy joins in the conversation about what he might expect while serving in the Army, and Walter and Father dive into the stew, tossing low mutters to one another. Jimmy, it seems, has decided to go, too.

Perhaps Father does not fully understand. By forcing us to journey out here without a moment to adjust, forced to follow the tools and stick under Father's roof … well, my brothers will take any option if it means they actually have one.

My own dinner mate sits across from me, stoic and silent as always, but tonight with the gleam of discontentment and frustration.

"Are you not pleased to become the master now? It is a great honor," I say, but Thaddeus only glowers.

"A timely honor. Father is a fool. He has left me no option." He stabs the rest of the stew, then sets down his fork with undue care, as if he is holding himself in check. His grey eyes meet mine, briefly and with tightness. "The soup sufficed." It is one of the few times he directs his attention at me, and I nod silently in return. He stands, his height and size making the movement more formidable than perhaps it is meant, but his words are heavy.

"I'll check the fires." The announcement seems unnecessary, and he walks out, leaving anger in his wake. The lively talk falters for a moment, and Jimmy starts to clean up. This is where I can be truly useful, so I pull the dirty plates toward me, catching up crumbles of bread with the cup of my hand. Outside where I empty the slops, the air feels cold and catches my breath. We likely only have a few weeks left before spring should start. I can feel it in the dampness of the breeze.

"Marie."

I look up, surprised Jimmy has followed me out.

He has the last of the potato peels in a shallow bowl. In a moment's breath, he comes next to me, our shoulders and arms brushing as he pours them into the bucket. The pigs snort and grunt at our feet.

"Marie," he says again, and his voice is quick and hurried. "If I go—you will wait for me, won't you?"

He speaks as though we have an understanding between us, as if somehow our slow flirtation has become something greater. Is this how it goes, then? One day I am nothing but a sister, and the next day a man is asking me to consider him? Is it always so immediate and hasty, with no time to truly speak to one another of romance, of preferences, of future plans? I know in some cases it is so quick, but I had always thought there'd be a sense of deeper affection, or at least, a chance to talk about our dreams.

"You won't be gone too long," I say, hedging. "I will wait for you all to come home. Do you truly wish to go? Now that your position here—"

"She's right."

We jump. How long has Thaddeus watched us from the inky shadows next to the front forge? He steps closer, invading our space.

"Does it not change your decision, Jimmy? Don't you want to stay and work the bellows?"

"I can be missed, I think, for the sake of our country's needs, to build forts," Jimmy lifts his face to catch Thaddeus' height. "And then I'll be back."

"Lord knows that there will be many orders for arms and horse shoes from Fort Randall come spring. Father won't—*can't*—be expected to take your place if you go on some damnable fool's march."

"I …" Jimmy looks at me, and even in the dark I see the plead in his eyes, caught by the lamplight from inside. He wants me to go in, and gives a subtle flick of his hands. I glance between the two, and duck in, but not before I hear his full rejoinder.

"I must prove myself a man, Tadeusz. You must understand."

The blacksmith's voice is a low, strained, response, and I cannot make it out. I wish I were able to stay by Jimmy and hear the whole discussion. If I were promised to him, would I be part of each decision? Would I be an equal? It's what I have always expected in a match, what I know of the marriages of my parents and others in our Chicago Polish community. A woman's stubbornness usually had some merit, her voice and preferences heard.

Now, my stubbornness feels oddly out of place.

When I come back in, I finish the rest of the tidying and my mind wanders over what Tom's departure will mean. Will I truly take over in the shop? The notion seems silly and unreal. Uncertainty snakes through my chest. Suppose they realize how unworthy I am to be working the shop? My fingers itch to try, anyway.

My brothers have lapsed into a satisfied, anticipatory slump, and Father and Walter lean toward one another, lost in conversation mostly in the old language. Father's eyes float and land on Tom and Al, sitting stoically side by side. I wonder how much this notion of the militia eats at him—my father, who craves the whole family together.

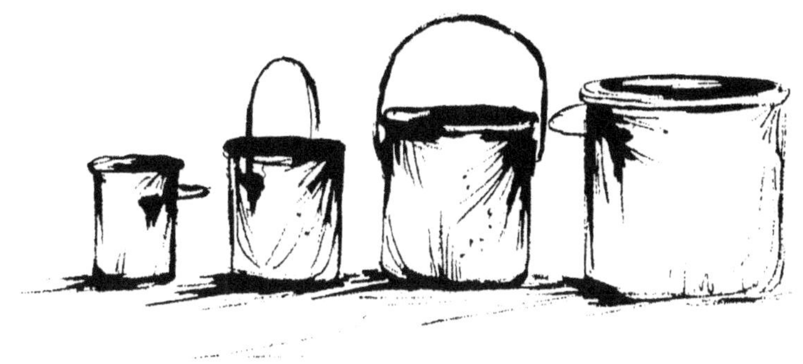

CHAPTER TWELVE

6 May 1866

"And then remember the one—what was it, that hilt? It was supposed to curve around the back of the hand and then twirl long. *Pamiętasz? Do you remember?*"

"*Tak, tak, yes,* but it was always to be breaking."

"So then. We ended up making the traditional kind— long and broad, and Stanisław made the handle look coiled with a round stamped end."

"Engraved."

"Yes, *tak.* But then we worked on the sabres."

Father and Walter delve deep into their memories, fondly swapping stories about swords. It is Sunday, and the boys leave in two weeks. They plan to arrive at Fort Laramie to enlist, and God knows when they'll be back. Before they go, Tom is scrambling to finish some tinkering for cash for the journey, and Al is sorting leather jigs for patterns. Sunday is anything but restful today, save the morning's Mass.

"You made *Szablas*? For the *szlachta*?" Al leans in. "You never told us, Father."

Jimmy shifts over to me, where I keep my hands busy on old darning. Tom's shirt is the worst of it. That hole from the journey west has only gotten bigger.

"What's a *Szabla*?"

I glance up at him, and then back down at my lap, feeling dizzy with his bright, earnest eyes.

"A particular type of sword, usually for the hussar cavalry back in *Polonia*. Many of the nobility—the *szlachta*—used them, too. They were very fancy."

"Oh yes," Walter folds his long frame deeper into the sheepskin-lined chair. He and Father have the best positions next to the hearth, and Walter smokes his long pipe thoughtfully. "Likely some of the *szlachta* used our swords. Stanisław made a very good handle from soft metals. One time even of gold."

Thaddeus snorts from his brooding corner, where he is taking out his frustrations by scraping down rust from old pliers, and pretending not to care or listen to the old stories.

"Did you keep patterns?" Tom wonders.

Father shakes his head. Unlike Walter, his hands are busy oiling snips.

"No. The patterns were belonging to our masters. But they were beautiful. The leaves and rosettes on the gold ... they were like what Marie is drawing in the margins of the ledger."

Seven pairs of eyes swerve to me.

"It's a bad habit," I say.

"Hah! And cluttered," Tom agrees.

"You are having a fair hand, daughter," Father says mildly.

It is a fine and generous compliment, and I can feel everyone weigh and consider it. Jimmy's presence is strong next to me, and I glance up at him. His face is, amazingly, full of pride, and the unexpected joy of his approval shoots through my chest.

"What I would give to make another sword," Walter sighs. "A beautiful one."

"You still are having a few on the wall," Father reminds him, but Walter shakes his head.

"They're done. It'd be something to be able to take up the iron and create just one more."

"Perhaps we will be doing it. One more time."

Later in the night, after the boys collapse on their freshly joined wooden beds and meanly stuffed mattresses, I escape the three snoring bodies. Creeping out of the rectangular living space, I sneak into the tinshop.

Father has pulled rank as master smith, and determined his preference for the shop's organization. There had been lengthy arguments about the placement of kettles and where to hang stakes along which walls. Father won every time, his stubbornness more practiced than Tom or Al.

Tonight, I run cold fingers over the colder iron of each machine in the moonlight. I've spent most days stirring oats and preparing the garden, but I also daydream on what it would be to create again, to be more than a woman of the hearth once more. Might be I'll find out soon enough.

CHAPTER THIRTEEN
9 May 1866

"And you think naming your damn brothel *The Powdered Rose* is cute? I'll show you *cute*! I'm naming my saloon *The Powdered Pig*! And I hope people understand that a pig *tastes* better than a rose!"

"How dare you!" Fortuna, newly arrived from Deadwood with two prostitutes in tow, brandishes a huge cast iron skillet and then shakes it, jiggling her gigantic bosom with the effort.

Dell Johnston stares, strangled for a moment, and his tangled beard works hard under dark eyes. He towers over Fortuna, but keeps his distance from her ironware and shouts instead.

"You gotta pick a new name, woman. I already got *The Powdered Keg*."

"I'm not changing it. I just painted the sign!" She quivers and swings the skillet once more. Dell takes an uncertain step backward, and then grits his teeth.

102

"Fine! Someone get me a gun!"

He's quickly handed a rifle by David Fawcett, who looks overly gleeful he's arrived from his Indian trading rounds in time to see something like this.

Fortuna's arms go out. "What the hell do you think you're doing?"

Dell ignores her, spins, and takes aim at his battered sign. With three shots, he's ripped the rotting wood from the edge of his saloon, and *The Powdered Keg's* sign crashes down and splinters.

"I—" He turns and finds me, where I'm mesmerized by the drama and my arms are full of tin deliveries. "Ah ha! You! The tinsmith's daughter! You go on and tell the boys at the smithy I want a new sign hanger. A solid *iron* one. One where I'll hang *my* new sign! From now on, it's *The Powdered Pig*!"

This last is a hoarse shout in Fortuna's direction and then Dell declares he'll be serving watered whiskey free if anyone cares to join him. Half the crowd does. The rest of us go back to our errands.

"Now that was worth leaving the Sioux for," David Fawcett says, his proper English accent out of place with his countless deer hides, buffalo furs, and tinkling trade beads. His wife, Caroline, grins and herds their passel of adopted Indian children, her chatter to them an unfamiliar Lakota dialect. As they move along Main Street, a woman screams, and a privy goes toppling from the top of the roof of one of the homes near the pig farm.

"Oh ho! That damn Horeb's at it again!"

"It wasn't empty. Someone find Doc Gunnarsen!"

"Someone find Horeb!"

The privy's contents spill along the side of the shack, emptying a mess and a very drunk cowboy onto the ground. Three young boys go sprinting toward the *Rusty Nail*. The doctor is typically found either on his small ranch or drinking whiskey.

I move to deliver a few goods to the general store, and Harry Turner leans on the porch railing, looking intrigued and laughing about the privy practical joke.

"Here's some of your wares," I tell him, handing over the watering cans he had hoped to sell. "And you wanted a lantern for your house."

Harry takes them up and glances over the handiwork. "Nicely done. I'd expect that for the wait I had."

"We ran out of tin sheet over the winter," I say, lifting my chin and pulling my shoulders back.

"So I've heard. I also heard you made Toot Warren her requests."

"She asked first!"

"Maybe."

His skepticism makes me feel mulish, and I push my mouth together at first.

"I suppose I should pay you our agreed price. Even with the wait."

"You know the first wagon train just arrived to camp at the old buffalo jump a week ago," I retort. "They brought our tin, which you're lucky we could get the money to pay for! If you want to cheap us out, you can expect an even longer delay next order."

Harry raises his eyebrows. "Don't you be playing games with me, girlie. You're too new for that. And don't be speaking so baldly about your money. It's vulgar."

Goddamn him and his condescending tone! I glue my lips closed and just wait for him to pay me. We desperately need the cash. We're behind on our loan to Percy Davies and the bank for the lumber, and heaven knows what kind of rent Father is paying. Plus the borrowed funds from Percy for the tin sheet to actually make more wares to sell. To make more money. It's an unending circle of shortages.

I know it's one more reason Tom needs to join the Army again. For all Father abhors the notion.

Harry hands me the coins, and I count them quickly.

"Well, we're settled up," I say.

He looks at me strangely and lifts the tin lantern. "You think this will be enough to cover your grocery credit over the winter?"

"It ought to. That's hours and hours of work."

"You all might have a big opinion of your time, but it costs dear to get grocery supplies out here too."

"It costs dearly to have the tin brought out!"

"Then you all should have thought of that before deciding to set up a shop out west," he says plainly.

"My Father—" Once again, I slap my mouth together and stare at Harry's faded vest. When I finally force myself to meet his eyes, his own soften under the bushy brows.

"I'll check the account," he says quietly, and turns to go into the mercantile.

I tighten my mouth and wait outside. Father should be the one soothing the customer! He's the reason we didn't have enough tin in the first place!

Turning back to the street, I watch the drama between the menfolk unfold, unable to care too much, chewing on my own inadequacies and my own lack of charisma. If I even had an ounce of Horeb's, I'd be better off …

"Someone gonna get Horeb at the lumberyard an' tell Mikey O'Donnell he'll be one man short! I'ma gonna … kill 'im!" The cowboy who was stuck in the privy Horeb locked and shoved on a roof last night stumbles down Main Street and swerves, still drunk and trailing a horrible stink. David Fawcett roars with laughter so loudly I'm sure he'll choke on his own spittle.

Doc Gunnarsen shambles over, freshly watered from the *Rusty Nail* and sniffs. "I'm not looking you over till you take a dip in the creek."

"Doc! I coulda be mean hurt!"

"You're walking, so not that hurt." The doctor turns back on his heel and ambles slightly sideways back into the *Nail*.

When I enter the general store to check on Harry and our account, I run into Lara O'Donnell and try not to cringe as she starts in immediately.

"Oh Marie Kotlarczyk! You're goin' to be speakin' with Father Jonathon about the summer picnic, then? Have ye already? No? Well, soon then. And be sure to catch Tina Brinkley at Mass, she's the best pie baker in town. After me, o' course."

"I haven't done a thing yet."

"Well, you should."

"Been busy," I tell her.

"How?" she says, her voice sing-song. "Ye have no husband or children an' you live in town. How hard can it be for you?"

"I have men to clean after and cook for!"

"Oh Marie," Lara laughs. "But everyone knows ye can't cook worth a damn."

She breezes out, and I sigh.

"You didn't have to say you'd help her with the church picnic," Sadie says at my elbow, leaning on a broom.

"I didn't. She assumed."

"Then tell her you can't."

"Sadie! You snipe! Do we pay you to gossip or sweep?" May Turner asks as she swings through from the back room. Sadie jumps into action, and I wander to Harry, where he's scratching down math next to our name in his great book.

"Heard about old Brinkley selling farmland?" Harry mentions to me as he runs his finger down the ledger.

"I have."

"Heard about Oddvar wanting to sell too?"

"Who?"

"Oddvar Svendsen. Your landlord."

My heart jumps. "I haven't heard of that."

Harry's eyes gleam and he looks very pleased that he's able to pass on new gossip. "Ohh, well, you should talk to your Father then. Or Percy Davies. Anyway, here's your balance." He points to the black mark and I sigh. We're still deep in debt to the general store and the bank, and though I hate the idea of my brother disappearing for a year or so, I will be glad for the money!

Waving to Sadie, I step back outside. Spring in Flats Town is muddy and wet, but the air is clear and clean and brushes the sky in a way that it never did in Chicago.

When I get home, I pull out raised dough rolls and get to work. I am baking bread two days early, so Tom and Jimmy can have something in their sacks when they leave for Fort Laramie. Colonel Henry Carrington, with almost nine officers under him, are to arrive there in June and the boys have received word they are to join Company K. Tom, from holding previous Army posts, is considered a contractor employee due to his specialty, though he and Jimmy will also be included as enlisted men in a fight. I can't tell if Tom is glad or resigned about re-enlisting. I only know he's angrier than usual.

Jimmy and Thaddeus help build the last of the interior walls in our barn-turned-shop, so the place is filled with hammering, floating sawdust, and sawing every late afternoon. The cacophony drives me next to madness, and I busy myself with as many kitchen chores as I can, so I might disappear to the large hearth in the blacksmith's house.

The silence in the kitchen is open and wide and overlarge. I put the risen loaves on the tin sheet and set it to bake in the copper biscuit oven. I am grateful Walter allows us to use his hearth, and in return, I usually leave some of the food behind. Bread is one of the few things I do not do poorly, and though there is no bread oven, I have mastered the smaller reflector biscuit oven next to the fire.

As I watch the metal gleam and quiver, I let the worries simmer through me. Where will I find help? If I'm to work a bit in the shop, and Jimmy is gone, someone will need to help me, though we cannot even afford it and no one seems to need work anyway. Everyone is busy with their own houses, scraping by and pushing against the elements. Perhaps I'll ask Susan Brinkley at Mass. She and her daughters-in-law, Cora and Marta, have been very kind. They've offered clippings of geraniums, and clumps of rosemary, and roots of roses for spring plantings.

I take out some mending from my possibilities bag, and as I do, my fingers feel the slice and prick of a piece of tin. Turning over the small sheet in my hand, I debate. The idea forms itself slowly, and I start to bend and curl the tin carefully around the handle of my knife, holding one of the edges down to lessen the chance of a warped corner. The piece is small, but neatly cut, and I ease it around without too much trouble.

When I'm finished with the curve, I know already what it will be. Glancing around the kitchen, I see the usual untidiness. For all Jimmy's cooking skills, he is still a man, and keeps the space full of odds and ends hovering between home and shop. There is always a bowl of nails. I go to the crock and lift the loose cover off to select a slender one.

Now if only I had a hammer! Even a rawhide one would do. I look around again in the hopes of spying one out, but the only option is a wooden spoon sitting in another crock on the sideboard. That crock is decorated and painted in the patterns of Poland. I wonder if Walter's wife did the design.

I take one of the larger spoons. Squatting down near the hearth again—both for warmth and to keep one eye on the loaves of bread—I start to aim and crack the small nail through the thin metallic sheet. The bang is muted against the soft wooden floor and the wood makes a dull popping sound against the nail. I pull it away and realize the dent is not through at all.

"So then, you'll want a true hammer." The low voice is filled with amusement.

Walter's craggy face looms over me.

"I haven't one." I hide my embarrassment under a tart response.

"Here you are, then." He pulls out a small hammer from his belt loop, and as he hands it over, his fingers shake with a noticeable tremor. Just as soon as I see it, it is gone.

"Thank you. I just ..." I look down at the metal in my hands, contorted and full of scratches. "Well, the bread is baking and I thought I'd see about puttering a bit."

Walter leans over me, the smell of fire and charcoal lingering on his shirt.

"You're making a *tarka do gałka muszkatołowej nutmeg grater?*"

"I'm going to try. I've seen many repaired and made, over the years."

"You should have hammered the holes before you curved the piece."

"Ah. Damn. I forgot the order of it," I curse myself. "I'll use it as is."

"Maybe, but you will have a distorted grate now instead, or at least, it will be hard to create a perfect half circle. One should always punch holes before shaping the metal."

I sigh, wishing in this moment I could be an apprentice and learn from everyone, at any time. "Well, it's what I have. How do you know all these little details anyway?"

"Well, then, we had our fair share of nutmeg grater repairs before the Kotlarczyk family arrived," Walter grins at me quickly with a smile reaching the depths of his dark eyes.

I return to the metal, slowly banging it flat again against the flagstone and then slamming holes using Walter's old hammer. He peers overhead. When I finish, I start to re-curve the grater. He stops me and hands over a few pieces of leather hide.

110

"To save your hands," he reasons.

It is hard to do such small work holding the leather, though, and without the proper stake. I recall the needlecase iron Father had pulled out on the wagon journey, and I know it would be the right one. Walter does not comment as I use the rounded handle of my knife again, nodding slightly as if he approves of my salvaging.

"You'll want to put a cover and a base on," he says. "So then, let me see what I have around the shop yet for scrap."

He disappears into the front forge, and I check on the bread. It has risen well and is on its way to turning a deep, golden, brown.

The side door swings open and I look up, half-hoping for Jimmy. He has been sparingly but endearingly attentive, as if he does not want to hope too much that I might give him a promise before he leaves. I still do not know if I might. I like him very much, and I like how he has no qualms about cooking, and I like that he does not care how I play around with the tin. His attentions are sweet and thrilling: the soft looks across the table, and when his hand brushes against mine as we manage the kitchen duties together.

"What are you smiling about?" Al's head pokes around the corner of the door.

"Why aren't you helping the others?" I counter, quickly hiding my disappointment.

He looks a little guilty, then steps in completely, his fingers flicking absently against the frayed seams of his broadcloth pants.

"I just ..." He shifts to take a view of what is baking on the pan bed under the oven hood. "How many are you making?"

It is an odd question. I frown, looking at the browning bread.

"I have enough for the two going toward Fort Randall, and then one for Walter and Thaddeus, and two for us."

Al looks uncomfortable and it puts me on edge.

"What is it?"

"I ... might you save one of the loaves for me?"

"Of course. Father and I can share the other."

He twists his hands behind him, and inhales, looking down at his feet. "No. Not for ... I am going to go, tomorrow."

I gape at him. "Al. You can't be serious."

"They'll let me. I mean, Carrington or his officers will take me. Or someone at Fort Laramie will. I'm sixteen, I have my two front teeth, and—"

"Father will never let you. He won't. He's already worrying about Tom going."

"He doesn't have a choice."

"You can't!" I wish to pause his rashness, to implore that he not leave me alone, that he and I will have a grand time playing at running the shop, that we will have so many moments of laughter. Would he give that up?

"I must. I have to, if I'm going to live out here."

"What?" I cannot fathom his reasoning. "But—you already *are* living out here, Al. How does going to fight ... whatever his name is ... this Red Cloud Indian have anything to do with it? How will raiding an Indian campsite make it easier to live in Flats Town?"

"It might be just building a fort."

"You have to build a business. Why, Al?"

"You always ask too many questions," he says lightly, and his dismissiveness hurts. A loud bang echoes from the

112

forge behind the door, and he looks up quickly. "Who's that?"

"Just Walter. Puttering." I gesture backward, and the half-finished nutmeg grater glitters against the copper hood and flame. Al's eyebrows lift, and he holds out his palm to take a closer look. I hand it over, nervous but a little proud of my initial try.

He turns it around, considering. Then he glances up toward the doorway between the living quarters and the forge, and he speaks terse and fast. "I need to go to face the Indians. The stories I heard on the journey here … they are too much to sleep well, to feel safe. You saw me the day the thieves tried to go in our wagon. I need to know I can stand against them, to face them, to hear their hollers and war cries for myself and know I will survive."

I stare at him. The deep fear splays across his face, pure and heavy. It seems to suffocate him. Is this why he has been less inclined to be so chatty around town, to leave the mailing of letters to Tom, to sit and work on the backlog of tinkering?

"How will you get Father to let you go? He will protest. Hell, he'll forbid it."

"I've thought on it. When the others leave, I will slip out. You won't even see me do it until it's done. At least you will know of my plans, so you will be able to put Father's mind at ease."

"So I'm to do with all the emotional baggage again?"

"You're the female."

"Females don't always like to deal with feelings," I tell him, shoving down my own. "It's stupid. You're going to make it worse for us. You're being selfish."

"At least I'll be away from your harsh tongue," he suddenly lashes out. "And your horrible cooking. And watching you sink the business with your terrible customer service!"

"I'm not ruining the business!"

"Sure." The sarcasm bites, and then Al hangs his head. "Damn it, Marie. I hate fighting with you."

"You will—you will hurt Father's heart, Al," I tell him. "You shouldn't go. I wish I could make you stay."

"Even your stubbornness can't stop me."

"I could tell Father."

"Don't! Please. Marie—I must do it, or I'll begrudge him, and I will forever feel like I'm not enough. Much like your Jimmy." He takes a moment to smirk at me, all arguing forgotten.

"Whose Jimmy?" Walter asks, and we both jump around. Walter ambles into the kitchen to offer me a few small pieces of tin. There are spots of rust on one—tiny, brownish red droplets that look like dried blood—but they will suffice for my little project.

"Oh—we all have seen that Jimmy has eyes for our Marie," Al says, and I reach out and slap him playfully, my head still pounding with the implications of what he has told me.

Walter's eyebrows go up, and he presses his lips together. "Is that so?"

"So he tells me, sir," I say softly, slipping into the formal in my embarrassment. Al has the presence of mind to realize he has spoken out of turn in his own nervousness, and backtracks.

"Well, he's made no declarations, and Marie has not given him any hope."

"Hm. Well then. I've brought some of our old snips too." Walter pulls a few straight tin scissors out of his belt. Most of them are oiled, and small enough for the daintier work. I take up a pliers and estimate the crease of the lap seam, bending to mark it. If I focus on the metalwork, maybe Al will see how I lack, and how he needs to stay and help me.

But Al walks out, and Walter and I are left in the quiet, with only the crackle of the hearth and the smell of bread rolling over us.

"That is very nice, Marie," Walter finally says, and I am at once grateful he will not tease me in the way of old men, and wind out a story about the possibilities between myself and Jimmy. Instead, he is intent on the grater, and the marking of the base and cover I do before I carefully cut out the circular shapes, pushing against the metal

"Good. You've left room for the burr?"

I nod, not taking my eyes from the work, watching the snips eat the skinny line of the circle. When it's finished, Walter takes the pieces and measures them against the tubed grater.

"You will be able to use your machine to finish this?"

"I think so. If Thaddeus is done fixing it." And if the boys let me touch it again. When they are gone west, I will have plenty of time with the machines. The thought is defiant, but also exhilarating and incredibly bittersweet.

"Solder it when you can. I will buy it from you." Walter's eyes are black and merry, and I feel a kinship with him I do not expect.

The bread smells done, and looks it, too. I poke it carefully. "There we are. At least I did not burn them."

"You are too hard on yourself, Marya. You've yet to make a poor meal since you've arrived." His use of my Polish name warms me, and I smile at him fully before pulling the bread pan off the biscuit oven, placing it on the pitted and worn surface of the kitchen trestle.

"That's because Jimmy has made most of the food, and I've only made things I know I will not mess. Truly, I generally ruin a lot of things. When Jimmy is away, and I will be in charge of cooking for you all … Well, then you will see my talent, or lack of it." I mean more than the food.

Walter does not rejoin, and in truth I am surprised he has been so talkative today. I place one of the loaves of bread on the mantel on a piece of cheesecloth. Pulling another off, I take out a heavier piece of cloth from my possibilities and wrap it up.

"This is for Jimmy, for tomorrow."

Walter nods once, shortly, and reaches for one of the tankards of ale. He always has one half-full permanently on the table. Once again, I notice the slight tremble to his fingers. I wonder if Thaddeus knows. Surely, he is observant enough to see it?

I leave the copper oven where it is, and put the pan back after scraping down any leftover residue into the fire. I gather up the other loaves in my apron, and head to the door, but before I can reach the latch, the door swings open, spilling in the twilight and the cold air as well as Thaddeus, who is glowering more than usual. He is a black shadow, and I pull back as he pounds past me, his height and size adding to the storm of anger.

"Marie. The new burring machine is set up. Think you can manage not to break it?" he says shortly, pausing briefly as he stalks in.

My chin goes up, and I clench my apron tighter around the loaves. "I didn't break the other on purpose last time."

"That so?"

"What do you take me for? A destructive woman?"

"Ha. Well, then." Thaddeus barrels toward his father, and I slip out. Still, the walls and door are only made of wood, and I am able to hear Thaddeus's voice carry as if he was booming into my ear.

"So, Father, you must be exceedingly pleased with yourself!"

Walter's response is calmer, but I can hear it just as well.

"I am not sure what you mean, Tadeusz."

"We're not going to dance around this topic any more. You know I'm stuck here as master now, and I will not be able to go fight at all. Already Army orders are trickling in, and surely Fort Randall will ask for additional wheels for supplies to wherever they're building the next fort, plus summer projects at Randall itself. I'll be tied to the forge for months."

"That is the way of the blacksmith."

"That is *your* planning, Father, *your* scheme. *Your* wish for me to stay behind and *safe* instead of considering how I might wish to strike out on my own. Maybe I want a good fight. Maybe I want to make fast money like Tom Kotlarczyk. What if I want to grow our nation my own way, with the other young men?"

"Your patriotism is misplaced."

"So you say! You! The one who wishes to see the railroad, the progress, and more trades come and grow this town?"

"My desire is to build in Flats Town what was lost in the Old Country. My loyalty is not to America so much. I want our life here in the west to be good and successful. Something small to you, maybe, but it is enough. It is foolishness to chase away a good business for the sake of the frontier."

"You calling Tom and Jimmy foolish?"

"I didn't say so."

"Someday the west will *be* America, Father. I care about it, and I want to show my loyalty. I want to—"

"Show your manhood?"

Even through the door, I am able to hear the sarcasm and disappointment filtering Walter's words. I can imagine him, sitting at the table with his head down and his eyes on his beer. Perhaps Thaddeus is pacing, or standing over his father with his hands on his hips, his eyes boring into his father's slowly balding crown.

Walter's voice continues, though more tired now.

"You are needed here. I am finished being the master and your *nauczyciel teacher*, though you think it premature. I have reasons, and they are more than what you say. I do indeed have a desire to keep you close, for you are my only son and my only family. But it is more than that."

Before I can eavesdrop further, a hand snakes around my waist, and I am spun into a loose embrace. Jimmy's cheek presses to mine, and the early stubble of a young man's beard chaffs my skin. He smells like fire and sawdust and sweat, and his long and lean arms catch me up with ease.

"I leave tomorrow, Marie," he says, stating the obvious. "Will you leave me with nothing, if you will not give me your promise?"

I am not quite sure what he asks of me, but I can sense it and anticipation trickles through my blood. The headiness of Jimmy's attentions rushes into my head, though it is not quite so titillating as I expect. Shouldn't my heart feel full and glad? Still, I am so very grateful I get a turn in the quiet stillness of moonlight, with the end of winter breathing around us. It is certainly exciting, and is filled with the potential of the future. My heart beats and stops at intervals, laced with the worry that someone will find us in such an embrace.

"I can leave you with a little something." It seems an appropriate response, but he takes me at my word and presses me close, so the tightness of his chest hits my bosom, and the hollow of his stomach curls against the gathers of my skirt. We are similar in height and he gazes into my eyes directly against the blue of the starlight.

He kisses me. It is both a tremor and an ache, and delightfully shivery, and my body pulls and catches at once. It is my first kiss, and I do like it. Jimmy's hands move to my waist, and one of his flat palms brushes against the side of my breast. Womanly instincts flash and burn into being. Suddenly, I fully understand what is the lust between a man and a woman. I can start to understand the need pooling, and the inability to see straight. Though I am unable to let myself go, as my nerves are too jumpy and my mind too buzzy with calculations, I still like the tingle, however slight it is.

But Jimmy kisses me as if he is a hungry man, and his lips are insistent. I allow him to open my mouth further with his, and I do not jump as his hand once more lightly touches my chest. I am interested in experiencing what I saw from across the wagon circle at night. I want to feel what it is to be kissed, to be wanted. It is a quiver and a hope, a whisper without words.

We break apart, and Jimmy's breath is fast and hot against my neck. It is a powerful feeling. I might ask much of him right now: a trinket, a lifetime, a piece of his character. Some women might. The idea is tempting, but what exactly would I beg of him? I do not want his promise yet, as I am not sure I want to tie his life with mine. For all the headiness of his embrace, there is still much to consider. Will Father approve? My brothers? Does he love me?

My reverie is broken when Jimmy dives back in for another kiss, this one more insistent. I allow him another moment of passion, but then push against him with the hand not holding up my apron. His chest is flat and hard against my palm, his breath wild and quick.

"Is that what you wished, then?" I ask softly.

He presses his forehead to mine, and nods silently, unable to speak. I feel a deep fondness unfold toward him. His earnest affection for me, coupled with his respect and desire, is a lovely combination. It is, truly, what I had wanted in a match. I find myself hoping he asks Father for permission to court or marry me when he returns.

I pull away from Jimmy and our arms drop away. The night chill creeps along my shoulders. The warmth from the bread is nearly gone, and I look toward the deep tawny light spilling from my family's space.

"Go ahead home. I will see you yet tonight for dinner," he says, following my eyes.

Before I walk into the lamplight, I look behind me. He's standing in the blue and black of falling night, watching me go, and my heart leaps a little higher.

CHAPTER FOURTEEN
10 May 1866

I spend more of the night awake than I care to be. It is a foolish thing to do. Even without much sleep, my duties in the morning will be there, with the same amount of water to be hauled from the Flats Basin stream, the same clothes to be washed and wrung, the same candles to prepare, the butter to churn, the pigs and damnable chickens to feed. And coffee will need to be roasted and ground again, and the Salomon's smokehouse needs to be cleared of the rabbits Jimmy brought back last week. I still need to speak to Father Jonathon about the church social, and Sadie has invited me to go berry picking with Grete and Bess—Bess, who just married Franklin Jones, so she's not plumping her breasts at my brothers anymore.

Al says he's going tomorrow. He shouldn't. He *can't.* The thought makes my stomach churn, and if I were a weepy woman, I would allow myself some tears of fear and distress, but my eyes are dry and scratchy. Instead, I steel myself, pulling up my resolve, as the questions still pour in. What about the shop? How can Al leave Father and me? Is Al's young pride—his peace of mind, his manhood—so unstable by the thought of the wild frontier? Is it so necessary to prove his mettle, that he is man enough to live here?

I cannot understand the workings of a man's heart, though I live with so many. They say a woman is not sensible, and must have her way carved out by a father or brother or husband. But there are times I do not believe it. There are times I believe the sensibility of our communities is rooted in the women. Many times, here in Flats Town, I've seen a woman speak a word, mind a business, or take control. I want to do the same, though no one listens to my ideas, and I'm painfully aware of my crude attempts.

I turn over in bed, and the blanket shifts to expose my foot. I kick it back against the creeping cold of the room. My bed is not near enough the potbelly stove, though its radiant heat wafts over us weakly. The boys have made the rough bed frames fast, and one of the legs of my bed is cut too short. They are so exact with their tinwork, but sloppy with wood.

Unlike my flowers. I've just planted the roses in a perfect row outside. Mrs. Andersen mentioned it when she stopped in a few days ago.

Mrs. Andersen seems very nice. She is the widowed mother of Grete; their faces are cut of the same cloth. Father's eyes followed her when she visited. She stopped by to say hello, bring food, and decided I needed help with making an early green soup. Tom pulled me aside later, and said I am to watch out, as Father might be interested in replacing Mother with a woman we do not know well. His worry may be misplaced. I noticed Mrs. Andersen pays the same amount of attention to Walter as she does Father.

I toss again, and remember my kiss with Jimmy tonight. It runs through me, a tingle of excitement when I recall his touch, his caress. I understand now how a body can awaken to the touch of another. My heart turns over the sense in tying myself to Jimmy. Eventually, he might open a second smithy when he returns from the Army. Goodness knows there is enough work. And he does not begrudge my poor cooking. He smiles at me, and he is attentive without being overbearing. It is what I would hope for in a husband. I know this. I just did not expect it to be so ... quick. I expected to feel something permanent and earthy. Well, perhaps Al and Tom will discourage him as they march out. Perhaps they will tell Jimmy that I am not available, as they have done so many times before. Perhaps my own heart will bloom with deep affection in his absence.

The night is old. I pinch my forehead and beg my heart to stop soaring, to let exhaustion consume me. Under the simmering of my racing, jumbled, thoughts, my worry for Al, and my fear for the future, I must sleep. My world will upend in the morning.

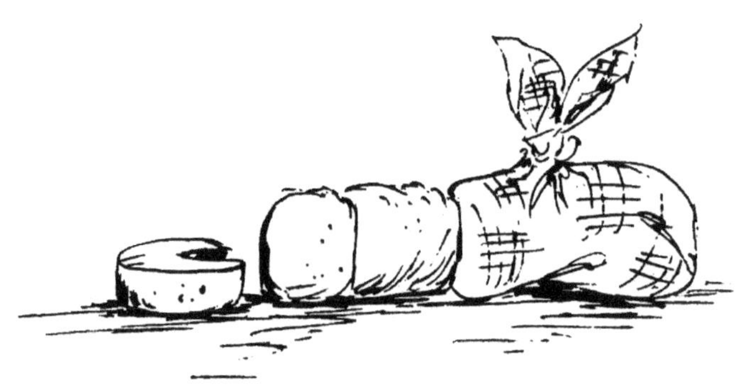

CHAPTER FIFTEEN
10 May 1866

"Don't you think everyone might waste away from poor vict-uals?" I say to Jimmy, trying to be humorous, and to keep from talking about the hundreds of miles between here and there.

He gives his bright smile.

"Just bake him bread. That you can do well." He raises a kerchief, where the fresh brown loaf is packed around hard cheese and dried meat and the last of the previous winter's salt pork from the Salomons.

"That at least," Tom nods as he passes by, his wide shoulders holding an expansive plank to serve as extra seats across the loaded wagon bed. Buckskinner David Fawcett will drive to Fort Randall with a few other local Army recruits anxious for the promised funds. His adopted children climb up and around one another, hanging on and shouting unin-telligibly to Caroline: *"Louŋčiŋpi! Ina! Louŋčiŋpi! We are hungry! Mother! We are hungry!"*

124

"*Loyačiŋpi he? Waštepe! You are all hungry? You all be good!*"

"You will be fine, Marie," Jimmy says. "We won't be gone forever. It's only a month's walk to Fort Laramie. I'm sure we'll get home at some time sooner than later. And your brother will send the money back."

The money, the money. It's all about the damn money.

"You can make fine things from tin in the meantime," Jimmy continues. "Though one can't eat tin."

"Unfortunately not," I agree, and grin back up at him. The cord between us strings tight with hope and uncertainty, and I feel my heart flutter again. Though he has not demanded a promise of me, I like him better for it. I turn to him so that we are very near each other. Would an embrace be so very inappropriate here? Now? In front of so many?

He seems to think so, and instead takes up my hand and bends over it as a gentleman would in the city. "I will think of you often, Marie. Be well, and hearty. I will see you soon."

I want to know if I've imagined the way my body reacts to his, and pull him toward me so he ends up hugging me anyway, just so I can try to feel it all over again. The spark is there, tempered. I wonder why, but there's not another moment. Tom claps a heavy hand on Jimmy's shoulder.

"We're to be off, Jim. Release my sister. It's my turn."

He fairly pushes the younger man away. With a backward glance, Jimmy hops up to the wagon with his agile speed. Tom hovers, his bear-like stance magnified by the messy hair hanging over his shoulders and bleeding into his beard. He glowers at first, then yanks me loosely to him.

"Be well, Marie. No boys until we're back, all right?" Tom wiggles his eyebrows once, and if the day weren't so somber, I'd laugh.

"I don't think you'll need to worry, Tomasz."

He offers a smile with the tight, careful grimace that passes as one, and climbs onto the wagon. I look around and realize Al has already slipped away, and indignation couples with anger. How could he go without at least saying something to me? Or has he changed his mind? Maybe he won't really go!

I wonder if Tom has any notion of Al's plans. Or perhaps Jimmy does, as he has become fast friends with my youngest brother. I stare at the two of them. They do not behave as if they are waiting on Al, but they do not seem worried that he is not here, either. Instead, Jimmy leans down in serious, low, conversation with Walter and Thaddeus, who looks thunderous.

The reins snap, and the wagon lurches forward. David Fawcett's rich British accent shouts out to the rest of the Fawcett family who live in Flats Town, and his siblings and elderly parents wave resignedly. Six young boys start to race alongside the wagon, but they're out of breath before the horse team makes it to the tannery on the west end of town. The handful of men on the wagon boards sway and bounce.

Along with several other townspeople, Father and I wave heartily, calling out the same words, the same farewells, the same wishes. I almost forget for a moment that Al means to leave with them. It is only when he comes tearing out of a side alley once the wagon is nearly off the street, and onto the prairie itself, that I remember.

Father goes completely still next to me, his waving hand frozen.

126

As Al makes to swing up into the jiggling, bouncing wagon, hands reach down and pull him up in one slick, fluid motion, and then he is there, sitting beside Jimmy and Tom. He is far enough away so I cannot see whether his face is triumphant or frightened. He raises an arm in our direction, and that is what it takes to move Father.

"Albert! Wojciech! You may not go! Get down now—I forbid it! *Może nie udać! You may not go!*" The Polish spills from him, an unending stream of anger and cursing, and he takes fast steps toward the wagon's retreat, though there is not a hope for stopping it now. He gives an angry, anguished, shout, and then seems to remember he has an audience. I want to slide into the dark grey shade of the nearest buildings, as so many people are watching this agonized response. If I could, I'd disappear into Walter's shadow.

"Marya!" He rounds on me, his eyes glazed. "Did you be knowing of this?"

"I … he told me last night."

"You are not thinking to tell me?" Father has the presence of mind to lower his voice, though it does not make him any less furious.

"I—" There were many reasons I found to stay silent last night, not least of which was Al's trust. Still, I cannot tell an outright lie, even though I would dearly like to keep my bit of complicity quiet. Walter and Thaddeus plod behind us and I don't like to admit my failures in the hearing of so many—my cooking aside. It is already all too embarrassing.

"He could have changed his mind when it came to it, Father. And he could have been turned away."

"Turned away?" Father's voice rises again with incredulousness. "There is being no chances he is going to be being turned away. The Army is being bled—*is bleeding*—men. They'll be taking all the recruits they are getting!"

"Father, please. What was I to do?"

"You're his big *siostra*. You are to be asking him to stay behind and help."

"But I did. I tried!"

"Not hard enough, then. If he will not be listening to me, he would be listening to you!"

"I did ask him not to go—" I clench my hands and swallow the rest of my words, folding my lips over my teeth. I did ask. And I had failed. That part is true.

"How will you be managing, Marie? Besides all the spring chores and the household, you will be needing to be helping me in the shop. There is being no other way around it now."

"But that was the plan from the first. I was to help with the tinkering."

"To be tinkering is one thing. You will be having to be starting full orders. Otherwise I won't be being able to keep up. Marie … Marya … He left! *On zostawił mnie! He left me!* He is leaving me alone!" Father's voice drops so low I can hardly hear it, and I want to take his arm, but I do not, for fear my touch will undo him in his grief.

"How will we be surviving? What will become of us if they do not return or send money? How will we be living? What will we be doing? Oh, my Jozefa. I have failed you! I was to be keeping them safe, away from the Army, and I have failed you! *Moja miłość, zawiodłem Cię! My love, I failed you!*"

He repeats this, over and over all the way home, and pushes open the door to the tin shop as if he does not see it. I pause, wondering what I should do, knowing the layers of chores still awaiting, and the list of orders to be filled. I shouldn't leave Father to it all alone, but I don't want to sit next to him while he fumes.

I turn to our blacksmith neighbors, and as I do, Thaddeus disappears into the smithy, his hands bunched in anger and dissatisfaction. Walter watches him go, and then looks to me.

"Stanisław … So then, do you need anything, Marya?"

I gulp in air. I do not dare give him the litany of my needs and my fears, unrolling through my mind in ropes.

"No. No, I think we will be all right, for now."

Walter nods once, and goes in, leaving me in the cavernous silence of the yard between the two buildings, listening to the splash of the nearby stream, and wondering what I should do next.

My head whirls, and I allow myself a moment against the door, where my forehead hits the rough prickle of aging wood. The enormity of what I must do hits my chest, catching the air I breathe. I send a hard reprimand to Al in my mind, berating him his selfishness and his desire to face his fears and yes, to prove his manhood. I compose a note to Jimmy, asking him to be safe and to find his pride in the firing of his gun. And I do desperately wish for Tom to come home once more, full of boasting war stories and countless escapades, if only that it means he is back in Flats Town whole and happy. The money seems secondary to it all in this exact moment.

I sigh. No one else is going to get the meal on, and I suppose I should see what is on the ledger for tinkering today even though I don't know if I can concentrate. As I push open the door, I look for Father, but he is only a gray shadow outside the back doorway. He sits outside, staring at the trees on the horizon, listening to the water and likely wishing Mother were here. I wish she were, too.

But she is gone, and so are the boys, for now. I put another roll into my sleeves and then, as an afterthought, move to the seed box. Today is a good day for hands to be in the earth, and the mindless, numbing, tilling of soil. If I am quick about it, I can get half the garden in, water heated, and bread mixed, all before breakfast.

CHAPTER SIXTEEN
19 June 1866

The bank door is formidable. It matches the fancy trim on Percy Davies's decorated, cake-like house on the west side of town, and is painted green, though the sand of the prairie has scoured most of it off.

I'm not sure which is worse: little, snotty-nosed Harold Ofsberger running into the shop a few minutes ago to tell me I'm needed by Percy Davies or actually standing here outside the bank.

"The door gonna bite you, is it?"

I swing around and instinctively wrap my arms around my chest. "No."

Horeb Harvey smirks up at me from the street and chortles again. "Then go on, you been standing there five minutes, and I have four pennies on you'll go in within the next two. Trusty Willy Warren's been counting with his fancy watch."

"Get your ass back in, you can't be forcing your bet to win!" Someone yells from the back window of the Rusty Nail.

I feel my face drain of color, but then the familiar flood of blood rushes up. "You've got a bet that I'll go in within the next two minutes?"

"Yup." Horeb spits and rocks back onto his heels, slinging his thumbs into his belt.

I spin and plunk down on the stairs of the bank, my skirts settling in a haphazard heap around my legs. Horeb's eyes immediately glue to my exposed ankles and stockings while I scramble to cover them up.

"Oh, so you're gonna make me lose on purpose, is it?" His chin goes out, pointy and sharp and grizzled.

I don't answer, just drill my eyes into the dark windows of the saloon, where the building angles across the alley people call General Street.

"Well, no mind. I got to see your whole leg, knee and all, and that was worth it," Horeb says, and saunters, loose-limbed and wobbly, back into the Rusty Nail. The hollers and whoops are inordinately loud when he walks in. I want to run back to our shop.

Not that it would help. All of the Rusty Nail customers will wander in at some point for repairs. Most of them will stare at my bosom, no matter it's not extraordinary.

I wait an extra few minutes just to be sure Horeb will lose his bet, and then walk into the dank, choking, musty bank.

"Marie Kotlarczyk. Thank you for comin' in." Percy Davies stands at once from the dark desk along the back wall, smoothing his rumpled velvet vest before hooking his fingers under it and through his suspenders. "How good of you. Come in and take a seat."

The bank teller, a chisel-faced, dark and handsome young man gives an austere nod as I go past. He looks familiar, and then I realize he's Tom Fawcett, the younger brother of the frontiersman. His stiff manner and brushed suit are a complete opposite of his older sibling.

I take a seat, settling as best I can into the polished leather of it, and brace my feet against the floorboards. Why is a bank so stuffy? It smells like ink and crumpled paper and old coffee, but mostly I smell my own fear.

"I need to speak to you. I'd take your father up with this business, but I've heard he's a bit ... indisposed."

At least Percy is civil about it.

"Yes. Father's a bit quiet since the boys left," I say, hedging and sweating.

"Well, I'm sorry to hear it. But time is marchin' and I need to keep movin' before things get too far gone. Have you spoken to your landlord recently?"

Confusion melts into my bones. "No. Usually that's Father."

Percy nods and braces his hip against the edge of his desk, folding his arms over his stomach and narrowing his eyes.

"I figured as much. Still. Miss Kotlarczyk. Have you heard of the railroad comin' through?"

"There's been talk, always," I say.

"Oh, it'll happen. I'm makin' sure of that." Percy waves a hand briefly. "But I need you to keep payin' rent to Oddvar Svendsen."

My eyebrows squeeze together. "Why wouldn't we?"

"Oh … in case he makes it too expensive. But you need to keep payin' it no matter what."

"I won't promise." I don't like to remind the banker of the loan we still have with him, especially since we have had to take out a bit more to cover our costs at the General.

"You can," Percy says comfortably, and sits in his chair. The wood creaks under his bottom and he leans into the spokes. "I'll be sure of it. If rent goes up, you pay. Oddvar won't kick you off the property, at least not while he can squeeze every cent from you in rent. Once you stop payin', he'll have you leave."

"I'm sorry. I'm confused. If he wants the rent, why would he raise it so we can't afford it?"

"Because, Miss Kotlarczyk, he has to put off how much the railroad surveyors will pay him."

"So let him sell to the damn railroad!"

Percy's eyes widen slightly at my curse, but he's gentlemanly enough to ignore it. "No. He's not to sell."

"Then *you* buy it." My words spill out, as blunt as always, no matter it's obvious I keep poking the only man in town who can run us out. No one is around to silence my lips. "Or the bank. Isn't that what you did for the Brinkley's?"

"I bought the Brinkley farm to be sure the right land is sold to the railroad. Not that it's your business."

My mind whirls, stops, and whirls again. "I'm pretty sure this is my business."

Percy sighs and spreads thick, wide, fingers on the rough board of the desk. "If Oddvar can get a decent monthly rent from you, it will eventually be worth more than a single sale to the railroad. So he will keep you on. Otherwise he's sellin'."

"The bank—"

"The bank can't take another purchase that big."

"Maybe we can buy—"

"Enough. I'm not givin' you a loan to purchase your little tract of land on top of the lumber money and rent loans. You won't buy it. I don't want him sellin' it. I want the railroad goin' through the south end of town where it belongs and not north. So Oddvar can't be sellin'."

His grit pounds into me heavily. I feel numb and want to nod, but it would be dishonest. I'm not happy with being caught in the middle of a land war. In fact, it puts me more on edge than I've ever been. I think of the money Tom promised, and stand up.

"But if we could buy our property, and pay our loans—"

"You won't. Not for a while. You're not buyin' that place from the Svendsens; I've got you locked into two loans already. You keep payin' rent and tell me if it goes up and I'll supply the funds till the railroad comes in."

"And then?"

Percy settles deeper into his chair. "Well, I won't charge you interest on the loan for extra rent, how's that?"

I want to run my fingers through my hair and shout with frustration. How can this man be more stubborn than me? Perhaps he isn't—perhaps he only has more money. I plant my own hands on the desk, inches from his and meet his eyes straight on.

"It's a horrible deal. I won't take it. My Father won't take it."

"It's what you're gettin'. I'll have my railroad where I want it, and if you're the excuse I can give Oddvar to not sell, that's enough for me. Thank you for comin' in, Miss Kotlarczyk."

I'm dismissed, but I'm frozen. "Your deal means we never get out from under our debts."

"Isn't that why your brothers left? To make enough money to pay me back?"

"When they do, we're buying that damn tract of land."

Percy grins slightly and ignores my threat. "I like the spunk in you, young lass."

He pulls out some tightly printed papers and clears his throat, but I'm burning inside.

"I mean it."

"I'm sure you do. Good day."

Unable to come up with anything else, I walk out and rudely ignore Tom Fawcett's proper farewell.

What do I do now?

How do I even contact this Oddvar Svendsen?

When will I find the time?

My days already stretch long. June stretches closer to July, and I am distracted by the constant worry of keeping up with the household chores and the needs of the tinshop. I'm hopeful we might find a woman willing to take on some of the home work, but so far the only help I've had is the occasional hour from nosy, chatty Mrs. Andersen. I'm not entirely certain how I will keep at it. These past weeks have me breathless with exhaustion. My only moments of enjoyment are with my flowers. They're already growing happily for all that they were recently transplanted.

At least Walter, in his retirement, takes care of the damn chickens, the few pigs, and the one bashful sheep. I've given him a bit of our precious cash money for their upkeep.

136

He took it grudgingly, but now at least I feel that I own part of the animals, since the food is shared between households.

Every week, I go to the Salomons' hearth to bake bread, and I'm there daily as well as to manage the cooking. Neither Walter nor Thaddeus are as well-disposed to home duties as Jimmy is, so my days split between tinwork and housework.

Most nights, Walter tries to draw Father out with memories of their old days as apprentices, but that is usually met with silence.

If I am around when customers come in, I do my best to sweep away doubts about our shop's competency. We cannot lose business so soon after arriving in Flats Town, and while some seem to understand, those who do not know us well yet are less kindly. I can hear their comments in my mind, circling and festering.

A woman, then? You're strong enough?

Can you handle the exactness?

I need my seams perfect. Are you sure you are up to the task? What about your father?

How long have you been working, then? A month? Two?

You need a man, young lady.

Yesterday I tore weeds up around my new roses and cursed under my breath when I recalled the snide remarks old farmer Simon Zalenski gave about Father's ragged mustache. Every bitter thought about my neighbors crowded my brain, and I knelt by the roses without seeing. It wasn't until Thaddeus had forcibly pulled me up so I might start dinner that I noticed a thorn plugged into one of my hands, which wept black-red blood after Thaddeus had impatiently ripped it out.

"Marie!"

I look around as I walk up small dusty Second Street, surprised someone greets me so familiarly.

It is Mrs. Andersen, her smile crinkling the hollow places under her cheekbones. I glance at the heavy basket on her sturdy arm, obviously laden with foodstuffs. If I were a tactile woman, I would embrace her in my relief.

"Mrs. Andersen."

"Call me Berit, dear *honning* honey, there's no need for ceremony here." She follows me into the tinshop and glances over at Father, who has not stirred to greet her, nor even acknowledge her arrival.

"I'll try." Her insistence toward casualness falls on my ears and out again. I don't really care. I need to think about how I will draw out information about my landlord from my newly-taciturn father.

"You've been busy, Marie, so my Grete says."

"Oh?"

"*Honning*, this may be a growing town that will some-day get its own railway station and tracks and even be a city in the Union, but we are still small enough to know every-one's business."

Mrs. Andersen's eyes rove over the messy shop, and then settle on me. I try to straighten my braids, but it's no use. They are frizzy from the heat of the coppers and solder and fires. And I'm too tired and worn and exhausted to care.

"I've brought some victuals for eating," she announces loudly, as if hoping to break Father out of his purposeful stupor. "So, Marie, I have heard you've been so busy trying to run the shop and keep up a house all on your own with-out a ... husband." She glances over at Father again, but he continues to stare at the charge casing in his hands. The ridges of the interior, where the papers of gunpowder and ball will go, are unsoldered yet, and they tinkle and shift as he breathes and ignores us.

"Well, that is very kind of you, truly," I say. "But we have our meals with the Salomons, and—"

"Oh, I know that." She waves her hand and puts the basket on the wooden counter at the front of the shop. "I brought enough for you all."

I stare at her. Surely, she has her own home to manage and her own work to accomplish before it gets dark? I ask as much and she waves her hand at me again.

"That's what having a grown unmarried daughter is for. Grete needs to practice a hand at making meals before her wedding this fall, and I could use a break from the house."

"Grete did mention she's getting married."

"Oh yes, my youngest, finally! Getting married to Lawrence Fawcett—you know, the biggest of the brothers. He's farming on the far north, just west of the Svendsen lands. They say he's grand for making cows mate. Lots of young ones every year. Isn't that a marvel?" Mrs. Andersen rolls up her sleeves to match my own, which are permanently in a crease.

"Now, do you want me to tackle laundry or any food preparations you've a need to do? I don't think you want my help in the shop." Her eyes actually twinkle, and I feel a cascade of warmth trickle down my body. Her kindness is genuine, it seems, and it gives me more heart than I care to admit.

"No, no, I can help Father finish up the rest of the orders we have planned for the day." I think about the amount of work waiting in the shop and in our private living quarters.

"If you wouldn't mind, you might check on the bread rising and then, perhaps, get some overnight oats ready?"

She nods, the smile still filling her face, and then her tall blonde head disappears into the gloom of the back room. Her puttering and the sound of crockery sliding makes me smile. I have not realized how lonely I have been.

I take the hot copper out of the small brazier forge. The coffee pot on the bench is nearly finished, save for the last soldering along the seam, and then this repair is ready for its owner. The long handle of the copper soldering iron is comfortable in my hand, and though the wooden covering keeps it from getting too hot, the heat is very warm. My cheeks feel permanently flushed after a handful of minutes, and the sweat runs down my arms and back.

It's hard to imagine Al, Tom, and Jimmy working far away with the Army. We have had only one letter with a few bills to cover some of our debt a week ago, I always hope for more: more news and more money. Colonel Carrington has them working along the Bozeman. Fort Philip has become Fort Phil Kearney. Though it sounds like the Sioux continually barrage the men, there have been few casualties so far, save for a woodcutting group. I pray each night for the boys, but usually I am too tired to do lengthy prayers.

There is a crick in my neck as I finish the last repair on the two teapots. They sit side by side, their interior tin gleaming like white ghosts against the blackening of use. They were difficult to clean before I could repair them, and I glance at Father to see if he notices or approves. Instead, he sits, staring at the tin in front of him, measuring and ignoring me.

"That's all, then, Marie." Mrs. Andersen interrupts me, coming brightly from the back room, the new, heavy door separating our living quarters from the shop slamming shut behind her. "Shall we all go over to the Salomons to eat?"

"We can."

"Oh, then, here we go. Won't you walk me over, Stanley?" she says sweetly, but without any flirting. She threads her arm with Father and he stands up dutifully.

I follow Mrs. Andersen and Father over to the Salomons. Walter is drinking weak ale in the kitchen, and nods. Mrs. Andersen leaves Father by the table and immediately empties her basket: bread and butter, smoked meat and potatoes, as well as unfamiliar Norwegian canned goods. Because I do not know what she wishes to do with her foodstuffs, I pull out the tinware plates, cups, and some knives. After filling cups with beer, it's very apparent I'm in Mrs. Andersen's way as she bustles between hearth and stove and table. Hearing Thaddeus' heavy bang and smack of metal, I slip through to let him know it is time for supper.

His back is to me, the strength and delicacy balanced in his movements as he smites the iron and turns it deftly. It does no good to break a man's rhythm, so I watch and wait for a moment to speak. The fire roars, but the larger bellows sits silent to the side where Jimmy left it.

With the iron to take his mind from his constant irritation, Thaddeus's face is smooth. His arms are cross-marked with white and pink scars, and his hands are patched with the shine of burns both old and new. Unlike my own, which are mostly sliver slices and cuts from the thin tin and copper gauges, his work leaves him with large, painful blisters. Jimmy will be the same in time.

As he pauses and then douses the iron in water, I take the moment to jump in.

"Thaddeus. It's time to eat."

He starts and then turns to look at me, squinting. "So soon?"

"Mrs. Andersen brought some supper over."

"Well, that explains it." He looks eager. "I'll be right in. Soon as I finish this." He glances at the work in his hands and then up at me. "More for the Army, of course."

He turns to the fire once more. I turn toward the back door, then pause, feeling I might have a moment to speak on Walter's behalf. For all that the older blacksmith is quiet, he has been continually kind to me since my brothers left, and I'd like to return the favor in more ways than just my planting of geraniums in the Salomons' front yard.

"Thaddeus, I wanted to say … I know you're angry you are not fighting." He stills and waits, but does not face me. "But your father—"

"My father does not understand." He cuts me down before I might say my piece, and it rankles at once.

"That is not what I was going to say. I think it's more than a desire to retire."

Thaddeus shakes his head, his brow drawn up in a line, creasing tightly between his eyebrows. "It is not more than that. My father won't give his own flesh and blood to this country. He forces my hand. Unlike your father." The bitterness lacing his voice slices the air between us.

"Well, you're the only family he has left."

"You're the only family Stanley has."

"And I don't count," I remind him. "You do. You're the only capable blacksmith in the surrounding area, and he knows you're needed here."

"You're wrong," he says simply.

"Have you not truly seen him?" I almost regret the words as I say them. If Walter will not swallow his pride to explain his reasons to his son, perhaps I shouldn't tell what I have guessed.

Thaddeus glares, his eyes narrowed. "I see him."

"No. I mean. His hands."

"What of them? They are burned overmuch, like mine." He holds out an arm and spreads out his fingers, the palm facing downwards. I look once more at all the scars and close my own into fists.

There is no going back now. "You're a blind fool, then. His hands and arms are not steady any longer. I think he's losing his strength."

Thaddeus stares at me as if I am wearing the latest new-fangled bustle fashion or silly leg-of-mutton sleeves.

"What do you mean?"

I can feel his stare burning into me, tangible and awkward. I shouldn't have spoken aloud. It was ridiculous to do so, to put myself in between father and son. Perhaps I should feel embarrassed, but I don't; I'm certain in what I've seen, and so I look back at Thaddeus squarely and I do not falter against his powerful annoyance.

"I believe … it seems as though he is no longer as strong, and able to twist the iron. That he does not trust himself to do the fine work that you must do—the curls and bends, to keep a steady beat to make a sword straight. To …" I trail off, recognizing my ramble.

"My father has confessed this to you? Why should he? He does not know you." Thaddeus steps toward me, his body tensed. I take a step backward in response.

"No. He has not said as much," I admit. "I only am telling you what I've observed. I'd not betray a confidence. It's just my own eyes seeing such things. And if you did not know, now you do. Now perhaps you might be less inclined to be ... angry."

The last word is soft, and against the bellow of the fire behind Thaddeus I'm uncertain if he has heard most of my words. The grey eyes look dark in the gloom of the evening, and he studies me as if trying to see if I am telling a truth, or if I am hiding something else in my mind. His scrutiny puts me ill at ease, and I don't detect his frustration to be lessened by my speculations.

"My anger at my father is not your concern."

His voice is low, too, and he takes another step forward so he towers and glowers over me, taking up space. He considers for a moment longer in silence, and then goes back to the forge.

"Well, if you're going to be angry, at least have the right reason for it."

"Go away, Marie."

My body collapses inside itself, and the familiar sense of failure rushes into me. There's a reason I generally don't put myself in between my father and brothers, as I never seem to play the woman's role properly. What did I possibly think would happen if I tried to soothe things between Walter and Thaddeus? Every time I open my mouth, I only cause irritation.

I stare at Thaddeus's shoulders, and wonder if he's remembered the reason I came to the forge in the first place, but he methodically banks the fire and pushes the coals back toward the furnace. Though he's asked me to leave, I wait for him anyway, as if it is a conciliatory thing given how I've pried my way into his personal life. My presence does not seem to affect him as he pays me no mind, nor glances my way.

We walk together through the dividing door into the kitchen, which envelops us in a bright, stifling, orange from the stoked fire in the hearth to the reflection of the copper oven sitting on the ground. Mrs. Andersen has warmed up the victuals she brought, and is chatting to Father and Walter as if they care to answer her. Sometimes Walter interjects, but Father remains quiet and pensive. I wonder if she craves company, for I have no notion why she stays.

"There you are!" Mrs. Andersen glows at us. "Just in time to eat!"

I help pass out the victuals. Walter and Thaddeus help themselves without preamble, though Mrs. Andersen clears her throat loud enough to demand pause and prayer, which she says in her own native tongue.

Pressing my lips together, I settle in to eat the delicious smoked meat, thankful beyond measure for Mrs. Andersen's kindness this night. I must find a way to thank her.

"Danny Svendsen is in town," she says into the space, her voice echoing. It is outlandishly quiet with the boys gone. Though it has been almost two months, I still can't get used to the silences, and they often gnaw at me in the shop and at night. Mrs. Andersen's chatting helps, but her announcement causes heads to jump up.

"Is he related to Oddvar?" I ask.

"Danny's his son." Thaddeus says tersely.

I feel uncertainty in my bones, and I put down my spoon. Damn. I have yet to figure out how to deal with Percival Davies and his scheme to trap us. To trap *me*.

Mrs. Andersen keeps on with her talk. Perhaps she cannot abide the quiet either. "Oh yes, old Oddvar's boy. They say he runs the properties now—Danny, that is—and he is doing a fine job even for his youth. He's returned from a successful long drive. The first time the ranchers have organized such a thing from Texas to the railhead in Sedalia." She nods toward Father, and then me. "You know he is handsome—tall and fair—and so much a businessman. The ranch has nearly doubled since '64."

What will happen when the Svendsen son visits? Will he demand we leave? That I rip up my flowers? That we pay more rent? The thoughts jumble and panic.

I look across the table at Father's laggard eating, and wish desperately he'd start to thaw toward me. He stares ahead. I want to shake him, to beg him to return to himself, to stop worrying on the boys. There is nothing to be done, and we have so much to manage, the two of us. The pile of orders and tinkering tomorrow overwhelms me on top of this new revelation, not least because I still feel as though I am swimming in a trade among tin patterns I barely understand. Can't Father look me in the eye, and give me a plan on how to deal with the landlord when he comes? Shouldn't we be thinking what it would cost to build a new shop if we are asked to leave? Will he listen to me if I explain Percy's plan for our loan and rent? Why should I have to speak up for us both? *What I would give for some help!*

There is a press to my boot, and when I ignore it in my reverie, a metal spoon raps across my knuckles. I jerk my hand backward and nearly upend the potato *klubb* Mrs. Andersen brought over.

"Don't fret yourself so. Danny's an old friend."

I glance up at Thaddeus. "To *you*. But maybe he'll want more rent. Or he won't want a smithy on his property."

"He'll take a smith if you can pay rent."

I think about Percy's half-threat. "I hope so."

Thaddeus's face melts under his beard, as if some of the uptight, wounded, anger has dissipated. He looks more like he did when I first met him. Calm and earnest and stoic like Walter. Has he been wearing his anger so profoundly? Did my words help him see beyond his own selfishness?

"You won't be set out of the shop if it comes to it, and there's no time for you to build something else right now. Danny will understand."

I look away. I wonder how the boys are doing in the west, in the growing heat of oncoming summer and surrounded by the buzzing of insects. I hope we will get more word of them before too long.

"What about next spring? In a year. Will he ask us to leave then?"

He frowns. "Are you always so worrisome?"

"No. Well. Usually. But, I have to be, now," I mutter, stabbing the meat with my knife. "There's no choice, what with all of the work in the shop, and—"

"I've been thinking on that," Mrs. Andersen speaks across the table, jumping into our quiet conversation. "You need more help, Marie, what with the boys still gone. Just something to consider, *kjære*, that's all." She smiles. "Harry Turner keeps talking about how poor you're getting on, and I might be able to help."

I smile back, the ghost of it whispering away as I glance up at Thaddeus. He is observing me again, his face neutral, his eyes hung with tiredness.

"What?" I raise my eyebrows at him. "Are *you* considering handling the housekeeping?"

He snorts and rises from the table. I do too, to help Mrs. Andersen with the dishes. Behind us, Walter pulls up the chair to sit next to Father, where he has not moved on the bench. They sit in silence, with Walter slowly feeding his worn pipe.

"It'll be summer soon enough," Mrs. Andersen tells me, her tone implying that she is ready to settle into a long chat. "And then the Army will come through again in a large group to change out their numbers perhaps, which usually means a boom of business for everyone. My son Jarle will be glad for the work at the tanner's. And you might get your father to your church again soon, Marie?"

"We'll see." These days I go without him, standing next to Walter and Thaddeus. Neither of them sing, like Al and Father used to do, so the Mass feels weak and stilted. Afterward, I always answer the same questions about whether I'm managing or not.

Mrs. Andersen continues chattering, dropping hints of her niece Astrid's eligibility, which I gather is meant for Thaddeus' ears, and of the new reverend coming to town on the heels of St. Diana's Lutheran Church's construction. She tells me news of people I do not know, and names I have not heard, mostly farming families from further out of town and the names trip over themselves in my ears.

The flow of her words washes over me, and reminds me of Mother's happy chatter. It feels so good to have someone to talk to instead of the singular banging of the shop work, and Father's ringing silences.

CHAPTER SEVENTEEN
1 August 1866

"Are you Marie Kotlarczyk?"

My hands are busy with heated coppers and I cannot look up at once. My heart leaps, though. I have been waiting for weeks for Danny Svendsen to arrive, and every time someone comes in that I do not recognize, I crackle with fear.

"In a moment," I breathe, my eyes stuck on the fine, thin, line of tin, hoping it releases from the copper tip of the iron. I run out of solder at the very end, a few more centimeters needed to make it airtight, but instead of going back in, I stick the coppers into the brazier and look up at the newcomer.

He is tall, and as handsome as Mrs. Andersen has warned: blond, square-jawed, and strong, with light eyes watching me carefully. Before I took over Father's shop, I would perhaps have found myself in a tizzy around such a man, flustered and flushing. But he is my landlord—or at least, speaks for his father. He is intimidating and he is unknown. I've been beyond anxious about what he will ask of us.

"I am Marya. Marie."

"I'm Danny Svendsen," he says, though it is unnecessary to do so. He is every bit the Norwegian, and is dressed like a rancher except for the polish on his belt, which looks newly applied to the brass.

"So we've heard you were in back the area. That you would be stopping."

"We? I heard all your brothers were gone to Fort Phil Kearney this past spring." He glances toward the back of the shop, where Father is sitting and carefully, slowly, cutting out the curve of a coffee pot from a pattern.

"They are."

He surveys me again, his eyes speculative. "Your Father's been keeping up with the orders?"

"And me. So far."

Danny has the grace not to be overtly shocked when I say I'm working as well. Instead, he just nods.

"And the tinkering. Copper and tin both—it's going well?"

"Yes. There's some backlog, but of course that is expected. We have the help of the tools."

He cocks his head. "There is talk of all the machines. They were expensive, I'm sure."

"It was my mother's inheritance."

"That is good. No debt, then."

I push my mouth closed. Debt! That's all I think about! Our damn debt!

Father stands and works around to the front and holds out his hand. "I have been speaking to your father. He is being a good man about this arrangement."

Danny bobs his head. "He's reasonable, usually."

"And he is hearing how we are doing well. Me and Marie. She is a help to me with her brothers gone. A very good one."

His words zoom through me, and melt inside the deepness of my bones. Has he forgiven me? Please it is so!

Danny glances around the room at large, taking in the additional partition along the back, where our private space hides. Unlike Tom or Thaddeus, Danny is clean-shaven like Jimmy. Or perhaps, like others of his heritage, he does not easily grow a beard. My heart beats fast, but it is not because I am taken with him and his general good looks. It's because I wish he'd tell me our fate. My feet feel glued to the dirt under my boots.

"I hope it is fine that we made some changes to the building," I wave my hand at the back, where the door stands ajar. Anything to fill his silence.

"Improvements." He nods again at me, then at Father, and a smile lights his face, transforming it completely. "Have you had your midday meal yet?"

The question throws me. "I—no. It is just Father and me, and to stop work to make a meal is a waste." Why am I telling him the mundane reasons behind my daily life?

He shifts his head side to side as I say this, though, as if he does not mind hearing it.

"That's well. I have plenty in the bags. Our housekeeper packs enough to feed three men. Might I share the meal here with you? I have more questions about your business."

Even if I wish to refuse him, I could not. His family owns the ground we walk on, the roof over our heads and the walls of our shop. He can ask much of me. I nod at his questions, and the heat of the day matches the heat spreading over my belly. It's fear and it's nerves, and I wish Father were his talkative self. I wish I was as sparkly as Mother.

He goes out to his horse, which I assume is hitched in front of the blacksmith forge, and returns quickly, a large leather saddlebag slung over a shoulder. I move to the back room, where our kitchen and beds combine, touching Father lightly on the shoulder, and he shrugs in agreement. Oh please! Is this the melting of it? The end of his silences?

In May, I had assumed Father would lash out with anger and hurt before reacting with his stoic calm. Instead, he sank into this undecipherable murk I cannot seem to break, at least not until today. His unending anger chafes me so hard I feel my spirit is bleeding. But we've a guest. There is no time to lament my family's issues. And he's talking!

"I'll clear the table, Mr. Svendsen," I say, bending over to pull yesterday's tinkering from the center. My own housekeeping has much to be desired as I now have no time at all for it. Mother would be so appalled. A good Polish woman should keep a neat house as a matter of pride! At least I had made paper lace curtains before the boys left. It gives the place a little touch of home and softness.

"Mr. Svendsen! You must call me Danny. It feels odd to hear you call me anything else."

"Well, let me get the plates." I turn away from him, dodging Father's soft shuffle as he comes into the living quarters.

"Well, Marie," Danny says calmly, piling out a small feast of cold duck, stuffed tomatoes, and baked beans with pork. "You've gone above and beyond with your brothers' absence. Though I am sure it is difficult to keep up with everything?"

Does he ask this to find out how well-equipped I am to manage everything? Or to gauge how much to charge us, now that we are making use of his land and coming up with a profit to boot? What will he say if I told about our debt?

"It is difficult to do it all, though with only Father to care for, it is easier than it might be. I hope my brothers will be back soon," I say slowly.

And I hope we get some more money, too.

Danny glances down at the goods on the table. He gestures, his long-fingered hands graceful and blemished with the calluses of a working man.

"Please—eat. There is more than enough."

He does not take anything until I serve Father and then put vittles on my own plate. After I'm finished choosing, he takes it upon himself to add another bit of beans on my plate. His offering is both intimate and careful, but it draws me up and makes my shoulders crease with tension. I've not had a man—*anyone*—do such a forward thing. Does he do it to intimidate me?

"I don't want any more beans," I say, and push them off and back into his crock. "What I have is enough."

He pauses, and then cleans the rest onto his plate. We fall to eating, and for a few awkward moments, there is silence until Danny starts to ask questions again. Perhaps he asks them for his father, the true landlord behind it all, but some of his questions are personal, such as whether I have a beau or children.

"I have neither, I suppose, though I am not sure why it matters."

"You *suppose* you have neither beau nor children?" He raises his eyebrows. "Children, for instance, either exist or not."

I flush. "I have no children, and any semblance of a beau disappeared with my brothers and the Army. But please, Mr. Svendsen—Danny—this dancing around the issue is trying my nerves. Will you let us stay here? Or should I look for a new space?"

His head comes up quickly. "Why on earth would I have you leave the premises?"

"I don't know. Perhaps you don't want a smithy on your land. Or you'll want some more rent money."

He sighs, and wipes his mouth with a kerchief before leaning away from the table slightly and bracing his wide, lean, shoulders against the wall.

"Look, Marie. I … it is my father who asks for rent from the land. We do more than ranch, and it is how we make a living, pay for more cattle, pay for feed in winter if we need it."

"And the railroad money helps."

He freezes. I stand to clear plates, but he puts a hand on my forearm. I yank out of his grasp.

Danny puts his hand back on the table and swallows. "The railroad money is tempting, yes," he admits finally.

"We are understanding. But we must be knowing what your plans are for us," Father finally jumps in.

Danny presses his lips together, then drinks slowly from his mug. Even though I am stacking dishes, I can feel his bright eyes on my back and the fuzzy black-brown braids on my head. He takes his time answering, and I'm halfway

154

through the few dishes when he appears next to me, his familiarity and closeness both disconcerting and surprising.

"There will be more rent, Marie and Mr. Kotlarczyk, but know you stay here as long as your family must—or wishes to. If you're holding your own with the work, it shouldn't be hard."

"How much more rent?" I look up at him, and he does not glance away, holding my eyes steadily and without blinking.

"Less than you might think. Father wishes eight dollars a month."

Eight? Impossible! I choke back a retort, covering my teeth with my lips, struggling to hold in a strangling type of scream. We might have afforded such a price in Chicago, with a long list of clients, but not here!

"We might be slow in getting you money, sometimes," I say instead, grinding my teeth as I promise, anyway. But I'm stuck so soundly I can't see straight. We owe money to Percy and the bank for the lumber on the place and our overages at the general store. Now more for the damn rent?! I admit part of me hoped the Svendsens would let us be without asking for anything more. But we are trapped.

There's no way we can afford to go home, or afford to build a new shop from scratch. We simply have more debt. I need to see the numbers, today.

"Take your time paying. I'll keep my father calm," Danny says. "I'm sure you're good for the funds, or I think you might have said otherwise. Aren't I right?"

His eyes twinkle at me. I want to go along with his incorrect judgement of my character, so I nod, guilt raining into me as I do.

"But—why?" I can't let it go completely, and my voice cracks into the tangible feelings stretching between us. I find him beautiful, overwhelming, and yet casual: a combination that befuddles me.

"Why what?" He stops at the door of the shop and looks at me squarely, smiling slightly, as if holding a secret I do not understand.

"Why will you ask your father to be patient? That is very generous."

His grin widens. "I'm a kind businessman."

"Or one that will go out of business," I say lightly. "Your father won't like it." I know nothing of the older Svendsen, but I can only imagine him as strict and hard-nosed.

Danny shakes his head, throwing a farewell over his shoulder. "I'm not concerned. Besides, he will be glad I've finally met a woman who captivates me."

When I turn around, Father is looking at me fully, in a way he has not in weeks. For that alone I am thankful for Danny Svendsen's visit.

Dear Marie,

It's like winter here already, though by the time this gets to you, it'll probably be winter by you, too. Please don't worry. We are warm in Fort P K, though we have to leave for woodcutting duty tomorrow. Have you heard from Al? They sent him out to Fort Sully and we haven't had word. Maybe he'll be home before we are. Your brothers send their affection.

With my own,
James

CHAPTER EIGHTEEN
13 November 1866

"Miss Kotlarczyk. How goes it?"

Percy Davies darkens the door and I swallow hard.

"Well enough, sir."

"Keepin' busy, it seems?" he asks pointedly, jutting his chin at the pattern I'm making. It's my first try to measure out frustums of cones without Father's help and it's slow going.

"Always."

"And the rent? It's still the same?"

I swallow even harder. "It hasn't gone up since we last spoke."

"Hm. I'm not sure how I feel about that." He tucks his thumbs under his vest and rocks onto his heels, surveying the work around us and nodding at Mrs. Andersen, whose queenly head watches us sharply from her butter churn next to the brazier. His eyes fall onto the machines and he wanders over, stepping beyond the counter without asking and nodding briefly at Father, who only gives one, curt tweak of his neck in return. I wish Father would actively take over this part of living in Flats Junction, and I wonder if he has lost all interest in living here without the boys underfoot right now.

"Which one is this?"

"A setting down machine." I stand and follow him.

"Ah ha. And it does?"

"It sets down seams, sir."

He gives me a shrewd once over, and narrows his eyes. "I wish you'd call me Percy. Everyone does."

I flatten my lips and run my hand over the oiled machine, touching the sideways gear briefly. "Did you want to see how it works?"

"Surely."

Feeling foolish, I take a scrap of tin and bend it at a ninety-degree angle, and then tack it to another bent in the opposite direction. Sliding the two pieces under the kissing wheels of the machine, I tighten the top crank and then wind the handle carefully. I'm not a master of any technique and doing anything in front of an audience always makes me squeamish. The two pieces squish together as I run them through over and over, tightening as I go, until the metal is pressed tightly. I only slip out twice and cut my hand once with my trembling fingers.

"There," I say, handing him the finished scrap. "Saved me likely at least one hundred hammer pounds, and it's smoother than I'd get by hand, anyway."

"Very nice, Marie, very nice," Mrs. Andersen says soothingly, nodding and bobbing her head all at the same time. "You know, Percy, my Dag is very much the artisan too, even though people say his buckets leak. He'll make a cooper yet, you'll see. He and young Franklin can set up a big cooperage, wouldn't that be nice? It would be good for the town, especially if the rail comes in."

"Yes. I'm sure." Percy heads her off and hands the tinwork back to me, his eyes gleaming and his Welsh thicker with firmness. "Assumin' we can keep the railroad comin' through as it is, and where we need it to go. If it goes north, it bypasses the General and the saloons, and Flats Town doesn't become a stop on the rail. We need it to be a stop. Don't we, Marie?"

My stomach clenches and my hands match it, but all I can do is nod. I wish I could be outspoken with this man. I wish my stubbornness would find the words to tell him I don't want to be stuck in the middle. But I'm trapped.

When will that damn Army money come? It was supposed to be every month!

"Well, carry on, then," he waves vaguely, and marches smartly out.

Mrs. Andersen waves at his back before clattering around me to settle in with the churn again, the milky curd sloshing along the interior.

"The Salomons are going to go for a goose from the farmyard for Christmas dinner. Do you think your Father would like to help select one?" Mrs. Andersen asks conversationally, as she churns and I scrabble over the mathematics of the new pattern. I look up at her from the tin in my hands and give a one-shouldered shrug.

"I'm not sure. Perhaps. Though I wish they'd kill the chickens. There's so very many. What do you think, Father?"

"Goose is being best."

"Well, it will be nice for you all to have a proper Christmas meal anyway, even if your boys don't come home this season."

"I wish you'd join us," I tell her earnestly. "But I don't know what Walter and Thaddeus do for Christmas, or if there'd be room for your whole family. If I were the woman of a household of my own, I could invite you in full."

Her warm face folds into a soft smile. "Perhaps you won't need to wait too much longer, Marie. How many times in the past months has Danny Svendsen stopped by for midday meal?"

I cannot deny what she sees. Mrs. Andersen is here at the shop daily now. Somewhere between my conversations with Harry Turner, and my obvious inability keep up the house, gave her the idea to just jump into the job. Now she keeps house for us, and the fires lit, the water drawn, and does the bone-weary work of constant food preparation. Walter splits some of her meager fee with Father and me, as Mrs. Andersen also prepares the morning and evening meals for the blacksmiths too.

"Does a man who is courting come for occasional lunches?"

"You know how it is at the churches, Marie, honey," she reminds. "Most young men bide their time at the back after the last prayer, and offer to walk a girl home. Danny doesn't go to the Catholic Mass with you, so he needs to find another way."

"Did Grete's new husband wait and watch for her before he begged for her hand?" I attempt to deflect the conversation.

"Honey *kjære*, we're talking about you. It wouldn't be such an awful thing," she adds, looking at my incredulous face. "You'd be able to keep the shop for your family, and likely not charge any rent on account of it belonging to your kin."

The idea pierces me with anxiety.

What would Percy Davies say if I married into the Svendsen family, and there'd be no more rent paid, and old Oddvar would sell to the railroad? I'd be Danny's wife, but in the banker's bad graces. I'd still be trapped.

Good heavens, imagine when Danny would discover I'm not a good cook!

"You'll help dress Christmas dinner, won't you?" I ask Mrs. Andersen suddenly. "And I'll ask Walter if you might stay for the meal."

"Don't you know what your family makes for the holiday? Or Walter should know, at least. And likely you all like your bird flavored differently. We often use apples and some plums as my mother taught me. It is an old Norwegian recipe."

"We are liking to make *półgęsek smoked goose breast*, traditionally. But perhaps we will be having black goose instead." Father's voice is rough and low for his lack of use.

My mouth opens. I want to tell him that I don't remember how to make black goose. Mother made it sometimes, only allowing me to watch, so it would be perfect for Christmas dinner.

"We'll come up with something," I say benignly instead. "It will be delicious."

Mrs. Andersen nods encouragingly at Father. "A goose is a goose. And Marie will manage splendidly on some sausages."

Her confidence in me is so misplaced. I shoot her a skeptical glance, but she grins and shrugs. She pumps the butter churn once more before opening the top and looking at the contents.

"We're about there, Marie. Your new cow is doing well."

We've traded in the last ox from the bull team for a cow, adding to the shared farm between us and the Salomon men. Some of the money from the sale went to pay the ongoing bank debt. The rest went to the cow. The animal gave birth last spring, and her milk is still new and fresh and creamy.

"Leave the churning for the day. It's late enough, and the light is getting low," I say, looking out the window at the slowly swelling evening. "Take the lantern home, and we'll see you in the morning."

She grabs her wide shawl before picking up the copper lantern and lighting the candle inside. The glow is warm and slightly dim inside the bone panels. It was one of my first attempts at a lantern. It only wobbles on two ends.

"Good night, Marie. Stanley," she says comfortably, and then disappears with a brisk, light step out the door.

Father says farewell so quietly I am not sure she hears him, and I swallow my annoyance at his rudeness. I no longer make excuses for his apathy to Mrs. Andersen, nor with Walter and Thaddeus. His quiet is a constant reprimand, reminding me of my guilt and my failings.

There are hours when my frustration boils and whips through me. I expect to feel helpless and sad and distraught, but instead my emotion is pure anger. Why is he leaving me to myself so often, when I need him the most? Does he think to give me independence and strength? I'm not sure I like the lesson, if that is so. Tonight though, Father seems to warm up, and he actually chatters about the upcoming needs for hot dip tin, and how he and I might build a copper cistern.

"And that Danny Svendsen will be wanting to marry you at some point. Will you be saying yes?" His comment is so casual, at first I miss it, and he plows on. "I know you will be wishing to be married," he says, surprising me. "I know you are wondering if you ever are to be being so. The boys used to be keeping most of the young men away." He echoes my sentiment and actually cracks a small smile. "There is something to be being said for making a match. A *szczęśliwy happy* one, a love match."

"Like yours and Mother's?" I'm embarrassed we are discussing my love interests at all. It'd be easier with the boys.

He smiles again, though his eyes slant with sadness. "There is being both good and bad with having a passionate marriage, my little Marya." The endearment feels like acceptance, finally. I breathe just a little easier. Maybe he is not quite so angry about my inability to help him keep things together after all.

I slide over along the tinner's bench so I can lean across from him. I wish to grip his hands, to keep him connected with me. Forgiving me. I hold my tongue, waiting and hoping he continues.

After a long moment, he inhales slowly.

"I'm sorry. The grief from her being gone … what is being the word? Overwhelming. The joy of all of you—with the boys and you—being together, and with no worry that you'd be leaving me … it was being enough. But then the boys leave. Both of them. I … I am breaking the promise to your mother."

"You promised her they'd never go to fight anywhere again? That's an odd thing to agree to, Father," I say softly.

"No, not that. I told her I'd be keeping us together. I'd be keeping you all safe."

"But Father—"

He holds up his hand. "I know, it is being a strange thing to promise. So she was dying, and it was meaning much to her for the family to be being together. We did not like Tom to be fighting in the war. The boys are so much prone to be doing what they wish instead of putting the family first. It is not being Polish to do so. So then I was to be worrying with the west being expanding perhaps one of the boys would be leaving to seek adventure, and another might be going to make master smith in a new city. This way … well. It was being a foolish thing to be promising your mother, and more foolish to be thinking I could keep it."

He clears his throat, and it is noisy and raspy. "We were having dreams of the Kotlarczyk family to be being a grand house of smiths. It is another reason why we were spending money on all the machines. And I was thinking we were having a bigger chance of building here, where it is being fresh and open. I was not to be thinking there was to be being something else to be taking them away. More wars. All of them, now. Gone."

Does he realize his stubbornness to keep the family together, to keep them from striking out on their own, is one of the reasons they went with the Army? It wasn't only the money. And yet, it seems he had hoped for just that.

"They'll come back," I reassure him, though the seeds of doubt curdle in my stomach.

"As you are saying, I hope it is being true," Father says, reaching over to pass his hand over my own work, glancing over the math I've sketched. "And in the while, you are being a good help, Marie. I am being grateful. Your mother would be being glad of this."

His memories clot inside my heart. What would Mother think of me now? Would she be upset that I am no lady? That I hold a job, of all things?

"She would be proud."

"Well, damn," I swear. I had not meant to use it aloud.

"Marya. Your bad words is getting worse! But no, she would be being proud. As I am. I know I've been being so silent. But I will be trying harder. The boys will be coming home soon, I'm sure. And then we can be being as I am imagining—as your mother is always hoping. And in the spring, you might be marrying."

We've come full circle, and I feel foolish.

"Father, I'm not sure about that. Danny is kind, but it's awfully soon to worry about it."

"And then is there Jimmy."

My head spins up, and Father meets my eyes.

"You think no one is noticing it?"

"I didn't know. I figured if the boys didn't like it …"

"They are seeing. They are encouraging it. They are liking the Salomons and Jimmy too."

I blow out a small huff of breath. "So they finally found someone they approved." I stop short of saying the rest: it is too late. They took Jimmy away with them. The words are invisible, unspoken and yet I feel them hang: a judgment I must ignore.

Father lets the air out of his nose, and shuffles around to me, putting his hand on my shoulder.

"It is not mattering, Marie. You will be being—you are *becoming*—a good smith. You'll be finding a husband, and your own way likely, too."

CHAPTER NINETEEN
24 December 1866

"It's beautiful."

"I thought it would match your eyes."

"You had a difficult color to match." I pat down the soft hazel wool draping in wide folds around my shoulders. It is a gorgeous, luxurious gift.

"I know I couldn't give you what you really want, but this is at least useful," Danny explains, and I smile at him. I'm always tongue-twisted around him, for so many reasons. He reaches out and runs a hand down the seam of the fabric. In truth, he is tracing my shoulder, and then my arm before reaching my hand. "Merry Christmas, Marie."

His long-boned fingers squeeze mine. The gesture is tentative and sweet, and I know I am blushing. Father is behind us in the shop, but has discretely turned away so I might open my gift in the privacy of an unobservant chaperone.

"I'm afraid your gift is not so fine, nor store bought," I tell him, and release his hand to reach under the counter.

166

The box is copper instead of tin, and gleams with new polish. Inside are a small boiler and mucket, as well as a place to put any foodstuffs.

"It's for your lunches, so you don't always have to pack in a loose sack, as you're rarely at your own house to eat," I explain as he opens it. His hands pass over the copper carefully and smoothly, leaving ghostly fingerprints against the shine.

"Marie, did you make this?"

"Well, Father helped with the handles on the two inside pieces. It's not something we've made before, but you will use it, perhaps?"

"Perhaps? Of course I will. Likely my father will want one, too," Danny winks. "You do enjoy the trade, don't you? Won't you miss it?"

"Miss it?"

"When your brothers return," he says. "Will it be hard to go back to the kitchen?"

"I was never much for the kitchen," I remind him, and he shakes his head, still disbelieving I am as incompetent as I say.

"Well, has Mrs. Andersen been cooking up quite a storm for the holiday?" The question is put as a reason to stay and talk a moment longer together. He states the obvious with the mouthwatering smells wafting between my little back kitchen and the big Salomon one. Mrs. Andersen flits constantly between the two, happy to have both a hearth as well as the potbelly here. Walter has agreed she should share the Christmas dinner with us, and strangely, she states she will enjoy a quiet dinner with our little group better than the large, sprawling party at her son's house this year.

"She says she is making buckwheat stuffed goose of all things. And I made a creamy kielbasa stew," I tell him.

"See? You are a grand cook," he grins, and his blue eyes go squinty with mirth and teasing. He reminds me very much of Al and Tom and their incessant poking. I wish I could get my most desired Christmas gift: to have more word of them, or to have any of them to return to us. Any—even Jimmy.

Jimmy! Will I still blush at his kisses? Be embarrassed to have him see me flushing in front of Danny? If I must decide between the two, whom would I choose? The fact that I have no answer for this question sometimes keeps me awake at night.

"Well, you must have a good time over the holiday yourself," I tell him, inching Danny toward the door.

"It will be a long winter, Marie. I'll have to think of other reasons to stop in and see you."

"You'll know where to find me. There's plenty to do." I wave my hand at the work that surrounds us. I wish he'd go. Sometimes, seeing him only reminds me what money we owe Percy to keep up with his father's demands. The rent has gone up the first of December, and likely will continue. Unless we get many orders over the winter and the tin sheet lasts, we will only sink further into debt even if the money from the boys comes in the next letters.

He smiles once more, hugging the copper box to his chest and then calls across the room. "Good Christmas to you, Mr. Kotlarczyk!"

"And to you," Father tosses over his shoulder.

As Danny leaves, I smooth the wool once more before taking it off. The color is deep. It must have been died in the wool and not after weaving.

"He is liking you very much, my daughter." Father is behind me, watching me place the cloak off to the side. "You will have to be thinking on an answer to him, for when he is asking."

"Has he mentioned anything to you?"

"No."

"Then I have some time. Thank God."

Father sits next to me, slowly and with a heavy breathing that makes me pause and take him in. He looks the same as always. Has he aged so quickly? Is he unwell and hiding it?

We sit quietly for a moment, before I blurt out a niggling fear.

"If I refuse Danny, Father, do you suppose he will ask us to leave? We'd have to start over. Build a new smithy and shop, and new living quarters. We'd have to buy land, take an even bigger loan if Percy Davies gives it to us, and ..." The enormity drowns my words.

"I am not sure, Marie. If you are knowing Danny's character, you might be guessing what he will be doing if you are not wishing to marry him."

My silence makes Father shift his uneven weight, and I hear the hitch and wheeze of his breath once more.

"Love is growing, sometimes, daughter, and is starting with such affections. Jimmy is not being here, and Danny is."

That doesn't matter. I want the choice.

"I hope he doesn't ask me for a long time," I mutter. "I've only just started to make decent headway into the more complicated pieces and I want to try a biscuit oven."

Father heaves himself up, the skin around his face sagging and flappy. He puts a hand on my shoulder again. "So stubborn so not to be letting a job go unfinished?"

We clean up the shop, and I put away the coppers and the sal ammoniac. There are five projects I'd put aside for Tom to do, as the lamps are his specialty. Putting away the unfinished wares always gives an icy jolt. I might have to do them.

"Ready?" Father fidgets by the door.

I nod, and pull out the large basket holding all my Christmas gifts. I have yet to finish the mitts I'm making Al, and I'm going to scramble to have them ready before the new year. It feels right to have something ready in case they come home. Tom's mittens are finished and stowed along with the other gifts. Father has his own sack of goods, and I smile at him as I light the extra lantern. In the crunch of snow below our boots, I pull myself out of my seriousness, and elbow Father gently in the arm. Before our trip west, before our money woes, before my loneliness, I used to be just as jovial as the boys. Why can't I find that piece of me? I should try, but there's no more time to fret. We are at the Salomons' door, and I open it without knocking. Their house is like a second home to me now, what with sharing a housekeeper and hearths.

"Merry Christmas!"

Both Walter and Mrs. Andersen nearly shout it aloud, and Father and I pause to take in the festivities. Besides the beer and wine, which has been making rounds between the two red-cheeked people at the table, there is goose for sure, and my stew attempt is sitting on the fire and looks as ready as it might. And there's pickles and mashed potatoes and turnips, boiled onions and applesauce, and a lovely pumpkin pudding.

Thaddeus comes in from the forge from the opposite side of the room, and his eyebrows shoot up as well. Even under his beard, I sense his surprise.

"It's a feast!" he exclaims, and I actually laugh out loud at the incredulousness written across his brow.

"Well, *honning* dears, it's been years since I've had anyone to cook for like this—all smaller, more manageable servings over the holiday," Mrs. Andersen says comfortably, and shoves small tankards of beer toward us all. "I thought I'd do it up."

Father takes his usual seat next to Walter, but before we start the meal in earnest, there are toasts. Each of us thanks the others in the room, gives a blessing, and no one tackles the giant, obvious hole of the absent boys hanging over us.

After the men are served, I take my seat across from Thaddeus, who wordlessly pushes the dishes toward me so I might pile my own plate. Mrs. Andersen keeps up her steady stream of chatter across from Father, her arms moving with great circles as she recounts the fight she had to butcher the goose.

"And then, if it weren't for Thaddeus here, I'd be still chasing him!" she finishes, and takes another well-earned bite of the tender, greasy meat.

"Oh really?" I squint at him. "How did you manage it?"

He shrugs with a shoulder. "I walked out of the forge with a hot poker, reached across the yard, and banged him on the head."

Our fathers roar with laughter, and as they explode in their re-telling of farm animal escapades in the Old Country, I turn back to Thaddeus.

"Where was your father during the whole goose chase?"

"Napping," he tells me, looking down at his food. His plate is half-covered with the kielbasa stew.

"Is it to your liking?" I press, poking a knife into his meat.

He swats my utensil away. "I haven't tried it yet."

"Taste it. I made it."

"That's why I haven't tried it yet, Marie," he says, and I press my lips together. He looks up at me sharply, his face hard but his eyes almost merry. "I'm jesting. Or, trying to, at least."

We fall to eating, and it is only after the meal is finished when I realize he ate it all and asked for seconds. Well, at least someone likes my cooking.

As we do the dishes, Father and Walter pull out their bags and exchange gifts, and then hand over Thaddeus his present. He nods gravely, running his hands along the handle of a new bellows to replace the raggedy one in the forge. Mrs. Andersen has done small things for everyone: scarves and some beeswax against the cracking and bleeding of our hands. I am deeply pleased she has thought to include me in these items instead of offering me the usual feminine presents of ribbon and other baubles.

I hand out my gifts: knit mittens for everyone, including Mrs. Andersen. Inside each pair is something small that I've made from scraps in the shop. Father exclaims over the pressed tinderbox with a Polish pattern drawn lightly on the top, and Mrs. Andersen seems to like the copper brooch I fashioned with a floral design matching her Norwegian dress print.

Thaddeus reaches his broad hand into the dark mitts and pulls out thick copper rings. He holds them up, his eyebrows high.

"They're a bit large for me, don't you think?" He twirls one around his heart finger, spinning it deftly.

Walter, his tongue quite loose from the beer and special plum wine, hoots. "Finally! Since my son won't find a woman, one has decided to ask him!"

I flush, and reach across to pluck the copper out of his hand.

"It's for the leather apron you have," I explain.

"What?"

"The one you use in the forge. The leather is wearing out of the slats because you tug at them so hard. If you use these, they should pull closed and the leather belt will last longer. I think," I add, and then hand the gift back.

He frowns, as if trying to understand exactly what I mean, but he looks up in a moment and nods, his face surprisingly clear.

Walter finds the old nutmeg grater inside his mitten, and he shakes his head.

"I said I'd buy it from you!"

"This is better," I say, and smile at him. He snorts and goes back to teasing Father about some old story, their voices in the old language spilling over the room.

Thaddeus turns over the copper rings. They look small in his expansive palms. He has a new burn.

"Merry Christmas, Tadeusz," I tell him, realizing I have not said so yet. The grey eyes meet mine, and he inches nearer.

"*Wesołych* Świąt," he returns lowly. "*Merry Christmas.* And thank you, too."

He reaches into his possibilities pocket and pulls out a long iron piece. It looks like a well-formed hunk of metal until he sets it in my palm. The weight surprises me, and I look at the edges. One side is square and the other tapered, ending in a dull slanted angle.

"But it's a setting down hammer head!" I am surprised and delighted at this.

"I have no talent with wood, and the cooper's been busy," he explains, looking into the fire and reciting calmly why his gift is only half-finished. "But he has been paid for the work. Make sure the handle he makes is strong, but not so heavy. In case you … ah … break your setting down machine."

The tool is valuable and I ignore the barb, feeling overwhelmed. "My gift to you is hardly anything compared to this."

"They are just as useful. More so, as I'll wear them every day." His reasoning is given without waver. "And I owe you for more than Christmas."

I watch his eyes slide over to Walter, who holds my nutmeg grater yet in one hand, gesturing with the other. A tremor runs through his fingers and up his arms, and we look at one another, sharing an understanding. Perhaps my prying did help Thaddeus surpass the anger he felt so keenly toward his father. If so, I'm glad for it.

CHAPTER TWENTY
11 January 1867

January stretches brittle and barren across the streets of Flats Town. The cold pours in my bones whenever I go outside, and my hands peel red and raw from dipping them into the water to cool tin and copper.

Walter feeds the handful of chickens and ducks and geese so I needn't battle the pecking, and the pig and cow intermingle happily in the small barn. Between Thaddeus and myself, we keep the small farm in working order, and many long evenings are spent in companionable silence as we throw clean straw and feed the animals. While he is silent most of the time, I feel he respects me and the strength of my arms. Working as a team with someone is heartening, though Thaddeus is not the same as my small army of brothers.

Watching Mrs. Andersen spin on the wheel she brings to our house, I often feel a stab of guilt at being unable to help her with her duties. But the need for my help with the

metal to make money is too important. There's no time for
me to sit and do the usual women's work. Father does not
mention it, and I know I shouldn't fret, but there are many
days when I feel unbalanced.

Who am I, really?

A woman? A smith? No one in between the two?

Both?

The door slides open, protesting against the cold and
frost and freezing wind. Thaddeus marches in without greeting. His arms are bare against the chill, and he wears his
leathers. The copper loops in the slats gleam in the white
winter sunlight. He seems flummoxed.

"The Army has asked for more wheels. And then
there's a fancy sword, Stanley."

I jump on his words, though he's speaking to Father
and not me. "If the Army is in town, then there must be mail?
Word of our boys?"

He glances at me. "I'm sure there is. I didn't ask. I was
... *commanded* to create a list of goods in short order, some
contraptions for those new Spencer rifles, and a sword to be
ready by midsummer."

His words mean nothing to me. Father and Walter are
the sword makers. I am just glad there will be letters. There
has to be.

I must find out any news. Surely someone will know
something at the general.

"I'm going to go see if anyone has word of the boys,"
I announce.

The men ignore me. Thaddeus pushes past the counter
and squeezes by, his hand pressing against my shoulder hard,
as Father nods and makes room on the tinner's bench for

drawings and plans of the sword, his hands quick and eager to find a pencil.

There is sleet today, a strange mix of rain and snow adding a layer of ice to the heavy coat of snow weighing on the earth. Already I miss the smell of the garden, and the color green, and the exploding heads of colorful geraniums.

Through the mist, lights bounce around a large crowd at the general. I hurry, hoping to hear news and dreading it all the same.

Harry Turner stands to the side of the store's porch, bundled in his buckskins but shivering all the same. The crowd won't all fit inside, so the bodies spill around, shuffling feet scuffing against the crackling ice and snow. Two young men stand on the porch, and I know neither. One is supported with a rough-hewn crutch, and the other is standing, feet planted apart, and has a sheet of paper in his hands. It is grubby and torn and blotted, as if reflecting the weariness of the man holding it.

"What are they doing?" I whisper to sweet young Else Henderssen. She doesn't even glance at me, her eyes glazed and wide with waiting and excitement.

"Calling off the names of the fellows who fell back in December with Captain Fetterman. And any others who they know who are captured or dead."

"But—I thought the Army might tell us when something happens!" I say, shocked that it is so unorganized and the news old. "Surely, when they asked for recruits and militia and local men, they'd have realized that the families will want to know—"

The two old spinsters, Lettie Zalenski and Emma Molhurst, spin around to shush my wonderings with angry hisses, and I press my mouth shut, but Else decides to take pity on me. She speaks quite low, though her attention remains fully committed to the young man on the top of the general's stairs.

"There's no money for the Army to embalm and ship back bodies and no real good way to find out where the boys are at. They say if you're lucky, you might get someone at the Missing Soldiers Office in Washington to take your case and find your menfolk."

Then there may be old news. Or no news. Or the Army may never tell us. It is worse than after the War Between the States! The air is crushed and squeezed out of me. There is no way to breathe for fear of hearing my brothers' names listed.

The sleet bears down miserably on us all, and the ebb and flow of the crowd makes me feel like a rock in a stream. It is a tedious and painful retelling. The young man reads off a name, and usually the family calls out for more information. Sometimes he has none, and other times he will recount the happenstance or skirmish that claimed the boy's life. One fell at a decisive massacre by the Sioux they call Red Cloud two weeks ago, and the fear curdles in my stomach. Surely my brothers would not be part of a company of fighting men? Surely they—and my Jimmy—would be safe within the walls of the new fort, building and forging?

He calls out a Samuel Baumann and Else crumples. I catch her around the waist.

"Dead or captured?" she manages to call out, trembling. Was he her sweetheart?

The young man's eyes rove over the crowd and finally land on her. He takes us both in, and then answers slowly. "Captured, miss. On woodcutting duty."

"He could still be alive, then," she says to no one in particular. "My Sammy might still be alive." It is only speculation, wildly hopeful, but hope just the same.

"You—you're Marie Kotlarczyk?" Somehow the young man recognizes me. It is a surprise. Do I know him? The lights of the general are greasy stains of yellow against the deep mist and heavy sleet. I almost wonder, for a strange, unearthly moment, if the young man is Jimmy all changed and battle hardened, but I blink again and know he is not, and I recognize him, finally, as Robert Newton, one of the farmers' sons who'd left with the others.

"I am," I say, and my voice is steadier than I expect.

"I have a name for you," he says simply. "Thomas Kotlarczyk. Tom died protecting the woodcutters on a trip for fuel."

The name is flung softly across, but rocks fill my stomach. His fingers go down the writing swiftly. The paper is nearly transparent, and I can see the uneven ink blooming into the parchment from the back side. Others call out, impatient and eager.

"Any word on Thunder?"

"Alive and well, ma'am."

"Aw, Chrissy, that man ain't coming back for you. He's his own counsel."

"He's a lonely cowboy just looking for money right now. He'll be back."

"What about James Petit?" The voice is deep, commanding, and shouts from the edge of the crowd, expressing the restlessness I felt while waiting for my own names to be called. I look up, but cannot focus. There should be no more names. Not after Tom's. His is the only one that matters.

The chatter goes on, and I struggle up toward the front, hoping I can hear about Al. There has to be some hope. It is impossible to think all my brothers are gone. Gone like Lou after the War Between the States. They cannot all be gone.

I push my tears back, smother my wailing, and clear my throat. When the crowd starts to shiver itself back into the saloons and the houses, I step up and touch Robert lightly.

"Any word on Al? My youngest brother. Maybe he's under a different name, his Polish one? Wojciech."

Robert's head jerks up, and the circles under his eyes shine purple and red. I feel nothing as I look at him, though, not even a stir of pity. There are no real thoughts at all, just panic.

"Didn't you get a letter?" he asks.

My heart stops, and my face must give away my fear. The lines carve deeper under Robert's cheeks as his shoulders curl down further.

"Ah, damn. I suppose ... word was he made it to Fort Reno after Sully. He was on a different list, but I remember what your brothers said."

"Then he's—"

"Dead. Sorry, Marie. I'm sorry. I thought the Army would have sent a notice with his last bit of money. We knew of it. Tom knew. I'm so sorry."

I want to close my eyes and feel the impact of their deaths, but I cannot. I am frozen and crackling with grief. It is too much to hear at once. Too many names have poured out, and too many gone in one, single list.

What will I do with this?

I'm lost and cut, as if I am suddenly and inexplicably without anchor or compass. Every week and month has been spent pushing toward the day when my brothers—one or both—tripped back into the shop. They were supposed to just make some money, to make a point to Father, to show how they did not have to obey him so completely.

But they were always to return.

How will we manage without them?

Who will tease me? Who will find me a good husband, and dance on my wedding day? Who will tousle the heads of my children, and help remember Mother's face? Who will gently help me with tricky tin projects, or make faces at my burned meat?

I want to cry and scream, but the sounds are so wide and impossible that they cannot make their way out. Instead, my chest curves in on itself and throttles my heartbeat, narrowing my eyes and deadening my ears.

Young Else has disappeared—before or after my brothers were called, I don't know. I see nothing. My vision flickers to blurriness, and I turn around, unable to say another word to Robert, but I stop after a step.

How will I get home? I can't think straight, let alone see straight.

The next thought trips on itself as it forms, and blows into my forehead.

How will I tell Father?

A hand grabs my arm, gentle and tender. It takes me a moment to register this, and to look up into Danny's worried gaze. He looks stricken and beside himself, but as usual he has words. They are hollow, like glass, and empty to my ears.

"Marie. I heard. I am ... there is nothing to say for such loss. Please—let me help you. I don't know what or how, but let me do *something*!"

He looks desperate to be useful, and yet I don't know what to tell him. Danny cannot take away my awful shock, nor help me save Father from the blow of it. I dread the repeating of it all, as though saying the words again will release the truth of their deaths once more.

Danny doesn't remove his arm, and walks us slowly toward the shop. We pick our way through the half-frozen mud, the slushy, sleety muck, and the deep wagon ruts of the roads. Though I am used to the uneven ground, I watch it with detailed fervor. It's brown and black and a frothy grey, speckled with snow and ice. Danny's presence is here, but it is as if he is a specter. I cannot even feel his fingers.

"Marya!"

Thaddeus's voice breaks through my numbness, and I stop and spin, twisting out of Danny's grip, stumbling as my boot catches on a clump of mud. The snowy rain blinds me briefly, and the cold slices through my bones, shattering my blood in pieces, numbing me against reality.

"Damn!"

Danny checks at my cussing, but he takes my arm again in silence, ignoring it, taking me around a large pile of half-frozen horse apples.

The realization that my brothers will no longer be around to both tease and teach me the naughty words eats at my composure, but Thaddeus reaches us and I am afraid to show him weakness. It is all I can do to muster a full breath. If I do more, I will begin to weep.

"Marie," he says again, his breathing short and fast from trying to catch up to us on the road. "I heard about the boys."

"You were there?" I ask the question blankly, wondering why he bothered. Thaddeus never wants for gossip, for all that he doesn't seek it out. I suspect, after Harry Turner, Thaddeus is the most informed tradesman in all of Flats Town. I think these things acutely, with perfect detail, if only to stem off reality.

"I had to find out if there was news of Jimmy at least," he explains, a hand pulling at his dark beard and then tangling in his hair. I swallow the tears threatening to overpower my voice. I hadn't expected to hear of Jimmy. It didn't seem my place to ask, anyway.

What more?

Is there any word on the young man who tried to sweep me off my feet?

Can I manage it if there is?

Thaddeus has the grace to look appalled and distraught, and he runs his rough, scarred hands across the flannel of his arms, hugging himself briefly before dropping them. It is the most vulnerable I've ever seen him, and for one moment it jars me out of my own stupor. I reach across the cold air to put a hand on his sleeve, but he jerks away before I can touch him, and the rain eats the space in between us.

"He's gone," he says simply.

"Gone?"

"Dead. Died weeks ago—woodcutting. The damn Indians. Damn it!"

For a moment, the vision of Percy Davies's quiet Sioux lover splashes across my mind, but it blurs and disappears at once. I cannot place the notion of screaming braves with the stately, calm woman who lives in the cake-house down our street.

All at once, I think I might lose the contents of my stomach. Bending over slightly, I grip at my belly, and

Danny's hand is on my elbow, as if waiting for my knees to give away. They don't, but my jaw is stuck while sour bile snakes its way up my lungs.

"You'll have to tell your father about Jimmy. And write his family in Vermillion," I wrench out between my teeth, and Thaddeus nods silently, falling into step at my right side.

My thoughts whirl and crash and swerve.

Jimmy gone too.

It's over, then. Life in the territory is cursed before it can start. Our debts growing, with no way to pay them. Death surrounding us.

What do I have left to wait for?

What else is there now but some poor remainder of what had been a thriving family business?

What should I do? How will I manage? What will Father decide?

Do we leave now, and return to Chicago? Do we try to carry on?

What about all our debt?

Do we have funerals, even without the bodies?

Jimmy's death cuts more acutely than I'd expected, too. The disappearance of our romance, however small it was, is a rift in my heart, piercing and crying deep within me.

In the last steps before we reach the smith shops, the wetness of the weather has bitten into my shift. Thaddeus takes my free hand, the gesture hidden in the gloaming. He is either taking or giving me comfort—I'm not sure which. His fingers are wide and bumpy with scars. Without breaking stride, I clench at him for a moment, and then he releases me. Perhaps he is able to get enough from one short, small touch. I feel a loss when he detaches, though, as if I need both him and Danny to keep me walking, but we are at the smithy anyway. Thaddeus ducks inside without a sound. Irritation speckles. I expect more of him, and of his friendship, and am oddly hurt he thinks to leave right now, in this moment of impossibility. I forget, and then remember through my own grief, how he sees Jimmy like a brother. That he must mourn in his own, angry way.

I pause at the entry to the tinshop. The orangey glow under it means Father is still awake.

"Do you want me to go in with you, Marie?" Danny looks apprehensively between the door and me, and I shake my head.

"I will have to tell him myself. Thank you."

Forgoing propriety, I take a liberty to reach up and touch his smooth face, and clap a hand to his neck. "And thank you for your kindness."

"I wish I could do more, sweet Marie." He captures my hand and presses it to his cheek. Briefly, he kisses my palm and in the middle of my sorrow I sense the attraction buried under grief. "But don't worry. You'll be fine. I'll see to it."

Does he mean that he will keep our rent low? Ask his father to remove the pressure from Percy so we aren't stuck in the middle? Marry me? I don't wish to know tonight, and I don't ask.

"Thank you," I repeat, and then go in. My steps are determined, but my spirit sags low and cumbersome with a new pain, which is outlandishly heavy even though it only confirms the deepest fear of my heart.

When Father looks up, it seems he can read my face at once, but a stern flatness takes over the planes of his cheekbones, as if he is steeling himself. Or unwilling to truly hear what I must tell him.

"There is news," I say, finding my voice has gone hoarse.

"Injuries?" Father asks, looking down at his hands. A deep tremble rumbles through his bones, visible even to me, pulsing through the purple-black veins rippling under his skin, as if pulsing with anticipation or dread. "Is one coming home? One is being dead? Who is it, Marie?"

One? Who? Damn it.

I must say it. It is on me. It will always be my duty, now.

"All," I whisper. "All gone. No one is alive, Father. Just you and me."

CHAPTER TWENTY-ONE
22 April 1867

The door slams open in Thaddeus's usual broad swipe, but there are two shadows crossing the threshold of the shop. The space smells of hot rosin flux and burning tin. I've been soldering and braising everything I can in one single day, and I push the coppers back into the fire as Thaddeus comes in.

"What is it?"

There cannot be any more bad news, at least.

The boys are dead, and Father as good as gone for all he still breathes. Still, each time someone enters, I feel my body tense with a deep agony. Months have passed since the news of my brothers' deaths and most nights sleep still eludes me. It helps to bury myself in the copper and the tin, to let my eyes sear with the brilliant glow of it. The trickiness of some orders keeps my mind drowning in fractions, so I will not find myself weeping.

I think, sometimes, the metal saves my sanity.

"Captain Bush is coming in to discuss the sword design," Thaddeus explains. "He's been in from Fort Randall as the weather holds—his annual trip into town for the season."

My heart beats with thuds ripping my ribs. The Captain has not met Father, who was supposed to be the one working on the decorations of his sabre commission. Since Father's illness dropped into him like a stone, and he lies with half his body frozen, I have taken on all the work, including the drawings for this decorative weapon. I'm ill-prepared and unwilling to meet the Army officer.

The doorway, which is halfway open, darkens again, and two men in deep navy blue uniforms step in. I take in the brass of the commander's buttons—well made, I see— and the stripes of banding on his cuffs and collar. His boots look as though they were polished before he left the fort, but now are covered in mud splashes from the last of the early spring rains.

It hurts to look at his eyes. They are bright and feverish and unnaturally focused on whatever he sees. I glance up at him, and feel inadequate to do so again. His eyes are too much.

"I've heard you're the one who will do the work on my sword." His voice is low, but it is not deep. It has a patina of off-handed swagger. Next to him, the lieutenant's chest swells importantly but silently.

"Just the decorating of it, sir."

"Yes, yes, I've seen Salomon's work. His father trained him well enough."

"Did you want to see the drawings?" Before he can answer, I pull out the fine vellum papers waiting and layered under the counter. My hands tremble, and I clench them into the leather of my apron and press my lips together before striking into the conversation with as much confidence as I can muster.

"There is floral, or leaves and scrollwork. And of course, any Latin you'd prefer." I ask, knowing Father would do so, but hope he does not ask for suggestions. My Latin non-existent.

Captain Bush ambles over, his hands behind his back, his uniform smelling like warm wool and whiskey. He bends over and peers closely, squinting hard at my sketches, which are drawn out in graphite and charcoal and not very perfectly. I hope he will understand the drawings for what they are: scribbled thoughts, done in my own haste, and with a mind half-gone with worry.

"The scrolls and leaves are by far my favorite," he decides. Thaddeus and I let out a single breath simultaneously. Captain Bush spins around.

"You've said you'll have it etched, or inlaid, or some other such beautification."

"We will. The design you've chosen will be the theme," Thaddeus says curtly. I want to soften his tone, to remind him that I, at least, need this man's money and his favor.

"Hm. Well, do try to have it to me by midsummer as discussed, Salomon."

The men walk out, and I sigh. Panic settles into my bones. I have no idea what I am going to do about the sword. I want to shake Father out of his stupor and beg him to take this project.

If only old Doc Gunnarsen understood what ails him. He's been by twice, shaking his head, jiggling with too much whiskey. He has no idea what it is, only that he cannot heal Father, and I wonder how he calls himself a doctor if he knows so little of the body.

The terror of my Father collapsing and crumpling on the floor still stalks my dreams. Has it already been a month since he fell, holding his head strangely, never to rise or speak again? And now, when he cannot speak, cannot move, the left side of his face sagging and melting off the bones ... now I am at a loss.

Damn that Doc Gunnarsen! What good is a doc if he cannot heal?

It's my brothers' fault. It's their choices that have led me to this: the uncertainty. They should have stayed and made money in the way we all know. Not some quick-rich idea!

How dare they leave?

How dare they die?

Now I must try to make a living doing something I still don't understand fully. Now I must support myself and father, and try to pay off loans, make rent, and somehow keep living.

Instead, I live my days as a strange, half-finished artisan, who knows next to nothing about making a sword decorative.

CHAPTER TWENTY-TWO
29 April 1867

Danny takes the letters from my hand, and glances at the names on the backs, his lips moving slightly, before passing them over to Douglas to post.

> *Dear Sonja,*
> *I do not know if Tom's death has reached you ...*
> *Do not come West ...*

He wrote for me, and I am grateful. I went chilly every time Danny put ink on paper, copying down my words. It was a grueling task, one that froze my bones and made me weep again at night. I won't sob, though. I won't let my sorrow loose. My stubbornness can be good for something.

And there is too much to do, anyway.

We walk out of the postmaster's into the chill of the late spring afternoon. I forget to buckle the clasp of my cloak, so Danny does it absently, and with a calm familiarity both comforting and exasperating. Sometimes I cannot bear his kindness, for it only exacerbates how much I wish to scream, to cry out, to give in to the appalling mess of my existence.

But for Danny, I will still be calm. I should not repay his sweetness by turning into a wild, sorrow-filled, half-mad woman. Those moments are caught in my pillow, silent and wrestling and black.

"How is the sword coming along?" he asks as we descend the steps. "Trusty Willy has been bragging how he has seen the finest in the world back in New York, except everyone's pretty sure he's never been there, and his wife won't say. The bets are on in the *Rusty Nail* that there will be gold on the handle, and they say Captain Bush boasted how he will have it for summer, and it will be the most decorated weapon in the territory. By the way, have you figured out how to use the acid yet?"

My hands clench at my sides, and I feel the roughness of the acid burns that never seem to heal against the water and cold and metal. I shake my head, and watch the ruts ahead of us.

Danny leans into the silence. "Well, have you asked Mrs. Andersen if you might join us for Sadie's taffy pull? By *us*, I mean the handful of unmarried folk in town. It's tonight."

"I know." To think there are jolly parties yet is beyond me, and I've put off answering Danny for weeks. I truly don't think I'll be good company, but he is insistent and I feel myself giving in. "I'll ask her. Likely she will be fine nursing Father by herself for an hour or two. It's not as though he takes much work," I say softly, and with bitterness.

"It'll be good to talk with friends again."

"You say all the unmarried people in town? It sounds suspicious."

The corners of his mouth tilt up at my attempt to be light-hearted. "It'll be perfectly chaperoned. You know Sadie. I hear she'll have refreshments, too."

"Very well. If it will stop your harping," I sigh.

Danny grins, the brightness of his blue eyes sparkling against the grey and pale brown and early green of the land around Flats Town. "You'll like it. I've got to run back to the near pasture for the afternoon to see if any grass is up, but Thaddeus can walk you over to Sadie's house at the right time."

This actually pulls me to attention.

"Thaddeus is attending a taffy-pulling?" The idea almost makes me laugh, a strange bubbling I barely remember.

Danny's eyebrows go up. "He says he might. I'm sure old Walter has a hand in suggesting it."

The dust of the first wagon train, arriving a week earlier than expected, sifts over us. Some families are peeling off to go further north, and others are pushing west. I wonder if any will stay, and pass by Horeb, who has taken his lunch break to speak to one of the ladies.

"All fancy, is it? You know, this town is fancy, too. We use golden-colored rope to hang the outlaws."

"Outlaws!"

"Sure. And there's only been … oh, about ten killings."

"Oh?"

"Yup. Ten killings just this week. Pretty tame and all, don't ya think?"

"My word! Pansy, find your father! And quick!"

Horeb sees me and winks, and I enjoy the panicked fluttering of the greenhorns myself too much to put him off his joking. If anything, it reminds me I'm not so green myself anymore.

I return home. It is acutely quiet in the shop now, punctured only by Mrs. Andersen's bubbling chatter when she comes in to help. Father himself only mutters and gurgles. His eyes do not focus, and his body is withering.

All my actions are just distractions. Everything I do is simply to numb my own disbelief and my own sorrow. It helps to be busy, as then I can give the semblance of stalwart strength to anyone who looks. No one questions my feelings overmuch when I am busy and if I am stoic. I hope to be accepted as simply the smith, and nothing more. Perhaps people will forget I had a big family, and they will cease to look at me speculatively when they drop off an order, and the Henderssen and Brinkley ladies will stop fluttering over me after church as if I am fragile. No one will see me for a woman, or for a spinster, or a girl without kin. I won't be a lost soul in the wilderness of a western town. When Lara O'Donnell speaks to me about church picnics, she sees Marie the tinsmith. Every time Toot or Elaine Warren ask for a repair, they only see someone who can fix their leaking pots. Douglas Ofsberger comes in drunk and yelling at everything and everyone, but he won't see me flinch.

I have to make a Whitworth cartridge box for old farmer Simon Zalenski, who wishes to splurge on something fancy, and the individual ridges inside the shallow rectangle give me a terrible time. Eventually I give up with the tools at hand. Seeking out the shared wood pile, I crumble through the debris to find a stick with the right diameter to use as

194

a jig for the curving interior slats. It is a cloudy spring day, smelling of wet earth and old manure and leftover rotting leaves. The thick muck sucks at my boots and an overcast, heavy, grey sky hangs like a moldy blanket. The damp chill seeps into the fabric of my dress, and I shiver.

"I've been meaning to catch you, Marie."

Thaddeus surprises me, and I jerk slightly before twisting to look up at him, where he stands just outside the forge door.

"My father says I ought to go to the damn little gathering tonight, and Danny is going as well," he snaps, his arms crossed.

"Danny mentioned it again this morning. I haven't asked Mrs. Andersen yet, but I thought I might go," I say.

"I would sit with Berit." Walter looms behind his son, his long arms and wide shoulders shadowing Thaddeus. "I'd do with some company."

That the quiet retired blacksmith seeks out my chatty housekeeper is odd, but people who are old are allowed their eccentricities. I shrug in answer.

"I'll ask her if I might go to the taffy pulling then," I say.

Walter nods, disappearing back into the gloomy depths of his house. Thaddeus still stands, his eyes matching the overcast sky, piercing between the darkness of his beard and his thick head of hair.

"I asked if I ought to walk you. Shall I, or will Danny?"

"You, please," I tell him, and then quickly add amend. "Danny is busy. He'll meet us there."

He doesn't answer me directly, just nodding before jumping into work. "I know you've other jobs to fill, Marie, but will you be ready on the etching soon?"

I sigh, fiddling with the stick I've chosen for the cartridge box. Our conversation on this thread is circular and repetitive.

"Suppose I ruin the sword with the acid?" And then, because I'm feeling irritable, I finally admit, "I don't want to make your work unsound."

"Do you really think you'd fail so badly?" he asks. "You've been practicing, haven't you?"

"Well, yes. But it's not perfect yet."

"We have only two more months. I'd like to have the sword to him by June."

"He wishes it in midsummer."

"Yes. June is just before."

"Damnit, Thaddeus," I say. "If I don't feel comfortable etching, might we try something else? Perhaps an inlay? You know I can make tinware, but this is altogether beyond my expertise."

"You don't really have expertise on anything."

"I'm better at copper work than you are!" I shoot back, ignoring his barb. "And making things pretty!"

"So then. What's the problem?"

"I don't want to do the acid. I want to carve it in," I tell him, standing from the woodpile to face him fully.

"Why do you have to push back on everything?" he grouses, then presses his lips together. "We'd have to cut a cavity and do a true damascening, heating the soft metal into the design."

"Could we, if I don't etch the iron?" My voice suddenly sounds desperate, even to me. "Would it be impossible?"

He looks pained, and steps closer so we don't have to speak loudly across the yard. Hooking his fingers into the copper loops of his apron, he rocks back and forth on his feet.

"Not impossible, but I'd worry about taking the temper out of the metal. It's some of the best steelwork I've done."

"It's all about *you* and your work, is that it?" I shoot back.

"I just don't see the sense in trying an experiment on good steel."

I throw my hands up. "It's *all* an experiment! What about simply cross-hatching the surface so I might just cover that, shallowly?"

I'm glad for our sparring. It finally feels like we're finding a conclusion.

He pulls on his beard, his wide fingers squeezing his chin as he considers, then shrugs. "Work on the etching, Marie. Try the acid first. Please."

It's the 'please' that finally chokes my argument. "Fine."

He turns away, appeased for now, and I go back into the shop with the long stick of wood, which I clamp down and push the metal around, curving and bending as I worry over the upcoming night's festivities, as well as the saber.

I'm not much for chatting or dancing, nor playing a tease. Surely, I can speak to customers in my own way, and I can tease—*could tease*—my brothers. I am passable, but passable has a large arc of acceptance. And the ability to make happy, simple conversation has alluded me for months. A taffy pull. I grimace when I think of all the flirtations normally had which lead to marriages more often than not.

I wish the true question was whether I wish to marry Danny—or *anyone*—at all. I'm almost a smith now. My independence, while at one time a burden, is now a strength. Suppose I might truly do something outlandish? Isn't that why Father moved us out here? To do something different with our lives?

That was *before*, when I might have had a choice. Soon, marriage to a rich man might be the only way to survive. It's such a cliché I want to laugh, but my laughter is buried.

"Marie! Dinner, and then I'll feed your father while you and Thaddeus are out." Mrs. Andersen calls, popping her head around the corner of the doorway.

"Oh!" I look up from my work. "You know?"

"I know, *honning* dear. Thaddeus already asked me of it, and of course I don't mind. You need to have a moment away. It'll do you good," she smiles.

I feel a slight relief to have had the matter settled, and am grateful Thaddeus handled the logistics. I bury the guilt of leaving Father. Should I enjoy myself at all when he is suffering and locked in some strange painful place, caught in an irreparable body? Will he notice I'm gone?

Dinner is a quiet affair. Even Mrs. Andersen is prone to moments of silence tonight. Thaddeus looks annoyed and Walter satisfied.

"Will you be ready after we eat?" Thaddeus breaks into my musings. "Do you need to do any womanly things?"

I give him a reproachful look. "Really? You need to ask?"

"How am I to know? Don't girls always do ... prettying up?"

Walter chortles over his beer. "And that, my son, is why you need to go to some social things. Find a wife. It'll do you good."

Thaddeus glowers at his father and refuses to acknowledge the nudge, and instead keeps his attention on me.

I shake my head. "No. I've no other dress, and no looking glass."

Mrs. Andersen pats my hand with her free one as she continues to eat. "That's very nice, honey dear, but I'll go get a ribbon or two for your hair at the least. Give yourself a few minutes to freshen up from the shop."

I glance down at our joined fingers before she pulls them away. Her long, strong hands, while rugged and raw and chapped, do not have the slices, burns, or scars of my own, nor does she have inescapable gummy blacking under her nails and in the deep creases of her palms. Will the men I'm paired with think me dirty and disgusting?

Still, she puts some pretty ribbon on me. It is thickly decorated in the blue, white, gold, and red pattern of her heritage, with dots and swirls and flowery leaves. It looks fine in my hair, she tells me, and I must believe her. After she sets it in, I recall that I have my own ribbon, buried in Mother's wooden chest and embroidered with the bright flowers of Poland. My fingers twist painfully against the new cuts on my fingers as I run over what I will say to the young men at the taffy pull, and what I will look like next to the fresh and pretty women.

I feel foolish with ribbons, reminding me of my girlishness and my unmarried status. But I dutifully leave them in without further protest. It is something Mother would have done for me, too.

"I'm ready," I tell Thaddeus, poking my head into the forge. He's fussing over the sword again, running his hands along the thin flatness of it. He nods but continues to finger the blade, considering and weighing.

"I think you might etch here and here," he says, without looking up. "On both sides."

I stare at the skinny metal. "I'm still not sure I can do it."

"It'll be a work of art when we're done," he says decisively. "A mastery to be sure."

"We'll see," I say, and look up at him. His face in profile carries enough of the Old Country to remind me of my brothers. "But you're stalling. Will you walk with me or no? You're so reluctant I'd think you were afraid of girls."

My gentle tease is enough to rouse him and he grunts, taking the lantern and walking to the front of the forge. I follow and close the heavy door behind us.

We are silent as we walk, as if once we banish the sword, we have nothing to say to one another. The grief of Jimmy's death, and of my brothers, is carried like a heavy bag. We do not speak of them, and we do not speak of my Father. He knows all of my mourning, and I know his, and we hide it, help each other to hide it. Though our quiet is heavy, it is shared.

"There you two are!" Danny waits for us at the front steps of Sadie's house. His face relaxes as we step into the circle of the house's lantern lights. "I'm glad you're here. I was thinking I'd have to fetch you."

I reflexively pull my arm out from Thaddeus's support in order to take Danny's. It feels like a trade, though I am not sure if it is me who is traded, or the men. The alliance of my heart wavers and shifts. What is truly my emotion, and what is an echo of my lost family and the life that might have been? I glance back as I take the porch steps, as if seeing Thaddeus will give me answers. Instead, it's only his familiar face, looking tight and uncomfortable. The rounded cheekbones above his beard gleam against the lamps, and his wide eyes stare into the house. Maybe he is trying to wish away all the festivities.

Sadie is just inside the door, her hands clasped tightly in front of a fresh apron. Inside, many friends and acquaintances mingle. There is sour Lettie Zalenski and her pretty sister Marion. The Brinkley girls have made it into town for this: young little Lucy and Susie. Else Henderssen is there, and her widowed sister Kjersti, looking for a husband, her great curves swinging around the room. Tom Fawcett is tall, dark, and handsome and plastered to a wall with shyness while Tim Bailey the farrier is already making eyes at newcomer Julie, fresh off the wagon train. And then there's Robert, home for good from the Army, and the boy who came home with him—Johnson, they call him—who is missing a leg.

After I put aside my wrap, Thaddeus, Danny, and I take a cup of punch each. It is quite a treat, sticky, with some precious cinnamon sprinkled throughout for additional special flavor. I sip, fearing the moment we are paired with one of the guests. The house smells of warm nutmeg and hot sugar and sweetness. We will all go home with taffy, but most will be sold at the general, as Harry Turner prefers to get it fresh whenever anyone makes excess, and Sadie is nothing if not overly helpful.

Sadie herself comes to the middle of the room, looking as nervous as I feel. She glances around and absently clears the sides of her skirt. Tom Fawcett stands up straighter. She announces her plan tentatively.

"We'll draw numbers for the first pairing, but I thought it might be fun to try something different this time. We all know how it can ... be ... to be paired with a single partner all the while. So we'll trade every so often. Everyone will have a better chance to mingle."

Eyebrows rise in a surprised murmur through the small crowd, but no one seems mightily displeased by the arrangement. I'm glad for it.

My first partner is a young man I know only on sight, and it is after a tedious pull and yank on the taffy when I learn his name is Benjamin. He is the new apprentice at the cooper's shop under Franklin Jones and Bess. He's very young, and kind, but also very boring.

Thankfully, my next partner is Thaddeus.

"Is this taking your mind from your precious sword?" I ask him, as we pull the elastic candy between us.

"No," he admits.

"How else will you find yourself a wife?" I ask reasonably. "Your father is right to get you out and about other than the occasional stop at the *Rusty Nail.*"

"Sometimes Father is right," he agrees. I must be staring because he looks up and almost smiles. "I've surprised you. Well, there is that, at least."

I look down at the taffy, which is starting to look white around the edges. We are close to finishing. I'm warm with happiness that Thaddeus can see past his frustration and notice the merit in what Walter asks of him. Family is important. I know this so strongly it can throttle me if I think of how little I have left.

"Do you hope to get one of the other ladies particularly?" I look around the room.

He sighs, and puts more force into the taffy between us. The vigor he uses is rough, and I plant my feet widely so I might keep from toppling as we knead the candy.

"I have no wish to talk of marrying them, or anything else romantic I should do. What about *you*? Is it only a matter of time before Danny asks you to be his bride?"

There is curiosity in his voice, but the direct question requires me to answer it.

"I have no damn idea."

He doesn't flinch at my cuss. "Well, then. You should give him some encouragement. Likely you can partner with him for the last bit of this nonsense."

"But I—well, I don't know what to … Thaddeus, you know I'm no tease."

He blows out through his nose, a huffy sound almost funny coming from such a large man. "No, that you most certainly are not. So to let a man know you are interested? You might touch his hand in passing, or put your fingers to his cheek, or allow a kiss on the stoop of the door. Or you might bake him a pie especially."

After he says the last, we both snort.

"You know my talents do not reach so far."

Thaddeus sizes me up. "How will you tell him you wish to wed him then?"

If I could, I would throw up my hands in exasperation. "I don't know. Must I do something? Must I say a word? I don't know what—"

"What to say? You've always plenty to say about your worries and your work, and even what to tell to the customers, but no words for the one who has eyes for you? You tell him that you desire to marry him, to be with him. That you like the romance he offers you."

My mouth hangs open. He says it so factually and baldly. "Are you trying to be my brother and offer such ideas?

If you are, you're doing it wrong. My brothers always kept the men at bay instead of offering love advice." As I say so, the bite of their deaths hits me again and I catch my breath.

Thaddeus yanks on the taffy, his wide, thick hands grabbing my fingers under the sugar roughly as he pulls with a speed that surpasses mine. He is quiet for a long moment, perhaps thinking on the loss of my brothers and of Jimmy.

"I am not your brother, Marie," he says finally. "But Danny is a lifelong friend, and he is your landlord, and someday you'll need to decide what you want from him."

"Do I have a choice?" I wonder softly. He looks at me sharply, but doesn't answer.

The call goes around for the last shift of bodies. Sure enough, Danny comes to claim me, his eyes bright with mirth and laughter.

"Marie! You'll finish with me?" he asks, hopeful and bouncing with energy. I release the taffy I'm holding with Thaddeus, and two girls jump to claim it. I didn't realize the blacksmith was so popular.

As we pick up the candy and work to find a rhythm, I glance over at Sadie, who is opposite Thaddeus, and wrinkle my nose. He meets my eyes and gives me a strange, small smile. Sadie talks incessantly, as if she will amuse him with her noise, and Tom Fawcett is sending dark looks their way.

"Do you not approve of Sadie?" Danny pokes into my reverie, and I look up at the tall, golden height of him.

"She's a nice friend. Besides, it's not up to me," I say.

Danny grins. "Oh, but you're eyeing her up to make sure she's good enough, aren't you, sweet Marie?"

"I suppose I am," I tell him, and flush a little. "But mainly deciding whether Tom will hit Thad when this is over."

204

We both look at Thaddeus in unison, where he is sitting silently, and then smirk at one another at the joke. I suppose I am as protective of Thaddeus as I might be of Al. Had Al lived. Had he married … I stop my thoughts quickly, and focus back on the candy.

"I understand your interest," Danny confides. "Thaddeus is a good friend to me, and I'd like him matched happily, too. This is fun, though, isn't it?"

"It's been good to get out of the shop," I agree, sweetly touched by his concern.

"And it's nice to talk with everyone—you especially— that's not about work or … family." He trails off.

"Well, thank you for asking me to this," I say quietly.

"What other girl would I want on my arm?"

I choke on my words, unable to give a hint to Danny about my heart. I only know that right now, it still does not belong to him.

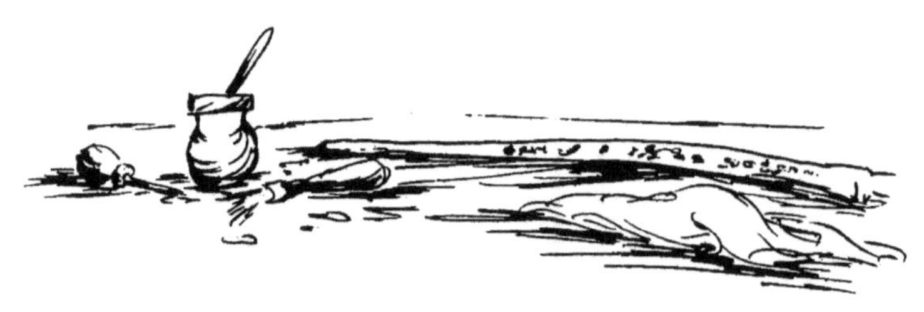

CHAPTER TWENTY-THREE
16 May 1867

"How is he today?" Mrs. Andersen sweeps through the door to our narrow private quarters. Even with my brothers gone, the space feels crowded with the tiny kitchen, long, unused trestle, and the four slim beds.

I shrug. "The same."

She gives a brisk "tsk" and heads to the sideboard with the basket of fresh vegetables of the season from the early garden, and I am glad for the change in taste it bodes. I am deathly tired of the crumpled root vegetables from last year's harvest. Spring also means my flowers will rise from their blank beds and bring color to the yard. It will be balm to bury my hands in earth.

"Did you see that, Father?" I ask, tucking the blanket around his skeletal frame. "Mrs. Andersen will be making new broth for sure, and you'll have something tasty. Perhaps you will actually eat some of it."

The heavy flesh that kept Father robust and healthy for so many years wilts around his bones and his face looks completely unlike the father I remember. He does not move when I ask him questions, but I do so anyway for my sanity. We've kept him alive since early March with nursing and force. I can't believe he's made it so many weeks already. I can't believe *I* have.

Every time I look at him, I feel anger and fear, pain and guilt. Perhaps I should not have told him about the boys' deaths all at once. Perhaps I should not have said anything about Jimmy, nor mentioned how none of them will be shipped home for a proper burial.

Doc Gunnarsen, slurring and cursing about his lack of leeches, says nothing would have stopped Father from crumpling to the ground, his beefy hand clutching his chest, foreshadowing the strange, unbreakable inability he has to move most of his body. My words had little to do with the way his face sags, and his eyes do not focus. The doc says a fit like that is unknowable.

It doesn't matter. Father has to get well. I can't be left alone.

To add to it all, today is the day I will etch that saber.

This sword is alive. It weighs on me, and feeds the fire in my belly. And yet it gives me an identity.

It is to be beautiful, useful, and unique. It is to be decorative and special.

It has been a painful process—both physically and in my mind—but it has also done one other thing. The sword distracts me from the sorrow of my brothers' deaths whenever I work on it. Somehow, months later and in the deep of spring, I am still mourning them. I wish I could shake it. I wonder if I ever will.

"Marie! Thaddeus is waiting!" Mrs. Andersen reminds me. I sigh again, dropping bits of tin, and walk to the Salomon's back door. He's there, standing, his arms crossed and the habitual sternness around his eyes. From the sound of it, the forge is crowded. The echoes of men's voices bounce through the space.

"Are you ready?"

"No. I wish I could be, Thaddeus," I say helplessly once more. He does not acknowledge my gripe, and follows me through his house into the smithy. Once in the forge, I nod at Walter, who is smoking his pipe, waiting. "Next time, you might want to let me follow my own thoughts on the final execution."

"Do well on this, and there will be a next time," he reminds.

"Must there be an audience?"

"You're always too nervous. What can go wrong?"

"Everything," I mutter, but he chooses not to hear me, or just ignores me, and nearly pushes me into the forge. No one quiets down as I enter, which is heartening. Perhaps it will be a casual thing, with the men just milling about and occasionally looking at my handiwork.

Thaddeus has waxed the sword. I have the design ready, and hope I can replicate it so it matches Captain Bush's expectations. Unlike engraving, which is a mechanical process, I must use a solution to etch. The only problem is I have no way to know if the chemical mixture I've cobbled together will work every time on steel. Sometimes it does, sometimes it doesn't. Sometimes it bleeds together and the design is lost, leaving an uneven pitting on small pieces of metal scrap. My practices have yielded mixed results, and this time I will be ruining the sword itself if it goes awry. I've made notes on each mixture I've made, and the one I use today is the culmination of many weeks of trial and error. It works *most* of the time. It's not foolproof, and it makes my skin crawl.

Taking the pot off the hook by the forge, I pour hot water into a small tin cup, and then add salt, stirring until it dissolves. Leaving the cup to the side, I then sit down by the sword with my drawings, pull the weapon into my lap, and begin to painstakingly carve into the wax.

I've Father's awl, which is sharp enough, and a few scribes from the shop. I must get all the way through the wax to the steel below for the design to take, and I plan to do the decorations in panels. As I work, the boisterous chatter stops and a general shuffling clatters as people take turns to see what I'm doing. But it's quickly clear nothing exciting is happening, so the hum and thrum of chatter soon fills the smithy. Men come and go as they wish, but a small crowd always remains.

"So, Thaddeus, you've got all the shoes for my horse finished?" Matthew Winters mentions over the counter.

The blacksmith leans casually against the wood to answer. "Yes, and a fine fat horse that is, what can wear them down so fast. I just made shoes for Tim to put on your beast not two weeks ago."

"Oh, no, Thad, it's the man who she's carrying what wears 'em down!" comes a hoot.

"So I'll make fatter shoes."

"A horse needs new shoes every six weeks, at least!" someone else reminds.

"What about those wheels on your wagon, Matt? Who wore those down?" Thaddeus wonders.

I don't look up, but I can hear the grin in Thaddeus' voice, which is as rare as his joshing.

"You're only jealous because my missus is the best cook in town," Matthew boasts, and everyone groans and smacks lips.

"Not as good as my mother," Trusty Willy mentions. "Toot's the best."

"As long as she's not too liberal with the cayenne."

"Wooo-weee!"

"Has anyone seen Sally Painter?" Nancy Ofsberger calls from the doorway. "Her catalog on fashions is in."

"Check the general!"

"Is the doc here?"

"At the *Nail*!" Trusty Willy roars.

The shadows shift around me as people move and peer and move back again.

"How long does this take anyway?" Alek Zalenski drawls mournfully.

I feel Thaddeus stand up straight. "Whatever it takes. There's no hurrying the artist."

I flush at his praise as Alek reminds, "Some of us have chores to do, if she can get on with it."

"What chores? Watching the crops grow?" I fire up, wishing they'd take Alek's advice and leave me in peace.

There is laughter and jeering, and the ebb and flow of their banter sharpens, then fades, as I concentrate on removing the wax and creating the decorative flourishes.

My hand is not as steady as I'd like, and I feel as though I am a charlatan and a fake to try my skill at making a blade like this. My work is best kept to tin and copper: broad boxes and curving mugs. Thaddeus is right. I'm no expert or master at any trade at all.

This display of craftsmanship threatens to expose me.

"Will you be ready soon, Marie?" Thaddeus approaches me slowly so I do not start and make a mistake, and I'm grateful for his thoughtfulness.

I don't dare look up, but I nod briefly.

Placing the sword on one of the large work tables, I stare at my handiwork and the quiet descending upon the room is a sudden contrast to the chatter.

Picking up the acid, I inhale the strange, medicinal, pungent scent. If I'm not careful, it can cause me to sneeze, or make my eyes water.

"They'll want to know what you're doing," Thaddeus murmurs as he hands over the brushes. Pressing my lips together, I shoot him an annoyed glance.

"I'm not a performer."

"Marie—"

"It's bad enough they're watching."

"Aw, come on, Marie. It's as good entertainment as we'll have all month," Horeb Harvey groans. "Don't be sour."

"I'm not!"

"Ha! It's her rosy personality coming through now, see that, boys?" Horeb chortles.

Thaddeus sighs loudly next to me. "Don't be so uptight. They'll otherwise start asking questions—"

"That's right. We will!" Trusty Willy agrees heartily.

"—and sometimes that's worse," Thaddeus finishes. He gives me a small, encouraging poke in the shoulder and takes his post by the counter. I look up over the room just as the doorway darkens again. This time I know the arrival. It is Danny, and he is smiling immediately at me, a bright beam of confidence shooting into my stomach.

"Well, then," I say. My voice is not strong or powerful, but the men quiet enough to hear me and lean in. My inhale catches, and I once again get a whiff of the acid. It inspires me, so I hold it up.

"This is what will be put into the design, which is now exposed from the wax." Swirling the acid around, it sloshes inside the clay jug. "It is a mixture of vinegar and calcium hypochlorite powder, as well as a tiny bit of water. While there is no exactness to make it, it is strong and will burn your skin if you're not careful."

I put down the pot, the small acid burns on my own hands rippling as I do. Taking yet another deep breath, I dip my brush into the pot and start to work through the designs, taking care not to let it drip to the other side, or go near the hilt. The work is slow and careful, but the men are watching interestedly, waiting to see how the design changes.

When I'm halfway across the blade, I sneeze and my eyes tear, which I expect when working with the mix. I don't dare wipe my hands across my eyes, so I blink hard a few times though the tears keep coming. Shaking my head, I bend back over the sword, fighting another sneeze. The stuff is strong today, but I'd made it so, to make sure it will work.

As I try to follow the path of the drawing and keep the acid from running, I hear Danny's voice, low and earnest.

"Have her clean off her eyes, would you? She can't see properly."

"Got anything clean?" Thaddeus mutters back.

"Sure. Good thing, too, as you never have anything clean on you."

"Still on about that? You know my mother would have noticed I was wearing your shirt."

"Still didn't stop her from taking a switch to both of us. Here."

Thaddeus arrives with a handkerchief. I recognize it as one of Danny's. He taps me on the back.

"Take a moment and wipe down."

"I don't wish to get acid in my eyes," I tell him. His face creases slightly, and then, quite kindly, he puts one of his paws on the back of my neck and uses the other to gently brush the tears off my lashes. For a man who hits metal with tremendous zeal, his ministration is soft. I smile at him, and then at Danny, thanking them both with my look before bending down.

The men are making more racket now that they can see I'm closer to the end of the sword, and I glance up the metal to see how it's burning. If all goes well, we can cover the other side with more wax and do the rest of the etching tomorrow. I feel restless, as though the idea of tackling the artwork is invigorating, and my chest tightens with excitement. These intense emotions are not like me, especially when it comes to metal work. Perhaps I am overwhelmed by the attention of the townsfolk. I take in deep breaths and try to focus.

"So the etchin' is today?" It's a new voice, but one everyone recognizes, and the crowd shifts. Percival Davies enters the smithy, and my heart lurches like it always does when I see the banker. Everyone clears a way for him as he strolls up, peering at the metal and hitching his fingers in suspenders under the patterned vest.

"She's nearly finished," Thaddeus announces in general, cutting off further inquiries from Mr. Davies.

"How is she doing?" Mrs. Andersen enters. Her presence is a balm to my ruffled spirit and hushes up a number of the men, who are muttering among themselves of general town gossip, which always includes a few choice cuss words.

The smell of the acid is making my stomach turn. It's too close to completion to stop now, but I feel nauseous with worry. I'm still uncertain about how long the acid will need to work, or whether we should go over the steel again with another layer of it. The scent of the mixture burns my throat, and I suppress a hard cough building under the sneezes.

Once more, Thaddeus carefully wipes my eyes.

"Thank you," I tell him breathlessly. My air comes fast and tight, my whole body quivering, as if I'm physically willing the etching to be finished and beautiful.

Mrs. Andersen makes her way to the counter to get a good view.

"It's looking very fine, Marie. All that practice must have helped."

I smile briefly up at her, and then bend close to the steel near the end, where the last few inches of the blade escape the wax. I don't wish to splatter when the raw metal is showing.

"It will be a very fine piece," she says, and I want to relax with the arrival of her familiar pattering of congenial chatter, but I must have somehow tied my corsets too tight today, because I truly am struggling to catch my breath.

"I'm nearly done, I should think," I say softly, and everyone surges forward, Mrs. Andersen the closest to the counter. I wait for her words of praise, and try to find her face, but a fit of coughing hooks me, and lightheadedness descends.

The next and last thing I hear is a warning. Danny shouts above the chatter of the other men.

"Thaddeus! Catch her up!"

CHAPTER TWENTY-FOUR
16 May 1867

I wake.

By the smell of iron and wool and leather, I know I am in the Salomon household. The wavering oval of each face is blurry, but my vision clears quickly and the burning sets in.

The pain is hard and intense and sharp.

"What happened?"

Mrs. Andersen peers over me, her brilliant eyes damp with worry and her forehead lifts in wrinkles. "You fainted, dear one, under the stress of it all."

I shake my head and try to sit up, but Danny's hand is at my shoulder, his long, strong fingers cupping the joint gently so I must lie back down. Thaddeus methodically winds clean rags over my wrist. The other hand is numb.

"You'll be needing a new dress," Mrs. Andersen sighs. "Though your apron caught the brunt of it." She gestures, and I see the leather across the chair nearby, large holes still eating away at the shape.

"I fainted?" I repeat, and Danny frames my vision, carefully taking up my free hand and pressing it lightly between his palms. The wrist Thaddeus binds stings fiercely, and I suck in my breath tightly with a hissing whistle.

"Nearly done," he mutters.

"Careful on her," Danny murmurs.

"I am!"

"Like you were with that baby bird you crushed?"

"We were eight! And Marie's not fragile."

"Boys. Enough." Walter stands at the foot of the bed, a pipe in his hand and a grim crease in the corners of his mouth where his beard gives way to his lips.

"It was a close moment, Marya. You could have been blinded. Disfigured at the least of it. The acid was a fool's idea."

He is cross, I realize. Angry he cannot do it himself. Angry at my ineptitude, perhaps. Perhaps even upset with Thaddeus—for the etching idea, and for asking me to do it.

Blind? I cannot fathom it.

"It wasn't the stress of creating the artwork," I object belatedly, glancing between Mrs. Andersen and Danny and Walter. Danny gives me a small smile. I realize he is quite worried and I try to placate his unspoken fear. "And it was not difficult, really. It was working so well! I can certainly manage the other side."

Thaddeus pauses, the hard callouses of his fingers curving into mine. He half turns and gives me a strange, unreadable pierce with his grey eyes.

"The sword is ruined."

The air goes out of me. "How?"

"When you fainted, you fell forward, Marie," Danny explains softly. "You knocked the acid over everything. You would have landed directly on the table and burned your face—or worse—had Thaddeus not caught you in time."

"Thanks to your warning," Thaddeus adds, and his voice is heavy. I cannot tell if he is frustrated or shocked, but he finishes the bandages and stands. As he walks toward the fireplace mantel to get a tankard of ale, I see red blisters on the back of his own hand, raw and bright against the old scars.

Mrs. Andersen stands over me again, offering water anxiously.

"It'll be all right," she soothes, but I'm blasted by guilt. I've destroyed the sword! I know how hard and long Thaddeus worked on that blade, and how proud he was of the craftsmanship. Captain Joseph Bush is expecting the finished piece shortly, and now he will be without it for the summer as he'd bragged. He will be outrageously angry.

Fear spills into me, familiar and sharp. Suppose Thaddeus is disgusted with my ineptitude and tells everyone I'm no good? Will Captain Bush demand a new sword? What of the cost the Salomons must swallow? To make a whole new steel blade will be difficult. I must repay them for their wasted effort. How will I afford it? What if people stop bringing me work because of this failure? I will not be able to afford rent, the loan … My business will die. I will starve …

How will I face everyone?

I've failed. Publicly, obviously, foolishly so.

Danny's hand is still over mine, and he is watching me closely, his eyes soft.

"I want to see it. I want to see what happened," I tell him.

"Not now, *kjære*," Mrs. Andersen says. "We'll take a meal, and you get some rest, *honning* dear." She heads to the hearth and begins to putter around the cutlery. "You'll want to sup too, Danny?"

He hesitates, and I can see he wishes to stay, if only to watch over me. His kindness is sweet and endearing, and I smile wanly at him, understanding his pause. "You must get home?"

He returns my smile. "Yes. Father is expecting me. But I'll come and see you soon."

With a few quiet words to Thaddeus and Walter, Danny departs, and I feel strangely alone without him, as if he has decidedly become part of my existence. It's hard to face Thaddeus, and even Walter. Danny would have helped to block their fiery anger.

"Well, you'll have to let it be for a while," I hear Mrs. Andersen say. She is talking to Thaddeus as he finally covers his own acid burns with bandages. "There's no use in hurrying another one."

"Captain Bush will be waiting, and wanting it," he says, and though he is quiet, the deepness of his voice carries. I feel chastised at once, even if he has not directed any ire in my direction. "I must start immediately again. We all need the money."

"Perhaps it will be a better one," Walter adds, from his seat at the table. "Now you've made a sword once, you'll have a trick for it."

"It was the best I've done," Thaddeus says without looking up.

No one is watching me now, and I slowly stand, testing my feet. I seem sure enough. The door into the forge is open next to the bed, and I slip through.

I want to see the sword for myself. I have to see the damage.

I wish my father were here, instead of wasting away, unaware and uncaring. I wish for my brothers and their presence at my humiliation. It would feel less of a humiliation with them, for though I've made a mess, I know they'd stand by me. Al would encourage. And though Tom would fuss and huff, he would not be truly angry. He would drive me to try again.

The table in the forge has been cleared, though I see evidence of the acid in the darkened wood grain of the trestle.

It is strangely quiet. With no one here and the fire banked, I feel as though I am floating. There is still the slight scent of acid in the air, as if it is burned into the fiber of the place now.

The sword is wrapped in old leather, cast off to a side bench, the ends of it poking out, a softened, dull, grey against the black soot of the shelf.

I pick it up. It does not feel alive any more. I've somehow killed it. The weight of the metal is familiar, and I am afraid to open the bindings. The dimness of the coming night gives it a ghostly glimmer.

"It's irreparable."

Thaddeus's voice makes me start hard, and I nearly drop the blade. He catches the iron as it slips, gripping it hard through the cowhide. It is still sharp steel, and it cuts through the animal skins and slices into his new bandage.

"I'm—so sorry." My voice sounds small and still in the quiet of the room. He opens the wrapping and I am aghast. My spill has pitted the metal and while the decoration remains intact within the wax, the ends are destroyed, and the other side, which had not been protected, is eaten in rivers and swirls and pockets wherever the acid touched and sat.

"It's awful," I say into his silence, as we both stare at the long sliver of iron. "I shouldn't have worked on it." The sight of his craftsmanship completely unusable, all because of me, makes my chest feel tight and flat.

He stares at it, perhaps wondering what it would have looked like had we finished. I wish he would say something, but instead he wraps it back up and sets it aside, then goes to push the coals of the forge fire around, the rasping shuffle of them crackling into the gloaming.

"Will you make another?"

He takes a moment, then nods as he stares into the fire.

"I'm sorry. Please. I'll have to repay you for the steel—you must let me. And ..." I reach out in spite of myself and touch the back of his hand, where the bandage covers the burns reflecting my own. "And I don't know how to thank you for protecting me from blindness. Scarring."

He freezes at my touch, and pulls his fingers away. "You'll have scars enough from this, Marie."

I glance down at my own bandages, and wonder how I will work the tin with such cumbersome wraps. Shock and realization hit me intensely.

How will I manage yet another setback?

If I were a different sort of woman, perhaps I'd collapse now, in the face of what tomorrow brings, but it is not the way of my family, or my people. Father would say that, as would the boys. They'd say there is no option. I want to rail against those words, even in my own mind. I refuse to be dictated to! *I want* ...

I want something different than what awaits me in the morning. Not weeks of agony as my blisters heal while I work the metal.

"Scars are better than blindness. Then I would have no trade to offer," I finally tell Thaddeus. He grunts.

"Please. Tell me how to repay you. Tell me what—"

"Stop." He turns to me, and emotion plays and pulls across his face. "There is no need to say more, Marie. It is done."

"But you're angry with me," I reason, finding my voice. "And I don't know how to fix it. I can't work the iron for you. I don't have the skills or tools to do it. I would, if I could. It was the most beautiful sword I've ever handled, but I—"

"You think I'm angry with you?" He looks surprised.

"Of course."

I expect only coldness from him in the future because of my blunder. Frostiness, until he gets over my mistake. I'll miss his quiet friendship.

"I'm not angry at you, Marya." He says this so softly I almost don't catch the words or his use of my given name. "I'm just dismayed. I'm uncertain I'll be able to forge another."

His lack of confidence is surprising, and I am touched he confesses so intimate a thought.

"I should not touch any other you make," I jump in, but he pulls himself up and places a hand on the black anvil in the center of the shop.

"No. You'll do the design on the next," he states firmly, and ignores the shaking of my head, plunging on. "You're the best soft metal artist in Flats Town, and the one who drew what Captain Bush wants. But we'll do something else. Engraving, perhaps, as you had hoped for from the first. I'll not have you fainting again."

"It was weak of me," I interrupt.

"How would you have known breathing in the acid so long would make you lightheaded? I cannot blame you. It is me who must prove to be as good a blacksmith as my father."

"You will create another. Likely better," I tell him. "I'm certain of it."

"It won't be done in time for the summer, as Captain Bush has hoped." His voice is mournful.

"Waiting a bit longer won't kill him," I reason, wondering how we have switched roles. Now I am reassuring Thaddeus, when it was me asking for absolution earlier. "He will wait for a superior blade."

"I hope so," he sighs, running a finger along the edge of the cowhide once more, then glancing out at the forge entry. "But anyway, Mrs. Andersen will be ready for us to eat shortly. She and my father took over supper for Stanley."

There is simplicity in the end of our discussion, and I'm grateful it went as well as it did. It strikes me that both Thaddeus and I often have no choice in most things.

We close up the front of the smithy, and the echoing of the doors bangs into the blackness. The dim orange wavering of the forge fire is now the only light.

"How long was I out of sorts?" I ask, and reach out to feel around the shop toward the door at the back, where yellow lamplight oozes around the cracks.

"Long enough," he says roughly, and grasps my elbow hard to steer me around the extra table and the anvil. "Danny was beside himself."

"It was good of him to stay to make sure I was well. And good of you to talk to me now, to put my mind at peace," I add, tripping over one of the fuel shovels for all Thaddeus' grip on me. He takes a firmer hold as I stumble, the thick band of his arm circling my shoulders calmly and guiding me the rest of the way. I like to think I would know my own tinshop as well as he knows his forge in the dark.

"If we are to work together, we should always discuss such things," he says, surprising me with his candidness.

As we reach the living quarters, he moves to open the door in the occasional gentleman's gesture he sometimes offers. He does not release me at once, his palm dropping briefly to my back as we pass through. The gesture is unexpected, but it is not distasteful and I glance up at him for some further connection.

But Thaddeus's eyes are on the hearth, where Mrs. Andersen bends over the large pot, and Walter is peering into the stew, his wide hand casually on her shoulder. The scent of venison and carrots and potato fills my nose, and finally chases away the last of the acid in my mouth.

CHAPTER TWENTY-FIVE
19 June 1867

Anette Zelenski, Mrs. Andersen's eldest daughter, walks into the shop and her hair sparkles like spun sugar. She is truly like her mother, with the height, gentleness, and warmth. It spills from her the minute she arrives with three children scattering before her skirts.

"Good morning! Well, it's certainly a treat to be here." She looks around as she enters familiarly, coming around the counter as if she is a long-time friend. "Mother thought you might like some company, and I have a few minutes to spare if I don't cook anything difficult for Jacob when he comes in from the field."

"You're taking time from your busy day to see me? I told your mother she shouldn't ask such a thing from you," I say, feeling both pleased and guilty. I haven't seen Anette since early spring, when the mud was fat and heavy on our boots and the planting just finished. She is so very busy on the farm she shares with her husband and in-laws.

"I don't mind. It's a bit of a lark. Everyone should have one of those here and there so I brought in the wagon for the morning. Mother thought you might like to go to the general with me and pick out some cloth for a new dress. You know I was a bit of a seamstress before I married. Let me help you. It'd be a treat."

The notion is frivolous at best, and I laugh. "Shall I pick out a silk?"

"Marie, you need to wear more than a scrappy dress."

"I didn't know you had a trade."

"Of course I did. Most of us do, to make the money. But Jacob needed a wife, not a working girl. All men do."

"All men …" I echo, my heart aching, knowing she's right.

She runs a finger along the lines of a tinderbox I have just finished. I glance down at the gown I'm wearing. It is dirty, of course, but it is the patched holes that make it look truly ratty. There was no reason to destroy it after the acid spattered it, and it is still quite serviceable.

"Let's go now, then," I shrug lightly, and return her wide grin with one of my own smaller ones. Her enthusiasm is infectious, for all it's absolutely silly to leave work undone. "But I must tell your mother."

Anette waits for me by the door, a child on her hip and the other two sprinting across the yard, yelling brightly.

"Babcia! Bestemor! Grandma!"

Mrs. Andersen stops outside the doorway of the Salomon house, a wide clay bowl cradled in her arms.

"Oh my! You did come down today, then? Anette, *kjære*, how good of you." She leans in to brush her cheek with her daughter as we approach, and then pats the heads of the children gathering around her.

"We are off to the general," I tell her. "Father is sleeping, and we won't be gone long, I should think."

"Marie!"

The shout carries through the quarters, and at first I think it is Walter. I peer past Mrs. Andersen's shoulder and see Thaddeus framing the space between the forge and their house.

"What?"

"Stop over when you're back," he says. "I want to go over the new sword with you."

He has worked quickly. I am surprised. And as nervous as I am to try again, I crave being done with the stress of the saber.

"I will," I tell him, and he disappears back to the fires. Damn him! Now my morning fun is ruined and filled with apprehension. But Anette pulls me along, and I try to shove down my anxiety to match her gaiety.

"My mother tells me she's enjoying working for you and taking care of your household," Anette says, her statement broken in half by a call to her little girl to keep up. "Which is very lovely to hear."

"She might not always enjoy working," I say honestly. "She will get tired of it."

"She adores it, and has been hankering to get back at it since my youngest sister found a man and planned to moved out." Anette waves a hand. As she says it, I realize Grete has been married almost a year. How has the time slipped by so smoothly, without an edge? Surely there have been problems? Horeb has since put five privies on top of houses, tied all the horse's tails in knots together at the livery, and

Dell Johnston is sporting a black eye from Fortuna's fist over another argument about the names of their establishments. There was a diphtheria epidemic that took the lives of seven children two months ago, and Calvin Johnston lost both his legs after falling from his horse. He died later from bad blood, with Doc Gunnarsen saying as how there's nothing to be done. It's never a dull week in the West.

We arrive at the general store, where the dusty floorboards creak and send up puffs of dirt to settle in the tucks of our skirts and in the creases of the bare feet of her children.

"Anette!" Harry Turner, wearing a long ivory apron, greets her happily.

Sadie runs in from the back room at the announcement, brimming with joy, work dress swinging and a broom dangling.

"Marie! Anette! You'll never guess!"

We glance at one another, and Anette opens her mouth to respond, but Sadie beats her.

"I'm getting married! Tom Fawcett has asked me!"

Harry's wife May, green-eyed and slim and somehow always giving the impression of being dust-free, smiles thinly at us. "Be as it may, Sadie, you're still my hired girl and paid by the hour. Move along."

Anette sends her children to stare at the candy, which sparkles and beckons from the side counter.

"Marie needs something for a new dress," she tells Harry. He grins and turns us over to May before meandering over to the candy counter, his eyes gleaming with excitement at his little customers.

"Something serviceable?" May glances over my worn flannel. I finger the holes in my sleeve, remembering the acid spill and feeling the apprehension of the next sword settle in my bones.

"This will last me a while," I reassure her, and look up the tall shelves, where bolts of colored fabric stretch into the brown-grey gloom of the ceiling. "But I suppose I ought to have something that is both serviceable *and* nice."

"There is a pretty green calico," Anette offers, pointing over our heads. "It's sprigged."

"Yes, there's that," May cranes her neck upward. "And then there's also a deep red, which will go well with your coloring."

I am dark, like my entire family. Black hair, brown eyes and slightly sallow, just like Father. Like Mother. I'm not fair cheeked and saffron haired like Anette is, and I couldn't wear the lovely light colors that are on one of the shelves where the silks and taffetas glisten. They'd not only fill with the blackened grime of western living, but they'd never last against the grease and the fires of the smithy.

"Perhaps the green? Oh, bring down both." I realize belatedly that I ought to take the advice of both women. I've no eye for color, only for design, and hope Anette will continue to take initiative and choose for me. What else are friends for?

"Yes, of course. And also the blue." May considers, then climbs the stool to bring down multiple folds of fabric.

"The blue would do lovely for you. It's very dark, so it would be practical." Anette fingers each as May spreads them out.

I touch them all with the very edges of my fingers, likely the cleanest part of my hands. "Well, that's fine then."

Both women look surprised at my immediate choice, and I look up at their hesitancy.

"What?"

Anette chuckles, glances at her children, and then turns to me.

"Usually there's much consideration of a new dress, Marie."

"It's a *dress*." I shrug, wondering at the price, hoping it will fit under our credit. "And I'm not wearing it to be fine. I've no idea of notions either, to be fair. You were the seamstress, Anette. You choose."

May stares at me, as if judging whether to be dismissive or helpful. She finally sighs, shakes her head, and begins to cut the bolt. I can't determine if she's happy with my choice or thinks I'm not making a very good one. Anette beckons me over to the case of buttons and ribbons.

"Don't look so discouraged. Didn't your mother care about the trimmings?"

"Yes," I tell her. "But she chose for the both of us."

She smiles at me with her own mother's easy grin, the corners of her eyes curving downward like blue crescent moons.

"I'll help you, Marie."

I'm grateful for her unencumbered kindness and matching truthfulness, so I let Anette choose the notions while I beg May to put the items on our credit. We walk out together, my package swinging with string from my arm, and each of her little ones licking a horehound sweet.

"That was a treat," she tells each of them, a twinkle in her eye. "Don't tell your big brothers at home."

"How many children do you have again?"

"Five living," she tells me proudly.

I consider her. She must be close to my age to be sure, but somehow has given birth many times over and kept so many babes alive. I'm impressed and a little in awe of her.

Our steps are light-hearted while we bounce between dry wagon tracks, and I catch up her youngest before we reach the forge. As we walk through the wide doorway, my eyes adjust to the change in light and Thaddeus looks up from his workbench, taking in me, Anette and the children.

"Keep them out of the back here," he orders her, and she nods.

"Of course, Thad. I'll get them around to Mother to say goodbye."

She wordlessly relieves me of my soft goods, and pats me on the shoulder before squeezing it.

"I'll see you around, Marie. This was great fun."

I cannot answer her, because she is immediately distracted by a child reaching for a hot metal poker. Scooping her baby from my hip, she disappears in a whirlwind of rose skirts and candy.

My eyes must be large, because Thaddeus smirks at me.

"Children too much for you?"

His tease is what my brothers would say, and it loosens my muscles and my worry at the upcoming discussion about the sword.

"They are," I admit.

"So, then. Here it is. The one side is ready and polished," he reveals, opening up the hides further so I might see the finished piece. It is still breathtaking, and he has obviously felt more confident forming the blade. There's a straightness to the upper part and a delicate curve to the tapering end. He has formed it well, the metal folded within itself, the weight of it balanced even in my unpracticed palms.

"I'm too afraid to decorate it," I tell him truthfully, echoing many discussions we've had over the dinner table. "It's more beautiful than your last."

"You must, Marie. It's your design," he says firmly. "And as we've decided, you won't be etching it. So, then. What about engraving it as you asked from the start? Or inlay? Or both?" He is eager with his ideas, his energy sudden and compelling.

"What would you want to inlay?" I wonder. "Bone? Tin? Copper?"

"You tell me what you'd be most comfortable doing," he says. "And I've spoken to Father about it. He said he'd show you how to do a false damascening—the cross-hatching of the iron and then laying the softer metal in, but I told him that it wouldn't hold for the pattern."

I nod, agreeing, running a finger along the flat end of the blade. "You're right. Father used to talk to the boys about engraving, and it's what I'm most familiar with."

"It'll be more expensive for the Captain."

"But prettier," I add. "If I can just get a cavity carved into the iron, and do it at an angle so the metal can be pressed or heated or hammered in, it might stay."

Thaddeus gazes at the sword with a mixture of pride and apprehension, and I hope he is not regretting allowing me to work on the piece.

How can he be so calm? Suppose I ruin it again?

"I could make you a burin for cutting in," he tells me suddenly. "And you could do a dovetail profile into the blade to keep the metal from chipping out."

I lean over the sword, noting the swirl of steel buried deep inside the iron. "It'd have to be a sharp burin. Then it would be a true damascening." I look up at him, where he towers over me.

"It's not a technique I'm familiar with."

"Are you sure you want me to tackle this?"

"*Yes*, Marie. And also to finish the inlay to the handle too, with copper wire, horn, or bone at the least. I don't think Captain Bush wants an old-fashioned saber. Something common, like what the men used in the War between the States."

He comes behind me, where I'm wedged against the wall and the bench. "At least I did not need to remake the handle itself, and it'll be near impossible to ruin it, so you needn't fret at all."

I feel solidness of his body, the brush of his chest on my back, and the brace of his arm curving around mine while he holds himself from toppling. He reaches high up for the handle. His closeness is a strange thing, a comfort, and an odd drop of something more before he moves away from me languidly, casually. I feel a flush spider along my bosom, hidden under the brown flannel.

It is time I make my exit quickly, my fingers working over the itchy new skin on the backs of my hands. After the day's mixed activities, I feel more at ease when I'm pressing sheets of copper. The golden-red metal oozes through the machines and the tin puddles along the seams in a way that is comforting and familiar.

And while I am glad for the money the saber will bring, I am choked by failure. I dread touching it. If the boys had sent more funds home before they died, if the Army had ever followed through, we would be free of most of our debt. Free from need for the sword at all. Whether I wish it or not, my survival now depends on the metal. And the failure of my sword eats at my confidence.

I still smart from the snide comments of my customers over the past few weeks. I'm not sure what's worse: Lettie Zalenski and Emma Molhurst's sniffs or Horeb Harvey's off-color teasing. While some jest to show their support, others are enjoying my failure, as if it is proof a woman should not be allowed to manage metal. It only makes me wish to hold onto my position harder.

What would Mother say? I know what I'd wish to hear. *"Marya, kochanie. My sweetheart. You're a smith. You have been for some time, whether you call yourself so or not. You will survive. You will find happiness."*

Truth and coldness mate in my heart. When Father dies, I will have nothing. Marriage is in my future. And will a husband expect me to set aside my newfound identity? Of course. No right-minded man in Flats Town would want a wife to continue working the machines and smacking copper. He would not even give me the choice. He would expect me to take over his own hearth, to move in with him and give him children.

Of course I will lose the shop when I marry.

These thoughts bury themselves in my soul, so I feel frozen, like the ice crystalizing across the top of the stream in winter, with currents hidden and unending below.

CHAPTER TWENTY-SIX
2 July 1867

"Stay within my sight!" Anette begs, causing another pause in our conversation while she instructs the toddling baby. The others have disappeared long ago into the thick deep velvet of the pines on top of the old buffalo jump, but she is somehow not concerned.

"Are you certain they'll be alright?" I ask, gazing about the deep green of the woods. In the distance, chattering voices can be heard bouncing off the wide bumpy bark.

"Of course. They know this area well enough," Anette dismisses. "And I've the older children with them, so they'll watch out."

My mind races, wondering about the wildlife, particularly the mountain lions that would see any of her children as easy prey, but I suppose if Anette isn't worried, I shouldn't be either. Perhaps it is a fine thing I have no children to fret over.

"Now, tell me plain what you're suspecting of Danny," she prompts.

"I think he wishes to ask me to marry him soon," I admit, saying it aloud for the first time. "And he might have done it sooner, but he wants to do it on his own merit, not as a way to release me from his father's new rent."

"How sweet of him! Danny Svendsen is a catch. And he's even tried to court you as prettily as the west allows."

"I know it," I tell her, staring up into the waving boughs of the pine trees, my eyes trying to see through the gloom.

"But ...?"

"Nothing. He is a catch."

"Then you should be encouraging him!" she bursts.

"You sound like Thaddeus. I don't really know how to flirt, Anette. My brothers never gave any young men a chance to court me, and I'm afraid if I tried now it would come as too forward or too false."

"I could have Mother say things," she offers. "Or I could start some whispers with Harry Turner, so Danny would know your answer to the question."

"He ought to be brave enough to ask me without such prompting," I retort, coming to the realization as I say it. "And to know my nature enough to know I will not play the role of blushing, simpering girl for him."

Anette shakes her head, following my lead by staring up into the trees. "All men need a little encouragement. How else do you think they know your heart? My own Jacob needed heavy helping to finally ask me."

"What did you do, then? To get Jacob to propose marriage?" I ask curiously.

"I smiled a lot," she reveals, then pauses and laughs. "Alright, I smiled very specifically at him. And I found ways to be near him, and obviously touched his arm or his hand."

"That's all?"

"Well, I may have eventually mentioned how I favored him above all the other young men in town." Anette smiles a little foolishly, likely thinking on her wide Polish husband, a man devoted to her, their children and his farm.

"If that's not encouragement, I don't know what is." I start to chuckle.

She has the grace to blush. "As I said, he needed a lot of help to know what I wished. You should do the same."

I shrug, unable to tell her how relieved I am that Danny is taking his time. If I am to consider a life as a housewife, I wish to be sure I am comfortable doing it. I want to *choose*, not be forced into it to save my family from money woes.

If I get just enough money from orders this summer with all the wagon trains coming in, and from the sword, I'm determined to get out from under Percy. Somehow. If I can, I'd have my reputation as a coppersmith and a tin tinker to sustain me so I'll have no need of a husband. Imagine not touching the copper, or shaping the tin? I find it hard to believe I might ever stop forming metal now.

"There! Is that a good area?" Anette interrupts my meandering mind by jerking her forefinger into the branches right above her head. She's almost a head taller than me, so she can see into boughs that I cannot.

I peer through the long, spicy needles and squint against the shadows.

"Yes—that's it!"

Climbing the lower part of the tree is work for children, but they've scattered, so I hike my outer skirt into my waistband and scale it myself. The tang of pine and greenery fills my nose and reminds me of Christmas, though the holiday is still half a year away.

There is a long scar dug into the tree's bark, creating a crusty, rough, pitted exterior with yellowy deposits of sap hardened into chunks or streams of stiff drips. Some of it has already started to turn dark to help the tree heal from whatever damaged it, and that is no use to me. What I want are the lighter pieces for rosin flux. I've nearly run out and it's pointless to send east for something I can find in the trees nearby.

"Hold out your apron, I'm going to break off what I can!" I call down to Anette, who dutifully steps up, preparing her wide piece of stained cloth to catch the pine resin.

Some of it comes free without issue, and other bits can be pried with my nails. When I want to get the last chunk, a golden-hued globule half hidden by dirt, I pull out a small paring knife to dig into the soft pine.

"Anette!"

She swings at the sound of her name, a manly shout neither of us expect.

"What is it?"

"I found one of yours all the way down by the water at the smithy, no doubt trying to find her grandmother. But Berit's out right now. I saw her myself by the general as I was leaving."

The top of Danny's head comes into view. It is a strange sight, to be higher than him, to see the full scalp of rich blonde hair shimmer through the needle branches.

"Thanks for returning her," Anette says comfortably. "They do wander. At least Flats Basin River isn't too deep."

"It's a *stream*," I laugh.

"Thaddeus near tripped over her on his way to it," Danny tells us ruefully, his eyes finding me and dancing. "There was some … ah … colorful language used."

"Oh dear. Well. Nothing she can't hear anywhere else in town if she's ears on her. Isn't that right, *kjæreste*?" Anette bends down, still holding the apron up to her waist. I've nearly finished prying the rest of the resin. As I shift on the branches, some of the debris from the loose bark rains down on Danny and Anette.

"Why on earth are you up there, Marie?" he calls up. "One of the littles is good for that."

"They'd disappeared," I say, climbing off the boughs slowly with the last piece in hand. "And I'd rather get it myself, really."

"Thaddeus said you were up the buffalo path looking for resin," he says, watching me descend closely, and then graciously taking my hand to help me the last bit. It's a romantic gesture to be sure, though certainly unnecessary. Behind his shoulder, I see Anette grinning and nodding. "I didn't think to find you up a tree, though."

"I need more rosin flux," I explain. Anette waves a hand, as if beckoning me to say something more, but words are stuck and tight in my throat.

"Well, do you need any more help?" he asks uncertainly, staring up at the towering conifers.

"You've the height for it," Anette says at once. "And I might get home myself to start dinner. I've taken enough time away from my duties. You can help Marie finish her hunt." Her smile widens. "I trust you both can be responsible, and don't need a chaperone?"

Her jibe, in the tone used by scolding mothers, is not lost. The three of us chuckle, though perhaps with some reservation on my part and Danny's. We are so rarely alone, for all the snippets of conversations we've had over the past few months. What will I say to him in such leisure?

"I'll stay and give aid where I can," he agrees, and gives me a small, hopeful smile. I am incredibly anxious and excited all at once. Should I treat him like a customer? Ask him about his day, and his plans? Perhaps I should discuss the logistics of his cattle the way I would the repair of a lantern.

"I'll be off!" she says cheerily. Anette's pronounced departure only heightens my heart's speed. My eyes are wide at her, and she waves again with additional cheer and a wink.

She calls sternly for her children, and pours her resin into my basket. The four children arrive in staggered gaps, though it feels far too quick for my preference. Danny is looking at me in a way that makes me weak and breathless, and I still don't know what I will say to him in the stagnant silence of the forest, when the lilting chatter of the children departs.

But depart it does, and then the soughing of the wind in the razor leaves of the pines is the only noise. A pop of sap, a buzz of a summer insect, and the trill of a horned lark cuts the lull between us. Danny still stares at me, as if he cannot get enough. It is unnerving. I can, now and in their deaths, be even more grateful for my brothers, who knew my nature better than I did, who kept men away so that I would not constantly be flustered.

"What are we looking for?" he asks, and his voice is lower than usual.

I clear my throat and look above at the trees. "Scars in the bark—like that one—where the tree is healing. The sap

239

is congealed within it, or dripping out. It is the tree's blood, and the clearer it is, the better."

"And you use this in the shop?"

"Yes. It gets the solder running when I work on seams."

"Leaves something sticky, though, I shouldn't wonder," he observes, and I look at him, impressed at his notion.

"You're right. It's difficult to remove the residue," I agree.

"How are you holding up on orders?" he asks me, as if trying to find purchase on a topic. I'm not sure if he truly believes in my talent or is simply humoring me.

"There's much to do," I tell him.

"It's good you have work," Danny says without preamble. "As Father wants to raise your rent. Again."

I wonder if my face drops its color.

"Have you told him that it's only me?"

"He knows," Danny says miserably. "But he's a businessman, and he sees his figures every week. If he charges good rents on all his properties, he can purchase more land for more cattle. It's that or sell to the railroad, and Percy Davies is giving him enough push on that so he's been saying no to the rail bosses so far. You know how it goes, Marie. I won't insult you by treating this as something else."

My own head is whirling with numbers.

"How much is he thinking?"

"He wants ten dollars a month."

"*What?*"

"I know, Marie." He looks truly pained. His blue eyes, the color of a clear prairie day, stare into mine as if trying to press into me his sincerity. In another moment he has captured both of my hands, running his thumbs over the bumpy scars on them, and couching my fingers with his calloused ones.

"I'm sorry, truly I am."

"I don't know if I can do that, Danny," I say.

I *know* I cannot. Even in the cities, ten dollars is more than a month's wage for a tinsmith. It's an impossible rent.

"I know, Marie, I know. I would offer you other notions on how to escape the cost, but they would be ill-placed in this moment." His hands grip mine tighter, as if he wishes to save me from myself, and all the worries coming with his news.

He starts to release me reluctantly, and then, as we are alone for the first time in months, he reaches and clasps me into his arms. I'm surprised at the strength of him, and the long confidence of his embrace. It's not anything I was expecting. I like it. I like being held by him, and the tenderness with which he cradles me.

I find myself interested in his smell. It is horses and dirt and leather and the leftover chaff of animal feed. It's a masculine smell, and his skin is warm under the calico shirt he wears. His body is strong and lean and firm against the yielding softness of my own. Part of my small attraction to him is matched with my fascination in the visceral responses of my body. Whether this is affection or love or something in between, it ought to be a good thing to be partnered with such a man, who is kind and strong and smart.

He circles me into his arms tighter, and lowers his lips to mine. It is a light kiss, careful and sincere, and fills me with the fluttering I expect from an embrace. Danny's hands are firm on my back, his mouth sure and then desperate. I want to melt into him, if only because he is a man and I wish to feel the desire I hope will come. I sense a tingle of it. Possible pleasure, budding breathlessness, and wonderment bubble within my stomach. I allow him to kiss me deeply, and close my eyes and my worries against the heat clattering across my shoulders and through my marrow.

I wish I were a brazen woman, who hides my buried carnal hopes below the veneer of tin and copper, willing and able to explode into the man who kisses me. But the joy and desire I yearn to know eludes me. My heart and head do not sing Danny's praises easily for all I find him kind and sweet. Is it enough for a lifetime? Enough to give up my trade?

Will it matter?

He is a gentleman, and pulls his face from mine before we can dive further into the kiss. When he releases my mouth, he leans his cheek on my head, his chest heaving with unspent passion. Goodness! That a man should desire me so! It is powerful, indeed.

We stay like this for a long while, swaying slightly and unevenly. I will myself to stay apart from the maelstrom in my belly, to think on what this moment means. A kiss with Danny Svendsen is not without strings.

There are difficult discussions to come, ones that would never have happened had my family been around me.

"Danny," I say softly. "We ought to continue looking."

He draws away slowly, and I see his mouth is pinker with use, as if our kiss has ripened his lips beyond the narrowness of his heritage. I smile at him, and he smiles back, though it is tremulous.

"Of course, Marie. Of course. Forgive me."

"There is nothing to forgive. I cannot lie and say I did not enjoy our embrace myself." After I say it, even though it is a truth, I realize it sounds very much like encouragement. I feel a new flush feather across my neck.

His eyes light with hope, and he grasps at my words. "Then—perhaps, in the spring—"

"Marie!"

The shout is loud, meant to scan a broad swathe of land, as if the caller hopes to find me in a hurry.

"It's Thaddeus." Danny states the obvious, and we turn toward the blacksmith's voice as one. A crashing through the brush accompanies the next yell, and I move forward.

"What is it? I'm here!"

"Marie! You must come—*chodź teraz! You must come now!*" Thaddeus comes into view, his apron still on and his hands black with soot. His face is unreadable, but his words are wild. "It's your father. Something's wrong. Mrs. Andersen sent me—you—Marie, I think he's dying."

CHAPTER TWENTY-SEVEN
3 July 1867

The summer heat swells and hangs. My flowers wilt but do not brown. There is no reason to wait to bury Father, and we put him to ground hours after he breathes his last.

I watch them cover the box of new, planed wood with the red and grey-tan of the Flats Town earth. It is my place to throw handfuls in. It feels a frivolous, emotional task. My body boils with fear and anger and helplessness. The day sags stolidly, and I expect the night will roll through sleeplessly. I am grateful for Mrs. Andersen, who stayed with me while we waited on Father's life to leave him.

Anette brings meat pies and sweet apple pie to our house. With the help of Sadie and May Turner, and the unwavering shadow of the Salomon men, I've had very little to do.

I'm supposed to be mourning. This I understand. But it is one thing to know it and another to do it. The tears won't come. Sometimes I think they should, and I think if I spend

244

time thinking on his death, I might start to weep. But then I feel myself draw up, as if shutting down the sorrow is the proper response. The agony of my aloneness is unspeakable, and will break me if I dwell on it.

I burned many candles to finish some metal work well into the late hours last night, hoping the numbers and the artistry will be enough to salvage my grief. Thaddeus has kept the sword away from me since Father started to fail. Likely that is wise.

Hymns are sung by people who knew Father only as their newest craftsman. The deep baritone under it all is Walter, who knew him in his youth. My lips won't even move, and I chafe under the fine black gown Sadie lent me so I might be properly dressed. Most married women have a black dress, but that is not my lot.

So I stand on the cliff's edge of Father's grave, wearing borrowed goods and feeling nothing proper at all inside.

I want to rage at the unfairness of my lot. Would it be considered ill-placed of me to scream? Is everyone watching and waiting for me to break? To be a weak woman? To leave town? To give up?

Does everyone feel this way when they bury the last remnant of their family?

"Marie—my dear. Are you ready to go?"

Danny is at my side, a place he has staked since the early morning. I am pleased to have him near, for he is gentle and does not overwhelm me. I know he will do anything within his power that I ask of him. His actions are obvious: he adores me, he loves me, he wishes to take care of me. The innate knowledge of this—the deepness of his feelings—is both a comfort and an obligation.

"No, I'd like to stay," I say quietly. "I know they've put together some vittles for everyone and it's the way of it to have a meal. I'd prefer to wait until the deed is done."

"I'll stay with you," he says lowly, and takes up a shovel to make the work go faster, even as most of the other folk drift toward the trestle groaning under the ironware weighted with food. Walter and Thaddeus were up with the first light putting out the boards. I had tried to answer questions and direct my preferences, but I mainly just wanted to be alone in the shop. It seems it has become my refuge. If I am thinking of fractions, I might not feel so ravaged.

How do I tell Danny I wish to be alone? There are no words to say it kindly. I wish to think of the last moments of Father's life, when he might have offered some words of affection, or given me some acceptance. Instead, it was only a garbled slur. Is it enough to sustain me the rest of my days? It doesn't matter, I suppose. Father would never have told me the shop is mine, even had he been able to speak. He would never have wanted my destiny to be so unusual and unorthodox.

Soon the only ones left are myself, Danny, Mrs. Andersen, and the Salomons, who have done most of the digging and burying, with Thaddeus bearing the brunt of the work. He is sweating through his yellowing shirt, and Walter's arms are shaking visibly with the physical effort. Danny does not seem to mind the labor, and his head is down as he finishes pitching dirt.

"Come, Marie," Mrs. Andersen says softly, taking my arm with hers and winding them together. "Let's get you something to eat."

I resist the urge to look back at Danny, to think of his father's increased rent on the property, to worry on how I will build a new shop by myself if I cannot stay. Percy Davies came to the funeral, and though he says nothing and his Indian lover looks at me with deep kindness, I can feel the festering of my loan. It eats and gnaws at me.

The void of my days stretches grey and unthinkable. To make any decision now is impossible, and I look at the packed grass at my feet, focusing on each blade of crushed green, and then at the softly wilted roses around the shop and the stemmy geraniums framing the doorway to the Salomon house.

My head rotates around such plain thoughts, as if by focusing on them I'll lose the fear running in dizzying circles around my head, and I will be able to hold in the screaming shriek building inside my chest.

Nothing is as it should be.

Nothing is as I expected.

And nothing will bring back Tom or Al or Father, or even Lou.

Or Mother.

No choice leads backward in time.

"Marie!" Anette waves to me, her brood of five scattering and congealing around her as waves around a rock. Jacob is short and steadfast behind her, two plates of food heaping on his wide flat hands as he patiently waits for her to find a place to lay down a blanket. I wave back, but Mrs. Andersen has a firm grip on my arm so I might not stop to chat.

Food is handed to me, some of which I don't even like. But I pick at it dutifully, sitting on the edge of a woven rug brought out from the Salomon house.

"He will be missed," Walter says wistfully, and I wonder how, when he has been like a dead man for months as it is.

"You'll miss the sharing of memories," Mrs. Andersen tells him, and the old blacksmith nods and presses his wavering hands together. She puts one of her own work hardened ones over his and squeezes.

"That. And he was a good smith," Walter finishes.

"Marie will manage," Thaddeus interjects. His eyes fill with questions as I look up into his hard face. "Though it is a blow to lose one's father."

I nod absently, and bite into an early apple. They are sweet and ripe, nearly juicy.

"Perhaps Marie won't have to manage," Danny says quietly. "If she marries, she won't need to work so hard." These words are spoken directly to me, but so soft I barely hear them. I find his earnest, genuine face and smile bleakly.

"She's not alone," Thaddeus counters.

"I meant—"

"It doesn't matter what you meant. She has us."

"And you're fine company. You never said much when we were young and you're not much better now." Danny's tone is light but his fingers close into fists.

"Better than talk for talk's sake."

"Do you suppose the harvest will get in without issue?" Mrs. Andersen asks casually, purposefully changing the course of the conversation but with an obviousness not lost on anyone.

"I hope so," Danny offers, playing along after one more glance at me. "Though it is a hot summer."

"We'll have a long Fall, mark my words," Walter adds.

Their chatter fades to a buzz in my ears. I watch the people milling around. Most I recognize as customers or general townfolk. Flats Town is not so large that there are many complete strangers, yet even so, I do not know everyone. I see several people look my way, sympathy and questions etching and stretching across their faces.

I'm not a particularly emotional woman, I like to think, but today I have feelings crackling within me. When will they all leave? When do I get a moment to myself?

"Marie," Anette plants herself in my line of vision. "You'll be all right? Do you need someone to stay with you tonight? A body isn't meant to do such mourning alone."

"I have no other choice!" The words sting.

Though she flinches, Anette still smiles. "That is true. But you can remedy it, if you wish." Her eyes flick at Danny. My ire rises further at her matchmaking today, of all days.

"I think any request put to me today would be met with a sour answer," I reply, and with that, the anger flees, and I want to weep.

Her arm reaches out and she hugs me with one side, as the other still holds a youngster. I smell the milk on her, and the cloying heaviness of cooking oil and dirt and sun. It is thoroughly comforting, and I sag into her, letting her shoulder take the weight of my sadness for one short moment.

"Thank you," I whisper into her coiled braid, and when she pulls away she's smiling widely and with affection.

"If you need anything, you know where to find me," she says, and stands fully, straightening the child she holds. Jacob comes to shake hands, speaking quietly and mildly with Danny and Thaddeus.

"The food is nearly gone anyway," Mrs. Andersen says, looking up from her grandchildren. "We might as well clean up. We can take care of everything in your little kitchen, Marie. It'll go quick if you heat the water in the copper boiler."

I do her bidding, glad to have someone thinking and giving orders. She washes and I dry, and though she chatters, I'm utterly silent. There seem to be only idle things to say. Why say them?

"… and then I saw Mary Brown's daughter. She's looking well after that nasty bout with croup—early in the season for such a thing too. Lucky it wasn't the diphtheria. That's the worst. And did you see how Sadie's dress was? It was so fine! The detail on the wrist and sleeves—so much fabric for a dress! How are such big-shouldered sleeves practical? Though I suppose if there is money, one can have such fashions. And Sadie has no children yet … and with Tom's salary …"

She does it to comfort me, and it works in a fashion. It's late afternoon by the time we hang up the wash pan, and Mrs. Andersen sighs and puts her hands on her hips.

"I'm thinking the men will be over at the Salomons'. Do you suppose they'll want supper after such a big dinner?"

"I … perhaps?"

What do I know of men's stomachs now? The only ones I've ever fed are gone. My lungs feel crushed again. "If you'd like to go and check? And take a moment to sit, Mrs. Andersen. You've done more than enough. I'll take off Sadie's nice frock before I head over."

Mrs. Andersen's face collapses into fine wrinkles as she smiles, though her forehead creases with concern.

"You're going to be fine, Marie."

"Of course I am," I agree, but I cannot match her soft smile.

She leaves in a bustle, the length and height of her still out of sorts with the amount of energy she exudes, even after a long day. I hope Walter gives her a small beer and a chance to sit down. I know he will.

Removing Sadie's finery, I press it carefully onto the bed and look it over. It is a lovely dress. She brought it from the East after she wedded Tom Fawcett. Her mother told her a black dress was important for a married woman. If I lived in Chicago yet and we had our family money again, I'd wish for something as fine.

Outside, the light has gone gold and ochre, with a deep pink cutting the sky at the edge of the horizon. It is a beautiful evening now, all crisp and breezy. When the sun hits just so, myriad specks of seed and dust and tiny bugs shift through the air.

I think of Father's grave on the edge of the property. St. Aloysius has a small graveyard, but I wanted Father near. I need to make a marker. Likely I'll do a copper cross in the way of our Catholicism. Perhaps something with flowers.

I'm drawn outside, walking toward the grave. Drawn to it. It is as if I cannot allow myself to believe it. As if seeing it once more will press upon me the finality of my situation.

No one is around anymore. It is a weekday after all, and everyone is home and preparing for the next day's activities, or eating again, or recouping tasks left undone because of my father's funeral.

"*Ojciec* ..." I whisper the word as I approach. I do what I wished to do earlier, and sink to my knees in the soft churned earth. "Why are you gone? *Co zrobiłeś? What have you done?*"

The accusation breaks me. My lack of strength should appall me. But the hole of my heart peels open, and consumes my eyes and my mouth and my breathing. Catching up my hands, I hold them tightly to my throat, willing the sorrow to wash through and empty out, so I do not need to revisit such pain ever again.

Let it be gone.

Let me be free of it.

Let me live.

The gloaming settles, and the shadows go long. My knees ache and my body shakes. I let myself go with the pouring tears: an avalanche of acceptance and resistance. I do not think. I do not worry or fret or consider. There is only *this*, the tearing of family cloth, and of familial ties.

There is only loss.

When Thaddeus takes a knee next to me, at first I do not see him. But his hand is heavy, and the smell of fire surrounds him, and then me.

"Marie. Mrs. Andersen is worried you haven't eaten anything all day, and she's sent Father to get a fish out of the smokehouse. Danny is fetching something stronger to drink from the cooper's. Did you want supper?"

I shake my head. Does he think I will have words? Why would I try to eat? What good is there in putting food in my mouth? I won't see it, or taste it, or feel it stack in my belly.

"I'll go get Danny. He must be on his way back soon enough," he says nervously into my silence, rising to his feet ponderously. Without truly having a reason, I grasp at his hand, keeping it at my shoulder. The slits and bumps and ridges of my fingers collide with the burns and callouses of his.

"... wait." My voice, hoarse and broken, rasps into the evening. He does, without hurry or impatience, and for some reason his steadfastness brings me to new tears. I cannot stop them, nor slow them, and the silent, wrenching cries tear the breath from me.

252

"Marya, please."

I'm not sure if he wishes me to release him, or to let him find Danny. Or perhaps he cannot abide the sight of a woman crying. I let him go. He rearranges himself to crouch next to me, and stares at the grave, now almost black in the falling dusk. His face is inscrutable, the beard hiding half of it. I look at him squarely, then back at my father's resting spot. The sight of it blinds me again, as the tears build high and I gag on the weeping, the sobs tangling in my lungs.

"Death is part of things. You know this," he says. "It is more a way of it here than back East. You will find peace."

"How do I wash away the anger?"

My question seems to surprise him, and he shifts to look at me fully. I dive in, now able to put the emotion out into the air.

"I am *furious*. Furious at my brothers for dying. They were stupid, and crazy, and selfish! They should have known they might not live! To go, with no money returning … And Father too, collapsing. And then dying! Leaving me alone! All because Mother—my glittering, perfect, beautiful mother—asked my Father to keep a ridiculous promise. And he *keeps* it! In the name of their love! What is the point of it all?"

He is stoic against my tirade, only blinking as I hurriedly whisper the blackness of my spirit to him, forcing the words out as if to cleanse myself by the releasing of them.

My breast heaves after I finish, and I clutch at my shoulders with my arms crossed, feeling the emptiness of my life in that simple gesture. I am breaking inside, and the loss of my brothers and my father mix with the desperate memory of my mother.

"I know you have lost your mother too, and that death is part of it all. But truly, Tadeusz. What comes next? What do I do with all of my anger ... and my *fear*? Now do you think I am wrong to worry so much?"

This last is a taunt, reminding him of our early friendship, and at that he finally comes to life.

"You are a thoughtful, fretful woman, Marya, I'll give you that. And it is not without reason. The anger. Well, that may come and go for years."

"Years?" I exclaim, throwing up my hands, and then smashing them into my skirts. "I can see how one becomes bitter."

"That is up to you," he tells me honestly. "When my own mother passed, Father was nearly inconsolable for a bit. Like your father. But time does pass, and while I miss her, and I am sometimes angry ... I know he has healed. And that is enough to wash away the anger. And there are other angers. At yourself, for instance. The regret that you did not do enough while they lived, that you did not tell them how much you appreciate them. That eats at you too, if you let it."

"Did you let it?" I ask, feeling tears curl from my eyes once more. It seems they will come no matter what I do or say. He has touched on my guilt, my appalling stoniness in the months of Father's illness. Is this why Thaddeus is always so irritable? He carries his pain as anger?

"No. Not about my mother. I found ways to feel settled."

"My shop," I say suddenly, glancing at the silent, dark walls of the old barn. "That settles me. I could fall into the work."

"If that's what you choose to do with your life," he shrugs. "Or perhaps you will marry and move on, like so many others do."

But the idea of marriage somehow sends a shiver and a sob through me, and I bend over Father's grave to swallow it. Thaddeus's hand fits on the line between my shoulder blades, gently moving up and down as though I am a child he is comforting. I let him placate me for a long moment, closing my wet eyes against the slide of his iron fingers on the bumps of my spine. I miss the casualness of touch: my Father's hand on my hair, my brothers' bumps and pokes.

"I should go get Danny," he says finally, sighing and grunting a little as he gets out of the crouch.

"I should go in too, regardless." I stand with him, smudging the remaining wetness from my jaw, where it beads and drips.

Looking down at the grave at our feet, I take in a great, shuddering sigh, and feel the anger collapse into a small, tight ball within my gut. It will spring up on me, this I can understand, but for now it is subdued.

Perhaps it will never surface so violently again, losing force and effect each time it arises from my belly. Or it will rear up and overtake me, and God knows what I'll contemplate if that happens.

We walk back to the Salomon house side by side. The yellow lamplight spills and pools against the blackening shadows of night. Mrs. Andersen is tinkering with pottery and tin, and the scent of venison oozes through the door where it sits ajar.

It's like returning to the living after looking down into emptiness. Tears pump against my eyes yet again, and I am certain I look puffy and red. Danny will know at once that I have been weeping fiercely. Still, I do not know if I could have dissembled so easily to him.

I'm very glad for Thaddeus's friendship, and in the last few paces of the yard, I reach across and link one of my fingers with his. He makes no indication of the action other than to let go as he allows me to proceed into the kitchen first. As we enter, Danny comes in from the other door, his brow tight and worried, relaxing only when he meets my face before concern races across his eyes.

The sincerity of his gaze jolts me. I realize, quite suddenly, that if I do want to end my future loneliness, I have to only ask.

CHAPTER TWENTY-EIGHT
1 August 1867

Thaddeus and Lieutenant Balsam step into the tinshop, and my heart patters and pops before thudding heavily. I cannot read the lieutenant's face, and I can only imagine what he has said to Thaddeus about the ruined and delayed sword. I wonder how irate Captain Bush will be as well. Failure crumbles into me once more.

"How are you today, sir?" I ask formally, and Lieutenant Balsam frowns.

"I've heard about the sword. As I mentioned to Salomon, I'm to see what's left of it, and report back to the Captain."

"Yes. The delay is my fault. I am so deeply sorry," I tell him. He stares around the shop, taking in the high rafters and the makeshift walls, and the layer of dust I always battle along the shining tops of the machines.

"Eh. Well. I'm told you've had a spot of bad luck recently. Some loss," he says grudgingly, with obvious reluctance. "Though I'd hoped to fetch the sword by now instead of finding it ruined."

"I know."

Thaddeus steps in. "Marie would like to use an engraving, and then pound in a softer metal. It would be finer."

"More expensive," Lieutenant Balsam snorts, but he doesn't refuse immediately, and instead takes to fingering the prettier work along some of the new nutmeg graters I've put out what with the harvest coming soon. "The Captain will want to know how much."

"There'd be no acid," I add. "And unless my hands stop working, I can carve the same design, but inlay it with a metal instead. Gold, perhaps, or silver or tin."

"You think we've got gold just sitting in a pouch somewhere, waiting to be melted down and used in a sword?" Lieutenant Balsam's fat black eyebrows rise incredulously. "Army men, even those with rank, aren't paid so handsomely."

"Don't I know it!"

"Just what is that supposed to mean, woman?" the lieutenant's eyebrows sink back down as he scowls.

"What Marie is saying is that she is aware of a soldier's wages, or lack of them," Thaddeus says quickly. "As her brothers were enlisted."

Lieutenant Balsam glances around once more before his eyes settle on me. "Your brothers serve? Not at Fort Randall."

"No. They were posted west."

"Were?"

"Gone. Without hardly a cent for any of them!" The frustration spills out, the old annoyance with customers replaced by a barely repressed irritation.

The lieutenant's mouth goes thin, and finally he breaks his stare and looks down at the sword. "So you want to put a soft metal into the design?"

"Tin," I offer, battling my resentment and my worry, hoping to seal the deal to make him leave. "And it won't cost you more. I'll supply it."

He surveys me tightly, his narrow eyes more squinted than ever. "I suppose it is the least you can do." Lieutenant Balsam sets down a grater and sighs. "The Captain's not happy about the extended wait, but as you're the nearest smiths around, he'll have to, eh? Mind you have it ready before the holidays. Come, Salomon, we'll settle the price."

He gives a curt, irritable nod and stalks out, the blacksmith trailing him. As soon as they leave, I drop onto the counter with my forearms.

The weight of the ledger bumps into my knee under the planks. I'm no expert at numbers, but even I know I cannot afford to keep on Mrs. Andersen and pay the new rent for another year. At some point, Percy Davies will get tired of giving me such a heavy loan, or the railroad plans will be settled and Percy won't have a need to keep me on Oddvar's land paying a ridiculous amount for our little plot, in which case I'll owe him all the money back. No interest of course, but it's piled high. And this sword will offer some cash, but not nearly enough.

Damn the boys, who promised to help by leaving! And damn the Army for not following through! And damn ...

"Marie, *honning* dear! Thaddeus is done sweet-talking that Army man. Won't you come in for the midday meal?" Mrs. Andersen is at the doorway, her head in disarray and her face grinning. She is wound tightly, expectantly.

I want to ask her what her excitement means as we walk to the Salomons' back door, but the walk is too short. In the wide kitchen, Thaddeus stares into the small fire in the hearth and doesn't look up as we enter. Walter is looking at him, his face oddly sensitive even under the greying beard.

"Ready to eat then?" Mrs. Andersen asks, immediately going to the sideboard. The men don't answer her, continuing their silent battle. I look between the two, wondering what the quarrel is about now. Has Captain Bush's sword caused another issue? Reminded Thaddeus that he had once wanted to join the skirmishes that seem to never end out west? I had thought that old argument was long buried.

But when Thaddeus comes to the table, I'm surprised with his calmness. His features are clear, and not the usual thunderous frown. Still, the conversation is stilted and muted, and I glance around, aware that I'm likely the only person at the table who is out of the news. I'm no hand at social graces, but even I can tell something is amiss.

"What is it? What's going on?" I ask when it's quiet.

Mrs. Andersen and Walter exchange a sly, quicksilver glance. Thaddeus sighs and straightens up from his plate.

"My father and Mrs. Andersen have decided to get married."

I stare at him. Surely he must be teasing me as my brothers used to do. Twisting my body to look at Mrs. Andersen, she nods and grins, her blue eyes glinting with happiness.

I had no notion they were so sweet on one another, and the announcement surprises me. I'm unprepared for the pangs and washes of emotion sputtering in my heart, sending shivers to bang and slither from my chest out to my arms.

I will lose her, too, and it is not even for my inability to pay my part of her wages. The thought is almost unbearable, and I shove it away, determined to pretend I am glad.

"I'm so—so happy for you," I tell Mrs. Andersen, including Walter in my statement, and reach the few inches to wrap my nearest arm around her. She is glowing, the way a new bride does. I am fascinated.

"Yes, thank you, Marie," she says joyfully. "It's not something an old widow woman looks for late in life, but there's no reason not to marry. I do all the wifely things around here anyway."

"That's not the only reason I asked you," Walter interrupts gruffly, but his face is tender as he looks at her across the table.

Their little romance is electric, young, and merry. I wish to catch some of the happiness for myself, if only to chase away a day of dull overwhelming sorrow and worry. My heart aches. I want to put my head down on the worn table and press my hot forehead into the grain.

Now is not the time to bemoan it though, so I raise my mug to them, circling it in the air at the center of our little group.

"Many cheers to you both, and a long and happy marriage," I toast.

After we all drink heartily, I try to tease them to hide the pulses of sadness eating at my veins and numbing my fingers.

"You know this means I'll have to bake the traditional bread for you to break at the wedding. And to have some salt on hand."

"Bread we know you can do," Walter guffaws, but he says it kindly, and they laugh.

"And you'll be inviting everyone. Even Horeb Harvey, is it?" I mimic.

Walter chokes on his beer, snorting. "That is how he talks!"

"I don't think we'll ask Horeb," Mrs. Andersen says, her blue eyes glowing. "I prefer my privies on the ground."

Thaddeus is still quiet through the chatter. He does not seem unhappy about the new arrangement, but it is still news to digest.

"So, then, that's settled. We'll perhaps do a little something soon," Mrs. Andersen plans. "Gives me time to pack up the old house and choose what I wish to fit in here. I don't take up much room, of course, but a woman does have a trunk of her own things."

Walter nods absently, calm and unflappable as usual. Suddenly I realize their engagement truly is brand new. He may have asked her only an hour or two ago among the rows of carrots and cabbage. I feel particularly fortunate to be included in the first announcement of it. They behave as if I'm family, and that small drop of inclusiveness is a smooth salve to the exhaustion pulling at my eyes.

Mrs. Andersen stands, and I follow. We manage the cutlery together in our typical rhythm, and she chatters with more vigor than usual about the details of the marriage, and the happiness she bubbles with spills into my spirit. How can I begrudge her this? I find myself smiling, forgetting my money woes, my concerns about the sword, and my loneliness. I focus on her joy, letting it caress me. For a moment, my thoughts drift to Danny. He must propose soon, I suppose. Will I happily go with him, as happily as Mrs. Andersen marries Walter? I like to think I will. I'd like to think it would be more than just using Danny for my debt.

My God! Is that what I am doing?

Is that why I string him along?

Another layer of sadness and guilt buries itself in my spirit.

If I truly do mean to marry Danny for his money, shouldn't I be truthful of it? Is my guilt on this why I am so soft-spoken with him? Is it why I can be hard and blunt to customers and friends alike, but not to Danny? Because I am acting on a lie?

When my meager house duties are finished at the Salomons' house, I take off the cotton apron and hang it on the hook to dry. Before I can disappear into my shop, Thaddeus pokes his head around the forge door.

"I have your burin ready. Did you want to take a look?"

"Oh. I would." I turn on my heel and walk back in and through to the smithy. It is empty save for the hot fires and Thaddeus, who is already black to the elbows in the time it takes me to help with dishes.

"Here you go." He fairly tosses the sharp object, and I grab at it just in time.

The tool is like an awl, but harder and sharper, with one side narrowed to a point and the other rounded for holding. It is also smaller than I expected, and tell him so.

His brow creases. "I figured you wouldn't want anything too heavy. You'll have to do fine work with it. Smaller is better. Besides, you don't have big hands anyway."

I raise my eyebrows at him incredulously.

"No? Mine are certainly not small." I raise my palms, then flip them, showing him the burns and scars rippling along my flesh, and the bunchy thick joints of my fingers.

He stares at them for a moment, then meets my eyes. "So?"

"So you might have made something bigger and sturdier. And what if something small can't hold up against the steel of the sword?"

Thaddeus finally cracks, spilling the frustration he's bottled inside all of the meal.

"Damn it, Marya, it'll work."

"I hope so, or else we'll be further behind."

"Then get to it," he bites, stalking to the back of the forge and yanking down the new sword, where it is carefully wrapped in a layer of soft sheepskin. "And mind, no wrecking it this time!"

It's been a long while since he's reminded me how I ruined his first piece of masterwork, and the accusation stings dully. After the wedding announcement, I don't think anything else will hurt today.

"And suppose I do destroy it?"

"So you keep saying. What good are you as a smith if you won't stand behind your own work?" he growls, gripping the cloaked sword with a strong hand.

"This is different, and you know it."

"Not really. Either you can work the soft metals or you can't, Marya. You either are a smith or no. Call yourself what you are and then *do* as you are!"

I hold his gaze, but perhaps something in my face remains unschooled, because he puts down the sword and braces his fists and arms around it, breathing heavily through his nose.

"Ahh ... *przekleństwo. Damn it.*" The curse in Polish is soft, even for his deep voice. "I'm being unkind, Marya."

264

"I know. I mean, I understand."

"Do you?"

"I think so. You're upset because your father is remarrying."

"No. Yes. Well. It is unsettling. I never thought he would. And he's made a good choice. But that's no excuse to pick a fight with you."

"I don't mind," I tell him, surprised I mean it. "That is, I don't mind having an honest conversation."

"I'm generally good for that," he agrees, sighing and standing fully. "You'll do fine. Take it over to your shop and start to work on it. Let me know how the burin goes."

The sword is heavy in my hands. Once more, it feels alive. My fingertips burn with the old memory of the acid, but confidence curdles and grows in my stomach, as if I know inherently I will not make a mess of it this time. Hopefully that feeling is true.

Carrying the sword out of the forge with both hands to escape back to my own smithy, I pause at the doorway.

"Congratulations, Tadeusz."

He glances up from the band of iron he's shoving deep into the coals.

"Whatever for?"

"For your father's marriage."

He snorts, and I walk home, the sword weighing like a long heavy rock in my arms.

CHAPTER TWENTY-NINE
12 October 1867

For all the simplicity of the wedding vows at St. Aloysius, Mrs. Andersen—Mrs. Salomon now—is glowing like a new bride. It astounds me. Should a woman of her age and with so many grown children be so joyful in marriage? But she is quite that, matching Walter's height as she stands near him at our small gathering in the yard. Walter himself is smiling more than I've ever seen. It makes me feel glad, and I forget my worries as I am pulled into chatter and other little tasks. Anette handles the majority of the foodstuffs, but I like to pretend I know how to help her.

"Need a hand?" Danny comes up beside me and relieves me of the platter of small rolls and a pot of jam. He winks and delivers the food to the trestle with flair, and grabs up an apple before immediately getting waylaid by the older Brinkley brothers. It sounds like Young Henry, John, and George all are bursting with energy and beer, and it sounds suspiciously like they plan to leave the party to find Horeb and lock him into a privy.

"Have you—oh! You put it out. Thank you," Anette slips by me with a whole bowl of baked beans cut with brown sugar. The wedding is more of a feast than I envisioned, likely thanks to the harvest. She surveys the table and nods, satisfied, and then picks up her youngest toddler clinging to her skirt.

"So that's done." She nods toward her mother and Walter, who are shaking hands carefully with Percy Davies and his very pregnant Sioux lover.

"It seems they'll be very happy," I say.

"Yes," Anette studies the pair. "I suppose so. It's a bit frivolous of her to marry at her age, but I can't fault her. And she does seem happy, doesn't she?" Her voice softens as she continues to stare.

"I suppose now this will be the talk of the season. The elderly couple who married."

"Yes." She smirks at me and whacks my arm. "We have to get the harvest in so we can squeeze together all winter and do what we all do best when married."

"Which is?"

"Make babies, of course!" She laughs at my startled expression, and then turns to her child, who is reaching for a sweet roll on the table.

I walk away, feeling awkward. Her tease only reminds me of the coming cold. It will be a lonely season to be sure. All those cold, long days! In that big shop! And my brother's empty beds in the back room. It's ghostly and eerie, and no matter how tightly I squeeze my blankets I'm still unable to quench the wish in my womb.

And what will I do when the orders slow over the snowy months? How will I keep the money flowing without

Father to help? That damn sword! I went over the numbers with Thaddeus last night, and while I'll make some cash, it won't be nearly what I'd hoped to make. My ruining of the first didn't help.

"A wedding is not a place to be serious or fret," Thaddeus mentions as he tromps by with a small table under one hand and a bucket of water in the other.

"You're one to speak. You're rarely in a good mood yourself."

He concedes my point without giving in, and follows my gaze. "They're going to be happy, I think. I'm glad for my father, truly, Marya. And you might as well call her Berit now. *Mrs. Salomon* has an odd sound to it."

I wonder if he simply doesn't wish me to give his mother's title to the new woman in his house, but the thought is too sweet to ask. Ribbing him is easier. "If I didn't know any better, I'd think you were saving the title for your own wife."

He scoffs. "No wife of mine would be so formal."

"You'd actually marry?"

He looks affronted, but instead of continuing on this line, he asks a question I have never prepared to hear. "Do you wish you'd married Jimmy?"

I am glad I'm not eating, or I might choke. As it is, I feel the air go out of me. No one has talked to me of Jimmy since his death.

"How can I know the answer to that?"

"You ought to. It's your heart," he says shrewdly.

"Well, then." I pause, trying to think back and remember the pounding of my heart, the eagerness in my blood, and the response of my body to Jimmy's. It feels like it was many years ago. The excitement that had tingled with his attentions has dulled. It was so brief it feels as though it never truly happened. But the truth of it is deeper. Even when Jimmy was alive and attentive, I had hesitated. I had had questions in my heart then, same as now. Is that my answer?

"Perhaps I should not have mentioned him," Thaddeus says, as if realizing he may be prying open painful memories, but I shake my head.

"It's all right. I just never considered such a thing." I look up at him. "No, then."

"No?"

I clarify. "No, I don't wish I'd married Jimmy. I never gave him my promise, and I suppose it was because I wasn't certain. I don't think I would be glowing so on my wedding day to him." I gesture outward and include Walter and Berit in the swirl of my palm.

Thaddeus inhales and nods, perhaps feeling as though his question was answered full enough, and wanders away, though I'm left pondering on Jimmy in a way I haven't in months. What would we have done, had we married? Would we grow together? Would he be making stews while I pound on copper? Would marriage to Jimmy be any different than marriage to Danny? As though I am thinking aloud, Danny himself appears next at my elbow, having extracted himself from the Brinkleys.

"How's that sword coming along, Marie?" he asks at once, likely knowing shop talk will put me at ease.

"It's doing fine. I wish I was working on it now."

"You can't always hide from people."

"I know."

"And it'll do you good to get out and be social," he pushes. "Just like at the harvest dance coming up. Now you don't have to worry about your father, either, so you might enjoy yourself." He pauses and then grips my arm. "I didn't mean to sound so flippant about it, Marie, I—"

"I know what you meant," I soothe. "And in fact, it is Father's passing and this marriage that makes me think on what must happen next. For instance, the barn. It's good for a shop—really lovely, truly—but completely impractical for me to have so much space."

Danny lifts his pale, golden eyebrows. "What are you saying?"

"That I might look for a smaller space. Mrs. Ander— that is to say, Berit—will have her old house to sell. I might be able to take it over."

"You mean, buy it?" Danny looks concerned. "And take yourself across town?"

I'm not sure why it matters. It's Percy I have to truly answer to.

"Flats Town isn't that big. Yes, I'd move a solid two minute walk away," I tease lightly.

Thoughts for my future are cut short. People are leaving. I jump in to help tidy up the yard, Danny shadowing me and helping Thaddeus move everything back into the house. I even take initiative around the stove, as the new Mrs. Salomon is too busy with the last guests. I don't break anything, and even do not forget to change out the brine in the meat barrel. There are so many details to keeping up a kitchen, even more when there is a party!

"I'll stop by this week, Marie," Danny tells me as he surveys the clean kitchen, his hands on his hips. "Just to see how you are, as always."

He smiles at me, hopeful and bright, and I smile back before lowering my head to the large iron pot that has held rabbit stew all afternoon. He squeezes my shoulder as he walks out for horse and home, and I can only look up at his back as he leaves.

I am not sure why his attentions still fluster me. Is it because I love him? Or because he loves me? I am stricken with these thoughts whirling around my mind much like the water I'm scouring does the same to the bottom of the pot. I'd never thought love would be so tentative and careful and sweet.

"I think it's clean, Marie," Mrs. Salomon—*Berit*—says, tapping my shoulder as she walks by with an empty plate.

I lift myself up and haul the pot outside to slosh out the dirty water, spilling half of it on the hem of my skirt. There's a rhythm to housework too, clearly one I am not accustomed to.

Walter sits outside against the building next to old Henry Brinkley. They are both puffing into their pipes with a contentedness brought on from age and full stomachs. Henry is perhaps a bit younger than the blacksmith, but the head of a brood, which gives him some sort of respect among the menfolk.

Walter himself is not so lost in thought that he ignores me though, and he shifts in his seat to twist and look up.

"Marya. *Dziękuję Ci. Thank you.* For all of your help today."

"It's the least I can do, after all you've done for me."

"Well then. With your father gone, you'll forgive me if I am particularly careful about you, even with me an old married man," he says seriously, in his slow, careful cadence. "I still want to make sure you're taken care of."

"I think I'll be alright. I have my craft and the shop," I say, wishing I could find deeper comfort in those facts as I say them.

"Well, that aside, Marya, know you've family in me and in Berit. We'll be sure you're happy and healthy as best we can. Perhaps get you married." His eyes actually twinkle, which makes me want to laugh.

"I'm not too concerned with that," I say. "You're the married one now, Wladisław. You might get in to your wife."

"Suppose I might. My thanks, Henry, and tell Susan the squash pies were mighty fine."

The farmer stands and half-stretches.

"There is that. So, Walter. Best to you." He tips his fingers to me and strolls out of the yard, gathering his wife and sons and daughters-in-law as he goes. Suddenly the grass is cleared of people and Walter is at the doorway, staring down at me with a quizzical expression visible even through his beard.

"Well, then. You'll be good for tonight?"

The shop is not very far away, and it will not be the first night I've slept alone since my father passed, but his question makes me stop. I realize that somehow I *do* feel more alone tonight.

"Of course," I say anyway. "I'll finish up this pot and then head home. Might even try to get some work done by candlelight."

He considers the sunset, and then shrugs. "Don't work so hard, Marya. *Będzie dobrze. It will be fine.*"

"I just like the work." Do I need to remind him of my debt?

"Well. Good night then," he says, and disappears into the soft gloom of the house.

I tip the rest of the water out of the pot. It likes to pool in the bottom, even after a first ditch. The porous iron holds water more than any other metal I work with, and even with the heavy black seasoning, it still is difficult to dry.

"*Mil*—Marya." Thaddeus comes around the side of the house, his arms hanging at his side, one fist closed on the bucket from the well. "You're still here?"

"Thought I'd help your ... Berit and Walter ... clean up."

He stops short next to me and looks inside the house briefly, making a face.

"Good of you. I'm going to leave the water and then head over to sleep at the general. May and Harry have an extra bed for travelers, and I should give them a night alone."

The embarrassment of his meaning hangs between us, and I'm short of breath. Discussing sex, however vaguely, makes me think of it entirely. The memories of others in the midst of lovemaking on the wagon trail—images of limbs and skirts and shadow—crowd my mind. I wonder if I'm flushed or pale with the remembering. Because he is the one standing in my vision, I immediately imagine Thaddeus in his marriage bed, taking a woman in her nakedness and running his hands along her hips. What an outrageous thought! I cough to cover my gape, and then clear my eyes with a wet hand.

"I'd offer you a bunk at the shop, but it wouldn't be proper," I say, and the same vision spills back into my mind without pause, except this time it is my own hips I imagine sandwiched with his, leaving me simmering oddly, and floating disjointedly.

He looks at me closely. "You'll be all right there alone?"

"Why does everyone wonder that? Your father asked, and so has Danny," I say, throwing irritation behind the words. "Does no one think I can manage these days?"

Thaddeus raises his hands in instant defeat. "Probably because whoever is asking is just worried about you."

"Well, I thank them. And you. And I'll be fine. *Będę! I will!*" I hand him the empty pot and he automatically grabs it with his free hand. "I'll see you soon, as the sword is coming along fine enough."

I stomp through the yard to the tinshop and slip in through the doorway. Surveying the glowing, blackened iron of the machines, the golden fire of the copper, and the silver white of the tin scattered around the benches and the floor, I feel as though I can breathe and be myself. It is a strange thing, to feel at home in such a place, for all that it truly is lonely.

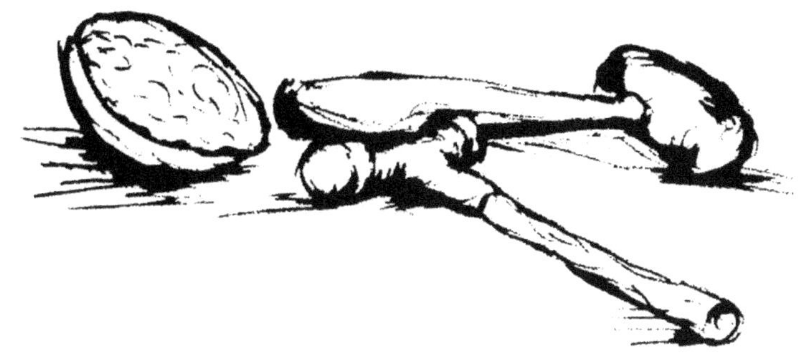

CHAPTER THIRTY
20 October 1867

Sliding a poker into the rounded belly of the stove, I wake the embers, and stare at the glow. It's a warm evening, for October, but I need some light if I'm to work past twilight. Opening the doors, I gaze across the yard. It's quiet. Sunday. And I'm exhausted.

It's tiredness brought on by worry. By pain. By loneliness.

I miss Father. And the boys. I don't even want the Army's money anymore, I just want to be free of my debt, my responsibilities, and the quiet of the shop.

I could warm the brazier and start some copper work, and fill my head with fractions and the slip of metal sheet in my fingers. I could dive into the mathematics and hide from the reality of my life. I could fly to Danny and beg him to marry me and save me from my debt.

No. *Nie.* No.

Should I bother to return? To Chicago? To what? For what? For whom?

I don't know.

Giving up my trade, the only thing I've ever done well, is a fool's notion, but staying here and digging myself further into debt is nearly as bad. I feel trapped within a circle of blackness, unable to see beyond, unable to discover a way out. There must be something. Must be a way to get out from under Percy's thumb, *must be.*

Marriage to Danny? That also feels like giving up. It feels unlike a choice.

It feels like a failure.

And I do not love him.

On the table, waiting for the last of the carving, the sword is so sharp, so fine and so pure. The steel gleams, and it will look like a mirror when it's polished.

I stare at the point. The tempting tendrils of the idea waft through my senses, as strong as the tantalizing smell of baked apple *jakbłecznik.*

It is a sin to think of ending it all.

But the thought is there, growing, taking form, a looming darkness curling around me, until it seems the shop disappears, and the only consideration is me, and whether or not I will use the sword the way it is meant.

Am I truly so tired? Tired of what? The work? Of being stubborn? Of fighting?

It would be the end. It would stop the questions, the worries, the fears.

Lifting the sword, an edge bites into my palm, but I do not feel it. The red of the blood seems to belong to someone else, and the river of it slides down my wrist and to the corner of my elbow.

A slice to the gut would be death too long in coming. The bowels would be worse.

The needle-point end flicks up toward the concave hollow of my chest, where my breasts swell just above my stays. It's as if the sword knows where to go. It is instinct, knowledge, surety. It is aware of my distress, and understands it must cut me fast, perfectly. It must use my strength against me, turning the power of my hands and my muscles inward.

"What the *fuck* are you doing?"

Thaddeus is an inky shadow, detaching from the gloom of the evening. Even in the darkness, I can feel the quivering of his body, the shock and anger and fear.

He's afraid.

Him! He has nothing to fear, damn him! He is not giving up his life, forced to marry someone he does not want. He is not drowning in debt, blackmailed beyond reason. He is not without family, alone and destitute and despairing.

The sword is stuck, suddenly far too heavy to move, and the press of the steel against my body is like a caress. And I'm frozen, too. Embarrassed. Appalled.

And yet longing for it to stab into my flesh.

Will it hurt?

Will it sting?

Surely it will not bite me the way the acid did. It won't scorch like the words of the people here who disapprove of me. It won't burn like the bile in my stomach when I think of marrying Danny. It will likely just throb. Slowly, like the heavy pulsing of my blood. I may not feel much at all.

Thaddeus strides across the shop in five gigantic steps. Wrenching the sword away from me, he glares at it, where it slides across his palms and catches the orange and red of my little stove's coals.

"Goddamn it, Marya. Damn it. What the hell are you doing? Trying to see if I've made it sharp enough? It's sharp enough!"

I have no words to offer him, and for once the stubborn rearing of an argument fails me. I can feel the last bit of strength in my body crumbling away, as if by tearing the sword from my chest, Thaddeus has ripped a hole into my soul.

"I cannot …" I gasp for a solid breath of air, find it, and finish. "I cannot go on like this."

"Of course you can. Everyone does," he dismisses.

"No," I shake my head. "It's asking too much."

"There are others who've had it far worse than you," he tells me flatly. "At least you've a roof over your head."

"That won't stay," I say softly. "Eventually. Money won't find itself. I have no way to pay Percy Davies back. I have … I'm trapped if I stay—"

"You've nowhere else to go."

"—and I'm alone."

"You've us," he repeats, echoing what he said at Father's funeral. "And if you leave, do you think you'll be less alone?"

He's so correct I cannot answer. Staring hard at the sword, and my half-carved designs, Thaddeus finally sighs and places the weapon on the tinner's bench, where the silver glints and winks in the dim light.

"Don't be so quick to give it up."

"Quick? I've been alone for months!" I want to laugh, and the sound comes out brittle and bitter. "But don't worry. I can't really leave. I don't have the cash. I'm stuck here, wallowing in debt for the rest of my days, surrounded by nothing but flowers and blasted chickens and empty air. I've only the metal." I wave my hand. "And what the hell am I supposed to do with that?"

"Impale yourself?"

I flinch, but Thaddeus doesn't seem to care. He stands over me, his arms crossed, his beard and hair blending with the black of the night, his eyes a hard glitter against the faint fire and single lantern.

"That's what you were doing," he accuses. "Isn't it?"

I fold my lips over my teeth, pressing my hands deep into my skirts to keep the trembling at bay. Hunching my shoulders, I curve into my own body, hoping I can keep in my tumultuous sobs until he leaves me be.

"*Isn't it*, Marya?" He's shouting now, his words almost as sharp as the sword. "You've given up, have you? Think it's worth the sin? You've nothing left, is that it? The talent in your hands, the business you've built, nearly single-handedly—that's not enough? Who are you trying to be? What else are you hoping to prove?"

"Go away, Thaddeus," I tell him suddenly, knowing if he continues I'll be weeping in front of him and unable to stop. This is nothing like when I stood at the precipice of Father's grave.

This is harder and deeper and darker.

His anger washes over me, as palpable and thick as ever. He spins on his heel, his boot grinding into the dirt of the floor, before turning back and grabbing the sword up in one huge hand.

"Hell if I'm leaving this here with you," he growls, and marches out into the night. By the time the back door of the Salomon house slams, my eyes are scratchy and dry and tearless.

Sleep fails me. The night insects sigh and chirp and sing a tune with the prairie grasses. The wind picks up sometime around midnight, seeping through the handful of cracks around the door and window, eddying in swirls along the floor, pulling up the old smells of stale and earthy musk.

Who am I trying to be?
What do I hope to prove?

I've always thought someday I'd be like Mother. If I tried hard enough and remembered her properly, I'd be just like her. Bright, vivacious, and beautiful. Sparkling and charismatic, brilliant and strong. I'd be able to spin a soup, cook a goose, and have dozens of friends. I'd have a love as deep and honest as she shared with Father. Something joyful and solid and real.

It doesn't matter.
I'm nothing like Mother.
I'm something else.

I must sleep, but it certainly doesn't feel like I might. Tossing often, I wake myself each hour until I find the churned blankets unbearable. The room is empty, a cavern of dust. The barren beds of my brothers lie flat and cold, Father's is wrinkled but lonely. And I'm lonely. And lost. And a failure at everything I touch except the metal. I might have to give that up, too, if Danny takes me. And then I'll be a wife, and will have to do everything I cannot do well.

Getting up and yanking on my clothes in the dark, I stalk into the tinshop, lurking like I used to when the boys would be asleep.

The burin gleams on the tinner's bench, catching the bits of moonlight. The end is duller now than it first was, but it is still sharp enough.

Will I be banished to hell?

Will it be cold if I use the tempered iron to rip open my veins?

Picking it up, I test the weight of the metal tool and place the end against the delicate flesh under my wrists, where there are no scars and the skin is unbroken and a soft white-gold. I can trace the rivers of blood underneath, visible even in the rusty orange of the low brazier coals. They are a deep purple-blue rippling up toward my elbow.

Will it hurt?

Pressing carefully, I draw a straight line, and the metal scratches across my flesh, not quite drawing blood. The coldness of the iron screeches through my body.

Dropping the burin, I shake my hands fast, willing them to warm. They are like ice and my body is a flame all at once. *Stop!* I must stop! I must get out of the house, and away from the tools.

I go outside into the chill of the fall morning. Father's grave is just visible, and when I kneel there, the old sorrow rises. It is a slow, wide bubble, forcing itself out until the cry releases. Draping my limbs across the dirt, I wish I could feel him hug me back.

Who would have suspected me to be a metalsmith? I'd started the trip to the Territory with a broken machine, but now it's me who is broken.

I'm sorry, Father! Mother—I want to give up!

Would I use the sword now? If Thaddeus had left it, would I slice my veins open and let myself go onto the earth, soaking it with my life, and letting the troubles slip away?

Do I really want to give up? Has my stubborn will left me, finally?

The sobs wrest themselves out of my body, painful and wretched.

Oh God! What do I do now?

What should I try next? I cannot think past this moment, this morning. The darkness is close, wrapping itself around me as thickly and thoroughly as death, overwhelming and choking and complete.

If I stop now, if I simply lie here, will anyone notice? Will they come and pick me up, and care for me? Would Danny think I am insane, or would he cradle me up and tend to my broken spirit?

"You're so loud I can't hear myself."

Once again, my emotions are harshly interrupted. Thaddeus stands in the barn doorway across the yard, his hands covered in manure and grime. The pinpricks of light from the barn lantern reveal his frown.

"Damn you!" I pull myself up to my knees. I expect to feel embarrassed again, but after the previous night, I don't know if I can this morning. "Can't a woman mourn in peace?"

"If she's quiet about it."

When I stand fully, the chickens suddenly scatter from the barnyard, spooked from their roost earlier than normal. The two biggest make a line for my shoes, their beaks lowered. Filled with frustration, I take a swing with my foot, catching one under the neck, hearing the crack as the body flies, flopping and shivering, into midair.

"I hate these damn *kurczaki*!"

Thaddeus is silent, watching the bird flip about and wobble its death throes until it stops. I am shaking as well, my hands quivering so violently I think the tremble will work its way through my whole body.

"I can't do this, Thaddeus," I say quietly. "I want to stay a smith, but I can't see how to make it work."

"So marry Danny," he shoots back, still immobile, still holding the lantern up so the light dimples on the ground, like golden pricks of starlight on the old grass. "And all your problems will be solved."

"No, they won't. And besides, Danny hasn't asked."

"It's better than using the sword to end it. *Jezus*, Marya." He shakes his head. "I'm afraid to give it back to you."

"I've settled," I promise him, realizing as I say the words that somehow they're true. "I don't know what I'll do, and I can't keep going like this, with all the debt, and all alone. But you needn't be worried about it."

He snorts and shakes his head again.

The embarrassment finally floods back, and I wonder what I might have done had he not entered the shop and stopped my dark thoughts. Warm relief and soft release ebb into my chest, and I look up at Thaddeus and smile.

"You seem to always catch me at my worst."

"I do."

"And yet you're still my *na*—friend." Another word nearly trips over itself to be said, but I manage a tamer one.

"I am."

"I suppose I should help with chores."

"You should." He stands aside from the barn door, swinging the lantern so I might pass first. As I head into the building, and the odor of musty straw and old hay fills my nose, Thaddeus glances back into the yard.

"Chicken for dinner today, then."

My laughter comes without warning, bursting out like a shot. It is nearly hysterical, but needed. I think I see Thaddeus grin under his beard, and goodwill swims in my chest. He is good-looking when he smiles. I wish he'd do it more often.

Yet his silence about my dark, unhappy moments is both a comfort and a sadness. It reminds me, once more, of my loneliness.

Najdroższy, I'd nearly called him. *Dearest.*

CHAPTER THIRTY-ONE
25 October 1867

"Marie!" Harry Turner greets me expansively, his eyes taking in my raggedy day dress. "What can I do for you?"

"A cone of sugar, for starters." I gaze up at the bolts of cloth. I can't truthfully afford anything, but I need leather for a larger apron. Sometimes Harry trades with the Sioux when they come through to visit Esther Flies-With-Hawks, Percy's lover, and then Harry has different hides for sale. This time of year, I'm in luck, but I've no money and hardly a shred of credit left.

"Been working along on the sword, I hear," he mentions off-handedly when I gesture for him to fill my sugar order.

"As I can."

He pulls the sweet over, but his bushy white eyebrows are still up. "Did you hear about Morten Henderssen?"

"No."

"His teeth have turned black! Doc Gunnarsen says he can pull them all, but old Mort went and hid. They found him two days later in a foxhole!"

"Ah."

"And you know Matthew Winters is re-opening the mess hall? I heard that his sister-in-law Doris has her sights set on Tommy Winters, but I say she's her work cut out for her for all she's a seasoned widow. It's her long face that does it, and Tommy's set on trying to be a cowboy, but if he'd pay more attention to his riding instead of his mustache designs, he'd get somewhere, don't you think?"

"Well, have you met Tilly and Eva Rose yet? Fortuna brought them in when she was buying flasks."

Harry shoots a sideways glance at May and clears his throat. "Ah, no. No, I have not been to Fortuna's *Powdered Rose*, nor met any of her girls. No, not at all. Never plan to, either. I've got me a wife, of course. No need for a brothel."

He stops his gossiping, though, and I can look over the goods in peace and quiet.

Harry binds up my purchase, marking it down in his great book on the counter. Watching my line of credit embed itself deeper is painful, but I gulp down the sourness in my gut.

As I walk out of the general, I nearly run into Danny. The soft package almost tumbles out of my arm. He catches it speedily, and tucks it under his elbow.

"Marie! I was going to meet you after I ran into the mercantile, but I'll take the opportunity to walk you home now," he says warmly.

"Fine then," I say, as if I am actually offering him permission, though we both know I wouldn't refuse him anyway.

We walk companionably. There's no use in having a private conversation along the soft dusty road, as we are constantly hailed from both sides. Sadie sweeps her front porch in the hopes of seeing passersby and to show off her early belly curling with pregnancy, and Doug Ofsberger the postmaster sits outside the office and shouts to anyone who has mail. Mrs. O'Donnell is working to manage her yard weeds by the fence with unusual zeal, and Elaine Warren is arguing so loudly with Toot she seems about to break the windows of the Rusty Nail.

"You've been well since I last saw you?" I finally ask Danny.

"Well enough," he nods. "And you too?"

"Yes, of course."

It's not a long walk to the tinshop, and when we arrive, he pauses at the threshold. I turn to look at him, waiting for him to follow me in. He does after a moment, and just like that, the world turns and tilts, with the ground tipping under my feet.

Change. It hovers around him and folds me into it. Before I can catch a breath, both his hands grab mine, and we stand hand-fasted in the middle of the shop.

"Marie, I ask this as it's in my heart. There's no reason to wait any longer. But—will you be mine? Marry me, be my bride, the woman of my home. I love you, truly, and I believe you feel affection for me, too. Will you?"

The words are rushed, his wide eyes brimming with hope, and his open face is strained with it. The relief that comes with the long-awaited proposal shocks me in its plainness.

So it is done. Finally. My answer sits on my lips, more a reaction than a true thought or decision, and with my pause, I find new, unexpected words.

"You want me to be your bride. What do you mean?"

He looks surprised, and his fingers tighten.

"Just that, of course. That you'll come home with me, and be mine. A wife. A mother. What else do you think?"

My eyes cast about the shop. The tin sparkles in the slant of light, and the copper is radiant in the shadows like small fires. This place—my trade—has been the strongest thing in my life since coming west.

"I wonder about this."

Danny follows my gaze. "Well, it's on my family property. I suppose you could leave it here if the shop is so sentimental, but likely my father will want to rent it, or use it, or tear it down, eventually. Perhaps he'll still sell to the railroad."

Percy would be absolutely livid.

"Who will take care of all the tinkering then, if I should stop the trade?" I wonder, finding jealousy tint my words at the imaginative specter of the tradesman who will replace me.

"Oh, probably Thad, as he used to." Danny's own voice starts to harden. I am sure he did not expect his proposal to be met with discussion or logistics or my worries and questions. If that is so, he does not know me well.

"That doesn't seem fair to ask of Thaddeus. He's alone now, not like it was when we first arrived in Flats Town."

Danny sighs, but he does not release my hands. I try to meet his blue eyes, but he casts about the shop, trying to stem the questions I shoot at him.

"Marie, honestly. It will work out. And I know you have debts, but I can help you settle them. And you might sell the tools. They are very valuable."

The notion that I'd rid myself of the machines my family painstakingly brought out west, that I oil with care every day, that were bought with my mother's money, snaps me out of my mulling.

"Suppose … well."

"Well what?" He leans in, his eyes suddenly bright again. "What can I do?"

"It's awkward, but I might like to tinker. I mean, I like to do the tin work, and the copper. Suppose I … I still work on it?" How am I daring to ask this? It is not what a woman would want, but it is something I must ask. I don't even know what I am asking of him, only that I cannot answer him without saying something about my craft, and the hard-won trade.

His smile is soft. "You like to make the pretty things?"

"No. I mean, yes, I do like to make the metal shine and beautiful designs. I like the job. I'd miss it."

"It's served you well," he agrees. "But you'll be married."

The final, genuine dismissiveness, gently offered, slaps me. The answer has come, though I do not understand it myself. I think I've known it for months, though I could not have said so until just now.

"So I'd not be working the metal?" I have to hear him say it again, my heart thumping ever harder and louder and quicker. "I'd give it up."

"Of course, my dear," he says, nodding twice, his finger pads softly circling the hard ridges of scars on my palms. "A married woman doesn't do a trade like this. But you know that. And you know the machine sales would help with your debt. You wouldn't be coming to the marriage so beholden." This part is true; he knows me enough to know how much such a debt would rub me raw.

I pull my hands out of Danny's, and he strings tight and wary. He backtracks quickly, looking extremely anxious.

"You don't have to sell them, of course. You won't need money once we're married, Marie. I can provide more than enough for you and any children."

"I'll not sell them," I say. "Who would buy them around here anyway?"

"Of course. You're right," he soothes, but the damage is done.

Is there a way to be soft about it? It's foolish of me to deny him, and I swallow the fright that comes with saying what I must, as it closes my chance at finding a husband and cancelling my debt.

"Danny, I want to stay a smith. I'm no good at the hearth, and I believe we would be unhappy."

My eyes go once more to all of the metal surrounding us. There are the ponderous machines, with their wheels and gears, and the brilliancy of the plates and sheets waiting for me to spin and curve to life. I've found a sense of self here, and I do not really need a husband to take care of me. I only need to pay my debts. It is a lonely choice, to be sure, but I would crave creativity each day I stirred soup and weeded a garden and chased children.

"My love isn't enough?" Danny stares, his own unhappiness dragging at his face and weighing on his shoulders.

My gut wrenches. It gives me no pleasure to hurt him, to serve him a dose of sorrow. But I cannot lie about what I want—or don't want, in this case. How can I tell him that in the dark of night, when a sword was pressed against my ribs, I understood how I must find my own way? I will not insult him by giving any sort of false hope. I won't marry him for money and nothing else. He deserves better. And I want something more from a match.

Working with my hands gives me strength. Danny cannot know that by asking me to marry him, I'd lose the last bit of familial identity I have left. He doesn't realize I cannot wed him if it means leaving the one thing that makes me feel like a person. The one thing in life that comes easily to me.

"Your love is more than enough for any woman," I reason. "But I'm not really a usual type of woman. I'm a smith. And I'm not going to marry someone I ..." It would be too much to tell him I do not love him back. He is hurting enough.

And I might love him in some way, but I love my work more, and the freedom it affords. I like having an identity beyond the stove of a woman's world, for all the hardships I face, and the ones yet to come. Marriage is not enough.

"You won't leave this?" he asks again, looking bewildered.

"Don't ask me to leave what I've built. To let go of my family's legacy. To leave all of myself behind." I gesture with my arm to encompass the whole of the tools and machines.

He looks about too, as if he cannot believe what he is hearing, as if the shop is somehow now his enemy for my affections. He doesn't understand. I see it in every fiber of him, but I cannot erase it by promising more than I can give.

Somehow, in odd, horrible twists of fate, I have more choice now than I have ever had before.

"You're sure, then? You won't marry me?"

"No. I'm sorry, Danny." My voice is so soft I am not sure he hears me, but he must, because he spins away and leaves me standing alone in the shop once more.

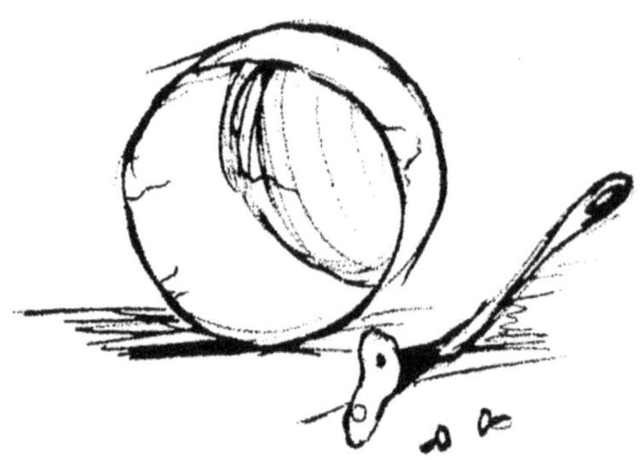

CHAPTER THIRTY-TWO
27 October 1867

With the design sliced into both sides, I must press the tin inside the cavities. If I've done it well, and the dovetailed cuts are proper, the tin will bury itself inside the carving. But if something's off or wrong, it'll show up at once.

Can I manage it if I fail at this once more?

I stare at the long slim metal. Do I melt the tin first, or just hammer it in? If I melt the tin and apply it hot, will I lose the temper of the sword's steel? What if the heat discolors the steel? It would be marred completely once more, and I cannot bear the thought of having a third made on account of my ineptitude.

I pull out a stick of pure solder, and remember flux at the last moment. If I plan to heat it at all, it will need the rosin to melt into any last remaining bubbles of air. But how do I make sure no rosin gets anywhere but in the thin decorative swirls, exactly where I want it?

It's foolish of me to try this alone, but I don't have Father to guide me, and Walter has exhausted his technical knowledge on engraving steel and meshing soft and hard metals together.

There's Thaddeus, of course, but I've been avoiding him whenever I might since he seems to befuddle me each time we work on the sword. Sometimes he is kind and reasonable, and other times so gruff and hard I want to cringe.

I hover for a long moment between decisions before finally taking up the warm woolen cloak Danny gave me last year and hiking across the crusty yard. The property is strangely quiet, unearthly so, and I wonder at it briefly before opening the door to the Salomon house.

Walter is at the fireplace putting in logs, and Berit hums and she starts the midday meal. Sometimes I try to pay for dry goods from Harry Turner's store, and sometimes Walter lets me, though I think he does not wish me to do so. He understands, perhaps, that I am trying to rescue my pride for all I can't afford it.

"I need—I mean, I'm looking for Thaddeus," I say, announcing my arrival at the back door.

"Go on through. I think there's a customer or two from the voices, but he's in the forge anyway," Berit offers, smiling warmly at me.

I walk through the familiar space, but pause on the edge of the door. What if it's Danny in the forge, visiting Thaddeus about another horse that needs shoeing? Or Lieutenant Balsam asking about the sword?

And then there is my own irrational reaction to Thaddeus himself, magnified by my deliberate separation from him over the past weeks. We have not had any other projects to work on together save the refitting of iron handles to some copper cookware Toot Warren needed repaired. And that was done efficiently, with sparse words. The silence I've stretched does not seem to bother him, and I'm both grateful and hurt by his reaction to my quiet.

Well, it serves the purpose I wished. I want to be able to pretend, at least, that I do not see him for more than what he has always been: a gruff, irritable friend and fellow tradesman.

By the silence in the room, it's apparent Walter and Berit note my pause. She stops stirring and waits for me to go through or speak.

"Marie? Is everything alright?"

"Yes," I say. "Of course it is."

Walking into the smithy, I don't let the door bang wildly, as I know he does not like to be interrupted in the middle of working iron. And working it he is. Tim the farrier waits for a set of shoes, and it looks as though Thaddeus is on the last one.

"How goes it, Marie?" Tim calls from across the room.

"Well enough," I say, taking an edge of the wall where I can be out of the way.

"Nearly done," Thaddeus says.

There is no rushing the work, though, and at least a quarter hour passes before Tim departs with his four shoes.

"What do you need, Marya?" Thaddeus's voice is calm and plain.

"*Usługa. Help.* I'd like your thoughts."

At this, he swings around to look at me, surprise inching across his face and body all at once. "Help with what? What can you possibly need from me?"

The bite in his words aches and binds my breath for a moment, shooting spikes of fizzling tightness across my ribs. He is so angry sometimes, an anger that sits just below his characteristic crustiness.

"I need help with the damn sword," I say. "I have ideas on how to press in the tin. Heat? Hammering? Both? In what order? I don't want to ruin your sword. I wanted to check once more."

He considers, rubbing his hands absently on the leather edge of his apron, then finally sighs and nods.

"Very well." He gestures that we should go out, and we do, walking as though we are on a funeral march, trekking across the strangely silent stretch of yard. I glance up, once, wondering if it's the quiet before a fall storm, but I cannot tell.

When we get to the tinshop, we go over the options once again. We consider cutting the rosin with whiskey to let it run into the crevasses, and I wonder how hard I should hit into the steel. I list my worries and my contradictory notions. Thaddeus listens without saying a word, picking up his work once again and checking its weight and balance.

"Even pure bars of tin need to be probably melted down," I finish. "And then hammered. Maybe."

Thaddeus looks cross. "Then hammer it in, Marya. Heating the sword won't work. The iron will pull the warmth off, which you'll need to keep the tin running. I think it's supposed to be pounded in from the start."

"Fine."

"Just fine?" he wonders. "No argument?"

"Should there be?"

He studies the sword again, then sighs and rises to his full height. "I expected more. What is it? Are you so worried about your work?"

"No. I'm not concerned. I just wanted to make sure to get a final opinion." If I do the decorations properly, I will not fail, and the saber will be even more beautiful than the original.

My eyes trickle down the line of the weapon, as if filling in the silvery tin by willpower alone. When Thaddeus taps my shoulder, it makes me jump.

"You won't be using the sword to end things, will you?" he asks gruffly. "I can trust you not to—"

"Damn it, I said I was settled there," I tell him shortly, unnerved by his reference to my moments of weakness. "You don't have to worry."

Thaddeus considers me, and I let myself meet his eyes briefly, the shock of their greyness sending shivers down my ribs. When he leans over to check on the design near the saber's hilt end, his chest and arm press into my back briefly. I am so taken with his closeness, it is as though I burn for it. I have not much before, and never like this. His nearness is extraordinary and tainted with sharpness and rejection.

"You've gooseflesh. How can you be cold?" He glances at my hands and forearms, white and striped with scars.

"It must be a draft."

He stares at me as though I am mad. "You are not unwell, are you?"

Desire courses through me. It is consuming and criss-crosses my breathing and my mind. "No, I'm not poorly," I reassure him instead.

"I've been thinking on your problems," he says,

suddenly. "The debt and loans and the like. As you were saying that night. The one you don't like to speak of."

I shrug. "What of it?"

"Well, I thought on how you hate the chickens so much." He digs into the deep pocket of his pants and pulls out a handful of shinplasters. "So I sold them. They were nearly past their laying time, anyway. Ornery bastards, the lot. Father and I can get pullets in the spring."

My mouth falls open as he places the squares of fractional currency on the tinner's bench. They flutter slightly, like colored, inky snow. Before I can form words, he dives into his other pocket, pulling out another pile of notes, a mix of legal tender and one greenback.

"What else did you sell?" I ask, finally finding my voice. "The cow?"

"I didn't sell anything else," he says testily. "It's Jimmy's pay. Finally. And back pay. I figure he'd want me to use it—give it—to you. Is it enough?"

The last name I expect to hear is Jimmy's, and it takes the air out of my lungs. Looking up at Thaddeus, the only emotion surging through me in this moment is how I want to grasp him near, to feel his strength, to offer my gratitude, to share my heady relief.

"It's Jimmy's?"

Thaddeus raises his eyebrows. "That's what I said."

"But—so the Army finally followed through on this? On his money, at least?"

"Obviously. To hell with all your wondering. Count it. Does this cover your damn debt?"

I pick up the papers, shuffling them, running the numbers through my mind and turning them over. "It covers most of it. The rest of the lumber loan, and a little over half of what I owe the bank for the months of rent."

Thaddeus inhales softly. "Well, it's something, then."

"You don't need any of Jimmy's money?"

"No. He'd want you to have it. I'm sure of that. So, now I can sleep knowing you won't be driving this sword into your belly. You can be settled, as you say."

I crush the money in my hands and then put it back on the wide bench next to the sword. If I could, I would kiss him for his sweetness. I'd like to think he's right. Jimmy would wish to take care of me. To be free of over half my loans from the bank solidifies my resolve. I will get out from under Percy, from my debt, from the Svendsens.

I can. I will. *I must.*

"Thank you, Tadeusz," I finally tell him, mustering as much emotion behind the words as I dare. "I feel very fortunate."

He nods briefly, dismissively, and moves toward the door. "Well then. So. You'll be finished with the sword soon. I'll send word to Fort Randall with David Fawcett." He gestures to the saber. "You did very well, Marya. It is lovely." He looks at me fully and completely. Perhaps he is surprised I have managed to make it this far with both the trade and the sword.

"Yes. I mean, thank you. Again."

As he leaves, I call out, feeling I should say something. Anything. *Encouragement.* That's what Anette would tell me to do. Give him something.

"I will be sorry that we no longer have an excuse to work together."

He swings around at my voice. "Why would we not? We are both a *kowal smith* in our own right. The sword is not the last project." A glimmer of humor flashes across his face. "You cannot be rid of me so quickly."

He leaves for his own forge, likely to make sure the coals don't go out with the early winter chill that creeps in the night's shade. I can breathe again with the solitude and stare at the money. It heartens me to see it, as if it offers me a new way out, new ideas, plans, notions.

Thank you, Jimmy. I say the blessing over and over. *Thank you.*

And what of Thaddeus? His kindness overwhelms me, even as he only means it in the way a brother might care for a sister in need. If I were to spill my yearning to him, would that make it all easy between us? Surely not. Besides, what will I say? That I find his friendship to be everything I want in a husband? That I wish his hand would crush me and the heat of his body cover mine? But it's not for me to chase. I have chosen to be the town tinsmith, to deny Danny marriage, and with that comes other consequences. Such desperate thoughts, I tell myself, such lonely ones. It is just my tired sadness that aches for something—someone, anyone—to fix it. Time will make it fade, and it would be foolish to speak. In the meantime, I must cover my fingertips with tin and finish what is started.

CHAPTER THIRTY-THREE
1 November 1867

"You should go, truly, Marie," Berit urges. She ladles a hearty fall soup onto my deep dish. It smells wonderful. Sometimes I try to remember the spices and herbs and garden pieces she adds, so I might recall how to cook it for myself when I ask for her empty house.

"I'm not sure I should," I say, stabbing at the carrots in the mix.

"Didn't Danny ask you?" Thaddeus asks around a mouthful.

"He did." I fill my own mouth so I am not required to elaborate.

No one seems to know I have refused Danny, and for some reason I have no inclination to tell them. Perhaps because it seems as though it never really happened. I had imagined his proposal for so long that it was otherworldly when it occurred.

Or maybe it is because I do not want to expose yet another area of life where I have failed.

300

"Well, I can walk you," Thaddeus offers. "I'll go, too. The Brinkley boys will be there. One of the new cowboys is all citified and supposed to have quite a horse, and I want to get a good look at him."

"The horse or the cowboy?" Berit quips.

"Both," he says. "See if I have another fat Easterner who will need a lot of orders."

"I thank you for your offer, Thaddeus," I say. "But I should really stay home and work."

"There's plenty of time for working," Berit determines. "You go. We're all going, in fact, as I've promised to take over some foodstuffs."

"We are?" Walter looks at her, surprise written across his raised brow. She nods at him, eyes bright and matching his, as though they have a secret language only they can hear.

"Yes, *min kjære*. Just a short time. It's nice to see everyone, and the family, too. Anette and Jacob will be there, as well as a few of the others you know, Marie," she cajoles.

"I am apparently going to go to the harvest dance," I sigh. "And will see the Army." I shudder. Will Percy be there as well? All my tormenters in one place?

"Why don't you go home and finish up? Then you'll have time to prepare for tonight," Berit says, pulling my empty plate toward her on the table. "Go on then."

I go, and I spend the rest of the afternoon fretting about the dance. I don't want to see Captain Bush or Lieutenant Balsam or any of the Army officers for that matter. I'm worried Danny will be there, and I'm concerned about doing the square dances instead of the traditional polkas I know well.

But nevertheless, I'm ready when Thaddeus shows up at the door of the shop, looking partially organized himself with a fresh shirt and an attempt to tame his dark beard and hair. He perhaps will always look like a backwoodsman who happens to have a trade, but he is my friend, and I am glad to have him walk me along with Berit and Walter.

As we all stroll along the main road toward the over-large part of street in front of the general, others detach from their homes with lanterns held high. Many I recognize as ones I have made or repaired. It oddly boosts my confidence.

"Do you dance?" Thaddeus asks, drawing me out of my reverie.

"No. That is to say, not well. Nor much," I tell him truthfully.

"You'll be asked by some of the Army men. They're starved for women's company at the Fort," he warns.

"They'll find my company lacking. I'm no good at small talk, or political chatter."

"You're female. That's probably enough."

We arrive at the steep steps of the general, and I look around apprehensively. The dusk is deepening, but the lanterns and torches make for oily puddles of light, so it does not seem nearly as late as it is. There's the air of the festival combined with the relief in getting the harvest in, paired with the coming settle of winter. The sky is smoky and fluffy with clouds, and the wind is slight but cool. I'm glad for my woolen layers.

In the corners of the gloom, two young lovebirds indulge in a full kiss, and I'm reminded of my embraces. First with Jimmy, and then with Danny. Was I a fool to send him away? The young woman melts into her beau in a way I never did.

Trusty Willy starts his fiddle, bendy Ivar Henderssen twangs his jaw harp, and Doc Gunnarsen himself takes up the banjo, and they all start in with an old song.

I go into the fray, and the commotion overwhelms me. Army uniforms dominate the visual, and skirts whirl to the beat immediately.

Come all girls, pay attention to my voice
Don't you fall in love with the Kansas boys.
For if you do your fortune it will be
Hoe-cake, hominy and sassafras tea!

Berit delivers her foodstuffs and is captured by the chatter of the townspeople. Anette waves vigorously from the table sagging with refreshments where she serves her children sweetened water. Young Mitch Brinkley, gangly at nine, bounces out onto the dance floor with a sweet, plump girl, and I realize it is Alice Winters, Matthew's youngest. Sadie hovers smugly next to Tom Fawcett, and Doug and Nancy Ofsberger fling sweat as they take over the middle of the dance floor with a complicated two-step.

But it's the Army officers and militia causing the most commotion. Those allowed into town from Fort Randall tonight are taking their hours off seriously, and there is beer and liquor flowing as well as a vigorous amount of food digested.

"Eat up, then! And be telling everyone back at your fancy Fort I'm the best you've tasted," Toot orders each young man as he passes by and fills his plate.

"You are, are you?" Horeb hoots. "Are you delicious, Toot?"

"Ain't so." Gilroy Greenman twists Horeb's ear hard and ambles away, but it's enough for Horeb to switch victims.

"Ooo, so it's you who wants a taste, is it Gil?"

"Ain't."

"Been to Fortuna's lately, then?"

"Ain't."

The argument is swallowed by more swarming bodies flowing on and off the roped-off square made for dancing, the stomping of boots, the joyful howling with the music, and the shouts of greeting.

One young man approaches Berit, and she glances at Walter briefly before taking the Army officer's arm. Walter's shaking hands and age likely leave him in no mood to spin around the floor, but he is smiling lightly as he watches his new wife spryly step to the singing tune of Trusty Willy's fiddle.

"So, then, Marya, I suppose I should take you around," Thaddeus says grudgingly, his taciturn mood soured by the fact that he's even at the festivities, let alone following some sort of beholden offer to dance with me.

"You don't have to, if you don't want," I say, just as tightly.

"Well, let's do it and be done," he determines, glancing at his father, who does not seem to notice we are even talking.

I wonder if Walter has said he must make me feel at ease. The idea makes me even more disgruntled.

"Very well," I resign myself to the inevitable, and allow him to take me out to the floor. The tune jostles and shifts, becoming a spinning, familiar ditty, and the couples line up accordingly. Thaddeus sets me up with the women, and takes his place across from me, his bunchy muscles resisting the pull of the melody though everyone else is clapping in preparation. The song picks up and fills feet with the beat, feeding us lines and calls as we go to the old refrain.

As you walk, my dearest dear,
> *and you lend to me your hand,*
We will travel on afar till we reach the better lands.
Till we reach the better lands,
> *till we reach the better lands,*
We'll travel on afar till we reach the better lands.
We'll shoot the buffalo, oh we'll shoot the buffalo,
We'll rally round the cane brake and shoot the buffalo.
The boys will plow and hoe
> *and the girls will knit and sew,*
And we'll all work together wherever we may go,
Wherever we may go, wherever we may go,
We'll all work together wherever we may go.

I concentrate on remembering the steps, and watch the girls around me for cues. I take Thaddeus's hands belatedly and completely fail to master the turns, tripping along stupidly behind the others in my inability to feel the beat to the music.

"Stop fretting. You're making it more difficult than it has to be," he commands, yanking me along as we spin and separate again. The other men are less kind, and toss me around haphazardly as I miss their arms and grasping hands half of the time.

I feel completely out of my element, and long to leave. When Thaddeus is my partner again, there is comfort in his thick hands and his arms around my waist, tucking me tightly next to his own body so our sides and hips bump in passing. It is a strange feeling to be so near him for all he is his usual stoic self. The song finishes, with the last verse teasing all the couples:

And the girls will sew and spin,
              and the boys will laugh and grin,
And will hug and kiss each other,
              and will run away again,
And will run away again, and will run away again,
Will hug and kiss each other and run away again.

The spins at the end are always full of flourish, but Thaddeus is not so flowery. Instead, he holds me near in the last movement of the square dance without dipping or giving a last whirl. I'm grateful. I might trip over my feet doing something so fancy. But instead of feeling my heart slow, I am in no hurry to have him release me. Perhaps it is the comforting smell of charcoal and fire hanging around him. Perhaps it is because I miss having casual, familiar touch. I think I want to push into him, to press my bosom to his chest, and tighten our embrace. His hand lingers—doesn't it? I ask myself the question just as he drops his arms and looks over the sea of heads. He is tall enough that he can see over the masses, and his face changes slightly.

"I see Danny. He'll likely want to dance with you now. Come on. We'll go catch up with him."

"No!"

I don't need to catch his sleeve to stop him. The force of my refusal pulls him up fast.

"Why not?"

"I don't think he'll wish to see me," I admit, finally freeing the secret. Thaddeus continues to look befuddled, and my embarrassment grows when I realize Walter is standing next to us, listening in unabashedly.

"What's happened?" Thaddeus presses.

"Nothing."

"I don't understand women," he huffs, then pushes around the throng, grabbing two cups of ale as he goes, making a direct line to where I must assume Danny is talking on the far side of the group.

I am miserable. I wish to go back to the shop and lose myself in the simplicity of work and of gleaming metal. Walter stares at me, inscrutable and calm as usual.

"Have you and Danny Svendsen had a lovers' quarrel, Marya?" he asks kindly, trying to be fatherly and understanding all at once, which only serves to dismantle my defenses further.

"No, not like that." I shake my head. "We've never been lovers."

"I don't mean of the flesh," Walter says, waving a hand. "Have you had a disagreement?"

"You might say that," I sigh, then decide to finish the story, so I might be done with the conversation. "I refused him. That's all."

Walter's eyebrows go up, and he looks genuinely shocked. "Refused to marry him?"

"What's going on?" Berit arrives, breathless and rosy-cheeked, and I see Walter check at her appearance, made lovely somehow by the glow of the lanterns and leftover laughter.

"Marie was just explaining how she's decided not to wed Danny," Walter says for me, and I'm thankful I don't need to start over. Berit's response is what I expect. She looks both amazed and appalled. Her reaction doesn't help my confidence.

Damn it! Why should I have to marry him? Debt? Should I wed for such a practical reason, and damn my own misgivings? I have no one to ask. No one left to offer advice.

"You've told him you won't?" Berit asks, disbelief creating a higher pitch to her voice. "Or just that you don't wish to marry him soon?"

"I told him I won't. I want to be a smith, not a goodwife," I admit, and look at my scuffed shoes and the worn dress with the holes still gaping from the summer's acid burns.

It's too hard to handle any more of Berit's questions, especially when anyone's ears can overhear. I excuse myself tersely, and head toward the refreshment table. I hope Anette is still there, but she's nowhere to be seen. Instead there are only Percy Davies and Doctor Gunnarsen, speaking earnestly about government politics, it sounds. I ignore them and help myself to a bit of new hard cider, but Percy notices me eventually.

"Miss Marie," he says into my quiet, sliding up like a shadow as Doc disappears into the crowd. His vest is velvet tonight, the buckles of his suspenders peeking out a brushed bronze.

"Good evening," I say, nodding at him, and the dark Indian at his side. She swells with her second child, though her size is hidden with the deer hides she's thrown over her calico dress. Her daughter, eleven, dark-eyed and straight, stands next to her.

The sight of Esther Flies-With-Hawks only reminds me of what her people did to my brothers. I am so often torn by her appearance, ripped by some strange guilt and sorrow at the same time. It is much to pretend to ignore, and leaves me oddly tongue-tied.

"Are you enjoyin' your evenin'?" the banker presses. "You've been doin' alright, alone? I'm sorry I haven't had a moment to stop by lately." He gestures to Esther's belly. "It's been busy all around."

"It's a fine night," I say neutrally. "And I'm doing the best I can."

How I wish I could swallow pride and stubbornness and fall to my knees in front of this man, grip those suspenders and beg. *Please, forgive my family's debts! Cancel my loans! Help me pay for tin for this winter, so I might have enough to make goods in order to pay off those loans! Let me get away from the Svendsens, away from your little scheme, away from the politics! Find me someone from the Army who will give me what I am owed! The blood money of my brothers' service and their deaths. What I will offer you is not enough. Help me!*

If I could even say such things, he likely wouldn't give me my requests. Swallowing hard and pressing my mouth tightly together briefly, I smile instead and latch onto gossip I've heard trickling through my shop. "I thought I heard a whisper, Percy, about the rail being postponed?"

He pulls on his necktie and tugs on the bottom of his vest. "A rumor, and bad gossip at that."

"But is it true?"

"Hard to tell."

"But if it's true, then—"

"Then you'll still owe me for the rent loan, Marie."

"Of course," I snap. "But if there's any inkling old Oddvar isn't going to get a sale anyway from the railroad, I want to get out."

"Out?"

"Out from under his house, his land."

"You have nothin' to use to get out from your debt. You know that," Percy's voice goes hard around the edges.

"I have things."

"You mean assets?"

I grab wildly at the terminology, feeling flustered as always in his oddly charismatic presence. "Yes. Those. If I must … I'll … I'll sell my machines!" I don't mean this at all, but feel I must say something.

Percy's face softens ever so slightly at what must be my obvious desperation. "I have heard whispers of my own. Is it true you and Danny won't wed? It would solve many of your problems, Marie, if you married him."

Good heaven! How does he know our courtship is over? Even Thaddeus and Walter didn't know!

I clear my throat. "He would have married my debt to you."

"But no more rent. He could pay off your loan easily. I know, I see his accounts."

"If there's no rail, and there's no reason to keep me on his land for your own purpose, then—"

"I was thinkin' we'd re-name the town," Percy interrupts. "Flats Junction. When the train comes through."

Esther murmurs something to him, her hand on her rolling, curving stomach; I cannot tell if it is English or her own tongue, and he rounds back to me. "Excuse me, please."

Thankfully, they disappear into the deep dusk. My palms are slick with sweat and old grime. Wiping them on my skirts, I breathe deeply. I'll have to face Percy soon enough. He cannot *make* me stay on the Svendsen ranch, especially if we go over the numbers and he can see that I will never pay off my debt as it is, now that I'm alone. I'll only dig deeper into it. If I'm not going to end it all with a sword, I can at least put my stubbornness to good use. I'll carve my own way. As I have been doing all along, it seems.

As I gaze around, I notice Danny and Thaddeus, somberly buried in beer. What if Danny is airing his grievances about me to Thaddeus? I find myself wishing I could silence it. I cannot, of course, and instead watch with self-conscious interest as they continue speaking. Danny talks fast and low, gesturing fluidly, the liquid in his mug splashing onto his wrist.

Suddenly, they both look my way, their gazes locking with mine. I am stuck, pinned, and must wait until they look away again before I can breathe. Danny gulps down his beer with a single, angry slurp and slinks away.

Have I broken his heart so deeply? Will he forever shove a grudge against me? Will he never look at me with kindness in those blue eyes again? The thought strikes me hard. I suppose that's true.

Remorse tickles at me, but it is not strong enough that I will take a step toward changing what I've told him. At least, not tonight.

I watch the dancing and the skirts, and hear the laughter and the music. My feet start to ache with standing so long. By now I have usually put up my legs after a full day of marching on the shop floor.

Instead, I let the visions wash over me. Fortuna and Dell are drunk, dancing and arguing at the same time, and Sadie has clasped Tom Fawcett to her tightly, her head on his chest. They are completely off the rhythm of the music but don't seem to care. Horeb argues with Gilroy about a lost wager that has something to do with somebody's bosom, and Bess and Franklin Jones are half-hidden next to the livery and her skirt is certainly not where it should be. I grin in spite of myself.

"Marie! I'll dance with you the next one if you've a wish!" Harry Turner calls out as he whirls past with May, and Doc Gunnarsen stumbles through the dancers with an entire bottle of whiskey in his hands. Toot Warren chases him and Elaine chases her. Everyone parts and laughs and then all four Brinkley brothers toss their wives and dance partners to an old jig only they know the steps to, except Young Henry drops his wife Marta just before the Zalenski family shoves them away to show off their own version. Dag Andersen argues with Orville Pavlock about which grain of wood is better to use for cabinet doors and which for boxes, while Nels Henderssen loudly boasts over their chatter about the number of children he and Clara plan to have. Marion Andersen, Dag's wife, catches my eye over Clara's red face, and we both end up laughing so loud that she snorts.

The fiddle and the jaw harp twist the songs and edit them, now missing Doc's banjo twang, the tunes familiar and lively or low and romantic, and suddenly my spirit feels very tired.

I'll sing you a song though it may be a sad one,
Of trials and troubles and where they first begun
I left my dear kindred, my friends and my home,
Across the wild deserts and mountains to roam.

I don't like this particular ballad; it reminds me of death. Perhaps no one will notice if I disappear into the evening.

Taking a step backward, I dig my heel into the hard dirt of the road, but a heavy hand stops me. It is a familiar one, and I sigh to myself before answering for my attempted break.

"I thought I might head home. It's been a long day, and I am not well suited for such—"

"You think I am?" Thaddeus looks incredulous. "Fine then. One more spin and we'll find Father to leave."

He takes me up for the ballad in a loose-armed embrace, his fingers grazing my waist and his face averted. I want to ask him what Danny told him, to explain myself, but he doesn't bring it up or speak of his lengthy conversation with his old friend. The silence balances in between us.

"The song's almost done," I say, grasping desperately.

"I know," he says tersely. "Then we'll finish the next one."

My mouth tightens, and I find I'm unable to fight him. Perhaps tomorrow I will ask him what he thinks I should do about the rest of my debts, my loans, and leaving the property. But then I'll have to explain myself, and why I told Danny I won't wed him. I don't know if I can handle Thaddeus's rancor about my romantic tangles. It's all too new and raw.

The next ballad begins, and I look out across the crowd, letting the patterns of the calicos and the dull leathers of the cowboys and wool of the Army men blur and soften. Somewhere between my daze and the middle of the song, I realize my cheek is only an inch from Thaddeus's chest, and his hands are firm on my hips. He is as calm as always, and he still will not look at me, so I'm not sure if I am the one who drew near, or if he has pulled me tighter.

Many times I have wondered what it would be like to push myself close to the blacksmith. The attraction to Thaddeus, which flickers and ebbs, is unlike Jimmy's fumbling embrace or even Danny's careful and gentle kisses. But I allow myself to grip his shoulders tighter and lean in so that my face just brushes the brown flannel of his shirt. It smells of him and the forge, and I smile. There is comfort here, in the familiarity of him and that he thinks of me as his family.

"There is the last of it," he says, the stanza ending on its mournful refrain. We sway with the rest of them, but he slows. For a moment, we stand still while the others finish the song, and I unwittingly step toward him just as he pulls away and drops his arms.

The loss of his nearness is a slap, and my chest plunges to my feet while chills sweep up my shoulders, freezing them. His refusal, however simply meant, draws me up severely. I look for his eyes, but Thaddeus is already turning away.

"There they are," he says. "We might all leave. It's enough frivolousness for me, anyway."

He stalks off, and I trail him, wondering at my new-found attachment. Likely it is just that he is accustomed to me, and one of the only men who has no qualms to offer me a dance. I am only reacting to the plainness of contact.

We find Walter, who waits patiently next to Berit. She's circled her daughters and daughters-in-law around her and the coiffed and braided heads bob and twitch with words.

"But I told Larry what with him so good at impregnating animals and getting them to mate that he should have expected the same to happen to me!" Grete complains. "I am going to end up with a brood!"

"What's wrong with that?" Anette asks. "It's *fun* to get a brood!"

"Not everyone is as lusty as your Jacob," Mary Andersen giggles.

Anette grins. "No, but thankfully he's mine."

"We're *all* thankful he's yours."

"How is this helping me tell Larry he's not to touch me after this one is born?" Grete wonders, but she's laughing.

Berit laughs too, and links her arm with Walter. The old blacksmith grins around, his cheeks flushed and eyes bright, and then he notices us and nods. I smirk at Anette, but Thaddeus pokes me in the arm.

"What are you going on about?" he asks. "It's not like you can add into the conversation."

"Someday I might."

"How?" he snorts, and his derision strikes my chest hard, choking back any type of joking reply, cutting off my smile.

Does he truly think I'm so unmarriageable?

Walter extracts Berit with surprising speed so we can all walk toward the north edge of town where our smithies and fires sit dark and quiet. Berit talks about the dancing. How it was livelier this year, how there seem to be more of the Army men. She wonders if it means more offensives or more skirmishes. Will they wish for men from Flats Town to build the Fort up? Will it mean more supply trains? That promised railroad? Or is it true it won't come, now?

Walter listens attentively, but doesn't offer much by the way of conversation. I stride next to Thaddeus, trying to match his wide pace.

I need to let myself cool from the heat of our last dance, when somehow my blood and heart seemed to cleave to Thaddeus, if only for a moment. What a silly thing, and impractical too. I've no need for a man as I've said to myself many times these past days, explaining to myself once again why I told Danny no. It's likely my loneliness begging me to think of such things. But it is indeed a strong thing, this attraction blooming and weighing on me. I find my whole body pulling toward him, and I resist the urge to bind my arm in his as we walk. Instead I slow my steps.

It will all pass, same as my interest in Danny and Jimmy. I have my smith work, and a life to build, and a confrontation with Percy Davies to come. There is a sword to finish, and a new house to barter for from Berit.

"Daj spokój! Come on!"

In the dark, I nearly run into Thaddeus as I mull, and I'm at once thankful the night doesn't reveal my bright eyes and flushed cheeks.

He is terse and tetchy at me, so I bite back in the same tone, regardless of my wonderings. "I'm coming!"

His hand clamps on my elbow in a most unromantic way, and we scurry to catch up with his father. At the blacksmith's place, I bid goodnight as quick as I might, and escape to the deep shadows of the tinshop. The stove in the kitchen is still warm. With a fast swirl I light the embers and open the iron door so I have an orange glow to see by.

As I slide under the blankets, I wonder once more what it might be to share a bed with a man. My thought first goes to Thaddeus's powerful frame and the wide smith's chest, but just as quickly I dismiss him. Instead, I focus on Danny, and what it would be to turn back to him, to beg him to take me back. He said he loved me. Would that love be enough? He is handsome, and he is doting, and he is ever so kind about my own needs as long as, it seems, it does not entail smith work. I am foolish to toss his declared affection aside for my pride.

Otherwise this, then, will be my future: a shop, metal that glows, and an empty bed. Is it worth it for the freedom I have now?

Drifting into sleep, I dream as I had hoped. There is a man in the night, bending me into his lap. In my dream, we are in my own private space, sitting on the bench. His urgency is both demanding and desirable, and his hands run up the sides of my skirts, trailing along the untried flesh of my thigh and daring to cup my bare bottom. In the stillness of my imagination, I am firm and sure. I pull on the wooden buttons of his breeches in an act both intimate and certain. In my dreaming, I can glance down at my leg, gleaming white in moonlight, and I see the path of sooty fingertip kisses in the crease of my knee. I bubble to wake, still holding tightly to this fantasy. As I leap into the gentle awareness of my bed, I see the bearded face of the man who holds me, and my heart cracks.

Fatigue is a gift once more, spilling into my mind and giving me respite from my worries. The dream disappears.

CHAPTER THIRTY-FOUR
2 November 1867

When I wake, it is the small hours of the day. Grey, quiet, and chill. The dance feels like it did not happen, though I recall enough of the night to make my cheeks go hot. As I tie on my clothing, there is a knock on the inner door. Someone has entered the shop without my knowing, so I go, expecting Berit.

Instead, it is Thaddeus, and he looks ferocious.

"Come on." He's urgent and brusque, and spins on his heel, leaving me to stand alone in the middle of the shop. "Well, *pośpiech! Come on!*"

"Good morning to you, too," I grouse. "What is it?"

"The damn Army. Come on, Marie. You're dressed. We don't want keep them waiting."

I go out with him mutely, forgetting a wrap in my dizziness, and my breath sucks in at the cold air. We hike around the building with Thaddeus marching ahead of me, fuming and irritable. As we circle to the forge, a babble of

318

voices ebbs and rises higher, Walter's among them. It's early for such heated discussion and for customers.

"I'm back with her. What do you need, now, exactly? And I promise you, it won't be done in the speed you ask." Thaddeus starts to speak as he crosses the threshold into the smithy, where men in uniform wait. My mind starts to clear from the fog of sleep, and my blood starts to thaw and pump overly fast. What now?

"Two weeks, then, at the most," Captain Bush stands in the middle of the forge, where yellow lamps and lanterns blaze already against the morning dim. He has three of his officers with him, including Lieutenant Balsam. Their presence seems to give him additional mettle and prestige, for he puffs his chest as he speaks. "My orders are to move immediately toward Fort Sully before the Missouri thaws, but I won't go back through any part of Indian Territory without the right equipment."

"That's not really Indian Territory you'll travel," Thaddeus counters.

Captain Bush looks smug. "You don't know of all the attacks. The natives have even dared to sabotage the railroads this past fall. We'll need the goods."

"You're asking the impossible," Walter throws his own weight into the discussion. "One smith cannot build what you're asking. And the new wheelwright, and the cooper— you want the whole town to stop everything and help you."

"Well, government's orders," Captain Bush says pointedly.

Thaddeus himself does not sway from standing down Captain Bush, and he crosses his massive arms with irritation. "I will do what I can in two weeks. Pay me for what I do, no more and no less. If you're fortunate, I'll have it all done. If not, you'll likely manage on what I finish."

"Wheels and horse shoes and ammunition," Captain Bush lists. "You won't get paid without any of those, at the very least."

"You shouldn't get any of them at all until you pay for your sword," Thaddeus counters, and Captain Bush loses a piece of his smugness.

"Yes, well. That, too. Too bad there's such a wait, no thanks to you, Miss Kotlarczyk."

The men all round on me, staring as if they have forgotten I am here, and forgotten I am a woman.

Now Captain Bush has me pinned with his crescent eyes. "You'll have to do simple things anyway for us. I'll need a set of spice boxes, and ten tin lanterns, a copper boiler, and two dozen tin cartridge holders. The standard. And the same amount in canteens. Ten mess kits and a half dozen tinder kits."

My mouth hangs open. "In two weeks?"

"At the most," he nods. "And all of it. No shirking on this. The lanterns and the water holders are needed, but the cartridge boxes are essential for our march as well."

"But—"

"It's orders from the government," he reminds, walking out into the cresting morning so we cannot protest further. "Not really mine."

The men file out, and I am filled with both panic and pain, shock and worry. It is too much for a single smith to do with too little time. And in the middle of it is some odd, frozen glee.

This means the end of my debt, if I can finish it all.

If I can finish.

"Marie." Thaddeus plants himself in front of me. "You know they can't make you do anything more than what is possible. If you don't finish it all they'll take what you've done."

"I suppose we should both get our fires lit," I say stoutly, caught in the frenzy of desperate hope and horrible worry piling into my throat, the cords strung tight to hold in the battling emotions. It is all I can do to maintain some dignity.

Thaddeus clears his throat and nods, glancing about the forge. "So then. No time to waste. I'll take stock of the iron I have ready for forming."

"Right," I say, sliding past Thaddeus and out the door, tucking my hands against the freezing wind scuttling across the roads and the open yard between the forge and the tin-shop. My feet crunch on the broken, rutted path and crash on the icy bits of snow.

When I get to the shop, it is still dark against the cloudy morning, and I light the lanterns methodically, stirring up the stove so I might warm the brazier. The straight sheets of copper and tin gleam and shimmer and rattle against the light.

Can I do this? Will I have enough time? Not only to finish the sword, but to manage such an enormous order? My family could have done this, together.

But will *I* be enough?

CHAPTER THIRTY-FIVE
13 November 1867

The afternoon stretches and contracts, and I bend backward from where I crouch over the fine cutting of copper. There is so much of it. My tidy shop is in disarray, covered with projects. Some are fully finished, and some partially so, and others are only traced sheets of metal. There is a method to some of my work. Heating the copper irons, for one, is best done when I can do all the soldering at once, so I must prepare all the copperware at the same time.

To add to my stress, an Army soldier comes around once a day to check on our progress. Captain Bush left Sergeant Ollin in town to keep an eye over all the craftsmen, and he comes gloating and boasting and speaking as if he owns my shop.

I have the door cracked against the sweat running down my back; I stoked the stove against the chill too much. The blacksmith's hammer and bellows cuts through our yard, and the orange blast of the fire Thaddeus stokes seems to spurt onto the street as he labors over the wheel edges he's making.

There is no understanding by the Army that our work takes time. They do not care for the other orders we must put on hold, or the people who must wait for their teapot or their washpans, or the horses needing shoes. They only think of their own order, and every time I list what I still must accomplish, I want to simply sit down and give up.

"And today?"

I jerk, and the end of the snips catches the soft spot of my left hand between forefinger and thumb, and slices into it. I curse under my breath, and yank my hand to my mouth, trying to stop the bleeding as well I might.

It's Sergeant Ollin, his flat, cunning face a mirror of his commanding officer.

"I am making progress, as always." I gesture around with my uninjured hand.

"Very good," he sniffs, then takes it upon himself to step in and handle some of the finished lanterns.

"The longer you loiter, the longer it will take me to do my job," I remind him finally, and he lifts his eyebrows and puts down the tinware.

"*If* you can finish it at all. I think you're missing canteens." He steps up to the counter and lays his elbows on it, looking up over the ceiling and across the machines before sizing me up. I'm glad I am messy and disheveled, and that the apron hides my shape.

He seems to think so too, for after a moment he sighs and languidly, insidiously, slides upright.

"Not worth my time anyway, to idle with you. You're no sweet little lady to brighten my day."

"She's not."

Thaddeus stands at the door, his arms black to the elbows, soot and ash threading through the creases of his pants and rolled shirtsleeves.

"We agree on that, at least, Salomon," laughs my mild tormenter, a conspiratorial, nasty wheeze to his chuckle. He stops when the blacksmith bends himself into the room, towering over him.

"We don't," Thaddeus says. "But she's no sweet girl. You can report back that we are doing as was asked and no less. Good day."

His tone is deep and final and dismissive, and at first Sergeant Ollin draws up, as if intending to pull some sort of rank. Instead he stumps out, injured pride trickling with him.

I look up at Thaddeus as he comes around the corner of the counter and holds out his hand.

"What?" I ask.

"Why are you sucking on your palm?"

"Oh." I pull the flesh out of my mouth again and peer at the slash. "He startled me and I slipped."

Thaddeus glances at his own dirty fingers and drops his outstretched arm.

"Well, that's not so bad. Put a bandage on it."

"Later. Too much to do now." I frown up at him. "And really? I'm 'no sweet girl'? What the hell was that about?"

"The truth," he says shortly. "You're not."

He might be right, but it stings worse than my cut to hear it.

"Is the sword ready?" he asks instead, glancing around.

"Soon."

"Soon, soon, you've been saying that for a while now," he grumbles, and marches back out.

Soon enough I'll have to actually finish it, which both frightens and exhilarates me. Can I trust myself to do the final touches? Will I be able to succeed or fail?

The question swirls around my head and I realize the lateness of the hour when I light the lanterns. It's nearly dinner time, and I still have so much to do. Fairly running across the yard, I send a thought of thankfulness for the lack of chickens and stick my head through the back door.

"I won't be eating," I say in general, and three heads spin to look at me.

"You're burning through enough candles already," Thaddeus accuses. "And you need some food. Everyone needs food."

"I am supposed to finish it all. I want to try."

"Not if it means you'll get ill," he pushes back. "Then how will you spend the next days? Not soldering, but in bed."

"Do you think pressing me will make me change my mind?" My feet tap with impatience.

"When it matters, I would expect it to do that."

"Thad, you know how stubborn I am."

"You don't need to remind me."

"Two more long nights," I mutter into the room. "Two more and then … maybe." My eyes go dark as I see the items I must yet finish in my mind, building and spinning into existence if only I could get to them. The darkness wavers, and I look up, blinking. It's only Thaddeus, though, up and standing directly in my vision, shielding me from the kitchen's buttery light. He seems overly annoyed.

"What are you trying to prove?" He is almost hissing.

"You've done it already. You're the smith for Flats Town and for over a hundred miles in any direction. There's nothing more you need to do. Finish what you can."

His words are jarring, and I jump to remind him of my reasons for pushing limbs and hands past my usual. "There's no payment without the work complete. I need the money, to finish my debt. You heard his threats."

"You have Jimmy's pay," Thaddeus reminds.

"It's not enough. Not at all."

There's no answer from him, so I turn around and go back to the shop, my chest aching. I dislike being at odds with Thaddeus, for so many reasons they choke me. And I don't like the notion that he plants, that I might not finish, and the order unfilled.

The night inches along, tearing at the edges of my vision and creating a fuzziness to the corners of my fingers. I get clumsier and clumsier as the time oozes past, and it is only after I burn myself on the edge of the brazier for the fifth time that I realize I'm trying to solder half asleep.

I cannot give up yet. If I stop now, I will fail …

I will fail!

The thought, constantly wavering in the dank corners of the shop, leaps up at me in the dark.

I might fail. I likely will.

Suppose I make a mistake? Have to start over on a whole batch? Break a tool?

I should have known my life was still broken. My foolishness from the start, for handling the damn burring machine and dropping it, has cursed me. I am nothing. Not a successful smith, not out of debt, not able to do anything right enough to matter.

I need this Army money. I desperately, horribly need it. It is a windfall of cash, a huge order that will give me my future back. I will be able to wash myself of Percy's overhanging presence, leave Danny's land, and find a new start.

Free, and alone. If I finish.

If.

The *if* suddenly seems impossible and improbable and immovable. If I finish? Of course I won't. It doesn't matter how much I need the cash, or the completed sword, or the prestige it will bring me. Not one person cares about whether this all comes together for me. I am alone in this, just as in everything else. The bottom of my stomach goes hollow, and a weight drops from my hips to the floor, yanking me downward to the dirt and darkness below, snarling back up to hit and blind me.

What am I doing? What am I proving? What will be enough?

It will never be enough.

I will never finish in time. Of course I won't. It's an outlandish expectation, a goal so high and unbelievable, I cannot fathom how I ever thought I'd manage.

The sword is too tricky, the Army order too large, the orders not enough, the debt too great.

Another hour passes and the first of the morning light grows through the eastern window. My eyes are crusty and dusty with sand and metal fumes. I grip the burin tightly to trace the next pattern out. The lack of sleep, the awfulness of my reality, the loneliness of my days and nights, all boil together to remind me of my failings. I don't know if I will ever make enough pots and pans to cover the holes in my heart, and to make me worthy of the craft and solid enough with my bearings.

If I am careful, I can get at least two canteens on one sheet of hot dip tin, and the small pieces out of the scrap. I twist the pattern again and finish the first twelve tracings and pinch my forehead, wishing I had better light. There is just enough of the early light to reflect against the bright edge of the tool in my hand.

The point of it is silver and bright, and suddenly, without pausing to consider, I draw the end of it against my flesh, ripping against the softness between my elbow and wrist, yanking the metal into the skin and pulling hard.

It's numb.

Staring at the deep red of the line, I watch the tiny beads of blood slowly grow, turning dark and blackish and thick as the moments slide by. It doesn't hurt, or tingle, or even sting.

What had I been so afraid of?

The next line is deeper than the first, and the blood comes faster. If I continue, if I go even harder into my skin, will it all end?

I'm nearly at the end, anyway. I wasn't enough to keep my family together. To save Mother or Father. To protect Al. To be the right wife for Danny. And I certainly am not enough for Thaddeus. Why not be done? I won't finish in time, and I'll never be free of the failures of my family. The sword will rust away, and likely be the better for it. At least I won't ruin it …

Another pull.

Another line of blood.

It pools and runs, shimmying onto the dirt of the floor and disappearing into the black ripeness of the earth.

I'm not enough. For anything or anyone.
Not enough.
Not good enough.

A fourth line matches the others in length, but the deepness is such that the thump of my heartbeat is visible. Each time my heart goes, so too does the line of bleeding. The redness is deep and ruby and opaque.

How long does it take for lifeblood to leave? How long before I see Mother again?

The force of the metal inside the rim of my flesh is almost satisfying. I deserve it. This is not a sin. It is rightful punishment. It is justified that I weep blood this way.

As I place the tip at the edge of my wrist, the throbbing begins. It thrums and pumps with the rhythm of my life, suddenly so loud I think it will drown my hearing.

What am I doing?

What the hell am I doing?

Mother ... she would be so disappointed in me. Not for my smith work, but for this. For this weakness.

Mother ...

What had Father said, once? It had slid over my ears and never settled into my body.

She would be proud.

Of me. The smith.

Would she really?

Oh God, maybe. Maybe she would be.

I want to believe it. I want to believe she would be so proud, that Father and the boys would be, too.

Another spurt of my heart, and the blood splatters onto my shoe.

What am I doing!

Gasping, grasping for a resin-sodden towel, I cover the telltale lines and run toward the door, hoping the cold of the morning will catch me before I fall into madness. I have to stop now or the next slash of metal will finish me. And I am the smith. I have work to do. Is this insanity? Grief? Sorrow? The darkness of night, the crazed end of endless hours of soldering? Have the fumes choked my mind?

I breathe in the air, quivering.

If I turn now and look at the burin, I will use it again. I cannot. Must not!

It would be the end. The next cut …

My fingers are shaking, almost violently, and I curl a hand over my forehead, surprised at the slickness of sweat there. The old towel has not truly stopped the bleeding, and it has begun to snake through onto the brown flannel of my sleeve's elbow. Shit! Someone will notice!

I press harder and wish I knew something of medicinal ways to stem the bleeding.

Stem the bleeding!

The thought shoots relief through me, as hard and fast as pellets of ice.

If I wish to stop the blood, then I must be back within my senses. I don't truly wish to let myself slip into the softness of death. It must be so. Isn't it? It's my own mind speaking so meanly only, and I can certainly be as stubborn as my own self!

Stubbornness indeed. I press my mouth together so tightly my teeth break the skin behind my lips as I push on my arm and take in the cool morning air. If I close my eyes I can focus on the little things, such as the tang of snow on the air and the puffs of woodsmoke from the cooper's and the farrier. There are clean rags in the basket by the door, put there by Berit when she last brought the wash. I catch up one and wrap it tightly around the skin, tugging the corners, and firmly sealing up the wound. The strength of my fingers serves me well, and the bleeding does not escape this binding.

I own my life again.

My whole body wilts against the doorframe, and I wish my heart would stop bumping and thrashing inside my chest.

It is done. I've lasted the night, and with the knowledge comes some strange, calm certainty.

I will finish it all, and my life will finally be my own, whatever it may mean.

CHAPTER THIRTY-SIX
15 November 1867

Sergeant Ollin, Lieutenant Balsam, and Captain Bush stand in a line, but it is Sergeant Ollin who is counting the wares. His hair is brushed back carefully for once and his buttons polished except for the last two on his jacket front. His eyes flicker over the shiny tin and copper, clearly counting the items against the list he has in his head. Next to the deep ebony of the blacksmith's items, my goods seem to particularly glow in the early morning.

I am so damn proud of it all.

I matched the challenge, buried deep and bubbling from the start. I wanted to prove how I am a good and able craftsman. That I ... that I *know* my mother and father would say that I am. That I am capable, as I finally believe myself to be. I suppose the last is all that matters.

And I did it.

Sergeant Ollin is sweating in the close heat of the forge and the scrutiny of us all as he tries to peer through the morning gloom to make sure all of Thaddeus's order is accounted for as well. Behind him, another three Army men cough, shift their feet, and fidget their gear, but the Lieutenant and the Captain are still as stone.

"It, ah. Ha. Looks to be right?" He is fumbling, and so much unlike the greasy person who has sidled into my shop for the past two weeks that I would smile, except I am still so nervous. Though I have completed the Army's order, I'm not completely set to meet them, and I'm doubly aware of it. My news for the Captain, and for Thaddeus, is still not perfect.

Lieutenant Balsam steps up and flicks a cursory glance at everything, then reaches into the stiff leather pouch at his side. My mouth dries and my spit becomes sawdust as he pulls out the mix of greenbacks, shinplasters, and coinage.

He lays it out with something like nonchalance, muttering and counting as he does, his thin lips slipping on the numbers. My eyes swim as the amount is piled on the table in a small mountain of pale ink. It is so much! I have never seen so much money all at once.

Thaddeus picks up most of it, peeling a chunk away and hands the papers to me. When my fingers fold over the wad, the weight of it feels as good as gold. I'm so damn close!

The joy is short-lived. Captain Bush sighs loudly, then shifts his torso toward me. "The sword, then? It's all decorated and ready as well?"

I cannot look at Thaddeus or Walter as I answer, but the Captain's hard, bright eyes are no matter. Instead, I pull a line through the soot of the smithy's floor with the worn toe of my boot and clench my hands under the folds of my skirts as I answer.

"Nearly done."

"Nearly?"

"It's not paid for."

My head shoots up when Thaddeus jumps into the conversation, but he ignores me completely.

"Paid? It's not done," the Captain says, managing to sound smug.

"It's done enough," I counter, finding my voice again. "I'll send it with David Fawcett and his wife before Christmas."

The Captain doesn't look convinced at all. "I'll have to see it before I pay you a penny."

I hesitate, then nod. "You can come, then, but leave your men here."

Even though the officers are there to be Captain Bush's flank, they all turn their eyes to their commander expectantly. He looks disgruntled and flustered, but finally closes his eyes briefly as if he cannot bear all the bother.

"Very well."

He walks just behind me on the way to my tinshop, and my nerves are strung so tightly they will be singing in another moment. A constant trill of shivers races up and down my spine and into my arms and down my elbow, tingling in the deep gouges under my wrist.

Entering the shop, I pull the sword from under the wrapping, and fold my mouth over my teeth against saying a word while Captain Bush inspects the tin decorations on one side, where they are bright and white against the unpolished steel. It is not yet polished but the lines of the sword are obvious, the bones of it true, and the curls unfurling with tin. The other side is still blank, but my ability is at least visual.

334

When he steps back, I let out my breath loudly, and he spares a look at me. "It suffices enough. I'll give two thirds payment now, the rest with Fawcett when he comes with it."

He doesn't even think to wait for Thaddeus, and instead takes his personal funds out of the leather pouch at his side and verbally counts out the cash. The respect of this alone is astounding to me, more so when he nods curtly and spins on his heel to leave.

Staring at the money, where it scatters limply in the cool breeze from the door the Captain left open, I suddenly have the wild need to shout aloud with celebration. I don't, swallowing it hard. But the joy is there, foreign and perhaps fleeting. It has been long since I've felt such pure relief, though, and with it comes the last of the confidence I need to finally finish the damn sword.

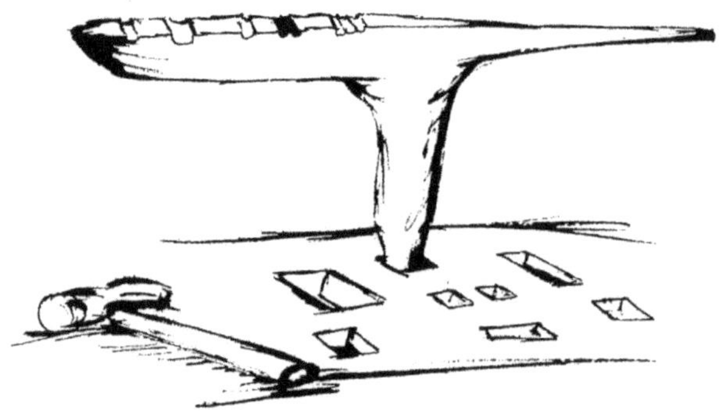

CHAPTER THIRTY-SEVEN
10 December 1867

"Marie! It looks beautiful!" Anette exclaims. Sadie nods encouragingly, Grete coos while holding a hand under her stomach, and even Clara is there with a babe on her hip, staring and grinning. Berit glows with praise, as if I am her own daughter, as if my achievements fill her with happiness. I bask in their amazement, and smile widely, the edges of my eyes pulling and folding into themselves as I grin, unable to be humble and demure.

"Thank you," I say, genuinely touched with their reaction to the finished sword. It truly is lovely, and I am both relieved and exhausted. It has taken me many days, nearly to the Christmas season, to be finished. But it is done.

"You've accomplished more than anyone could have imagined," Berit says, her long slender finger trailing the top of the saber where the tin sits shiny and silver inside the engraving. It twirls and swirls and whispers inside the steel, warming it and gilding it with light.

336

"I am very pleased, myself," I admit to them all, feeling ensconced within a womanly circle, and at peace for the moment.

The comfort is partly because they are so amazed with the artwork, of course. But also because these women are my dearest friends in Flats Town, and they do not care that I am both woman and smith. It seems it will not matter that I straddle both trade and sex. Perhaps I have put too much stock in it, anyway. Perhaps it might never have mattered here in the west. Still, the relief of it all pounds me, and rules my heartbeat in this moment.

"There will be so much gossip," Anette prophesies. "Just wait."

"I heard it's done!" Toot and Elaine Warren darken the doorway—one tiny and wrinkled and covered in food stains, and the other tall and commanding and buxom. Both look winded. Elaine explains as her mother-in-law comes to examine my work.

"Sally Painter said she saw it this morning when she came to pick up her order. We had to dash over before the supper rush."

"Ah, I'm the first man to see it, am I?" Horeb leers into the space, his green eyes splashing around the corners. "Tell me true, Marie, am I the first?"

I laugh. "Actually, you are."

"Ah ha! Gil! I win!" He spins and disappears toward the *Rusty Nail*, and Gilroy Greenman's rumbling answer gets louder as he ambles nearer, too.

Soon I have most of the *Nail's* customers inside the shop, and I want to cover the sword with my body to keep it from all the fingers. Lara O'Donnell ends up slicing open her hand as she touches the wrong end, and I pull out my rag box and bind it before blood gets on the steel.

"Behold what the Lord has helped Marie Kotlarczyk make with her hands!" Father Jonathon intones as he steps in, silencing the argument and removing his wide black hat against the heat inside the tinshop.

"Aaah, Father, did the Lord forget to help her the first time, then?" Horeb quips and all the cowboys guffaw loudly in response.

Everyone stares and touches until rumbling stomachs and the shift of the sun remind them all of their hungry stomachs or their duty and the shop empties again.

"I should do the same and make some food," Berit mentions, pulling her cloak back on. It is cold and frigid outside, perhaps worse than other Decembers past.

"I was wondering if you've sold your house yet?" I ask quickly.

She looks at me strangely, but stops putting on her wrap. "No. No one needed it when the last wagon train went through, as you know. What does it matter, Marie?"

The asking is hard, as it changes things. It will sever something comfortable and easy between us.

"I was thinking I need a smaller space. It is just me, after all."

She surveys the shop, skeptical. "How would you ever fit all of this in my old house?"

"I might take out a wall or two in your main room. Make it one big space, with a bed in the corner. It's small, and simple. You needn't take as much care of me—"

"But I *like* to take care of you, honey. It gives me—and Walter—joy to have you here."

"Where is she going?" Both Berit and I swing around to look toward the door, which is dark with Walter's height.

"Oh, Marie was considering ... *is* considering ... moving herself and the shop to my old house, as it hasn't been taken over."

Walter's thick eyebrows shoot up. "Is that so?"

I feel strange and disjointed now that my thought is out in the open, as if I am betraying him, too. I shake my head.

"It's just an idea."

Berit stares at me, weighing, then turns to Walter.

"I'll be over shortly, *min kjære*. It'll be a simple meal. I just need to do up the pudding with some nutmeg."

He glances between us, and then lumbers away, letting the late afternoon light in again. Berit looks at me closely, her head moving to the side as she considers.

"Marie, do you wish you'd married Danny?"

"Why can't everyone leave that be? I didn't want to marry him."

"And you will part ways with Percy as well, I suppose?" When I nod, she does, too. "Well, *honning*, I can understand that."

"Good." I rub my fingers together before twisting them. "Then I can buy your old place from you?"

She pauses once more. "Are you feeling you need to make your life smaller because you are alone here?"

It's partially true. "Yes, there is that."

"But you've us. We're family."

Her belief is touching and filling, but it also makes my body tighten. They are my family in a way, but not really. Not in the way I wish them to be. And I want to shrink away from the memories clouding the shop.

"I know, Berit. And I'm thankful."

"Well, of course, I can't make you stay in this old barn by yourself," she sighs, looking around again. "You needn't decide right now anyway, *honning* dear."

She pats my hand, and then calls over her shoulder. "Come on over, then. Thaddeus will be glad to know the sword is done if he hasn't heard already. I've got to grab up water, so I'll meet you inside."

I grab my wool cape and follow her out, still not certain if she will sell me her place, but unable to press the issue without sounding desperate. She heads to the well, her greying, queenly head bent against the chilly breeze, and I move toward the Salomon house, pausing outside the door to scrape the muddy slush from my boots.

"… said she'd take Berit's old place." Walter's rumble is deep and loud through the boards, and I pause, listening without meaning to, but needing to at the same time.

"*Czemu? Why?*"

"She wants something smaller. Can't say I blame her."

"But then who will cook and care for her? She can't do both."

I smile at Thaddeus' concern, though it is only because he knows that I am no hand at making up a home.

"I don't know, son. I'm sure my wife would look in on her. Now, Berit was going to add nutmeg to the pudding. Handle it, will you? I'll pull the coffee."

There is a snort, likely from Thaddeus at his father's newfound inclination to help around the hearth. I don't want Berit to see me eavesdropping, so I open the door, lifting my face to the blast of warmth from their living area. Walter looks up and smiles before going to measure the beans into the pot. Thaddeus is on the far end of the room, and he does not look up. Perhaps he does not hear me.

I watch him take down the nutmeg grater—the one I've made and given to Walter, I realize—and carefully shave the spice into the pudding. He pauses, considering how much to put in, then peers at the grater itself.

Likely I've left a seam poorly soldered or it is already coming apart. I sigh, but then catch the sigh halfway as I watch him rub his thick thumb over the curved edge of the grater. It is a thoughtful thing he does before palming the tool and pressing it back carefully into place among the cutlery. I wish … well, there is nothing to be done. What am I supposed to do? Tell him that I wish he might touch my body so gently? That I wish to be with him? If I were alone, I'd laugh aloud at the ridiculousness of it. I may be unorthodox with my career, but I'm no fool. I can only imagine how such a plead would sound, and how dismissive Thaddeus would be.

"Time to eat?" I ask.

Thaddeus turns, at once surly. "Father says you might leave your shop and move."

"Just across the town." I'm unprepared for the bitterness in his voice. I've forgotten how much he dislikes change of any kind. Well, it's not his life.

Walter straightens slowly too, facing his son. Even in profile, he looks surprised. "It's not a sure thing, Tadeusz."

The younger blacksmith stares at the pair of us, and then shakes his head. "I just didn't expect you to leave a good thing, Marie. Between the shops and Berit taking care of everything, it'd be foolish to disrupt it. You know you belong here, by the smithy. You may have your moments, but you never struck me as a *nierosądny foolish* woman."

"I—"

My retort is cut as Berit bursts into the room, and we end up all eating in complicated silence. Even Walter tries to be talkative, but both Thaddeus and I are brooding for our own separate reasons. Berit finally gives up.

"Well, since half of us at the table are in no mood to be happy, I suppose I should serve the pudding and be done with it and no ceremony."

I shake my head, wishing I could be livelier in the face of her obvious attempts.

"I'd adore some pudding, but perhaps tomorrow."

She doesn't argue, and instead winks at her husband. "More for myself and Walter. Go on then. And you, too, Thaddeus? You'll want to see the sword?"

His head comes up fast. "It's done then? You didn't think to mention it, Marie? I had to hear through gossip. Fine. I've only to add the hilt."

"Whenever you'd like to have it back, I'll bring it over to the forge," I tell him.

He looks more than annoyed. "Why should I want to wait to finish the damn thing?"

His anger bites and slashes my heart. What would it be to have him gentle again, the way he sometimes is—*was*? Not recently, of course. And it's been slightly worse since I decided to deny Danny a marriage.

"Then I'll bring it over," I say, and head out immediately, forgetting my cloak in my rush to finish this whole ordeal.

I'm proud of the work, indeed. But I am also embarrassed by my attraction to the blacksmith, and I am afraid of what it will mean to be done working so closely with him.

The air is cold and clear, and the evening falls quick and grey and blue. I walk into the shop, which is still warm from the brazier and the stove. In the cool brush of winter light, the sword looks otherworldly. I am actually fond of it now. It rather turned me into a full smith. I feel confident about my trade, and my ability. Though Al and Father and even Tom cannot see this masterpiece, I think they'd be proud too. It is enough.

I wrap the sword in the sheepskin, and carry it back to the smithy, going around the house instead of through it. It's good to have the time in the cold to gather myself a little longer.

Thaddeus is not in the forge. The coals spin hot and undulating in the chimney. I put the sword down on the bench, and unwrap it to see it once more. It will be grand when the hilt is on.

I turn to the outer door to go, but it is blocked by the smith himself, the grey eyes dark in the growing cloudiness. My cloak hangs limply over his arm.

"You forgot this. Must have missed you somehow going and coming," he says, then sees the sword. His arm drops and he carelessly lets the hem of the cape drag in the thick soot of the floor. "You were just going to leave it there? Not a word to me?" The disbelief is thick in his voice, the anger.

I try to face his annoyance head on. "I didn't think you needed to speak of it. It's done." I gesture lightly, and then look up at him. "I figured you'd be glad of it."

"That I am," he agrees, and moves inside from the cold, pulling the doors closed against the chill with my cape still hanging haphazardly from his forearm. "But it is unlike you to just drop and run. You've been a friend to me, Marie, but not lately. And this only is another moment of it." He has stopped calling me *Marya* since the dance, and that bothers me more than I admit.

The glow of the coals flickers across the exposed skin of his face. He's both familiar and ghostly in the darkness and I instinctively step backward, hoping I don't hit anything sharp or hot as I do.

"I think you've been strange too," I accuse, not sure if it's true, but then decide to grasp at the words anyway. "Ever since the dance. Since I refused your *other* friend. Since I said I won't marry Danny."

"I know. You have no wish to be married at all. Danny told me." The harshness in his voice is rough. I knew I'd be facing his irritation about this, and the frustration wrought by his loyalty to Danny. It might be best to be done with it.

"I never said such a thing to him."

"Didn't you?" He looks at me with hardness around his long slash of a mouth. "He was particular about it."

"When? He hasn't been back since the harvest festival."

"Oh, he told me then."

I remember them staring at me and into their beers at the dance before Danny departed, dejected and angry. The untruth of the statement squeezes me, and I push back.

"But I *do* wish to be married! Danny's wrong."

"How so? Danny was quite clear about the notions you had, that you don't wish to be a woman at a hearth all your days. You want to be a smith."

"Well, that part is true."

The fight seems to go out of Thaddeus. I wish he might light a lantern, but he seems disinclined to it.

"I don't blame you that. You're good at your trade."

The compliment warms me. And thankfully, the storm of his testiness appears to be over, at least for tonight.

"And you know I am not a good cook," I add.

"Many women aren't. But that doesn't mean you cannot take a marriage."

Why does he push into this discussion, as if he is accusing me? Old anger of my own boils up, the tetchiness hiding my stifling dejection.

"I know it. I never told him I didn't want to marry. Only that I did not wish to marry *him*. Danny is very kind, but I wish to love the man. It is a silly thing, of course." I tack on the last to temper my hope for an impossible match. "Besides, you helped me with my debt. It's thanks to you, Thaddeus, that I had a choice about marriage to Danny at all."

"And this is how you thank me? By refusing him?"

"I do not love him!"

He's quiet, brooding, then scoffs. "Love, you say. It *is* a silly thing." He turns away from me and toward his fire.

I grab my cloak from his arm, yanking hard. "Is it too much to ask? I'd like for a man to see me as a smith. Not just a smith, but a woman, too, and care for me as both. *Both* things, together. Anything else I will not cleave to. It wouldn't make sense anymore."

I spin away from him, feeling tears convulse inside my throat, as if the sorrow of my father's death is once more pulling upwards, to remind me to pity myself, to tempt me to drown in the pain of loneliness. It is sharp this time, and an ache. I reach the door to the living quarters and can hear the soft murmuring of Berit and Walter through the wood planks.

When I yank it open and stomp through, Berit and Walter fall silent, and I half expect Berit to stop me, but she stays quiet. And while I wish to hear Thaddeus pound after me, if only to continue our argument, that is another half-hope that falls flat.

The tinshop itself is not comforting when I arrive. Now that everything is finished, I have nothing left to fill my mind and my hands. The emptiness is loud and almost painful.

CHAPTER THIRTY-EIGHT
20 December 1867

Marching into the bank is easier this time. And slapping the pad of cash on the hard, rough wood of Percy Davies's desk is just as fulfilling as I could have wanted, giving me the courage to spit out the blunt demand.

"I want to leave."

"Excuse me?" He stares first at the money, then me.

"I want to leave the Svendsens' land. It's not possible to stay."

Percy looks a bit blown about, and his hair is not slick today. Esther Flies-With-Hawks has had a child just the other night, and I try to remember the gossip.

"Ah … and congratulations. On your son."

Percy grins widely. "Why thank you, Miss Marie." He settles back into his chair, the creak echoing through the bank, as he thumbs through the bills.

"I mean what I say. I can't play the game anymore."

"I won't have Oddvar selling to the rail. It'll end up

bypassin' the town and Flats Town'll die. It has to go through on Brinkley land."

"But—"

"I'm sorry, Marie. You need to stay there so Oddvar won't sell. He's no fool. A monthly rent that never ends eventually will be worth more than a one-time sum from the railroad."

I fold my mouth over my teeth briefly, tightly, and then let out the air hard. Panic marries frustration and I let the anger blast outward. "Damn you, Percy Davies! I'm telling you I'm done. And even if I wanted to stay, I can't afford it!"

"Yes, you can. I'm giving you the loan."

"It won't work. I'll just keep in debt to you—more and more! I need to stop."

"Marie, you owe me, and the bank, for your family's old lumber loans, the initial rent, the back rent and the interest on it. It's a large sum."

I choke down my scream and cross my arms, glaring at him as darkly as I can. "Damn you to hell. It was blackmail. I'm done with it."

"It's practical. I do what I can to build this town into somethin', to keep it alive."

"I—"

"You should have married Danny Svendsen."

I fume, filling with indignation. "It's a poor reason to marry."

"But then you could have paid off your debt to me and spent your marriage convincin' him that his father doesn't need to sell, that the place is rentable and the money would keep comin' in for decades. You would have been—"

"You put so much power in a woman's role, do you?" I counter.

348

"Why, I—"

"Just because you—you've been knocked over by an apron string—"

Percy grins again. "Ah, Esther's not exactly one for wearin' an apron."

"Damn it, you know what I mean."

He sighs and crosses his arms across his stomach, which is just starting to round with age. "I can't make you stay on the Svendsen land, I suppose, if you've a place to go, and you've served a purpose for a good while. The rail men won't be back now for at least another six months to speak to anyone, so I've got time for another scheme."

"A new one without me," I demand. "I can count and so can you. I've paid everything. Even the fucking interest."

Percy's blue eyes go wide at my curse, but ignores it and slowly reaches for the wad of notes. Flicking his wrist and licking his fingers between every fourth scrap of paper, his lips move soundlessly as he adds.

As he reaches the end, his face almost melts. "It covers."

"So I said."

He ignores my tartness and gazes at me frankly. "Back to Chicago, then?"

"No. I'll stay." I grip the sides of my skirt, my palms sweating, my knees tremble once, and I slide into the chair across the wide desk, pinning Percy with my eyes. "I understand what you've been trying to do in Flats Town, and I am in favor of it."

The chair pops and cracks under him as he shifts, and Percy frowns slightly. He waves a finger, as if dismissing my half-compliment into the cool air.

"If you won't stay on the Svendsen land, will you live somewhere else? And how will you buy another little place?" he asks, but he is not rancorous, and seems honestly interested.

"I don't know yet, but I'll manage. I always do."

He cocks his head. "I'll be frank. I won't be lendin' you money for a different house. You've reneged on this deal we had about stayin' on the Svendsen land. Do you understand, Marie?"

I stand, feeling both exultant and very tired. "I understand."

Marching past a stunned Tom Fawcett, I stride into the street before I say anything else obstinate, and let my breath out again in one agonized, light-headed whoosh as I hit the edge of First Street.

"Let him have it, did you?"

I look up, winded. Seven faces peer out of the doorway of the *Rusty Nail*, and Horeb is grinning wider than any of them.

"What?"

"We could hear you clear across the street and then some, Marie!" Toot calls. "Good for you, but maybe a little hot-headed at the first?"

If I was flushed before, I must certainly be now. "Well, all of it is true."

"No one is denying that, but you watch your next steps, you hear?" Horeb shouts. "Don't be too overly hasty to make things more difficult for yourself."

For once, his advice is sound, and I nod briefly before stumbling home. Difficult? For some reason, my life has felt never so clearly staked.

CHAPTER THIRTY-NINE
23 December 1867

With Christmas looming, and a flurry of new orders from people hoping to have gifts, repairs, or who have simply heard of all I did for the Army, I'm busier than I've ever been. It is a good thing, for many reasons. There is little time to think of the quiet in the shop during the holidays, or how it will be my first Christmas alone.

Berit and Walter have not yet told me about any dinner plans for Christmas, though I make myself scarce at the Salomon house in hopes I will be able to ignore my unrequited attachment to Thaddeus. He is surlier than ever since our quarrel, so when I slip over to drop off the copper kettles for their wrought handles to be attached, I do so in the lateness of the hour, hoping to avoid any discussion, or even be around Thaddeus's frostiness longer than needed.

There is no luck with me tonight, as he is still in the forge. I drop the copper on the bench and jerk my chin at them.

"Handles for these."

He steps over and inspects the bottom seam of the largest piece. "It's good work."

For some reason defiance trips over itself, and I cannot help but retort. "Good enough considering a woman did it?"

His eyebrows go up. "You're a smith. Everyone knows that now."

It might be the stress of facing the holidays alone or the relief of finally being free of debt, or the worry of moving my shop to Berit's house if she will let me. But the words spill out on their own.

"Of course. A smith. That's me, now," I say. "It doesn't bear thinking that I am more than that. A woman, for instance. An orphan. A ... a strange, unmatched ... unwanted ..." The rest of the words disappear and I spin to the door, tugging the caramel cloak around my shoulders.

But his voice is calm, coming out of the darkness of the forge, and it stops me for a moment.

"I have always seen you as a woman as well as a tinsmith, Marya."

"That is very well, Thaddeus."

"*Tadeusz.* As my family calls me."

I close my eyes against the familiarity. "Tadeusz." *Family, am I?* I have no wish to be his sister, or even his friend. It is not enough.

He continues, lowly and slowly. "If it is true that you wish to be ... as you said the other day. Well. I suppose I cannot tell you who to love."

"You can't."

"And romance does not come easy."

"No, it seems I ..." I turn back to stare at him, though I

352

can only see the bare outline of his right side, where it gleams orange and peach with coal glow.

Has he ever tried to romance me?

"What did you say?"

He is silent. I've pressed my luck.

One time he thought to romance me—is that what he hints? It is something to hold to. I press a hand to my stomach against the feeling of a lost appetite, and go for the latch once more.

"Święty *piekło! Holy hell!*" His cuss is over my shoulder as he pushes his wide palm on the door, blocking and towering over me all at once. His height and size are no longer frightening or intimidating. It is all I want, but how can I find the words for him? I know the sighs and the deep kisses along the dance floor and understand what I hope to have from him. But now faced in the dim dark with the man himself? Well, that is something new.

"I don't know what to say, Marya," he admits quietly. "I'm no good when it comes to fancy words or gestures. And Danny had me thinking you wouldn't wish to share your life with anyone. And before that … Well. Danny wished to marry you."

"Well, as you said—I want to be a tradesman."

"So be what you are," he says bluntly. "But suppose you married someone who might even prefer you to work in the shop?"

The darkness of the forge feels crowded, half-blind, fuzzy. My vision goes dim and soft with the shock of his suggestion. The hope is almost as choking as any sadness.

"Is there such a choice?" I ask, facing him fully, allowing the dare and the wish to believe. "If there is, tell me, because then I'd marry after all."

Please.

Let me be enough. Let him want me.

Let him understand me.

He is quiet again for a long moment, but I can hear his breathing, unsteady and deep in his chest.

"When Danny said you would not marry him, I was happy about it," he finally admits. "But when he mentioned you did not wish any marriage at all, I was angry." His voice is low and careful, as the statements are romantic in their own right and not his usual.

"You're always angry, Tadeusz."

"Well. *Tak. Yes.* Look, *I* wanted to marry you. So now. *Tak*, I am asking."

"Oh. Good. Yes."

My head swirls with the agreement. I am suddenly light, full of feathers, and yet my feet dig into the hard-pressed dirt of the smithy.

It is happening.

I had not even an inkling it was possible, and now, suddenly, just like that, I am to be wedded. Perhaps this, then, is love. If not, then it is wonderful friendship and affection, which is perhaps better, as Father once said. Perhaps it will grow to something even deeper. I simply know I do not question this arrangement at all. I want him and what he offers in all his soot and fire and surliness.

His left arm curls around me without warning, the right ripping the cloak away from my shoulders and tossing it onto the anvil before he tangles all his fingers in the folds of my skirt, where it bunches around my hip.

"Yes, Marya?"

"If it is you who is asking. Though I have many

questions and worries," I say, pushing up to his body the way I have wanted. "But yes, *mój najdroższy, my dearest,* I'll marry you." The endearment slips. It does not feel like a lie, and is a release. A joyful, surreal one.

"I would expect some fretfulness on your side of it," he says, pulling me even tighter, so our hip bones bump and our heartbeats intermingle. "But not more than small worries, I should hope. Especially since you call me your dearest."

"Affection doesn't solve everything," I echo him, but I'm smiling now, feeling free and excitable. I cannot believe I have revealed myself to him, and he isn't turning away. Some women might faint with the extraordinary exposing of affection, but instead I am fluttering with something like desire.

"No, *miłość.*" He returns a deeper beloved sentiment and fills my heart. "But it goes a long way, however silly. I know you wish to talk over many things. In a moment."

He bends down to kiss me, and it is by far the best kiss I know. It is hot and fiery and delicious. My fingers inch along his elbows and dance across his wrists. His arms are bulky and overlarge, tough with muscle and strength. I smell the charcoal on his beard, the ash on his clothes, and bend up to him without restraint. There is a swirl in my mind, blinding me against the darkness of the room, allowing me to brace into his mouth.

As there is no customer to come this late, and Walter and Berit do not think to chaperone us, we have no interruptions. It is the longest kiss I've ever received, and Thaddeus seems to have no plans to stop soon. *Miłość,* he says. *His love.*

"*Mój Boże. My God.*" He breathes once to the side of my mouth before pressing his lips back to mine. His beard is softer than I expect. I run my hand up the side of his cheek and jaw, tracing his ear and grasping his neck. My arms grab at him, shuffling along the hard, rounded muscles of his shoulders. His hands spread along my waist and hip, digging into the thick flannel as if he might physically attach me to him. The strength of his body and the satisfaction of his acceptance is more than I hoped for when I imagined his embrace and his affection. I want to hear it again, to know that he did not jest.

"So, then, you mean it?" I ask, as he pauses the kiss once more. "We're to marry? What of children?" Apprehension bubbles up. Marriage comes with pregnancy, all that goes with it. Plus, I am no hand with little ones, same as the kitchen. Even as I ask it, the thought of holding Thaddeus's babes strikes as manageable.

"What of them?" He does the unthinkable and bends to press a kiss to my neck and then my shoulders through the cloth, sending tingles and shivers down my body. "Of course I'd like some. As many as we might."

As he says so, he wraps me tighter into the circle of his arms, and I feel his desire and his need, surprising and delightful all at once. I ought to make more of his passion for me. In fact, the idea of doing so is both wild and feasible, but I push it away, trying to maintain some semblance of the barter.

"Tadeusz, if I am a smith, how will I care for babes?" I ask. It draws him up from another kiss, though he does not release me. I can feel him considering. It is nice to not worry for once, and to let him do the thinking. I press my cheek into the buttons of his shirt, smelling the sweat and coal and heat of him.

"You'll be a mother, of course," he finally says. "But Berit can help. She'll enjoy it. And she'd be their grandmother," he says into my half-protest. "If it comes to it, we'll pay a housekeeper. With both of us working, we won't be hard-pressed to hire one."

The notion of both husband and wife working astounds me. Is he really suggesting it?

It is not usual. It is unexpected.

"And where will I work?"

I feel him shrug. The coal is dying in the forge, and the blood-orange light is lower.

"We can build onto the forge. I'll knock a wall and make a place for your tinsmithing next to mine. And then we can add to the living quarters here."

He says it like it is so practical, so obvious. He speaks of our marriage bed simply and without frills, and of our work together as if it is the only way. It works, of course, now that he says it. And it adds another layer of acceptance of me, of my trade, and my existence. It means he cares for me for what and who I am, including my failings and my talents.

That I will be both tinsmith and wife is intoxicating, and I throw my arms about him, pulling him down to kiss him with fervor, allowing myself to melt. I know how his legs are hard, and his hands are overly strong, and his back is a maze of planked muscle. The nape of his neck has skin as smooth and soft as a child's. I wonder what else is allowed now in the plundering of our kisses. I remember hands on hands and under clothes, casting strange shadows in the wagon firelight, or against muted curtains of cloth. Couplings and tumblings wiggle across my mind. Will that be me?

My hands go up, tugging on the corners of his flannel shirt, wondering what his stomach feels like and the strength of his broad body. He stops me, pressing his forehead to mine as he breathes deeply through his nose.

"I know what comes after too much of this," he says. "Men will talk and brag after too much liquor and I've heard my fair share. But first, you know we should marry."

"When?" I ask, slipping my arms around his waist, keeping a firm grasp on what has seemed so unlikely. He is to be mine. I think I am happy, *know* I am happy. Happier than I've been in a long while. For once, I have received good news. I cannot absorb it. It's all impossibly wonderful.

"Tomorrow. No *Oświadczyny engagement*. We're not in the Old Country. There's no point in dragging out some long wait, and I'm not going to waste time courting you like Danny did."

"Very well."

He straightens. "All right?"

"Yes," I nod against his chest. "I want to marry you. But we should tell your father."

"Berit will be beyond herself," he says, and there is amusement in his voice. "But, before we go through. Again." He comes down from his height to kiss me more, to take my air and crush me to him. I know Thaddeus is often frustrated, and angry, and sometimes he can temper it with tenderness. But I did not ever think that it all might translate to passion for me.

When we next pause, I gulp, but decide to tell him all. "I am glad for this match, Tadeusz. I have wished to be with you for a long time."

He stills as I speak, and his eyes lock with mine. As I finish, he smiles: a wide, brilliant grin that lights his face and shows flat, strong teeth. "Well, then. I might start to romance you by saying you are a good-looking woman, Marya," he says, almost jovial now, before pulling me up for more embraces.

I try to kiss him as heartily again, so he can feel how I am so thrilled to make this match and to join with his life. It is another long kiss, and when he pulls away, it is slowly and reluctantly.

He opens the door before us, his hand firmly on my waist, and we go through to where Walter and Berit sit companionably on the hard, wooden chairs by the hearth. Walter's pipe is clenched in his mouth in the small curve on his lower teeth, as his hands are busy holding a skein of yarn. Berit has him helping her with womanly work more and more, but he seems content with it.

"Father. Mother."

I did not know he was going to give Berit such a title. Her head snaps up, surprised, and then a wide smile stretches across her cheekbones as she sees us, and her eyes glint merrily. Walter grunts and turns too, and his own eyes immediately settle to Thaddeus's hand encasing my waist, firmly and tightly.

"*Co to jest? What is this?*" Walter hides a smile under his beard.

Thaddeus shifts, sheepish, perhaps, or uncomfortable. I expect he does not like to explain our little romance, for all his gentle words with me. Perhaps he is irritated that his father forces him to speak what must be obvious.

But I when I tilt back my head, he looks calm. He meets my glance and half-smiles—a rare thing yet, but something filled with satisfaction. And when he tells Walter we are to be wed, and his father speaks teasingly of coming children, Thaddeus actually throws back his head and laughs. It is a boom and a roar all at once, and I laugh, too. I do not think I have ever seen him fully laugh, and I hope I can make him do so often.

CHAPTER FORTY
27 December 1867

Thaddeus and I wed in a brief and simple ceremony with the priest and Walter and Berit as witnesses at St. Aloysius. Elaine Warren, Sadie, and Tim the farrier were there as well. In the days after it, I think of my wedding often. It is crystalline and acute in my mind. I tingle when I recall how proudly Thaddeus spoke his vows, and how strongly he gripped my hands, his eyes intent and sincere on mine under the traditional Polish cap and a tight-fitting long coat of our heritage. I think I smiled the entire time with my hair in Mother's ribbons and a tall kerchief. Father Jonathon was good enough not to ask me to stop grinning.

Though I am married, the rhythm of my life is still the same. There is still work and math and the sugary customer service.

I take a moment to stop and stare at the completed work. The piles of curving tin and bended copper glisten against the candles, catching the yellow and orange and white of the light and throwing it back into my eyes.

I truly am a smith. It is still hard to realize. But it is true in so many ways.

"Marya," Thaddeus's voice shoots out of the dark from the crack in the door, and though I know it's him, he still surprises me. "I thought I said at dinner to not stay up so late."

"How far into the night is it?" I ask as he shoves open the door and latches it behind him.

"Long enough. How much more do you have?" He surveys the work.

"Just a bit. I'd like to finish David Fawcett's order."

He stands quietly, looking and likely calculating.

"I'll help now, too."

My eyebrows go up. "Really?"

"I haven't forgotten how to use soft metals." He flexes his fingers. "Though my hands may need some reminding. It won't take much. What is needed?"

I don't bother to walk him through the use of the machines so late in the night, and instead enlist him to solder the pieces as I finish them. He is slower than I expect, though perhaps that is because he is out of practice. We are mostly silent, save for the sift and shift of our feet and the mutter of reminders as we pass. Still, it is the most wonderful experience I've had in the shop since Father took ill. I find myself even more pleased for the future, when we will share our shops and our trade side by side. He was a good choice. The right choice.

"I'll get lanterns in. Finish that one, and then come to bed," Thaddeus says, suddenly standing and brushing past. He is casual, and I do not settle on his words until I hear the scraping of bedposts and wood against one another. Setting down the canteen, I hurry toward the living quarters. Thaddeus is combining two of the small beds so that it becomes a larger one. He stands and puts his hands at his sides, cocking his head and considering.

"It's not perfect, but it'll do," he puts calmly, then glances over at me. "Did you put out the rest of the lights?"

He means to sleep with me here tonight, I realize, instead of the loft over Berit and Walter, and fluttering excitement wraps around my head at the idea of all the privacy. Yearning sizzles in my blood.

"I did. Except this. We can leave it lit for bed, if you wish," I tell him, feeling brazen.

He turns around, and his grey eyes go stormy. "I'd grab you up now if I wasn't so blackened," he says, and the heat behind the words reminds me of his forge.

I shake my head at his excuse and approach him. "Do you think I care? Besides, I've on my own work apron. You didn't marry a lady with fine dresses."

"True." He considers me. "Well, then." He yanks me to him, rubbing the charcoal onto my leathers and the back of my dress, pluming it into the folds of my skirt. His arms are iron, and his mouth is warm and hard, and I know he wants me in the way a man desires a woman.

There is a deliciousness in knowing we are married, for all we only touch lips. The same fire sizzles through my arms and down my stomach, and I swim light-headedly in longing. The sharing of air, of tongues, of soot, magnifies with the knowledge that no one will bother us here, and no one will think we are wrong to caress so. When his hands fill with my breasts, I press toward him, wishing so many fabric barriers didn't hinder his explorations. He seems to feel the same, for his fingers inch up my outer skirts until only a thin fabric separates his hands from my flesh, and his strong fingers press at the curves of my waist.

"*Moje serce, my heart*, Marya!" He pulls away, and drops his head to the top of mine. "If I am not careful, I'll take you to the sheets before we wash, and one of us will have to explain to Berit why your set is so black and dirty."

He peels himself away and heads to the bucket, glancing around as he does. "We'll have to move you out soon enough and build onto the forge for your tinshop. I'll get the lumber from Mikey O'Donnell as soon. I figure we'll knock out a wall so the heat of my coals will reach to you."

"You say you are not romantic, but your planning for all of that is so," I tell him, smiling at him fully.

"Only you, Marya, would think that the addition of a metal shop is romantic," he snorts, but I can see I've pleased him. That I can do so warms my heart and sends ribbons of desire curling in my stomach.

Thaddeus's back is to me, but he strips down to his shirt, where it hangs long and low to his mid-thigh. I am intrigued at the sight of his wide legs and stout hips, outlined against the thin cotton as he bends to remove his socks. That his skin will soon touch mine sends me flurrying around the tiny kitchen, tidying up in my nerves and excitement. When I turn from stoking the fire in the small old potbelly, he's standing and waiting.

"Now, to bed, or I'll drag you," he says. "Though I admit I've still no hand at undressing a woman's things." He waves fluttering fingers at my layers, turning to the bed easily and comfortably, getting in and thumping the covers over his long frame. I hear a mutter about the unimpressive height of my brothers who cut shorter beds than he prefers, and I want to giggle.

When I slide next to him in nothing but my chemise, the roughness of his legs chafes, and the solidness of his body sinks the mattresses. His hands, while bumpy and tough, caress and brush my skin, and somewhere during our kiss he manages to slip them up my garment to touch the rest of me. His frankness leaves me room to be as forward, and I run my own chipped hands along the strong, thick muscles rolling off his bones. His entire body is one of tall power, broad and wide.

He pulls the strings of my neckline, stretching it wide. Trailing fingers down my collarbone, he dives a hand below the fabric and fills it with my bare breast. The anticipation of his touch melts with contact, shooting both shivers and blazes of flame in my blood.

"You've a good bosom," he says. "Full, and heavy." He kisses me again, gently, and with his heart in it, and I relax against his mouth and the familiar tickle of his beard against my neck.

Naked, his own form is beautiful. He is handsome, and he is mine. And he burns for me. He wants me. He desires me. I want everything we do to be slow and beautifully savored, while at the same time I wish to eat his lips and squeeze his chest and become his immediately, wantonly.

Thaddeus guides our bodies inexpertly, but his clumsiness is matched by his kindness and his willingness to let me actively participate in the touching. I'm no stranger to the notion of sex itself, and I yearn for him deeply and honestly, so that when he presses up and into me, I feel only pleasure. He is still for a moment, as if relishing our connection, and then he moves. For some strange reason, the rocking of our bodies and the memory of his caressing hands create a blinding flash, and I succumb gladly and thrillingly, trembling with it, sweating with it.

Thaddeus grabs up my mouth, gasping. "And again, Marya. With me!" He crushes me, rolling his hips, pressing on my body with his, which seems to trigger a carnal response. We are alone here, so I am free with my voice. I feel him give in too, hear his hoarse shout, the wetness of our lovemaking spilling onto the sheets.

We are silent, panting, and he shifts slightly so his elbows brace his face inches from mine. His body is shivering, and I feel buttery.

"That was exceptional," I tell him. "Might we do it again soon?"

"Tomorrow?" he offers, and then chuckles. "Later tonight?"

He kisses me soundly, melting me into him and deeper into the bedding.

"Tadeusz," I sigh into the side of his face. "I must have loved you without knowing what it was. I thought it was a friendship—a good one, a true one—but nothing more. That perhaps my attraction to you was simply my desire to be with a man."

"I'm glad you didn't wed Danny, then," he says, serious.

"Me too."

Our night is restless, as with only a week of marriage, neither of us is used to another body in the bed. It will take some adjusting. Once Thaddeus wakes me as he rolls. He touches me strongly and with purpose then, and joins his body to mine again. The next time it is me who urges, though he is more than willing and falls into my body as though it was made for his arms and his lips.

At the last, we lie in the dim muddle that heralds another day, sated and unable to sleep. I run my fingers through his beard and up along his jaw, pressing against his forehead and his skull while his own hands lazily circle my hip and thigh. He says nothing of my ministrations, but does not shift away.

"Well then. The sun's up enough." He rises, bringing me with him.

Practical, short with words, and a bit rough. He is the same, though he now has a wife. It is comforting, the sameness. *And he is mine. I am no longer alone. I have family again.* He reaches for his shirt, and I watch the broad muscles move as he pulls it on, and then he stands for his trousers and stockings. My body sings with the remainders of him, and I am loath to get out of bed.

"Marya?" He glances back, his eyebrows raised. "You should get up."

I rise, feeling the ghost of his hands on me, and his seed inside. Someday he will get me with child. To my surprise, the idea fills me with excitement, and I smile to myself. Thaddeus might be beyond pleased with such news. In fact, he may laugh. I hope he laughs with happiness.

"I will likely work late again. May as well use as much light as I can before January," I say.

He nods, belting his pants and tugging on his apron. "I'll help if I can. I know what it will take."

We look squarely at one another. I realize we both are content with our choices in this moment, and it is satisfying in a way that fills up my spirit. Perhaps this is what fulfillment is—somehow both fleeting and solid.

CHAPTER FORTY-ONE
2 March 1868

The wood is brittle from the years of fire heat, and the residue of old dust from the blacksmith forge falls onto my shoulders and Thaddeus's beard. What is it about taking a hammer to something meant to crumble? I find strange pleasure in smacking the iron against the wood, and Thaddeus does more than his share with something I can only describe as glee. Still, we are careful to hit only where the old nails rust in their holes, to hopefully reuse as many pieces as possible. I didn't get out of debt only to dive back in.

The early spring air whistles over our shoulders as we break the planks, and behind us, Walter is offering instructions if only to keep everyone else quiet. It doesn't work, though, and Horeb is the most audible with his nasal tone.

"Not gonna tear down the whole wall, is it?"

"Ain't."

"Aw, shut it, Gil, you ain't never broke down a wall in your own life."

"There's supposed to be a new drill they use in the mines," Trusty Willy offers helpfully. "If you have to go into the foundation maybe."

"They're not going into the foundation," Sadie says, her voice tighter than usual today. She must still not be pregnant. "Even an idiot could see that."

I am surprised at the sweat on my forehead, and wipe away the grit and dust from my skin. I'd follow my husband's lead and roll up my sleeves at least, but then our audience would see the deep red lines on my forearm, and even Thaddeus hasn't spoken of them. I could not bear a reminder of my weakest moments today.

Tim the farrier is standing on the other side of the wall, where his supposed property line extends, to be sure we don't stake the walls of the new tinshop on his land. Percy is there to approve of the changes and Mikey O'Donnell is on hand to estimate the amount of lumber needed. Tina Brinkley, Lara O'Donnell, and Toot Warren have taken it upon themselves to bake up a storm to feed the group, and everyone is debating who made the best pie. So far, Tina's dried apple confection seems to be winning.

My shop will most certainly not happen without the nosy influence of half of Flats Town, it seems, but that is beside the point. Thaddeus is doing as he said: giving me a real place of my own for my own trade. It is the type of wedding gift I never thought I'd receive, let alone be able to request.

"Another few planks, and the rest will need the handsaw," he tells me, pointing with his hammer, and his brief smile warms me as much as the afternoon sun. Before us, the ground is nearly budding with the promise of new grass, my flowers are poking out of the ground around the smithy, and for the first time in quite a while, I rise every day without the same worries I've known for years.

Now I can see a future, and how it might grow. I can imagine the tinshop, with the grey-black shadowy corners, the raw oil slipping around my family's machines, the soft curve of a new pot on the shelf, awaiting a sale. The space will be much smaller than I have had, with a low ceiling, and likely without a window, but it is worth it. And every morning and evening, I break my fast with Berit and Walter, and with Thaddeus, too. Every day, I will bang along the ridge of a strip of copper and hear the matching boom of his hammer and the huff of his bellows.

"Should be enough space to frame the entry," Walter says, his gravelly voice cutting into my daydream. "May as well stop here for now. Berit has hot coffee on for everyone to take away the chill."

Horeb fairly dances through to the Salomon kitchen and the rest of the onlookers either join him or disappear into the glow of the late spring afternoon. I can't move at once, still stuck at the yawning hole that will soon lead to the shop. It makes me giddy with hope, and for once I know my hope is not misplaced.

"What are you doing, Marya?" Thaddeus wonders, slinging his hammer onto one of his benches. "Come on through for coffee."

He pushes into the kitchen and I move to follow, glancing once more at where my future will build. I can imagine it so clearly, indeed. It will be my own shop, the way a proper trade should be housed. I will put the tinner's bench in the middle, and use a wide, fat plank for the counter. The shelves will be sanded so they do not scratch the bottoms of my wares, and I will hang jumbles of tin cups from the rafters, to tinkle with the breeze from the forge's open doors. I will be busy. There will be no time or reason to ever think I am not enough.

And at night, before I curl inside Thaddeus's frame, I will make sure the doors to the shop are closed against the elements, so that the tools will not rust, and the tin and copper will gleam and glow and glimmer.

The End

Historical Note

Machinery for tinsmiths and coppersmiths first became available at the very beginning of the 1800's. Pamphlets from the 1840's show tools costing between \$8.00 to \$15.50, which was more than a single smith made in one month. Today, those same machines are available intermittently on Ebay or at tinsmith convergences. They still work very well if they've been well oiled and taken care of over the years, but now the price per machine is several hundred dollars.

In remote areas, pioneers would hobble together their own smithing as required, but because of the need for metalwork, towns and large settlements would have had a blacksmith (or five!) nearby. Most of the tin and copper work done in the Territories in the 1860's would have been managed by those blacksmiths, such as the Salomon men. Summertime might have offered a peddler or tinker wandering around a given area to repair or sell tin and copper wares made over the winter. Eventually, tinsmithing stretched all the way through the territories, though the trade changed dramatically each decade.

Many Poles and Czechs settled in the Dakotas and there are whole communities there yet today who hold tight to their heritage. It's also true that the same potato blight that hit Ireland in the 1840's and 1850's hit Poland extremely hard as well, and added to the diaspora of Poles to America. Polish pioneers were especially noted for their strength and work ethic, and Marya's floral gardening hobby is a nod to the fact that flowers are an important part of their national identity. Beyond the traditional male/female roles of the time, Poles were recognized for the equality that balanced between husband and wife: women frequently helped with the family businesses, particularly in farming, and had a say in financial decisions.

There never was a town called Flats Town between Yankton and Fort Randall, though it was a well-used path between those two settlements starting in the 1850's. Later, the Milwaukee Road rail lines crisscrossed in the area where there could have been a town called Flats Town—or, later, Flats Junction. And though the Kotlarczyk family built their business in Flats Town, they would have likely tried their hand at farming or ranching in addition to a full tinshop or tinkering.

All the tools and methods of metalcraft mentioned in *Smith* exist now, and did exist, in the 1860's. Women would, on occasion, become tinsmiths or coppersmiths under duress, such as the loss of a husband or father and no other male family members to take over the business. By the 1870's, a woman who worked was not considered a "lady" in larger cities, but the pioneer mentality was more robust, forgiving, and centered around hard work, big families, and love. No one writes of them, but the women tinsmiths worked and survived, however few there were.

All of the songs mentioned in *Smith* are actual ditties sung during wagon trains west or in pioneer villages prior to 1870. Carrington's march into present-day Wyoming truly did happen while the tribes were in negotiations with government officials. Fort Phil Kearney boasted up to 500 men at one point in its short history, including craftsmen and civilians, and was constantly under siege from combined Indian bands. Fetterman's rash behavior outside that fort resulted in a complete massacre of his small force by over 2,000 braves, and catapulted the area to additional wars and skirmishes. Woodcutting excursions were necessary at Fort Phil Kearney but also ended badly for the Army. Still, history repeats itself every generation as our government continues to chip away at the rights and culture of the original Native American people that still hold tight to their land in the Dakotas. It is no wonder they push back.

Captain Joseph Bush was the commanding officer of Fort Randall during the mid-1860's, though I have no way to know his personality. Likely he did have a sword. Etching steel does require a particular kind of acid, though it is poisonous to breathe, creating the same reactions Marya experiences when she is trying to use it. It's akin to combining vinegar, water, and bleach, which even today is not recommended when cleaning. People who try to etch metal are warned of the side effects of the combination, and the need for proper ventilation and breathing equipment.

The kitchen tools, food, and even taffy pulling events are all historical, and I've included a bibliography of books I've used to research *Smith*. Some are short, full of photographs and illustrations, and are entertaining.

At the end, I hope you've had a good time growing with Marie—learning, enjoying, and fantasizing about the years our country was young and wild.

With joy—Sara Dahmen
in the copper shop, Wisconsin

Author's Thanks

Tinsmith could not have been finished or even fleshed out without my apprenticeship under Bob, a master tinsmith and coppersmith, the support of his wife, Marilyn, and all the men who answered my random questions on the tintinkers weekly online chat. When I first started apprenticing under Bob, it was mainly to understand the workings of original smiths, to better respect and learn the background of the trade that transformed into modern cookware. I wanted to capture the essence of early smiths who were constantly striking out with new machines, new territory and new ideas. Since the apprenticeship began, House Copper & Cookware has grown into so much more, thanks to the incredible hands-on guidance.

A wonderful thanks to Ben and the team at Promontory Press, who believed in this novel and supported it from the first day. Without my mother, who gives invaluable insight, and Christy, Valerie, Katie, and Heather for always reading the earliest versions, this book would not have made it further than the first draft. To my first editor, Craig, who drove me to make Marya more intense, and Richard, who discovered all the archaic meanings of the old words during his edits, I am endebted.

I must also thank my husband for giving me the long nights of writing this book needed. I'm so grateful for the help of my parents and my in-laws so I could network, write, and learn. It takes more than a village, and I'm well aware of it.

Language Glossary

POLISH

Babcia – Grandma

Będę – I will

Będzie dobrze – It will be fine, It will be alright

Chodź teraz – Come on, now

Co to jest – what is this?

Co zrobiłeś – What have you done?

Cyna – tin

Czemu – why?

Człowieku – man

Daj spokój – Come on! (exclamation)

Dobranoc – Good Night

Dziękuję Ci – thank you

Głupi – stupid

Gówno – shit / refuse

Kochanie – honey, sweetheart

Kowal – smith

Kurczaki – chickens

Miłość – love

Mój Boże – My God

Mój najdroższy – my dearest

Mój syn – my son

Moja miłość, zawiodłem Cię – My love, I failed you

Moje serce – my heart

Może nie udać – you may not go

Nauczyciel – teacher, master

Nie – no

Nierosądny – foolish

Odpieprz się! – fuck off!

Ojciec – Father

On zostawił mnie – he left me

Oświadczyny – traditional engagement period before marriage

Pamiętasz – Do you remember

Pieprzyć go – fuck it

Pierdoła – asshole

Półgęsek – smoked goose breast

Polonia – Poland

Pośpiech – hurry

Prosić – please

Przekleństwo – damn, damnation

Siostra – sister

Święty *piekło* – holy hell

Szablas – saber, sword

Szlachta – nobility

Szczęśliwy – happy, lucky, good

Tak – yes

Tarka do gałka muszkatołowej – loosely translates to
        "grate the nutmeg" or nutmeg grater

Usługa – help

Wesołych Świąt – Merry Christmas

Wynoś się – get the hell out!

NORWEGIAN

Bestemor – Grandma

Honning – honey

Kjæreste – dearest

Kjære – dear

Klubb – a type of potato dumpling

A Trade Glossary & Terminology for Tinsmiths and Coppersmiths

Beading Machine: a bead may be applied to a piece of tin or copper ware to strengthen tall sides or floppy forms, but often it is used to create a bit of a design or pattern as well. The beading machine comes with a variety of "beads" that can be interchanged on one side and can create different types of beads/lines in the metal. The most common are the single, double, and triple bead.

Burin: like an awl, it is a short, stocky piece of iron or steel with a very pointy end for drawing on softer metal sheet or carving into harder metals with pressure.

Burnish: to polish or make flat.

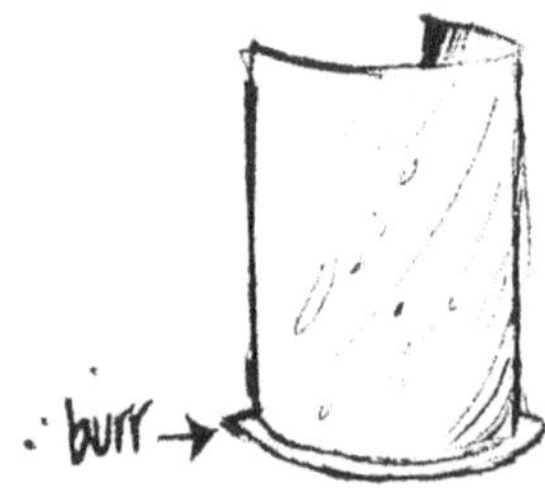

Burr: pulling a metal edge out so it is ready for a seam. Typically a burr is at a right angle from a cookware pot, and is where a seam or fold is formed along a top or bottom. However, burr can also mean a place on a metal cut that is sharp and not smooth, causing problems during the building of a ware.

Burring Machine: a machine for tinsmithing and coppersmithing that creates a burr along the edge of a metal sheet. This speeds up the process of burring considerably, which is need for most seams in the trade.

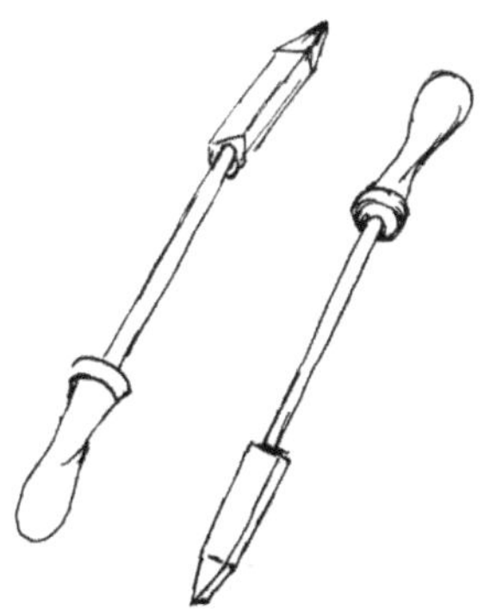

Coppers: copper shapes hammered into different sizes and tips for getting tin solder into the corners and seams of cookware. The copper heads were usually attached to long iron handles that were tempered by wooden handholds. They were heated by being put into a hot coal brazier before use. Today modern tinners often use electric soldering irons for the same job.

Cross-Hatching: creating very light criss-crosses into a harder metal and then heating or pushing a softer metal on top.

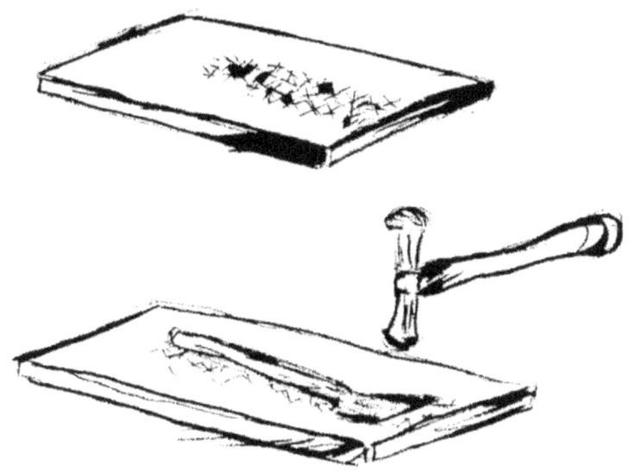

Similar to false damascening, it gives a rougher surface for the softer metal to cling to without actually having to go through the work of carving into the steel or iron.

Damascening: inlaying one metal into another without actually heating the two metals or melting them together. 
Usually a cut in the metal would be made with a slight angle or dovetail, so the softer metal inlayed inside the cut will get "stuck" inside the groove. Usually seen with gold, silver, or other soft metals being pounded into a harder metal like steel or iron or even bronze.

Encrusting: instead of laying a softer metal flush with a harder one when making a design, a smith would allow the softer metal to pile up on top, cre- 
ating texture—but in reality it is simply another way to do a false damascening.

False Damascening: giving the impression of damascening, but the softer metal is actually laid on top of the hard metal, not inlaying it inside.

Flux: a substance needed on tin or copper so the tin solder runs along tin and copper plate and can seal seams, cracks, and repairs.

Gauge: the thickness measurement of a metal sheet. 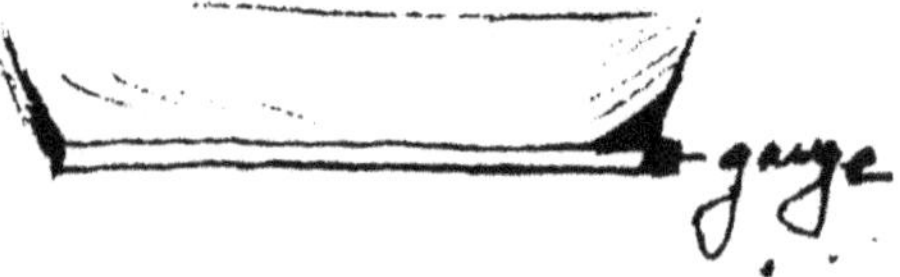

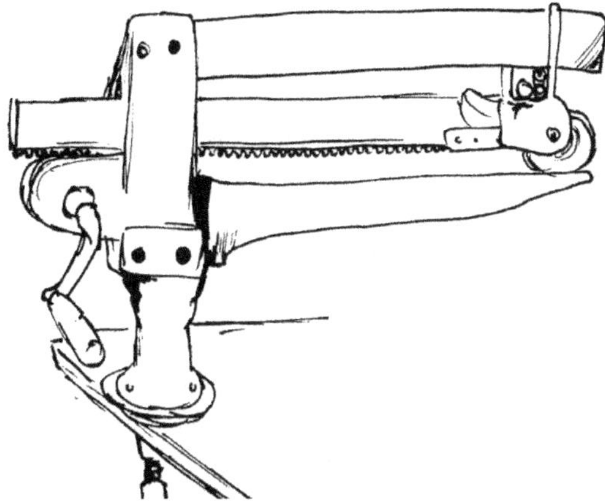

Grooving Machine: When creating a crimp seam, or a seam where the metals are folded into each other to create a seam, the grooving machine will set down the metal around the folded seam all in one quick swipe.

Hot-Dip: traditional tinsmiths only had access to thin sheets of steel that were dipped in vats of melted tin (hence "hot dip"). Today the same tin sheets are usually electroplated, but you can  sometimes see hot dipping done at tinsmith convergences.

Rosin: a type of flux used specifically for tin and copper, made from the resin of pine trees. Typically it was pulverized into a powder for ease of use.

Sal ammoniac: a soft, white mineral used in the tinning process to keep copper soldering irons clean.

Setting Down Machine: Once two pieces of metal are folded and joined properly, the two separate burrs or folds need to be compressed together. This is always done at first with a setting down hammer, but to create a very smooth finish, one then, after hammering, "sets down" the seam with the machine.

Snips: tinner's scissors, meant for cutting metal. These come in myriad sizes.

Solder: tin put in bars or sticks that melt easily with heat for sealing seams and cracks. Sometimes it was bought as "shot" or small pebbles of tin (my children call solder "metal glue").

Tinner's Bench: a heavy wooden bench with shelves and rectangular spaces for a tinner's stake plate, where the stakes are set for use in a shop.

Tinner's Stakes: long, specially formed iron pieces meant to fit within the holes of a tinner's bench stake plate (holder of stakes), which come in a variety of sizes and shapes and uses. Some look like elongated blacksmith anvils, while others have grooves for writing, and still others are for

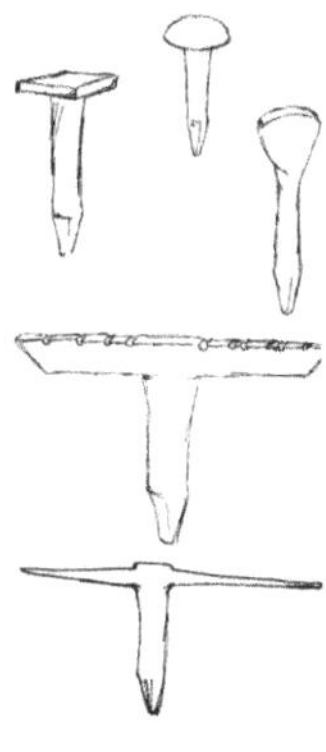

forming often-made tinware. The needlecase stake, for instance, was often uses for making needlecases.

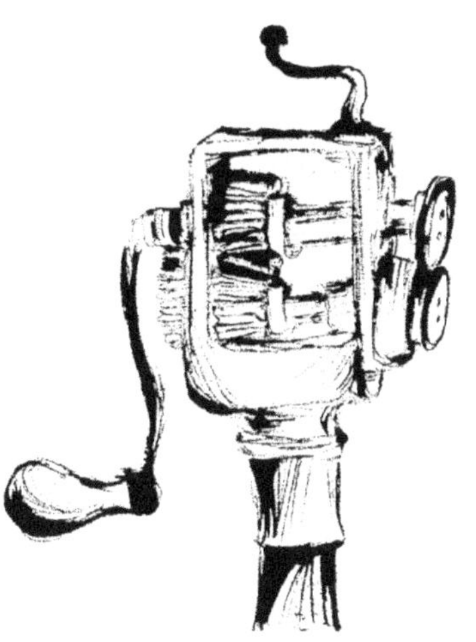

Turning Machine: Before a piece is wired, typically a turning machine would half-curl and press open the end of a piece so it would be prepared for a wire to be applied to strengthen the ware. It generally prepares a tin or copper piece to have a wire put in. The turning machine is best used for round objects.

Wiring Machine: best for round objects, a wiring machine will set down metal around a wire, with the smith's guidance, in order to finish a piece's top, for instance, and strengthen it, as well as remove any sharp edges.

Bibliography

Barr, Roger. *The American Frontier.* San Diego: Lucent Books, 1996.

Bartlett, Richard A. *The New Country: A Social History of the American Frontier 1776-1890.* New York: Oxford University Press, 1974.

Brady, Cyrus Townsend. *The Sioux Indian Wars: From the Powder River to the Little Big Horn.* New York: Indian Head Books, 1992.

Carmichael, Marcia C. *Putting Down Roots: Gardening Insights.* Madison WI: Wisconsin Historical Society Press, 2011.

Fife, Austin E. and Alta S. Fife. *Cowboy and Western Songs: A Comprehensive Anthology.* New York: Bramhall House, 1982.

Hasluck, Paul N. *Tinplate Work.* London: Cassel and Company Limited, 1907.

Hoover, Herbert T. *The Yankton Sioux.* New York: Chelsea House Publisher, 1998.

Hyslop, Stephen G. *The Old West*. Washington DC: National Geographic Society, 2015.

Kallen, Stuart A. *Women of the American Frontier*. Farmington Hills MI: Lucent Books, 2004.

Kalman, Bobbie. *19th Century Clothing*. New York: Crabtree Publishing Company, 1993.

Kalman, Bobbie. *A Visual Dictionary of a Pioneer Community*. New York: Crabtree Publishing Company, 2008.

Kalman, Bobbie, and Lynda Hale. *Pioneer Recipes*. New York: Crabtree Publishing Company, 2001.

Kalman, Bobbie. *Food for the Settler*. New York: Crabtree Publishing Company, 1982.

Kalman, Bobbie. *Settler Sayings*. New York: Crabtree Publishing Company, 1994.

Langum, David J. "Pioneer Justice on the Overland Trails." *Western Historical Quarterly* Vol. 5 (1974): 421-439.

Lubetkin, John M. *Jay Cooke's Gamble: The Northern Pacific Railroad, the Sioux and the Panic of 1873*. Oklahoma City: University of Oklahoma Press, 2006.

Nadeau, Remi. *Fort Laramie and the Sioux Indians*. Englewood Cliffs NJ: Prentice-Hall Inc., 1967.

Neihardt, John G. *Black Elk Speaks.* Albany NY: State University of New York Press, 1932.

Treur, Anton, *Indian Nations of North America.* Washington DC: National Geographic Society, 2010.

Treuer, Anton. *The Indian Wars: Battles, Bloodshed and the Fight for Freedom on the American Frontier.* Washington DC: National Geographic Partners, 2016.

The Flats Junction Series

Tinsmith 1865
Medicineman 1876
Widow 1881
Outcast 1883
Trader 1884
Stranger 1886

For more information,
visit www.flatsjunction.com.

To connect with Sara,
visit www.saradahmen.com.
Find her on Twitter at @saradahmenbooks,
on Facebook, or Instagram at @sara_dahmen.

To learn about Sara's cookware line
inspired by her research for Flats Junction,
visit www.housecopper.com.

www.ingramcontent.com/pod-product-compliance
Lightning Source LLC
Chambersburg PA
CBHW061053100726
47911CB00012B/207